WITHDRAWN

Heroes of the Nations

A Series of Biographical Studies presenting the lives and work of certain representative historical characters, about whom have gathered the traditions of the nations to which they belong, and who have, in the majority of instances, been accepted as types of the several national ideals.

12°, Illustrated, cloth, each . . $1.50
Half Leather, gilt top, each. . . $1.75
No. 33 and following Nos. . . net $1.35
   Each . . . (By mail, $1.50)
Half Leather, gilt top, . . . net $1.60
                                (By mail, $1.75)

FOR FULL LIST SEE END OF THIS VOLUME

Heroes of the Nations

EDITED BY

H. W. C. Davis

> FACTA DUCIS VIVENT, OPEROSAQUE
> GLORIA RERUM——OVID, IN LIVIAM, 255.
> THE HERO'S DEEDS AND HARD-WON
> FAME SHALL LIVE.

CHARLES THE BOLD

CHARLES THE BOLD OF BURGUNDY (1433-1477)
(FROM MS. STATUTE BOOK OF THE ORDER OF THE GOLDEN FLEECE, VIENNA)
PAINTED BETWEEN 1518-1531

Charles the Bold

LAST DUKE OF BURGUNDY

1433-1477

BY

RUTH PUTNAM

Author of "William the Silent," "A Mediæval Princess," etc.

G. P. PUTNAM'S SONS
NEW YORK AND LONDON
The Knickerbocker Press
1908

COPYRIGHT 1908,

BY

G. P. PUTNAM'S SONS

DC
611
B781
P8

The Knickerbocker Press, New York

PREFACE

THE admission of Charles, Duke of Burgundy into the series of Heroes of the Nations, is justified by his relation to events rather than by his national or his heroic qualities. "*Il n'avait pas assez de sens ni de malice pour conduire ses entreprises,*" is one phrase of Philip de Commines in regard to the master he had once served. Render *sens* by *genius* and *malice* by *diplomacy* and the words are not far wrong. Yet in spite of the failure to obtain either a kingly or an imperial crown, the story of those same unaccomplished enterprises contains the germs of much that has happened later in the borderlands of France and Germany where the projected "middle kingdom" might have been erected. A sketch of the duke's character with its traits of ambition and shortcomings may therefore be placed, not unfitly, among the pen portraits of individuals who have attempted to change the map of Europe.

The materials for an exhaustive study of the times, and of the participants in the scenes thereof, are almost overwhelming in quantity. Into this narrative, I have woven the words of contemporaries when these related what they saw and thought, or at least what they said they saw or thought, about events passing within their sight or their ken. The veracity attained is only that of a mosaic of bits, each with its morsel of truth. And the rim in which these bits are set is too slender to contain all the illumination necessary. The narrative is, of necessity, partial and fragmentary, for a complete story would require a series of biographies presented in parallel columns. My own preliminary chapter to this book—a mere explanation of the presence of the dukes of Burgundy in the Netherlands—grew into an account of a sovereign whom they deposed and was published under the title of *A Mediæval Princess*.

John Foster Kirk gave 1713 pages to his record of Charles the Bold, Duke of Burgundy. Forty years have elapsed since that publication appeared and a mass of interesting material pertinent to the subject has been given out to the public, while separate phases of it have been minutely discussed by competent critics, so that at every point there is new temptation for the biographer to expand the theme where the scope of his work demands brevity.

In using the later fruit of historical investigation, it is delightful for an American to find that scholars of all nations do justice to Mr. Kirk's accuracy and industry even when they may differ from his conclusions. It has been my privilege to be permitted free access to this scholar's collection of books, and I would here express my deep gratitude to the Kirk family for their generosity and courtesy towards me.

Preface

After some preliminary reading at Brussels and Paris and in England, the work for this volume has been completed in America, where the opportunity of securing the latest results of research and criticism is constantly increasing, although these results are still lodged under many roofs. I have had many reasons to thank the librarians of New York, Boston, and Washington, and also those of Harvard, Columbia, and Cornell universities for courtesies and for serviceable aid; and just as many reasons to regret the meagreness of what can be put between two covers as the gleanings from so rich a harvest.

One word further in explanation of the use of *Bold*. The adjective has been retained simply because it has been so long identified with Charles in English usage. I should have preferred the word *Rash* as a better equivalent for the contemporary term, applied to the duke in his lifetime,—*le téméraire*.

R. P.

WASHINGTON, D. C., 1908.

CONTENTS

	PAGE
CHAPTER I	
CHILDHOOD	1
CHAPTER II	
YOUTH	24
CHAPTER III	
THE FEAST OF THE PHEASANT	45
CHAPTER IV	
BURGUNDY AND FRANCE	67
CHAPTER V	
THE COUNT AND THE DAUPHIN	86
CHAPTER VI	
THE WAR OF PUBLIC WEAL	109
CHAPTER VII	
LIEGE AND ITS FATE	130
CHAPTER VIII	
THE NEW DUKE	154
CHAPTER IX	
THE UNJOYOUS ENTRY	170

CHAPTER X
THE DUKE'S MARRIAGE 183

CHAPTER XI
THE MEETING AT PERONNE 197

CHAPTER XII
AN EASY VICTORY 227

CHAPTER XIII
A NEW ACQUISITION 244

CHAPTER XIV
ENGLISH AFFAIRS 261

CHAPTER XV
NEGOTIATIONS AND TREACHERY 293

CHAPTER XVI
GUELDERS 320

CHAPTER XVII
THE MEETING AT TRÈVES 339

CHAPTER XVIII
COLOGNE, LORRAINE, AND ALSACE . . . 362

CHAPTER XIX
THE FIRST REVERSES 382

CHAPTER XX
THE CAMPAIGNS OF 1475 AND 1476 . . . 402

CHAPTER XXI
THE BATTLE OF NANCY 427

							PAGE
BIBLIOGRAPHY	.	.	.	.	.	.	463
INDEX	.	.	.	.	.	.	469

ILLUSTRATIONS

PAGE

CHARLES THE BOLD, DUKE OF BURGUNDY *Frontispiece*
> From MS. statute book of the Order of the Golden Fleece at Vienna. The artist is unknown. Date of the codex is between 1518 and 1565. This portrait is possibly redrawn from that attributed to Roger van der Weyden. That, however, shows a much stronger face.

PHILIP THE GOOD AS FOUNDER OF THE ORDER OF THE GOLDEN FLEECE 4
> From a reproduction of a miniature in MS. at Brussels.

A DUKE OF BURGUNDY AND THE POPE AT AVIGNON 16
> From a contemporary miniature reproduced in Petit's *Hist. de Bourgogne*.

PHILIP THE GOOD, DUKE OF BURGUNDY, AS PATRON OF LETTERS 18
> From a reproduction of part of a miniature in a beautiful MS. copy in Brussels Library of Jacques de Guise's *Annales*. The author is depicted presenting his book to the duke, who is attended by his son and his courtiers. The miniature is attributed by turns to Roger van der Weyden, to Guillaume Wijelant or Vrelant, and to Hans Memling.

Illustrations

	PAGE
A CASTLE IN BURGUNDY	24
From Petit's *Hist. de Bourgogne*.	
FRONTISPIECE OF A XVTH CENTURY ACCOUNT BOOK	30
COUNT OF ST. POL AND HIS JESTER	46
From reproduction of a miniature in Barante, *Les ducs de Bourgogne*.	
THE STATUE OF CHARLES OF BURGUNDY AT INNSBRUCK	68
LOUIS XI.	84
From an engraving by A. Boilly after a drawing by G. Boilly.	
PHILIP AND CHARLES OF BURGUNDY	100
From a drawing in a MS. at Arras.	
BATTLE OF MONTL'HÉRY (JULY 16, 1465)	124
From a contemporary miniature reproduced in Comines-Lenglet.	
LOUIS XI. WITH THE PRINCES AND SEIGNEURS OF THE WAR OF THE PUBLIC WEAL	128
From a contemporary miniature reproduced in Comines-Lenglet.	
ANTHONY OF BURGUNDY	150
After Hans Memling, Dresden Gallery.	
CHARLES, DUKE OF BURGUNDY, PRESIDING OVER A CHAPTER OF THE ORDER OF THE GOLDEN FLEECE	188
From reproduction of a miniature in MS. at Brussels.	
PHILIP DE COMMINES	210
OLIVIER DE LA MARCHE	232
From sketch in MS. at Arras reproduced in *Mémoires couronnés de l'acad. royale de Belgique*, xlix.	

Illustrations   xiii

	PAGE
MARY OF BURGUNDY	250
From a contemporary miniature reproduced in Barante, *Les ducs de Bourgogne*.	
MAP OF ALSACE AND ADJACENT TERRITORIES	260
From Toutey, *Charles le téméraire*.	
MEDAL OF CHARLES, DUKE OF BURGUNDY	280
BURGUNDIAN STANDARD CAPTURED AT BEAUVAIS	310
ARNOLD, DUKE OF GUELDERS	322
From engraving by G. Robert in Comines-Lenglet.	
MARY OF BURGUNDY	336
After design by C. Laplante.	
CHARLES THE BOLD	340
Idealised by P. P. Rubens, Vienna Gallery. (By permission of J. J. Löwy, Vienna.)	
MAXIMILIAN OF AUSTRIA	350
Medal.	
A FORTIFIED CHURCH IN BURGUNDY	382
From Petit's *Hist. de Bourgogne*.	
KING RUHMREICH AND HIS DAUGHTER EHRENREICH	406
(These characters in Maximilian's poem of *Theuerdank* represent Charles and Mary of Burgundy.) From a reproduction of a wood engraving by Schäufelein in edition of 1517.	
A PLAN OF THE BATTLE OF MORAT	422
Used by kind permission of Miss Sophia Kirk and J. B. Lippincott Company.	
PHILIBERT, DUKE OF SAVOY	430
After a design by Matthey reproduced in Comines-Lenglet.	

Illustrations

	PAGE
PLAN OF THE BATTLE OF NANCY	432
Used by kind permission of Miss Sophia Kirk and the J. B. Lippincott Company.	
PLAN OF THE BATTLE OF NANCY	434
From contemporary miniature reproduced in Comines-Lenglet.	
A MONUMENT ON THE BATTLEFIELD AT NANCY	436
From Barante, *Les ducs de Bourgogne*.	
THE TOMB OF CHARLES OF BURGUNDY	460
Church of Notre Dame, Bruges	

CHARLES THE BOLD

CHARLES THE BOLD

CHAPTER I

CHILDHOOD

1433–1440

ON St. Andrew's Eve, in the year 1433, the good people of Dijon were abroad, eager to catch what glimpses they might of certain stately functions to be formally celebrated by the Duke of Burgundy. The mere presence of the sovereign in the capital of his duchy was in itself a gala event from its rarity. Various cities of the dominions agglomerated under his sway claimed his attentions successively. His residence was now here and now there, without long tarrying anywhere. His coming was usually very welcome. In times of peaceful submission to his behest, the city of his sojourn reaped many advantages besides the amusement of seeing her streets alive beyond their wont. In the outlay for the necessities and the luxuries of the peripatetic ducal court, the expenditures were lavish, and in the temporary commercial activity enjoyed by the merchants, the fact that the burghers' own contributions to this luxury were heavy, passed into temporary oblivion.[1]

This autumn visit of Philip the Good to Dijon was more significant than usual. It had lasted several weeks, and among its notable occasions was an assembly of the Knights of the Golden Fleece for the third anniversary of their Order. On this November 30th, Burgundy was to witness for the first time the pompous ceremonials inaugurated at Bruges in January, 1430. Three years had sufficed to render the new institution almost as well known as its senior English rival, the Order of the Garter, which it was destined to outshine for a brief period at least. Its foundation had formed part of the elaborate festivities accompanying the celebration of the marriage of Philip, Duke of Burgundy, to Isabella of Portugal. As a signal honour to his bride, Philip published his intention of creating a new order of knighthood which would evince "his great and perfect love for the noble state of chivalry."

Rumour, indeed, told various tales about the duke's real motives. It was whispered that a certain lady of Bruges, whom he had distinguished

[1] The indefatigable Gachard has published an itinerary of Philip the Good, so far as he could make it. (*Collection des voyages des souverains des Pays Bas*, i., 71.) Unfortunately, owing to the destruction of papers, only a few years are complete. Between 1428–1441, there is nothing. But the itinerary for 1441 and for other years shows how often the duke changed his residences. Sometimes he is accompanied by Madame de Bourgogne, sometimes by M. and Madame de Charolais.

by his attentions, was ridiculed for her red hair by a few merry courtiers, whereupon Philip declared that her tresses should be immortally honoured in the golden emblem of a new society.[1] But that may be set down as gossip. Philip's own assertion, when he instituted the Order of the Golden Fleece, was that he intended to create a bulwark

"for the reverence of God and the sustenance of our Christian faith, and to honour and enhance the noble order of chivalry, and also for three reasons hereafter declared; first, to honour the ancient knights . . . ; second, to the end that these present . . . . may exercise the deeds of chivalry and constantly improve; third, that all gentlemen marking the honour paid to the knights will exert themselves to attain the dignity." [2]

The special homage to the new duchess was expressed in the device

*Aultre n'aray
Dame Isabeau tant que vivray* [3]

This pledge of absolute fidelity to Dame Isabella was, indeed, utterly disregarded by the bridegroom, but in outward and formal honour to her he never failed.

The new institution was, from the beginning, pre-eminently significant of the duke's magnifi-

[1] It was also said that the woollen manufactures of Flanders were denoted by the emblem of the golden fleece.

[2] Reiffenberg, *Histoire de l'Ordre de la Toison d'Or*, p. xxi.

[3] *Hist. de l'Ordre*, etc., p. i.

cent state existence, wherein his Portuguese consort proved herself an efficient and able helpmeet. Again and again during a period of thirty years, rich in diplomatic parleying, did Isabella act as confidential ambassador for her husband, and many were the negotiations conducted by her to his satisfaction.[1]

But it must be noted that whatever lay at the exact root of Philip's motives when he conceived the plan of his Order, the actual result of his foundation was not affected. He failed, indeed, to bring back into the world the ancient system of knighthood in its ideal purity and strength. Rather did he make a notable contribution to its decadence and speed its parting. What was brought into existence was a house of peers for the head of the Burgundian family, a body of faithful satellites who did not hamper their chief overmuch with the criticism permitted by the rules of their society, while their own glory added shining rays to the brilliant centre of the Burgundian court.

Twenty-five, inclusive of the duke, was the original number appointed to form the chosen circle of knights. This was speedily increased

[1] All the Burgundian embassies were not as patent to the public as were Isabella's. An item like the following from the accounts of 1448–49 whets the reader's curiosity:

"To Jehan Lanternier, barber and varlet of the chamber, for delivering to a certain person for certain causes and for secret matters of which Monseigneur does not wish further declaration to be made, 53 pounds 17 sous."

(Laborde, *Les Ducs de Bourgogne*, etc., "Preuves," i. xlii.)

PHILIP THE GOOD

Childhood

to thirty-one, and a duty to be performed in the session of 1433, was the election of new members to fill vacancies and to round out the allotted tale.

In their manner of accomplishing the appointed task, the new chevaliers had, from the outset, evinced a readiness to cast their votes to the satisfaction of their chief, even if his pleasure directly conflicted with the regulations they had sworn to obey. No candidate was to be eligible whose birth was not legitimate,[1] a regulation quite ignored when the duke proposed the names of his sons Cornelius and Anthony. For his obedient knights did not refuse to open their ranks to these great bastards of Burgundy, who carried a bar sinister proudly on their escutcheon. So, too, others of Philip's many illegitimate descendants were not rejected when their father proposed their names.

Again, it was plainly stipulated that the new member should have proven himself a knight of renown. Yet, in this session of 1433, one of the candidates proposed for election, though nominally a knight, had assuredly had no time to show his mettle. The dignity was his only because his spurs had been thrown right royally into his cradle before his tiny hands had sufficient baby strength to grasp a rattle, and before he was even old

[1] "Vingt-quatre chevaliers gentilshommes de nom et d'armes et sans reproches nés et procrées en léal mariage". (*see* description of the first list).—*Hist. de l'Ordre*, p. xxi.

enough to use the pleasant gold to cut his teeth upon.[1]

Among the eight elected at Dijon in 1433, was Charles of Burgundy, Count of Charolais, son of the sovereign duke, born at Dijon on the previous St. Martin's Eve, November 10th.[2]

"The new chevaliers, with the exception of the Count of Virnenbourg who was absent, took the accustomed oath at the hands of the sovereign in a room of his palace."

So runs the record. Jean le Févre, Seigneur de St. Remy, present on the occasion in his capacity of king-at-arms of the Order, is a trifle more communicative.[3] According to him, all the gentlemen were very joyous at their election as they received their collars and made their vows as stated. He excepted no member in the phrase about the joy displayed, though, as a matter of inference, the pleasure experienced by the Count of Charolais may be reckoned as somewhat problematical.

The heir of Burgundy had attained the ripe age of just twenty days when thus officially listed

[1] Jacquemin Dauxonne, a merchant of Lombardy living at Dijon, received twenty-two francs and a half for a rich cloth of black silk draped about the baptismal font. Why mourning was used on this joyful occasion does not appear. (Laborde, i., 321.)

[2] Summary of a register containing the acts of the Order of the Golden Fleece quoted in *Histoire de l'Ordre*, pp. 12, 13.

[3] St. Remy, *Chronique*, ii., 284. St. Remy is usually called *Toison d'Or*.

Childhood

among the chevaliers present at the festival. Born on November 10th of this same year, 1433,[1] he had been knighted on the very day of his baptism, when Charles, Count of Nevers, and the Seigneur of Croy were his sponsors. The former gave his name to the infant while the latter's name was destined to be identified with many unpleasant incidents in the career of the future man. This brief span of life is sufficient reason for the further item in the archives of the Golden Fleece:

"As to the Count of Charolais, he was carried into the same room. There the sovereign, his father, and the duchess, his mother, took the oath on his behalf. Afterwards the duke put the collars upon all."[2]

Thus was emphasised at birth the parental conviction that Charles of Burgundy was of different metal than the rest of the world. The great duke of the Occident made a distinct epoch in the history of chivalry when he conferred its dignities upon a speechless, unconscious infant. The theory that knighthood was a personal acquisition had been maintained up to this period, the Children of France[3] alone being excepted from the rule, though in his *Lay de Vaillance* Eustache Deschamps

[1] His full name was Charles Martin. One tower alone remains of the palace where he was born.

[2] *Hist. de l'Ordre*, p. 13.

[3] Selden (*Titles of Honor*, p. 457), however, says he knows not by what authority this statement is made and that he knows nothing of it. Seven is the earliest age mentioned by Gautier for receiving knighthood.

complains that the degree of knighthood is actually conferred on those who are only ten or twelve years old, and who do not know what to do with the honour.[1] That plaint was written not later than the first years of the fifteenth century, and the poet's prediction that ruin of the institution was imminent when affected by such disorders seemed justified if, in 1433, even the years of the eligible age had shrunk to days. Philip himself had not received the accolade until he was twenty-five.

How his predecessor in Holland, Count William VI., had acquitted himself valiantly the moment that he was dubbed knight is told by Froissart, and the tales of other accolades of the period are too well known to need reference.

It is said that the baby cavalier was nourished by his own mother. Having lost her first two infants, Isabella was solicitous for the welfare of this third child, who also proved her last. He was, moreover, Philip's sole legal heir, as Michelle of France and Bonne of Artois, his first wives, had left no offspring. The care and devotion expended on the boy were repaid. Charles became a sturdy child who developed into youthful vigour. In person, he strangely resembled his mother and her Portuguese ancestors, rather than the English Lancastrians, from whom she was equally descended.

His dark hair and his features were very different from the fair type of his paternal ancestors,

[1] Deschamps, *Œuvres Complètes*, ii., 214.

Childhood

the vigorous branch of the Valois family. Possibly other characteristics suggesting his Portuguese origin were intensified by close association with his mother, who supervised the education directed by the Seigneur d' Auxy. They often lived at The Hague, where Isabella acted as chief and official adviser to the duke's stadtholder in the administration.[1]

Charles was a diligent pupil, if we may believe his contemporaries, surprisingly so, considering his early taste for all martial pursuits and his intense interest in military operations.

At two years of age he received his first lesson in horsemanship, on a wooden steed constructed for his especial use by Jean Rampart, a saddler of Brussels.

His biographers repeat from each other statements of his proficiency in Latin. This must be balanced by noting that the only texts which he could have read were probably not classic. In the inventory of the various Burgundian libraries of the period, there are not six Greek and Latin classical texts all told, and excepting Sallust, not a single Roman historian in the original.[2] There

---

[1] The ancient quarrel between the old Holland parties of Hooks and Cods continually blazed out anew. On one notable occasion, to show her impartiality, the duchess appeared in public accompanied by the stadtholder, Lelaing, a partisan of the Hooks, and by Frank van Borselen, himself a Cod, the widower of Jacqueline, the late Countess of Holland.

[2] Barante, *Histoire des Ducs de Bourgogne*, vi., 2, note by Reiffenberg.

was a translation of Livy by the Prior of St. Eloi and late abridgments of Sallust, Suetonius, Lucan, and Cæsar,[1] with a French version of Valerius Maximus, but nothing of Tacitus. Doubtless these versions and a volume called *Les faits des Romains* were used as text-books to teach the young count about the world's conquerors. The last mentioned book shows what travesties of Roman history were gravely read in the fifteenth century.

There are stories[2] that the bit of history most enjoyed by the pupil was the narrative of Alexander. Books about that hero were easy to come by long before the invention of printing, though Alexander would have had difficulty in recognising his identity under the strange mediæval motley in which his namesake wandered over the land. No single man, with the possible exception of Charlemagne, was so much written about or played so brilliantly the part of a hero to the Middle Ages and after.[3] The simplicity and universality of his success were of a type to appeal to the boy Charles, himself built on simple lines. The fact, too, that Alexander was the son of a Philip stimulated his imagination and instilled in his breast hopes of conquering, not the whole world perhaps, but a good slice of territory which should enable him to hold his own between the emperor

[1] See *Catalogue des manuscrits des Ducs de Bourgogne*, "Résumé historique," i., lxxix.

[2] Barante, vi., 2, note.

[3] Loomis, *Medieval Hellenism*.

Childhood

and the French king. Tales of definite schemes of early ambition are often fabricated in the later life of a conqueror, but in this case they may be believed, as all threads of testimony lead to the same conclusion.

The air breathed by the boy when he first became conscious of his own individuality was certainly heavy with the aroma of satisfied ambition. The period of his childhood was a time when his father stood at the very zenith of his power. In 1435, was signed the Treaty of Arras, the death-blow to the long coalition existing between Burgundy and England to the continual detriment of France. Philip was reconciled with great solemnity to the king, responsible in his dauphin days for the murder of the late Duke of Burgundy. After ostentatiously parading his filial resentment sixteen long years, Philip forgave Charles VII. his share in the death of John the Fearless, on the bridge at Montereau, and swore to lend his support to keep the French monarch on the throne whither the efforts of Joan of Arc had carried him from Bourges, the forlorn court of his exile.

England's pretensions were repudiated. To be sure, the recent coronation of Henry VI. at Paris was not immediately forgotten, but while the Duke of Bedford had actually administered the government as regent, in behalf of his infant nephew, it was a mere shadow of his office that passed to his successor. Bedford's death, in 1435, was almost coincident with the compact at Arras when the English Henry's realms across the Channel shrank to Normandy and the outlying fortresses of Picardy and Maine. Later events on English soil were to prove how little fitted was the son of Henry V. for sovereignty of any kind.

Out of the negotiations at Arras, Philip of Burgundy rose triumphant with a seal set upon his personal importance.[1] His recognition of Charles VII. as lawful sovereign of France, and his reconciliation did not pass without signal gain to himself.

The king declared his own hands unstained by the blood of John of Burgundy, agreed to punish all those designated by Philip as actually responsible for that treacherous murder, and pledged himself to erect a cross on the bridge at Montereau, the scene of the crime. Further, he relinquished various revenues in Burgundy, hitherto retained by the crown from the moment when the junior branch of the Valois had been invested with the duchy (1364); and he ceded the counties of Boulogne, Artois, and all the seigniories belonging to the French sovereign on both banks of the Somme. To this last cession, however, was appended the condition that the towns included in this clause could be redeemed at the king's pleasure, for the sum of four hundred thousand gold crowns. Further, Charles exempted Philip from acts of homage to himself, promised to demand no *aides* from the duke's subjects in case of war, and to

[1] Pirenne, *Histoire de Belgique*, ii., 231.

Childhood

assist his cousin if he were attacked from England. Lastly, he renounced an alliance lately contracted with the emperor to Philip's disadvantage.[1]

One clause in the treaty crowned the royal submissiveness towards the powerful vassal. It provided that in case of Charles's failure to observe all the stipulated conditions, his own subjects would be justified in taking arms against him at the duke's orders. A similar clause occurs in certain treaties between an earlier French king and his Flemish vassals, but always to the advantage of the suzerain, not to that of the lesser lords.

The duke was left in a position infinitely superior to that of the king, whose realm was terribly exhausted by the long contest with England, a contest wherein one nation alone had felt the invader's foot. French prosperity had been nibbled off like green foliage before a swarm of locusts, and the whole north-eastern portion of France was in a sorry state of desolation by 1435. On the other hand, the territories covered by Burgundy as an overlord had greatly increased during the sixteen years that Philip had worn the title. An aggregation of duchies, counties, and lordships formed his domain, loosely hung together by reason of their several titles being vested in one person—titles which the bearer had inherited or assumed under various pretexts.

[1] It was in June, 1434, that this alliance had been made. Sigismund claimed that Philip had no right in Brabant, Holland, Zealand, and Hainaut, which in his opinion were lapsed fiefs, of the empire.

Flanders and Artois, together with the duchy and county of Burgundy, came to him from his father, John the Fearless, in 1419. In 1421, he bought Namur. In 1430, he declared himself heir to his cousins in Brabant and Limbourg when Duke Anthony's second son followed his equally childless brother into a premature grave, and the claims were made good in spite of all opposition. Holland, Zealand, and Hainaut became his through the unwilling abdication of his other cousin, Jacqueline, in 1433. To save the life of her husband, Frank van Borselen, the last representative of the Bavarian House then formally resigned her titles, which she had already divested of all significance five years previously, when Philip of Burgundy had become her *ruward*, to relieve a "poor feminine person" of a weight of responsibility too heavy for her shoulders.[1]

Antwerp and Mechlin were included in Brabant. Luxemburg was a later acquisition obtained through Elizabeth of Görlitz.

There were very shady bits in the chapters about Philip's entry into many of his possessions, but it is interesting to note how cleverly the best colour is given to his actions by Olivier de la Marche and other writers who enjoyed Burgundian pa-

[1] Putnam, *A Mediæval Princess*.

Divers items in the accounts show what Philip expended in having the titles of Holland, Zealand, and Hainaut added to his other designations. Also there were various places where his predecessor's name had to be effaced to make room for his. (Laborde, i., 345).

Childhood

tronage. Very gentle are the adjectives employed, and a nice cloak of legality is thrown over the naked facts as they are ushered into history. Contemporary criticism did occasionally make itself heard, especially from the emperor, who declared that the Netherland provinces must come to him as a lapsed imperial fief. For a time Philip denied that any links existed between his domain and the empire, but in 1449 he finally found it convenient to discuss the question with Frederic III. at Besançon; still he never came to the point of paying homage.

All these territories made a goodly realm for a mere duke. But they were individual entities centred around one head with little interconnection.

Philip thought that the one thing needed to bring his possessions into a national life, as coherent as that of France, was a unity of legal existence among the dissimilar parts, and the effort to attain this unity was the one thought dominating the career of his successor, whose pompous introduction to life naturally inspired him with a high idea of his own rank, and led him to dream of greater dignities for himself and his successor than a bundle of titles,—a splendid, vain, fatal dream as it proved.

As a final cement to the new friendship between Burgundy and France, it was also agreed at Arras that the heir of the former should wed a daughter of Charles VII. When the Count of Charolais was five years old, the Seigneur of Crèvecœur,[1] "a wise and prudent gentleman" was despatched to the French court on divers missions, among which was the business of negotiating the projected alliance. A very joyous reception was accorded the envoy by the king and the queen, and his proposal was accepted in behalf of the second daughter, Catherine, easily substituted for an older sister, deceased between the first and second stages of negotiation.

A year later, a formal betrothal took place at St. Omer, whither the young bride was conducted, most honourably accompanied by the archbishops of Rheims and of Narbonne, by the counts of Vendôme, Tonnerre, and Dunois, the young son of the Duke of Bourbon, named the Lord of Beaujeu, and various other distinguished nobles, besides a train of noble dames and demoiselles in special attendance on the princess, and an escort of three hundred horse.

At the various cities where the party made halt they were graciously received, and all honour was paid to the ten-year-old Daughter of France. At Cambray, she was met by the duke's envoys and as she travelled on towards her destination, all the towns of Philip's obedience contributed their quota of welcome.

At St. Omer, the duke was awaiting her coming. When her approach was announced he rode out in person to greet her, attended by a brilliant escort.

[1] Monstrelet, *La Chronique*, v., 344.

A DUKE OF BURGUNDY AND THE POPE AT AVIGNON
FROM PETIT'S "HIST. DE BOURGOGNE"

Childhood

Within the city, "melodious festivals" were ready to burst into tune; the betrothal was confirmed amid joyousness and the ceremony was followed by tourneys and jousts, all at the expense of the duke.

What a series of pompous betrothals between infant parties the fifteenth and sixteenth centuries can show! Poor little puppets, in whose persons national interests were supposed to be centred, were made to lisp out their rôles in international dramas whose final acts rarely were consistent with the promise of the prologue.

Catherine did not live to become Duchess of Burgundy nor to temper the duel between her husband and her brother Louis. The remainder of her short existence was passed under the care of Duchess Isabella, sometimes in one city of the Netherlands, sometimes in another.

La Marche[1] records one return of Philip to Brussels when his arrival was greeted by Charles of Burgundy, honourably accompanied by children of high birth about his age or less, some only eleven or twelve years old. There were with him Jehan de la Trémoille, Philip de Croy, Philip de Crèvecœur, Philip de Wavrin, and many others. All were mounted on little horses harnessed like that of their governor, a very honest and wise gentleman, named Messire Jehan, Seigneur et Ber d' Auxy. This gentleman was a fine man, well known, of good lineage, ready of speech and able to discuss matters of honour and of state.

[1] La Marche, *Mémoires*, ii., 50.

He was both hunter and falconer, skilled in all exercise and sport.

"Never [asserts La Marche] have I met a gentleman better adapted to supervise the education of a young prince than he. . . . Among his pupils were also Anthony, Bastard of Burgundy,[1] son of Philip, and the Marquis Hugues de Rottelin. These lads were older than the first mentioned."

La Marche dilates on the pleasure the duke felt in this youthful band of horse, and then tells how, within Brussels,

"he was received by the magistrates and conducted to his palace, where the Duchess of Burgundy awaited him holding by the hand Madame Catherine of France, Countess of Charolais. She was about twelve and seemed a lady grown, for she was good and wise, and well conditioned for her age."

At various state functions the Count and Countess of Charolais appeared together in public, and witnessed certain of the gorgeous and costly entertainments which were almost the daily food of the gay Burgundian court. One of these occasions was calculated to make a deep impression on the boy and to arouse his pride at the spectacle of a proud city wooing his father's favour, in deep humiliation.

In 1436, an insurrection had occurred in Bruges, when the animosity of the burghers had caused

[1] Reiffenberg, *Essai sur les enfants naturels de Philippe de Bourgogne.*

PHILIP THE GOOD AS PATRON OF LETTERS
THE YOUNG COUNT OF CHAROLAIS IS IN THE BACKGROUND WITH ONE OF PHILIP'S SONS
FROM MINIATURE REPRODUCED IN BARANTE, "HIST. DES DUCS DE BOURGOGNE"

Childhood

the duchess to flee from their midst, holding her little son in her arms, alarmed for his personal safety. Philip suppressed the revolt, but, in his anger at its insolence, declared that never again would he set foot within the gates unless in company with his superior.

Among the many negotiations wherein Isabella played a prominent part as her husband's representative, were those concerning the liberation of the Duke of Orleans, who had remained in England, a prisoner, after the battle of Agincourt in 1415. The last advice given by Henry V. to his brothers was that they should make this captivity perpetual. Therefore, whenever overtures were made for his redemption, a strong party, headed by Humphrey of Gloucester, rejected them vehemently.

In 1440, however, there was a turn in the tide of sentiment. Possibly the low state of the English exchequer made the duke's ransom more attractive than his person. At any rate, 120,000 golden crowns were accepted as his equivalent, and the exile of twenty-five years returned to France, having pledged himself never to bear arms against England.

Isabella of Burgundy was at Calais to welcome him, and to escort him to St. Omer, where high revels were held in his honour and in that of his alliance with Marie of Cleves, Philip's niece.

The week intervening between the betrothal and the nuptials was passed in a succession of banquets and tourneys, gorgeous in their elaboration. Moreover, St. Andrew's Day chancing to fall just then, the new Burgundian Order was convened and the Duke of Orleans was elected a Knight of the Golden Fleece, while in his turn he presented his cousin with the collar of his own Order of the Porcupine. Lord Cornwallis and other English gentlemen who had accompanied Orleans across the Channel participated in these gaieties, nor were they among the least favoured guests, adds Barante.

Amity was triumphant, and there was a general feeling abroad that the returned exile was henceforth to be the ruling power in France. People began to look to him to act as the go-between in their behalf, to be their mediator with Charles VII., still little known at his best. Many towns turned towards him in hopes of finding a friend, and among them was Bruges. But it was not royal favours that Bruges sought. Her burghers felt great inconvenience from the breach with their sovereign duke. Anxious to be reinstated in his grace, they seized the opportunity of reminding Philip of his assertion, and they besought him to enter their gates in company with the Duke of Orleans, a prince of the blood, closer to the French sovereign than the Duke of Burgundy.

After some demur, Philip consented to grant their petition. Possibly he was not loth to be persuaded. The deputies hastened back to Bruges to rejoice their fellow-citizens with the news, and

Childhood

to prepare a reception for their appeased sovereign, calculated to make him content with the late rebels.

Before the grand cortège, composed of the two dukes, their consorts, and the dignitaries who had assisted in the feasts of marriage and of chivalry, reached the gates of Bruges, the citizens were ready with a touching spectacle of humility and repentance.[1]

A league from the gates, the magistrates and burghers stood in the road awaiting the travellers from St. Omer. All were barefooted and bareheaded. Under the December sky they waited the approach of the stately procession. When the duke arrived, they all fell upon their knees and implored him to forgive the late troubles and to reinstate their city in his favour. Philip did not answer immediately—delay was always a feature of these episodes. Thereupon, the Duke of Orleans, both duchesses, and all the gentlemen joined their entreaties to the citizens' prayers. Again a pause, and then, as if generously yielding to pressure, Philip bade the burghers put on their shoes and their hats while he accepted at their hands the keys of all the gates. Then the long procession moved on towards Bruges. At the gate were the clergy, followed by the monks, nuns, and beguins of the various convents and foundations, bearing crosses, banners, reliquaries, and many precious ecclesiastical treasures. There, too, were

[1] Meyer, *Commentarii sive Annales rerum Flandricarum*, p. 296.

the gilds and merchants, on horseback, with magnificent accoutrements freshly burnished to do honour to the welcome they offered their forgiving overlord.

Throughout Bruges, at convenient places, platforms and stages were erected, whereon were enacted dramatic performances, given continuously, to provide amusement for the collected crowds. Sometimes the presentation carried significance beyond mere entertainment. Here a maid, garbed as a wood nymph, appeared leading a swan which wore the collar of the Golden Fleece and a porcupine. This last beast was to symbolise the Orleans device, *Near and Far*, as the creature was supposed to project his spines to a distance.

One enthusiastic citizen covered his whole house with gold and the roof with silver leaves to betoken his satisfaction. Indeed, if we may believe the chroniclers, never in the memory of man had any city incurred so much expense to honour its lord. The duke permitted his heart to be touched by these proofs of devotion, and on the very evening of his arrival he evinced that his confidence was restored by sending the civic keys and a gracious message to the magistrates. At the news of this condescension the cries of "*Noël*" re-echoed afresh through the illuminated streets.

Charles was not present at this entry, which took place on Saturday, December 11th, but Philip was so much entertained with the performance that he sent for his son, and on the following Saturday he and the Countess of Charolais came from Ghent to join the party. The Duke of Orleans and many nobles rode out of the city to meet the young couple, who were formally escorted to the palace by magistrates and citizens in a body. On the Sunday there were repetitions of some of the plays and every attention was offered by the Bruges burghers to their young guests. When Orleans departed with his bride on Tuesday, December 14th, what wonder that the lady wept in sorrow at leaving these gay Burgundian doings!

While Charles did not actually witness the humiliation of the citizens, the seven-year-old boy would, undoubtedly, have heard and known sufficient of the cause of the festivals to be fully aware that the citizens who had dared defy his father were glad to buy back his smiles at any cost to their pride and purse. He would have known, too, that merchants from Venice, Genoa, Florence, and elsewhere joined the Bruges burghers in the welcome to the mollified overlord. It was a spectacle of the relations between a city and the ducal father not to be easily forgotten by the son.

CHAPTER II

YOUTH

1440-1453

THE heir of Burgundy was still in very tender years when he began to take official part in public affairs, sometimes associated with one parent, sometimes with the other.

There was a practical advantage in bringing the boy to the fore by which the duke was glad to profit. With his own manifold interests, it was impossible for him to be present in his various capitals as often as was demanded by the usage of the diverse individual seigniories. It was politic, therefore, to magnify the representative capacity of his son and of his consort in order to obtain the grants and *aides* which certain of his subjects declared could be given only when requested orally by their sovereign lord. Thus, in 1444, it was Count Charles and the duchess who appeared in Holland to ask an *aide*.[1] In the following year, Charles accompanied his father when Philip made one of his rare visits—there were only three between 1428 and 1466—to Holland and Zealand.

[1] Blok, *Eene Hollandsche stad onder de Bourg. Oostenrijksche Heerschappij*, p. 84.

A CASTLE IN BURGUNDY

Olivier de la Marche was among the attendants on this occasion, and he describes with great detail how rejoiced were the inhabitants to have their absentee count in their land.[1] Many matters could only be set aright by his authority. Among the complaints brought to him at Middelburg were accusations against a certain knight of high birth, Jehan de Dombourc. Philip ordered that the man be arrested at once and brought before him for trial. This was easier said than done. Warned of his danger, Dombourc, with four or five comrades, took refuge in the clock tower of the church of the Cordeliers, a sanctuary that could not be taken by storm.[2] He was provided with a good store of food, this audacious criminal, and prepared to stand a siege. There he remained three days, because, for the honour of the Church, they could not fire upon him.

"And I remember [adds La Marche] seeing a nun come out and call to Jehan Dombourc, her brother, advising him to perish defending himself rather than to dishonour their lineage by falling into the hands of the executioner. Nevertheless, finally he was forced to surrender to his prince, and he was beheaded in the market-place at Middelburg, but, at the plea of his sister, the said nun, his body was delivered to her to be buried in consecrated ground."

In this same visit Philip presided over the Zea-

---

[1] La Marche, ii., 79, etc.

[2] See also *Chronijcke van Nederlant*, p. 76, and *Vlaamsche Kronijk*, p. 203. Ed. C. Piot.

land estates and the young count sat by his side, not as an idle spectator, but because usage required the presence of the heir as well as that of the Count of Zealand.

When Charles was twelve he was present at an assembly of the Order of the Golden Fleece held in Ghent. It was the first occasion of the kind witnessed by La Marche, and very minute is his description of the lavish magnificence of the affair, undoubtedly intended to awe the citizens into complying with the requests of their Count of Flanders.

Charles played a prominent part in all the functions, and assisted in the election of his tutor, Seigneur et Ber d' Auxy. Another candidate of that year was Frank van Borselen, Count of Ostrevant, widower of Jacqueline, late Countess of Holland.

In 1446, the little Countess of Charolais died at Brussels. "Honourably as befitted a king's daughter" was she buried at Ste. Gudule.[1]

"Tireless in their devotion were the duke and duchess in her last illness, and Charles VII. despatched two skilled doctors to her aid but all efforts were vain.

"Much bemourned was the princess for she was virtuous. God have pity on her soul"

piously ejaculates La Marche.

A little item[2] in the accounts suggests that a

[1] D'Escouchy, *Chronique*, i., 110.
[2] The items of the funeral expenses can be found in Laborde, i., 380. There were 600 masses at two sous apiece.

pleasant friendship had existed between the two young people:

"To Jehan de la Court, harper of Mme. the Countess of Charolais, for a harp which she had bought from him and given to Ms. the Count of Charolais for him to play and take his amusement, xii francs."[1]

It is easy to surmise that music was not, however, the young count's favourite amusement. In Philip's court, tournaments were still held and afforded a fascinating entertainment for a lad whose bent was undoubtedly towards a military career.

One valiant actor in these tourneys where were revived the ancient traditions of knighthood, was Jacques de Lalaing, a chevalier with all the characteristics of times past, fighting for fame in the present. In his youth, this aspirant for reputation swore a vow to meet thirty knights in combat before he attained his thirtieth year. Dominated by a desire to fulfil his vow, Lalaing haunted the court of Burgundy, because the Netherlands were on the highroad between England and many points in Germany, Italy, and the East, and there he had the best chance of falling in with all the prowess

[1] In that same year, 1440, in which this gift is recorded, there is another item showing how Charles took his amusement not only on the harp but in planning some of the elaborate surprises regularly introduced between courses in the banquets. "To Barthelmy the painter, for making the cover of a pasty for the Count of Charolais to present to Monseigneur on the night of St. Martin in the previous year, v francs" (Laborde, i., 381).

that might be abroad. For stay-at-home prowess he cared naught. A delightful personage is Messire Jacques and a brave rôle does he play in the series of jousts, sporting gaily on the pages of the various Burgundian chroniclers, who recorded in their old age what they had seen in their youth. One description, however, of these encounters reads much like another and they need not be repeated.

During his childhood Charles was a spectator only on the days of mimic battle. In his seventeenth year he was permitted to enter the lists as a regular combatant, a permission shared by his fellow pupils all eager to flesh their maiden spears. The duke arranged that his son should have a preliminary tilt a few days before the public affair in order to test his ability. All the courtiers—and apparently ladies were not excluded from the discussion on the matter—agreed that no better knight could be found for this purpose than Jacques de Lalaing, who, on his part, was highly honoured by being selected to gauge the untried capabilities of the prince.[1]

In the park at Brussels with the duke and duchess as onlookers, the preliminary encounter took place. At the very first attack, Charles struck Messire Jacques on the shield and shattered his lance into many pieces. The duke was displeased because he thought that the knight had not exerted his full strength and was favouring his son. He

[1] La Marche, ii., 214.

accordingly sent word to Jacques that he must play in earnest and not hold his force in leash. Fresh lances were brought; again did the count withstand the attack so sturdily that both lances were shattered. This time the boy's mother was the dissatisfied one, thinking that the knight was too hard with his junior, but the duke only laughed.

"Thus differed the parents. The one desired him to prove his manhood, the other was preoccupied with his safety. With these two courses the trial ended amid rounds of applause for the prince."[1]

The actual tourney was held on the Marketplace in Brussels before a distinguished assembly. Count Charles was escorted into the arena by his cousin, the Count d'Estampes, and other nobles. Seigneur d' Auxy, his tutor, stood near to watch the maiden efforts of the prince and his mates. He had reason to be proud of Charles, both for his bearing and his skill. He gave and received excellent thrusts, broke more than ten lances, and did his duty so valiantly that in the evening he received the prize from two princesses, and "Montjoye" was cried by the heralds in his honour. From that time forth, the count was considered a puissant and rude jouster and gained great renown.

"And that is the reason why I commence my me-

[1] Gachard puts this tournament in Lent, 1452. Charles's outfit cost 360 livres.

moirs about him and his deeds[1] [continues La Marche, on concluding his description of the tournament], and I do not speak from hearsay and rumour. As one who has been brought up with him from his youth in his father's service and in his own, I will touch upon his education, his morals, his character, and his habits from the moment when I first saw him as appears above in my memoirs.

"As to his character, I will commence at the worst features. He was hot, active, and impetuous: as a child he was very eager to have his own way. Nevertheless, he had so much understanding and good sense that he resisted his inclinations and in his youth no one could be found sweeter or more courteous than he. He did not take the name of God or the saints in vain, and held God in great fear and reverence. He learned well and had a retentive memory. He was fond of reading and of hearing read the stories of Lancelot and Gawain, but to both he preferred the sea and boats. Falconry, too, he loved and he hunted whenever he had leave. In archery he early excelled his comrades and was good at other sports. Thus was the count educated, trained, and taught, and thus did he devote himself to good and excellent exercise."

That the report of the lavishness and extravagance of the Burgundian court was no idle rumour, exaggerated by frequent repetitions, is attested to by every bit of contemporary evidence. Enthusiastic and loyal chroniclers dwell on the magnificence, and the arid details of bills paid show what it cost to attain the vaunted perfection, while

[1] La Marche, i., ch. 21.

FRONTISPIECE OF AN ACCOUNT-BOOK
XVTH CENTURY

Youth

the protests from taxpayers prove that this splendour did not grow like the lilies of the field.

Philip's treasury had many separate compartments. There were many quarters to which he could turn for his needed supplies, but there were times when his exchequer ran very threateningly low, and his financial stress led him to be very conciliatory towards the burghers with full purses.

In 1445, Ghent had been honoured by the celebration of the feast of the Order of the Golden Fleece within her gates. Two years later, Philip appeared in person at a meeting of the *collace*, or municipal assembly, and delivered a harangue to the Ghentish magistrates and burghers, flattering them, moreover, by using their vernacular. The tenor of this speech was as follows[1]:

"My good and faithful friends, you know how I have been brought up among you from my infancy. That is why I have always loved you more than the inhabitants of all my other cities, and I have proved this by acceding to all your requests. I believe then that I am justified in hoping that you will not abandon me to-day when I have need of your support. Doubtless you are not ignorant of the condition of my father's treasury at the period of his death. The majority of his possessions had been sold. His jewels were in pawn. Nevertheless, the demands of a legitimate vengeance compelled me to undertake a long and bloody war, during which the defence of my fortresses

[1] Kervyn, *Histoire de Flandre*, iv. Kervyn quotes from the *Dagboek des gentsche collatie*, M. Schayes.

and of my cities, and the pay of my army have necessitated outlays so large that it is impossible to estimate them. You know, too, that at the very moment when the war on France was at its height, I was obliged, in order to assure the protection of my country of Flanders, to take arms against the English in Hainaut, in Zealand, and in Friesland, a proceeding costing me more than 10,000 *saluts d'or*, which I raised with difficulty. Was I not equally obliged to proceed against Liege, in behalf of my countship of Namur, which sprang from the bosom of Flanders? It is not necessary to add to all these outlays those which I assume daily for the cause of the Christians in Jerusalem, and the maintenance of the Holy Sepulchre.

"It is true, however, that, yielding to the persuasions of the pope and the Council, I have now consented to put an end to the evils multiplied by war by forgetting my father's death, and by reconciling myself with the king. Since the conclusion of this treaty, I considered that while I had succeeded in preserving to my subjects during the war the advantages of industry and of peace, they had submitted to heavy burdens in taxes and in voluntary contributions, and that it was my duty to re-establish order and justice in the administration. But everything went on as though the war had not ceased. All my frontiers have been menaced, and I found myself obliged to make good my rights in Luxemburg, so useful to the defence of my other lands, especially of Brabant and Flanders.

"In this way, my expenses continued to increase; all my resources are now exhausted, and the saddest part of it all is that the good cities and communes of Flanders and especially the country folk are at the very end of their sacrifices. With grief I see many of my subjects unable to pay their taxes, and obliged to emigrate. Nevertheless, my receipts are so scanty that I have little advantage from them. Nor do I reap more from my hereditary lands, for all are equally impoverished.

"A way must be found to ease the poor people, and at the same time to protect Flanders from insult, Flanders for whose sake I would risk my own person, although to arrive at this end, important measures have become imperative."

After this affectionate preamble, Philip finally states that, in order to raise the requisite revenues, no method seemed to him so good and so simple as a tax on salt, three sous on every measure for a term of twelve years. He promised to dispense with all other subsidies and to make his son swear to demand nothing further as long as the *gabelle* was imposed.

"Know [he added in conclusion] that even if you consent to it I will renounce it if others prove of a different opinion, for I do not desire that the communes of Flanders be more heavily weighted than any other portion of my territory."

The duke might have spared his trouble and his elaborate condescension. The answer to his conciliatory request was a flat refusal to consider the matter at all. Salt was a vital necessity to Flemish fisheries, and its cost could not be increased to the least degree without serious inconvenience. The Flemings were wroth at his imitating the worst custom of his French kinsmen.

Philip departed from Ghent in great dudgeon. After a time he was persuaded that the indisposition of the town to meet his reasonable wishes was not due to the citizens at large, but to the machinations of a few unruly agitators among the magistrates. In 1449, therefore, he took a high-handed course of trying to direct the issue of the regular municipal elections, so as to ensure the choice of magistrates on whose obedience he could rely. The appearance of Burgundian troops in Ghent, before the election of mid-August, aroused the wrath of the community, who thought that their most cherished franchises were in jeopardy.

This was the beginning of a bitter struggle between Ghent and Philip. The duke found it no light matter to coerce the independent burghers into remembering that they were simply part of the Burgundian state. "*Tantæ molis erat liberam gentem in servitutem adigere!*" ejaculates Meyer in the midst of his chronicle of the details of fourteen months of active hostilities.[1] Matters were long in coming to an outbreak. Various points had been contended over, when Philip had endeavoured to change the seat of the great council, or to take divers measures tending to concentrate certain judicial or legislative functions for his own convenience, but in a manner prejudicial to the autonomy of Ghent. His centripetal policy was

[1] Meyer, xvi., 303.

disliked, but when his policy went further, and he attempted to control purely civic offices, dislike grew into resentment and the Ghenters rose in open revolt.

For a time, their opposition passed in Philip's estimation as mere insignificant unruliness. By 1452, however, the date of the tourney above described, it became evident that a vital issue was at stake. The Estates of Flanders endeavoured to mediate between overlord and town, but without success. Owing to Philip's interference in the elections, the results were declared void, and when a new election was appointed, the Burgundians accused the city of hastily augmenting its number of legal voters by over-facile naturalisation laws. The gilds, too, evinced a readiness to be very lenient in their scrutiny of candidates for admission to their cherished privileges, preferring, for the nonce, numbers to quality. Occupancy of furnished rooms was declared sufficient for enfranchisement, and there were cases where mere guests of a bourgeois were hastily recorded on the lists as full-fledged citizens.

By these means the popular party waxed very strong numerically. The sheriffs found themselves quite unequal to holding the rampant spirit of democracy in check. The regular government was overthrown, and the demagogues succeeded in electing three captains (*hooftmans*) invested with arbitrary power for the time being. The decrees of the ex-sheriffs were suspended, and a mass of very radical measures promulgated and joyfully confirmed by the populace, assembled on the Friday market. It was to be the judgment of the town meeting that ruled, not deputed authority. One ordinance stipulated that at the sound of the bell every burgher must hasten to the marketplace, to lend his voice to the deliberations.

For a time various negotiations went on between Philip and envoys from Ghent. The latter took a high hand and insinuated in unmistakable terms that if the duke refused an accommodation with them, they would appeal to their suzerain, the King of France. No act of rebellion, overt or covert, exasperated Philip more than this suggestion. Charles VII. was only too ready to ignore those clauses in the treaty of Arras, releasing the duke from homage, and virtually acknowledging his complete independence in his French territories. The king accepted missives from his late vassal's city, without reprimanding the writers for their presumption in signing themselves "Seigneurs of Ghent."[1] His action, however, was confined to mild attempts at mediation.

It was plain to the duke that his other towns would follow Ghent's resistance to his authority if there were hopes of her success. Therefore he threw aside all other interests for the time being, and exerted himself to levy a body of troops to

[1] They were charged with using this phrase. Gachard says that they placed at the top of their letter their titles of sheriffs and deans, as princes and lords take the title of their seignories.—(La Marche, ii., 221. *See also* d'Escouchy, ii., 25.)

crush Flemish pretensions. His counsellors advised him to sound the temper of other citizens and to ascertain whether their sympathies were with Ghent. Answers of feeble loyalty came back to him from the majority of the other towns. Undoubtedly they highly approved Ghent's efforts. They, too, could not afford to pay taxes fraught with danger to their commerce, nor to relinquish one jot of privileges dearly bought at successive crises throughout a long period of years. The only doubt in their minds was as to the ultimate success of the burghers to stem the course of Burgundian usurpation. Therefore, they first hedged, and then consented to aid the duke. This course was pursued by the Hollanders and the Zealanders, all alike short-sighted.

The Ghenters succeeded in possessing themselves of the castle of Poucque by force, and of the village of Gaveren by stratagem, taking advantage in the latter case of the castellan's absence at church.

When every part of his dominions had been canvassed for troops, and Philip was prepared for his first active campaign against Ghent, he was anxious to leave his heir under the protection of the duchess, conscious that the imminent contest would be bitter and deadly. A pretence was made that the young count's accoutrements were not ready, and that, therefore, he would have to remain in Brussels.

"But he whose ambitions waxed, hastened the completion of his accoutrements, and swore by St. George, the greatest oath he ever used, that he would rather go in his shirt than not accompany his father to punish his impudent rebel subjects."[1]

The approaching hostilities were watched by foreign merchants in dread of commercial disaster.

"On May 18th, the *nations*[2] of the merchants of Bruges departed thence to go to Ghent to try to make peace between that city and the Duke of Burgundy, and there were *nations* of Spain, Aragon, Portugal, and Scotland, besides the Venetians, Milanese, Genoese, and Luccans."[3]

But the men of Ghent were beyond the point where commercial arguments could stem their course. The very day that this company arrived in the city, the burghers sallied forth six or seven thousand strong, fully equipped for offensive warfare.

Both the actual engagements and guerilla skirmishes that raged over a minute stretch of territory were characterised by an extraordinary ferocity. Around Oudenarde, which town Philip was determined to relieve, men were beheaded like sheep.

In the first regular engagement in which Charles took part, he showed a brave front and learned the duties of a prince by rewarding others with the honour of knighthood. Among those slain in the course of the war, were Cornelius, Bastard of Bur-

[1] La Marche, ii., 230.
[2] Associations of merchants in foreign cities.
[3] Chastellain, *Œuvres*, ii., 221.

gundy, and the gallant Jacques de Lalaing. Philip grieved deeply over the death of the former, his favourite among his natural sons, and buried him with all honours in the Church of Ste-Gudule in Brussels. The title by which he was known, hardly a proud one it would seem, passed to his brother Anthony. Lalaing, too, was greatly mourned, thus prematurely cut down in his thirty-third year.

There was so much fear lest the duke's sole legitimate heir might also perish in these conflicts where there was no mercy, that Charles was persuaded to go to visit his mother in the hope that she would keep him by her side. She made a feast in his honour, but, to the surprise of all, the duchess, who had wished to protect her son from the mild perils of a tourney, now encouraged him with brave words to return to fight in all earnest for his inheritance.[1] He himself was very indignant at the efforts to treat him as a child.

The first truce and negotiations for peace, initiated in the summer of 1452, were broken off because the conditions were unbearable to the Ghenters. Another year of warfare followed before the decisive battle of Gaveren, in July, 1453, forced them sadly to succumb. There was no other course open to them. Not only were they defeated but their numbers were decimated.[2] With

[1] La Marche, ii., 312. Chastellain, ii., 278. See also *Chronique d'Adrian de Budt*, p. 242, etc.

[2] Meyer, p. 313. La Marche, ii., 313. Lavisse, *Histoire de France*, accepts 13,000 as the number slain. Chastellain (ii., 375) puts the number at 22–30,000, including those

full allowance for exaggeration, it is certain that the loss was very heavy. Terms scornfully rejected at an earlier date were, in 1453, accepted with every humiliating detail. More, the defeated rebels were bidden to be grateful that their kind sovereign had imposed nothing further to the conditions. As to abating the severity of the articles, he declared that he would not change an *a* for a *b*.[1]

The chief provisions were as follows: The deans of the gilds were deprived of participation in the election of sheriffs. The privileges of the naturalisation laws were considerably abridged. No sentence of banishment could be pronounced without the intervention of the duke's bailiff, whose authorisation, too, was required before the publication of edicts, ordinances, etc. The sheriffs were forbidden to place their names at the head of letters to the officers of the duke. The banners were to be delivered to the duke and placed under five locks, whose several keys should be deposited with as many different people, without whose consensus the banners could not be brought forth to lead the burghers to sedition. One gate was to be closed every Thursday in memory of the day when the citizens had marched through it to attack their liege lord, and another was to be barred up in perpetuity or at the pleasure of their sovereign. To reimburse the duke for his

drowned by the duke's order. Du Clercq lets a certain sympathy for the rebellious people escape his pen. Chastellain and La Marche treat the antagonism to taxes as unreasonable.

[1] Chastellain, ii., 387.

enforced outlay, a heavy indemnity was to be paid by the city.

July 30th was the date appointed for the final act of submission, the *amende honorable* of the unfortunate city. The scene was very similar to that played at Bruges in 1440. Two thousand citizens headed by the sheriffs, councillors, and captains of the burgher guard met the duke and his suite a league without the walls of Ghent. Bareheaded, barefooted, and divested of all their robes of office and of dignity, clad only in shirts and small clothes, these magistrates confessed that they had wronged their loving lord by unruly rebellion, and begged his pardon most humbly.

The duke spent the night of July 29th at Gaveren, prepared to march out in the morning with his whole army in handsome array. Philip was magnificently apparelled, but he rode the same horse which he had used on the day of battle, with the various wounds received on that day ostentatiously plastered over to make a dramatic show of what the injured sovereign had suffered at the hands of his disloyal subjects.

The civic procession was headed by the Abbot of St. Bavon and the Prior of the Carthusians. The burghers who followed the half-clad officials were fully dressed but they, too, were barefoot and ungirdled. All prostrated themselves in the dust and cried, "Mercy on the town of Ghent." While they were thus prostrate, the town spokesman of the council made an elaborate speech in French, assuring the duke that if, out of his benign grace, he would take his loving and repentant subjects again into his favour, they would never again give him cause for reproach.

"At the conclusion of this harangue, the duke and the Count of Charolais, there present, pardoned the petitioners for their evil deeds. The men of Ghent re-entered their town more happy and rejoiced than can be expressed, and the duke departed for Lille, having disbanded his army, that every one might return to their several homes."[1]

The joy experienced by the conquered, here described by La Marche, as he looked back at the event from the calm retirement of his old age, was not visible to all eye-witnesses. The progress of this war was watched eagerly from other parts of Philip's dominion. His army was full of men from both the Burgundies, who sent frequent reports to their own homes. Some passages from one of these reports by an unknown war correspondent run as follows:

"As to news from here, Monday after St. Magdalen's Day, Monseigneur the duke got the better of the Ghenters near Gaveren between ten and eleven o'clock. They attacked him near his quarters. . . . The duke risked his own person in advance of his company in the very worst of the slaughter, which lasted from the said place up to Ghent, a distance of about two leagues. The slain number three or four thousand, more or less, and those drowned in the river of Quaux about two hundred. . . . This Tuesday,

[1] La Marche, ii., 331. The Chastellain MS. is lacking for this event.

the date of writing, the army departs from their quarters to advance on Ghent to demand the conditions lately offered them, and the bearer of this letter will tell you what is the result. M. the duke and his army marched up to Ghent and I have seen the bearing of the citizens. They are very bitter and despondent. M. the marshall has been parleying. I hear that matters have been settled. I hear that the Ghenters' loss is thirteen to fourteen thousand men. I cannot write more for I have no time owing to the haste of the messenger."

This was written July 23d. There is another despatch of July 31st, giving the last news, which was "very joyous." The public apology had just been enacted—

"and afterwards, in token of being conquered and as a confession that my said seigneur was victorious, those of Ghent have delivered up all their banners to the number of eighty. And on this day my said lord has created seven or eight knights and heralds in honour of his triumph, which is inestimable."[1]

The duke's victory was certainly "inestimable" in its value to him, yet, in spite of the rigour enforced on this defeated people, they were not

[1] *Revue des sociétés savantes des départements*, 7me. série, 6, p. 209.

These two reports were enclosed with brief notes dated July 31 and August 8, 1453, from the ducal attorney at Amont to the magistrates of Baume. The former was one of the highest officials in the Franche-Comté. The reporter might have been one of his secretaries. The two notes with their unsigned enclosures were discovered (1881) in the archives of the town of Baume-les-Dames.

as crushed as they might have been had they submitted in 1445. Philip was clever enough to be more lenient than appeared at first. Ancient privileges were confirmed in a special compact, and the duke swore to maintain all former concessions in their entirety except in the points above specified. Liberty of person was guaranteed, and it was expressly stipulated that if the bailiff refused to sustain the sheriffs in their exercise of justice, or tried to arrogate to himself more than his due authority, he should forfeit his office. Lastly, and more important than all, the duke made no attempt to revive the demand for the *gabelle* —salt was left free and untaxed. As a matter of fact, too, the duke was not exigeant in the fulfilment of every item of the treaty and, two years later, he increased certain privileges. He had cut the lion's claws but he had no desire to pit his strength again with Flemish communes. He had taught the audacious rebels a lesson and that sufficed him.[1]

[1] Kervyn, *Histoire de Flandre*, iv., 494.

CHAPTER III

THE FEAST OF THE PHEASANT

1454

AFTER the fatigues of this contest with Ghent, followed a period of relaxation for the Burgundian nobles at Lille, where a notable round of gay festivities was enjoyed by the court. Adolph of Cleves inaugurated the series with an entertainment where, among other things, he delighted his friends by a representation of the tale of the miraculous swan,[1] famous in the annals of his house for bringing the opportune knight down the Rhine to wed the forlorn heiress.

When his satisfied guests took their leave, Adolph placed a chaplet on the head of one of the gentlemen, thus designating him to devise a new amusement for the company; and under the invitation lurked a tacit challenge to make the coming occasion more brilliant than the first. Again and again was this process repeated. Entertainment followed entertainment, all a mixture of repasts and vaudeville shows in whose preparation the successive hosts vied with each other to attain perfection.

The hard times, the stress of ready money, so eloquently painted when the merchants were im-

[1] A performance repeated in our modern Lohengrin.

plored to take pity on their poverty-stricken lord, were cast into utter oblivion. It was harvest tide for skilled craftsmen and artisans. Any one blessed with a clever or fantastic idea easily found a market for the product of his brain. He could see his poetic or quaint conception presented to an applauding public with a wealth of paraphernalia that a modern stage manager would not scorn. How much the nobles spent can only be inferred from the ducal accounts, which are eloquent with information about the creators of all this mimic pomp. About six sous a day was the wage earned by a painter, while the plumbers received eight. These latter were called upon to coax pliable lead into all sorts of shapes, often more grotesque than graceful.

One fête followed another from the early autumn of 1453 to February, 1454, when "The Feast of the Pheasant," as the ducal entertainment was called, crowned the series with an elaborate magnificence that has never been surpassed.

Undoubtedly Philip possessed a genius for dramatic effect and it is more than possible that he instigated the progressive banquets for the express purpose of leading up to the occasion with which he intended to dazzle Europe.[1]

For the duke's thoughts were now turned from civic revolts to a great international movement which he hoped to see set in motion. Almost coincident with the capitulation of Ghent to Philip's will had been the capitulation of Constanti-

[1] The chroniclers are not at one on this point.

COUNT OF ST. POL AND HIS JESTER

The Feast of the Pheasant 47

nople to the Turks. The event long dreaded by pope and Christendom had happened at last (May 29, 1453). Again and again was the necessity for a united opposition to the inroads of the dangerous infidels urged by Rome. On the eve of St. Martin, 1453, a legate arrived in Lille bringing an official letter from the pope, setting forth the dire stress of the Christian Church, and imploring the mightiest duke of the Occident to be her saviour, and to assume the leadership of a crusade in her behalf against the encroaching Turk.[1]

Philip was ready to give heed to the prayer. Whatever the exact sequence of his plans in relation to the court revels, the result was that his own banquet was utilised as a proper occasion for blazoning forth to the world with a flourish of trumpets his august intention of dislodging the invader from the ancient capital of the Eastern empire.

The superintendence of the arrangements for this all-eclipsing fête was entrusted, as La Marche relates,

"to Messire Jehan, Seigneur de Lannoy, Knight of the Golden Fleece, and a skilful ingenious gentleman, and to one Squire Jehan Boudault, a notable and discreet man. And the duke honoured me so far that he desired me to be consulted. Several councils were held for the matter to which the chancellor and the first chamberlain were invited. The latter had just returned from the war in Luxemburg already described.

"These council meetings were very important and very private, and after discussion it was decided what

[1] Du Clercq, *Mémoires*, ii., 159.

ceremonies and mysteries were to be presented. The duke desired that I should personate the character of Holy Church of which he wished to make use at this assembly."

As in many half amateur affairs the preparations took more time than was expected. At the first date set, all was not in readiness and the performance was postponed until February 17th. This entailed serious loss upon the provision merchants and they received compensation for the spoiled birds and other perishable edibles.[1]

The gala-day opened with a tournament at which Adolph of Cleves again sported as Knight of the Swan to the applause of the onlookers. After the jousting, the guests adjourned to the banqueting hall, where fancy had indeed, run riot, to make ready for their admiring eyes and their sagacious palates. *Entremets* is the term ap-

[1] This banquet at Lille was the subject of several descriptions by spectators or at least contemporary authors.

The Royal Library at the Hague possesses a manuscript copied from an older one which contains the order of proceedings together with the text of all vows. There is a minute description in Mathieu d'Escouchy, who claims to have been present, and in a manuscript coming from Baluze, whose anonymous author might also have been an eye-witness. Of the various versions, that of La Marche seems to be the most original. One record shows that "a clerk living at Dijon, called Dion du Cret, received, in 1455, a sum of five francs and a half for having, at the order of the accountants, copied and written in parchment the history of the banquet of my said seigneur, held at Lille, February 17, 1453, containing fifty-six leaves of parchment" (La Marche, ii., 340 note). It is possible that all the authors refreshed their memory with this account, which seems to have been merely a copy.

plied to the elaborate set pieces and side-shows provided to entertain the feasters between courses, and these were on an unprecedented scale.

Three tables stood prepared respectively for the duke and his suite, for the Count of Charolais, his cousins, and their comrades, and for the knights and ladies. The first table was decorated with marvellous constructions, among which was a cruciform church whose mimic clock tower was capacious enough to hold a whole chorus of singers. The enormous pie in which twenty-eight musicians were discovered when the crust was cut may have been the original of that pasty whose opening revealed four-and-twenty blackbirds in a similar plight. Wild animals wandered gravely at a machinist's will through deep forests, but in the midst of the counterfeit brutes there was at least one live lion, for Gilles le Cat[1] received twenty shillings from the duke for the chain and locks he made to hold the savage beast fast "on the day of the said banquet."

Again there was an anchored ship, manned with a full crew and rigged completely. "I hardly think," observes La Marche, "that the greatest ship in the world has a greater number of ropes and sails."

Before the guests seated themselves they wandered around the hall and inspected the decorations one by one. Nor was their admiration exhausted when they turned to the discussion of the toothsome dainties provided for their delectation.

[1] Laborde, i., 127.

During the progress of the banquet, the story of Jason was enacted. Time there certainly was for the play. La Marche estimated forty-eight dishes to every course, though he qualifies his statement by the admission that his memory might be inexact. These dishes were wheeled over the tables in little chariots before each person in turn.

"Such were the mundane marvels that graced the fête," is the conclusion of La Marche's[1] exhaustive enumeration of the masterpieces from artists' workshops and ducal kitchen

"I will leave them now to record a pity moving *entremets* which seemed to be more special than the others. Through the portal whence the previous actors had made their entrance, came a giant larger without artifice than any I had ever seen, clad in a long green silk robe, a turban on his head like a Saracen in Granada. His left hand held a great, old-fashioned two-bladed axe, his right hand led an elephant covered with silk. On its back was a castle wherein sat a lady looking like a nun, wearing a mantle of black cloth and a white head-dress like a recluse.[2]

"Once within the hall and in sight of the noble company, like one who had work before her, she said to the giant, her conductor:

"'Giant, prithee let me stay
For I spy a noble throng
To whom I wish to speak.'

"At these words her guide conducted his charge

[1] II., 361.
[2] The text says in the Burgundian or recluse fashion. *Béguine* is probably the right reading.

The Feast of the Pheasant

before the ducal table and there she made a piteous appeal to all assembled to come to rescue her, Holy Church, fallen into the hands of unbelieving miscreants. As soon as she ceased speaking a body of officers entered the hall, Toison d'Or, king-at-arms, bringing up the rear. This last carried a live pheasant ornamented with a rich collar of gold studded with jewels. Toison d'Or was followed by two maidens, Mademoiselle Yolande, bastard daughter of the duke, and Isabelle of Neufchâtel, escorted by two gentlemen of the Order. They all proceeded to the host. After greetings, Toison d'Or then said:

"'High and puissant prince and my redoubtable lord, here are ladies who recommend themselves very humbly to you because it is, and has been, the custom at great feasts and noble assemblies to present to the lords and nobles a peacock or some other noble bird whereon useful and valid vows may be made. I am sent hither with these two demoiselles to present to you this noble pheasant, praying you to remember them.'

"When these words were said, Monseigneur the duke, who knew for what purpose he had given the banquet, looked at the personified Church, and then, as though in pity for her stress, drew from his bosom a document containing his vow to succour Christianity, as will appear later. The Church manifested her joy, and seeing that my said seigneur had given his vow to Toison d'Or, she again burst forth forth into rhyme:

"'God be praised and highly served
    By thee, my son, the foremost peer in France.
Thy sumptuous bearing have I close observed
Until it seemed thou wert reserved

>   To bring me my deliverànce.
>   Near and far I seek alliance
>   And pray to God to grant thee grace
>   To work His pleasure in thy place.
>
> "'O every prince and noble, man and knight,
>   Ye see your master pledged to worthy deed.
>   Abandon ease, abjure delight,
>   Lift up your hand, each in his right,
>   Offer God the savings from thy greed.
>   I take my leave, imploring each, indeed,
>   To risk his life for Christian gain,
>   To serve his God and 'suage my pain.'

"At this the giant led off the elephant and departed by the same way in which he had entered.

"When I had seen this *entremets*, that is, the Church and a castle on the back of such a strange beast, I pondered as to whether I could understand what it meant and could not make it out otherwise except that she had brought this beast, rare among us, in sign that she toiled and laboured in great adversity in the region of Constantinople, whose trials we know, and the castle in which she was signified Faith. Moreover, because this lady was conducted by this mighty giant, armed, I inferred that she wished to denote her dread of the Turkish arms which had chased her away and sought her destruction.

"As soon as this play was played out, the noble gentlemen, moved by pity and compassion, hastened to make vows, each in his own fashion."

The vow of the Count of Charolais was as follows:

"I swear to God my creator, and to His glorious

The Feast of the Pheasant

mother, to the ladies and to the pheasant, that, if my very redoubtable lord and father embark on this holy journey, and if it be his pleasure that I accompany him, I will go and will serve him as well as I can and know how to do."

Other vows were less simple: all kinds of fantastic conditions being appended according to individual fancy. One gentleman decided never to go to bed on a Saturday until his pledge were accomplished. Another that he would eat nothing on Fridays that had ever lived until he had had an opportunity of meeting the enemy hand to hand, and of attacking, at peril of his life, the banner of the Grand Turk.

Philip Pot vowed never to sit at table on a Tuesday and to wear no protection on his right arm. This last the duke refused to permit. Hugues de Longueval vowed that when he had once turned his face to the East he would abstain from wine until he had plunged his sword in an infidel's blood, and that he would devote two years to the crusade even if he had to remain all alone, provided Constantinople were not recovered. Louis de Chevelast swore that no covering should protect his head until he had come to within four leagues of the infidels, and that he would fight a Turk on foot with nothing on his arm but a glove. There was the same emulation in the vows as in the banquets and many of the self-imposed penalties were as bizarre as the side-shows.

There were so many chevaliers eager to bind themselves to the enterprise that the prolonged ceremony threatened to become tedious. The duke, therefore, declared that the morrow would be equally valid as the day.[1]

"To abridge my tale [continues La Marche], the banquet was finished and the cloth removed and every one began to walk around the room. To me it seemed like a dream, for, of all the decorations, soon nothing remained but the crystal fountain. When there was no further spectacle to distract me, then my understanding began to work and various considerations touching this business came into my mind. First, I pondered upon the outrageous excess and great expense incurred in a brief space by these banquets, for this fashion of progressive entertainments, with the hosts designated by chaplets, had lasted a long time. All had tried to outshine their predecessors, and all, especially my said lord, had spent so much that I considered the whole thing outrageous and without any justification for the expense, except as regarded the *entremets* of the Church and the vows. Even that seemed to me too lightly treated for an important enterprise.

"Meditating thus I found myself by chance near a gentleman, councillor and chamberlain, who was in my lord's confidence and with whom I had some acquaintance. To him I imparted my thoughts in the course of a friendly chat and his comment was as follows:

"'My friend, I know positively that these chaplet

[1] Mathieu d'Escouchy (ii., 222) gives all the vows as though made then, and differs in many unessential points from La Marche's account.

The Count of St. Pol was the only knight present who made his going dependent on the consent of the King of France, a condition very displeasing to his liege lord of Burgundy.

The Feast of the Pheasant 55

entertainments would never have occurred except by the secret desire of the duke to lead up to this very banquet where he hoped to achieve a holy purpose and to resist the enemies of our faith. It is three years now since the distress of our Church was presented to the Knights of the Golden Fleece at Mons. My lord there dedicated his person and his wealth to her service. Since then occurred the rebellion of Ghent, which entailed upon him a loss of time and money. Thanks be to God, he has attained there a good and honourable peace, as every one knows. Now it has chanced that, during this very period, the Turks have encroached on Christianity still further in their capture of Constantinople. The need of succour is very pressing and all that you have witnessed to-day is proof that the good duke is intent on the weal of Christendom.'"

During the progress of this conversation, a new company was ushered into the hall, preceded by musicians. Here came *Grâce Dieu*, clad as a nun followed by twelve knights dressed in grey and black velvet ornamented with jewels. Not alone did they come. Each gentleman escorted a dame wearing a coat of satin cramoisy over a fur-edged round skirt *à la Portuguaise*. *Grâce Dieu* declared in rhyme that God had heard the pious resolution of Duke Philip of Burgundy. He had forthwith sent her with her twelve attendants to promise him a happy termination to his enterprise. Her ladies, Faith, Charity, Justice, Reason, Prudence, and their sisters, were then presented to him. *Grâce Dieu* departs alone and no sooner has she disappeared than Philip's new attributes begin to dance to add to the good cheer. Among the knights was Charles and one of his half-brothers; among the ladies was Margaret, Bastard of Burgundy, and the others were all of high birth. Not until two o'clock did the revels finally cease.

It must be noted that La Marche's reflections upon the extravagance of the entertainment occur also in Escouchy's memoirs. Probably both drew their moralising from another author. It is stated by several reputable chroniclers that Olivier de la Marche himself represented the Church. That he merely wrote her lines is far more probable. Female performers certainly appeared freely in these as in other masques, and there was no reason for putting a handsome youth in this rôle of the captive Church. In mentioning the plans that La Marche claims to have heard discussed in the council meeting, he says plainly that he was to play the rôle of Holy Church, but as he makes no further allusion to the fact, it may be dismissed as one of his careless statements.

This pompous announcement of big plans was the prelude to nothing! Yet it was by no means a farce when enacted. Philip fully intended to make this crusade the crowning event of his life, and his proceedings immediately after the great fête were all to further that end. To obtain allies abroad, to raise money at home, and to ensure a peaceful succession for his son in case of his own death in the East—such were the cares demanding the duke's attention.

The twenty-year-old Count of Charolais was entrusted with the regency for the term of his father's sojourn abroad in quest of allies, and he hastened to Holland to assume the reins of government, but he was speedily recalled to Lille to submit once more to paternal authority before being left to his own devices and to maternal bias.

For the ducal pair disagreed seriously on the subject of their son's second marriage. Isabella wished that a bride should be sought in England, and this wish was apparently echoed by Charles himself. The important topic was discussed with more or less freedom among the young courtiers, until the drift of the conversations, whose burden was wholly adverse to his own fixed purpose, came to Philip's ears, together with the information that one of his own children was among those who incited the count to independent desires about his future wife. Very stern was the duke in his reprimand to the two young men. He acknowledged that force of circumstances had once led him into friendly bonds with the foes of his own France, but never had he been "English at heart." Charles must accept his father's decision on pain of disinheritance. "As for this bastard," Philip added, turning to the other son, destitute of status in the eyes of the law, "if I find that he counsels you to oppose my will, I will have him tied up in a sack and thrown into the sea."[1]

[1] Du Clercq, ii., 203.

The bride selected for the heir was Isabella of Bourbon, daughter of the duke's sister, and the betrothal was hastily made. Even the approval of the bride's parents was dispensed with. This passed the more easily as the young lady herself was conveniently present in the Burgundian court under the guardianship of her aunt, the duchess, who had superintended her education. A papal dispensation was more necessary than paternal consent, but that, too, was waived as far as the betrothal was concerned. To that extent was Philip obeyed. Then Charles returned to Holland and his father proceeded to Germany to obtain imperial co-operation in his Eastern enterprise.

The duke's departure from Lille was made very privately at five o'clock in the morning. He was off before his courtiers were aware of his last preparations. That was a surprise, but not the only one in store for those left behind. In order to save every penny for his journey, Philip ordered radical retrenchment in his household expenses. The luxurious repasts served to his retainers were abolished and all alike found themselves forced to restrict their appetites to the dainties they could purchase with the table allowance accorded them. "The court's leg is broken," said Michel, the rhetorician.[1]

In his own outlay there was no stinting; the duke's progress was pompous and stately as

[1] "Michel dit que le gigot de la cour était rompu."—La Marche, i., ch. xiv.

The Feast of the Pheasant 59

was his wont. As he traversed Switzerland, Berne, Zurich, and Constance asked and obtained permission to show their friendship with ceremonious receptions. Loud were the cries of "*Vive Bourgogne.*" Equally hospitable were the German cities. Game, wine, fodder, were offered for the traveller's use at every stage, as he and his suite rode to the imperial diet.

At Ratisbon, disappointment greeted him. The emperor whom he had come so far to see in person failed to appear. Unwilling to accede to the plan of co-operation, afraid to give an open refusal, Frederic simply avoided hearing the request. Essentially lazy, he shrank from committing himself to a difficult enterprise, nor was his ambition tempted by possible glory. It had cost no pang to refuse the crown of Bohemia and Hungary. But even had he been personally ambitious he might still have been slow to lend his adherence to the duke's project, in the not unnatural dread lest the flashing renown of the greatest duke of the Occident might throw a poor emperor as ally into the shade. The very warmth of Philip's reception in Germany had chilled Frederic. From a retreat in Austria, he sent his secretary, Æneas Sylvius, to represent him at Ratisbon, a substitution far from pleasing to the visitor.

There were other defections, too, from the diet. None of those present was in a position to aid Philip in furthering his schemes. The matter was brought forward and laid on the table to be discussed at the next diet, appointed to meet in

November at Frankfort. But Philip would not wait for that. Germany did not agree with him. He was not well. Rumours there were of various kinds about his reasons for returning home. They do not seem to require much explanation, however. He had not been met half way in Germany and was highly displeased at the failure. Declining all further entertainment proffered by the cities, he travelled back to Besançon by way of Stuttgart and Basel. In the early autumn he was at Dijon.

During this summer, negotiations about Charles's marriage had continued. The Duke of Bourbon was inclined to chaffer about the dowry demanded by Philip. One of the estates asked for was Chinon, and it was urged that it, a male fief, was not capable of alienation. Philip was not inclined to accept this reason as final and the negotiations hung fire, much to the distress of the Duchess of Bourbon, who feared a breach between her husband and brother. Naïve are the phrases in one of her letters as quoted by Chastellain[1]:

"My very dear Seigneur and Brother,

"I have heard all Boudault's message from you. . . To be brief, Monseigneur is content and ready to accede the points that you demand. It seems to me that you ought to give him easy terms and that you ought to put aside any grudge you may cherish against him. Monseigneur, since I consider the thing as done, I beg you to celebrate the nuptials as soon as

[1] Chastellain, iii., 20, note.

The Feast of the Pheasant

possible although not without me as you have promised me."[1]

The king, too, was interested in the matter, and wrote as follows to Duke Philip:

"Dear and much loved Brother:

"Some time ago my cousin of Bourbon informed me of the negotiations for the marriage of my cousin of Charolais, your son, to my cousin Isabella of Bourbon, his daughter, which marriage has been deferred, as he writes me, because he does not wish to alienate to his daughter the seignory of Château-Chinon. It is not possible for him to do this on account of the marriage agreement of our daughter Jeanne and my cousin of Clermont, his son, wherein it was stipulated that Château-Chinon should go to them and their heirs. Moreover, it cannot descend in the female line, and in default of heirs male it must return to the crown as a true appanage of France.

"Lest, peradventure, you may doubt the truth of this, and imagine that the point is urged by our cousin of Bourbon simply as an excuse for not ceding the estate, we assure you that it is true, and was considered in arranging the alliance of our daughter so that it is beyond the power of our cousin of Bourbon to make any alienation or transfer of the territory at the marriage of his daughter. We never would have permitted the marriage of our daughter without this express settlement. With this consideration it seems to me that you ought not to block the marriage in question, especially as my cousin says he is offering you an equivalent. He cannot do more as we have charged our councillor, the bailiff of Berry, to explain to you in full. So pray do not postpone the marriage

[1] "Toute fois que ce ne soit pas sans moy."

for the above cause or for any cause, if by the permission of the Church and of our Holy Father it can be lawfully completed.

"Given at Romorantin, Oct. 17.

"CHARLES.[1]

CHALIGAUT."

As the marriage was an event of importance, and the circumstances are simple historic facts, it is strange that there should be any uncertainty regarding the details of its solemnisation. But there is a certain vagueness about the narratives. One version is so amusing that it deserves a slight consideration.[2] The chronicler relates how Charles VII. felt some uneasiness at the delay in the negotiations. Conscious of the sentiments of the Duchess of Burgundy, he feared lest her well-known sympathies for England might prevail in the final decision.

When Philip had returned to Dijon, the bailiff of Berry came as the king's special envoy to discuss some aspects of the subject with him. The mission was gladly undertaken as the messenger had never seen Philip nor his court and he was pleased at the chance of meeting a personage whose fame rang through Europe. Very graciously was he received by the duke, who read the king's letters attentively and replied to the envoy's messages in general terms of courteous recognition, without making his own intention manifest. The

[1] The original, signed, is in the *Archives de la Côte-d'Or*, B. 200. *See* Du Fresne de Beaucourt, *Histoire de Charles VII.*, v. 470.

[2] Chastellain, iii., 23, etc.

The Feast of the Pheasant 63

bailiff waited for an answer, finding, in the meanwhile, that his days passed very agreeably.

As a matter of fact, before his arrival at Dijon Philip Pot had set out for the Netherlands, bearing the duke's orders to his son to celebrate his nuptials without further delay. The duke did not intend to be influenced by any one. It was his will that his son should accept the bride selected and that was all sufficient. The reason why the duke detained the king's messenger was that he "awaited news from Messire Philip de Pot, whom he had sent in all speed to his son to hasten the wedding."[1] The said gentleman found the count at Lille with the duchess, his mother, and he was so diligent in the discharge of his mission that he made all the arrangements himself and saw the wedding rites solemnised immediately. The bridegroom did not even know of the plan until the night preceding the important day. Then Philip Pot rode back to Dijon.

When the duke was assured that the alliance was irrevocably sealed he was quite ready to answer the king's messenger, whom he at once invited to an audience. In a casual fashion Philip remarked:

"Now bailiff, the king sent you hither about a matter which I am humbly grateful for his interest in. You know my opinion. I had no desire to dissemble. Here is a gentleman fresh from Flanders; ask him his news and note his reply."

"What tidings, Monsieur, do you bring us?

[1] Chastellain, iii., 24

Prithee impart it " said the bailiff to the chevalier. And the gentleman, laughing, replied: "By my faith, Monsieur bailiff, the greatest news that I know is that Monseigneur de Charolais is married!"

"Married! to whom?"

"To whom?" responded the chevalier, "why, to his first cousin, Monseigneur's niece."

Merry was the duke over the Frenchman's blank amazement. Again the latter had to be reassured of the truth of the statement. Philip Pot told him that it was so true that the wedded pair had spent the night together according to their lawful right.

The bailiff did not know which way to turn. "So he acted out his two rôles. Returning thanks to the duke in the king's name with all formality, he then joined in the general laugh over the unsuspected trick. He was a man of the world and knew how to take advantage of sense and of folly."

It was on the morrow of this hasty tying of the wedding knot that the Countess of Charolais sent a messenger to announce the fact to her parents. They seem to have been perfectly satisfied, made no further objection to any point, and the mooted territory of Chinon made part of the dower in spite of the reasons urged against it.

As to the bailiff, when he made his adieux at Dijon, Philip presented him with a round dozen stirrup cups, each worth three silver marks, and he went home a surprised and delighted man.

"About this time [says Alienor de Poictiers] Monsieur de Charolais married Mademoiselle de Bourbon and he married her on the eve of All Saints[1] at Lille, and there was no festival because Duke Philip was then in Germany. Eight days after the nuptials the duchess gave a splendid banquet where were all the ladies of Lille, but they were seated all together, as is usually done at an ordinary banquet, without mesdames holding state as would have been proper for such an occasion."

It is evident from all the stories that Charles protested against his father's orders as much as he dared and then obeyed simply because he could not help himself.

Yet, strange to say, the unwilling bridegroom proved a faithful husband in a court where marital fidelity was a rare trait.

Philip's plans for the international union against the Turk were less easily completed than those for the union of his son and his niece. In November, the diet met at Frankfort; the expedition was discussed and some resolutions were passed, but nothing further was achieved.

Charles VII. would not even promise co-operation on paper. He had gradually extended his own domain in French-speaking territory and had dislodged the English from every stronghold except Guisnes and Calais. Under him France was

[1] The chroniclers differ as to this date. Chastellain (iii., 25) says the first Sunday in Lent. D'Escouchy (ii., 270, ch. cxxii) the night of St. Martin. Alienor de Poictiers, Hallowe'en (*Les Honneurs de la Cour*, p. 187). The last was one of Isabella's ladies in waiting.

regaining her prestige. Charles had much to lose, therefore, in joining the undertaking urged by Philip and he was wholly unwilling to risk it. From him Philip obtained only expressions of general interest in the repulse of the Turks, and more definite suggestions of the dangers that would menace Western Europe if all her natural defenders carried their arms and their fortunes to the East.

When the anniversary of the great fête came round not a vow was yet fulfilled!

CHAPTER IV.

BURGUNDY AND FRANCE

1455-1456.

THE duke's journey failed in accomplishing its object, but it proved an important factor in the development of the character of Charles of Burgundy. The opportunity to administer the government in his father's absence changed him from a youth to a man, and the manner of man he was, was plain to see.

His character was built on singularly simple lines. Vigorous of body, intense of purpose, inclined to melancholy, he was profoundly convinced of his own importance as heir to the greatest duke in Christendom, as future successor to an uncrowned potentate, who could afford to treat lightly the authority of both king and emperor whose nominal vassal he was.

The Ghent episode, too, undoubtedly had an immense effect in enhancing the count's belief in his father's power, in causing him to forget that the communes of Flanders did not owe their existence to their overlord. As yet, Charles of Burgundy had not met a single check to his self-esteem, to his family pride. As a governor, he probably exercised his brief authority with the rigour of one new to the helm.

"And the Count of Charolais bore himself so well and so virtuously in the task, that nothing deteriorated under his hand, and when the good duke returned from his journey, he found his lands as intact as before."

Such is La Marche's testimony.[1] Intact undoubtedly, but possibly the satisfaction was not quite perfect. Du Clercq[2] declares that Count Charles acquitted himself honourably of his charge and made himself respected as a magistrate. Above all, he insisted that justice should be dealt out to all alike. The only danger in his methods was that he acted on impulse without sufficiently informing himself of the matter in hand, or hearing both sides of a controversy. As a result, his decisions were not always impartial and the father was preferred to the strenuous and impetuous son. "Not that Philip was often inclined to recognise other law than his own will, but he was more tranquil, more gentle than his son, and more guided by reason," adds a later author.[3] There was an evident dread as to what might be the outcome of the count's untrained, youthful ardour.

The duke's chief measures after his return in February, 1455, seemed hardly calculated to arouse any great personal devotion to himself or a profound trust that his first consideration was for the advantage of his Netherland subjects. His thoughts were still turned to the East, and his main interest in the individual countships was as sources of supply for his Holy War. Considerable

[1] I., ch. xxxi. [2] II., 204. [3] Barante, vi., 50.

STATUE OF CHARLES THE BOLD AT INNSBRUCK

sums flowed into his exchequer that were never used for their destined purpose, but the duke cannot be justly accused of actual bad faith in amassing them. His intention to make the Eastern campaign remained firm for some years.

In another matter, his despotic exercise of personal authority, far without the pale of his jurisdiction inherited or acquired, shows no shadow of excuse.

In the bishropic of Utrecht the ecclesiastical head was also lay lord. Here the counts of Holland possessed no voice. They were near neighbours, that was all. Philip ardently desired to be more in this tiny independent state in the midst of territories acknowledging his sway.

In 1455, the see of Utrecht became vacant and Philip was most anxious to have it filled by his son David, whom he had already made Bishop of Thérouanne by somewhat questionable methods. The Duke of Guelders also had a neighbourly interest in Utrecht and he, too, had a pet candidate, Stephen of Bavaria, whose election he urged. The chapter resolutely ignored the wishes of both dukes and the canons were almost unanimous in their choice of Gijsbrecht of Brederode.[1]

A very few votes were cast for Stephen of Bavaria, but not a single one for David of Burgundy.

[1] Some of the canons wrote their reasons after their recorded vote: "Because Duke Philip had made the candidate member of his council of Holland, Zealand, and Friesland, in which office Gijsbrecht had acquitted himself well." "Because all the Sticht nobles were his relations," etc.—(Wagenaar, *Vaderlandsche Historie*, iv., 50.)

Brederode was already archdeacon of the cathedral and an eminently worthy choice, both for his attainments and for his character. He was proclaimed in the cathedral, installed in the palace, and confirmed, as regarded his temporal power, by the emperor.

Philip, however, refused to accept the returns, although not a single suffrage had been cast by the qualified electors for his son. He despatched the Bishop of Arras to Rome to petition the new pope, Calixtus III., to refuse to ratify the late election and to confer the see upon David, out of hand. Philip's tender conscience found Gijsbrecht ineligible to an episcopal office because he had participated in the war against Ghent, certainly a weak plea in an age of militant bishops!

The pope was afraid to offend the one man in Europe upon whose immediate aid he counted in the Turkish campaign. He accepted the gift of four thousand ducats offered by Gijsbrecht's envoys, the customary gift in asking papal confirmation for a bishop-elect, but secretly he delivered to Philip's ambassador letters patent creating David of Burgundy Bishop of Utrecht.[1]

The Burgundian La Marche states euphemistically that David was elected to the see, and the Deventer people would not obey him, therefore Philip had to levy an army and come in person to support the new bishop.[2] Du Clercq puts a different colour on the story and d'Escouchy[3]

[1] Du Clercq, ii., 210.   [2] *Mémoires*, i., ch. xxxiii.   [3] II., 315.

Burgundy and France

implies that the whole trouble arose from party strife which had to be quelled in the interests of law and order.

Apart from any question of insult to the Utrechters by imposing upon them a spiritual director of acknowledged base birth, the right of choice lay with them and the emperor had confirmed their choice as far as the lay office was concerned. While the issue was undecided, the Estates of Utrecht appointed Gijsbrecht guardian and defender of the see to assure him a legal status pending the papal ratification. The people were prepared to support their candidate with arms, a game that Philip did not refuse, and the force of thirty thousand men with which he invaded the bishopric proved the stronger argument of the two and able to carry David of Burgundy to the episcopal throne, upon which he was seated in his father's presence, October 16, 1455.

Some of Philip's allies reaped certain advantages from the situation. Alkmaar and Kennemerland redeemed certain forfeited privileges by means of their contributions to the duke's army. The city of Utrecht preferred a compromise to the risk of war. The bishop-elect, Gijsbrecht, consented to withdraw his claim, being permitted to retain the humbler office of provost of Utrecht and an annuity of four thousand guilders out of the episcopal revenues.

Deventer was the only place which was obstinate enough to persist in her rebellion and Philip was engaged in bringing her citizens to terms by a siege when news was brought to him that a visitor had arrived at Brussels under circumstances which imperatively demanded his personal attention.

In the twenty years that had elapsed since the Treaty of Arras, there had been great changes in France in the character both of the realm and of the ruler. Little by little the latter had proved himself to be a very different person from the inert king of Bourges.[1] Old at twenty, Charles VII. seemed young and vigorous at forty. Bad advisers were replaced by others better chosen and his administration gradually became effective. Fortune favoured him in depriving England of the Duke of Bedford (1435), the one man who might have maintained English prestige abroad and peace at home during the youth of Henry VI. It was at a time of civil dissensions in England, that Charles VII. succeeded in assuming the offensive on the Continent and in wresting Normandy and Guienne from the late invader.

But this territorial advantage was not all. Distinct progress had been made towards a national existence in France. The establishment of the nucleus of a regular army was an immense aid in curbing the depredations of the "*écorcheurs*," the devastating, marauding bands which had harassed the provinces. There was new activity in agriculture and industry and commerce.[2] The revival of letters and art, never completely stifled, proved the real vitality of France in spite of the

[1] See Lavisse, iv ii., 317. [2] For the effects of operations on a large scale see *Jacques Cœur and Charles VII.*, by Pierre Clémart.

depression of the Hundred Years' War. Royal justice was reorganised, public finance was better administered. By 1456, misery had not, indeed, disappeared, but it was less dominant.

The years of growing union between king and his kingdom were, however, years of discord between Charles and his son. The dauphin Louis had not enjoyed the pampered, petted life of his Burgundian cousin. Very poor and forlorn was his father at the time of the birth of his heir (1423).[1] There was nothing in the treasury to pay the chaplain who baptised the child or the woman who nourished him. The latter received no pension as was usual but a modest gratuity of fifteen pounds. The first allowance settled on the heir to his unconsecrated royal father's uncertain fortunes was ten crowns a month. Every feature of his infancy was a marked contrast to the early life of the Count of Charolais.

From his seventeenth year Louis was in active opposition to the king, heading organised rebellion against him in the war called the *Praguerie*. Finally, Charles VII. entrusted to his charge the administration of Dauphiné, thus practically banishing him honourably from the court where he was, evidently, a disturbing element. The only restrictions placed upon him in his provincial government were such as were necessary to preserve the ultimate authority of the crown. To these restrictions, however, Louis paid not the slightest heed. He assumed all the airs of

[2] *Duclos*, "Hist. de Louis XI.," *Œuvres Complètes* v., 8.

an independent sovereign. He made wars and treaties with his neighbours and at last proceeded to arrange his own marriage.

At this time Louis was already a widower, having been married at the age of thirteen to Margaret of Scotland, who led a mournful existence at the French court, where she felt herself a desolate alien. Her death at the age of twenty was possibly due to slander. "Fie upon life," she said on her deathbed, when urged to rouse herself to resist the languor into which she was sinking. "Talk to me no more of it."

Her husband cared less for her life than did Margaret herself. He took no interest in the inquiry set on foot to ascertain the truth of the charges against the princess, and was more than ready to turn to a new alliance. At the date of his widowerhood he was in Dauphiné and his own choice for a wife was Charlotte, daughter of the Duke of Savoy. After negotiations in his own behalf he informed his father of his matrimonial project. It did not meet the views of Charles VII., who ordered his son to abandon the idea immediately.

A messenger was despatched post haste to Chambéry to stop the dauphin's nuptials.[1] The duke evaded an interview and the envoy was forced to deliver his letter to the chancellor of Savoy. On the morrow of his arrival, he was taken to church, where the wedding ceremony was performed (March 10, 1451), but his seat was in such a remote

[1] Duclos, iii., 78.

place that he could barely catch a glimpse of the bridal procession, though he saw that Louis was clad in crimson velvet trimmed with ermine. Two days later the envoy carried a pleasant letter to the king, expressing regrets on the part of the Duke of Savoy that the alliance was made before the paternal prohibition arrived.

Nine years were spent by Louis in Dauphiné. He introduced many administrative and judicial reforms, excellent in themselves but not popular. There were various protests and when he dared to impose taxes without the consent of the Estates, an appeal was made to the king begging him to check his son in his illegal assumptions. Charles summoned his son to his presence. Instead of obeying this order in person, Louis sent envoys who were dismissed by his father with a curt response: "Let my son return to his duty and he shall be treated as a son. As to his fears, security to his person is pledged by my word, which my foes have never refused to accept."[1]

Louis showed himself less compliant than his father's foes. As Charles approached Dauphiné, and made his preparations to enforce obedience, Louis appealed to the mediation of the pope, of the Duke of Burgundy, and of the King of Castile, beside sending offerings to all the chief shrines in Christendom, imploring aid against parental wrath. Then his thoughts took a less peaceful turn. He called the nobles of his principality to arms and bade the fortified towns prepare for siege, while

[1] See Lavisse, iv^{ii}., 292.

he loftily declared that he would not trouble his father to seek him. He would meet him at Lyons.

Meanwhile, the Count of Dammartin was directed by the king to take military possession of Dauphiné and to put the dauphin under arrest. As he was *en route* to fulfil these orders, the count heard that a day had been set by Louis for a great hunt. That an excellent opportunity might be afforded for securing his quarry in the course of the chase, was the immediate thought of the king's lieutenant. So there might have been had not the wily hunter received timely warning of the project for making *him* the game.

At the hour appointed for the meet, the dauphin's suite rode to the rendezvous, but the prince turned his horse in the opposite direction and galloped away at full speed, attended by a few trusty followers. He hardly stopped even to take breath until he was out of his father's domain, and made no pause until he reached St. Claude, a small town in the Franche-Comté, where he threw himself on the kindness of the Prince of Orange.

How gossip about this strange departure of the French heir fluttered here and there! Du Clercq[1] tells the story with some variation from the above outline, laying more stress on the popular appeal to the king for relief from Louis's transgressions as governor of Dauphiné, and enlarging on the accusation that Louis was responsible for the death of *La belle Agnès*, "the first lady of the land possessing the king's perfect love." He adds

[1] II., 223.

Burgundy and France

that the dauphin was further displeased because the niece of this same Agnes, the Demoiselle de Villeclerc, was kept at court after her aunt's death. Wherever the king went he was followed by this lady, accompanied by a train of beauties. It was this conduct of his father that had forced the son to absent himself from court life for twelve years and more, during which time he received no allowance as was his rightful due, and thus he had been obliged to make his own requisitions from his seigniory.

There were other reports that the king was quite ready to accord his son his full state; others, again, that Charles drove Louis into exile from mere dislike and intended to make his second son his heir and successor. At this point Du Clercq's manuscript is broken off abruptly and the remainder of his conjectures are lost to posterity. Where the text begins again, the author dismisses all this contradictory hearsay and says in his own character as veracious chronicler, "I concern myself only with what actually occurred. The dauphin gave a feast in the forest and then departed secretly to avoid being arrested by Dammartin."

This flight was the not unnatural termination of a long series of misunderstandings between a father whose private conduct was not above criticism, and a son, clever, unscrupulous, destitute of respect for any person or thing except for the superstitious side of his religion.

Charles VII. was a curious instance of a man whose mental development occurred during the later years of his life. When his son was under his personal influence his character was not one to instil filial deference, and Louis certainly cherished neither respect nor affection for the father whose inert years he remembered vividly.

Whether, indeed, the dauphin had any part in Agnes Sorel's death which gave him especial reason to dread the king's anger, is uncertain, but of his action there is no doubt. To St. Claude he travelled as rapidly as his steed could go, and from that spot on Burgundian soil he despatched the following exemplary letter to his father:

"MY VERY REDOUBTABLE LORD:

"To your good grace I recommend myself as humbly as I can. Be pleased to know, my very redoubtable lord, that because, as you know, my uncle of Burgundy intends shortly to go on a crusade against the Turk in defence of the Catholic Faith and because my desire is to go, your good pleasure permitting, considering that our Holy Father the Pope bade me so to do, and that I am standard bearer of the Church, and that I took the oath by your command, I am now on my way to join my uncle to learn his plans so that I can take steps for the defence of the Catholic Faith.

"Also, I wish to implore him to find means of reinstating me in your good grace, which is something that I desire most in the world. My very redoubtable lord, I pray God to give you good life and long.

"Written at St. Claude the last day of August.

"Your very humble and obedient son,

"LOYS."[1]

[1] *Lettres de Louis XI.*, i., 77.
According to the editor, Vaesen, the original of this letter shows that *September 2nd* was written first and erased.

Burgundy and France

This letter hardly succeeded in carrying conviction to the king. He characterised the projected expedition to Turkey as a farce, a pretence, and a frivolous excuse.[1] Probably, too, he did not contradict his courtiers when they declared that the project had been in the wind a long time, and that the Duke of Burgundy would be prouder than ever to have the heir to France dependent on his protection.

The epistle despatched, Louis continued his journey under the escort of the Seigneur de Blaumont, Marshal of Burgundy, at the head of thirty horse. Their pace was rapid to elude the pursuit of Tristan l'Hermite. The prince needed no spurs to make him flee. Even if his father did not intend to have him drowned in a sack his immediate liberty was certainly in jeopardy. "In truth this thing was a marvellous business. The Prince of Orange and the Marshal of Burgundy were the two men whom the dauphin hated more than any one else, but necessity, which knows no law, overcame the distaste of the dauphin."[2]

Louvain was the next place where Louis felt safe enough to rest. Here he wrote to the Duke of Burgundy to announce his arrival within his territory. The letter found Philip in camp before Deventer. It is evident that he was entirely taken by surprise, and was prepared to be very cautious in his correspondence with the French king. He assured him that he was willing to re-

[1] Chastellain, iii., 185.
[2] Du Clercq, ii., 228.

ceive and honour Louis as his suzerain's heir, but he implored that suzerain not to blame him, the duke, for that heir's flight to his protection.

His envoy, Perrenet, was charged with many reassuring messages in addition to the epistle. Before he reached the French court, his news was no novelty. Rumour had preceded him. The messenger was very eloquent in his assurances to the king that Philip was wholly innocent in the affair and a good peer and true. Perrenet

"stayed at the French court until Epiphany and I do not know what they discussed, but during that time news came that the king had garrisoned Compiègne, Lyons, and places where his lands touched the duke's territories. When the envoy returned to the duke, he published a manifesto ordering all who could bear arms to be in readiness."[1]

Philip sent messages of welcome to Louis with apologies for his own inevitable absence, and the visitor was profuse in his return assurances to his uncle that he understood the delay and would not disturb his business for the world. "I have leisure enough to wait and it does not weary me. I am safe in a pleasant land and in a fine town which I have long wished to see." He showed his courtesy when the Count d'Étampes, Philip's nephew-in-law, presented his suite, by pronouncing each individual name and assuring its bearer that he had heard about him.[2]

[1] Chastellain iii., 197.

[2] See *Séjour de Louis XI. aux Pays-Bas;* Reiffenberg: Nouveaux mem. de l'Acad. Royale, 1829.

Burgundy and France

The count was commissioned to conduct the dauphin to Brussels and we have the story of an eye-witness of his reception by the ladies of the ducal family:

"I saw the King of France, father of the present King Charles, chased away by his father Charles for some difference of which they say that the fair Agnes was the cause, and on account of which he took refuge with Duke Philip, for he had no means of subsistence.[1]

"The said King Louis, being dauphin, came to Brussels accompanied by about ten cavaliers and by the Marshal of Burgundy. At this time Duke Philip was at Utrecht in war and there was no one to receive the visitor but Madame the Duchess Isabella and Madame de Charolais, her daughter-in-law, pregnant with Madame Mary of Burgundy, since then Duchess of Austria.

"Monsieur the dauphin arrived at Brussels, where were the ladies, at eight o'clock in the evening, about St. Martin's Day.[2] When the ladies heard that he was in the city they hastened down to the courtyard to await him. As soon as he saw them he dismounted and saluted Madame the Duchess and Mme. de Charolais and Mme. de Ravestein. All kneeled and then he kissed the other ladies of the court."

Alienor goes on to describe how a whole quarter of an hour was consumed by a friendly altercation between Isabella and her guest as to the exact

[1] Alienor de Poictiers, *Les Honneurs de la Cour*, ii., 208. It was early in October.

[2] This date, November 11th, does not agree with the others.

way in which they should enter the door, the dauphin resolute in his refusal to take precedence and Isabella equally resolute not even to walk by the side of the future king. "Monsieur, it seems to me you desire to make me a laughing stock, for you wish me to do what befits me not." To this the dauphin replied that it was incumbent upon him to pay honour for there was none in the realm of France so poor as he, and that he would not have known whither to flee if not to his uncle Philip and to her.

Louis prevailed in his argument, and hostess and guest finally proceeded hand in hand to the chamber prepared for the latter and Isabella then took leave on bended knee.

When the duke returned to Brussels this contention as to the proper etiquette was renewed. Isabella tried to retain the dauphin in his own apartment so that the duke should greet him there as befitted their relative rank. She was greatly chagrined, therefore, when Louis rushed down to the courtyard on hearing the signs of arrival. This punctilious hostess actually held the prince back by his coat to prevent his advancing towards the duke.

Throughout the visit the minor points of etiquette were observed with the utmost care. Both duchess and countess refrained from employing their train-bearers when they entered the dauphin's presence. When he insisted that his hostess should walk by his side, she managed her own train if possible. If she accepted any aid from

Burgundy and France

her gentlemen she was very careful to keep her hand upon the dress, so that technically she was still her own train-bearer. Then, too, when the duchess ate in the dauphin's presence, there was no cover to her dish and nothing was tasted in her behalf.

The Duke of Burgundy had to supply Louis with every requisite, but he, too, never forgot for a moment that this dependent visitor was future monarch of France. Without doors as within, every minor detail of etiquette was observed. The duke never so far forgot himself in the ardour of the chase as to permit his horse's head to advance beyond the tail of the prince's steed.

In February, 1457, on St. Valentine's Eve, Mary of Burgundy was born. Our observant court lady describes in detail the ceremonial observed in the chamber of the Countess of Charolais and at the baptism. Brussels rang with joyful bells and blazed with torches, four hundred supplied by the city and two hundred by the young father. Each torch weighed four or five pounds.

The Count of Charolais was his own messenger to announce the birth of his daughter to the dauphin and to ask him to stand god-father. Joyful was Louis to accept the invitation and to bestow his mother's name on the baby-girl. Ste. Gudule was so far from the palace that the Church of the Caudenberg was selected for the ceremony and richly adorned with Holland linen, velvet, and cloth of gold. The duchess carried her grandchild to the font,—a font draped with cramoisy velvet.

"Monsieur the dauphin stood on the right and I heard it said that there was no one on the left because there was none his equal. On that day, the duchess wore a round skirt *à la Portuguaise*, edged with fur. There was no train of cloth nor of silk, so I cannot state who carried it,"

sagely remarks Alienor with incontrovertible logic.

Later events made later chroniclers less enthusiastic about the honour paid to Mademoiselle[1] Mary by the dauphin. In a manuscript of La Marche's *Mémoires* at The Hague, the words "Lord! what a god-father!" appear in the margin of the page describing the baptism.[2] But in these early days of his five years' sojourn, Louis seems to have been a pleasant person and to have posed as the ruined poor relation, entirely free from pride at his high birth and delighted to repay hospitality by his general complaisance.

Charles VII. received all the reports with somewhat cynical amusement. He had no great trust in his son. "Louis is fickle and changeable and I do not doubt that he will return here before long. I am not at all pleased with those who influence him," are his words as quoted by d'Escouchy.[3]

Undoubtedly, though, the king was much surprised at his son's action. He had rather expected him to take refuge somewhere but he never thought that the Duke of Burgundy would be his

[1] "At that time they did not say Madame, for Monsieur was not the son of a sovereign."—La Marche, ii., 410, note.

[2] La Marche, ii., 410: "Dieu quel parrain!"

[3] II., 343.

LOUIS XI
FROM THE ENGRAVING BY A. BOILLY, AFTER THE DRAWING BY J. BOILLY

protector—a strange choice to his mind. "My cousin of Burgundy nourishes a fox who will eat his chickens" is reported as another comment of this impartial father.[1] Like many a phrase, possibly the fruit of later harvests, this is an excellent epitome of the situation.

[1] Chastellain, iii., 185; Lavisse iv[ii]., 299.

CHAPTER V

THE COUNT AND THE DAUPHIN

1456-1461

THE picture of the Burgundian court rejoicing in happy unison over the advent of an heiress to carry on the Burgundian traditions, with the dauphin participating in the family joy, shows the tranquil side of the first months of the long visit. Before Mary's birth, however, an incident had occurred, betraying the fact that the dauphin and Charles VII. were not the only father and son between whom relations were strained, and that a moment had arrived when the attitude of the Count of Charolais to the duke was no longer characterised by unquestioning filial obedience.

Charles was on his way to Nuremberg[1] to fulfil a mission with certain German princes when the dauphin alighted in Brabant, like "a bird of ill omen," as he designated himself on one occasion. The count did not return to Brussels until January 12, 1457. Thus he took no part in the hearty welcome accorded to the visitor. It is more than possible that the heir of Burgundy was not wholly pleased with the state of affairs placidly existing by mid-winter.

[1] He had departed with Adolph de la Marck on November 19th.—*Archives du Nord*. See Du Fresne de Beaucourt, vi., 113. No mention of this seems to appear elsewhere.

Instead of resuming the first position which he had enjoyed during his brief regency, or the honoured second that had been his after Philip came back, Charles was now relegated to a third place. Further, without having been consulted as to the policy, he found that he was forced into following his father's lead in treating a penniless refugee like an invited guest, whose visit was an honour and a joy. It is more than probable that Charles was already feeling somewhat hurt at the duke's warmth towards Louis when a serious breach occurred between father and son about another matter.

It chanced that a chamberlain's post fell vacant in his own household, and the count assumed that the appointment of a successor was something that lay wholly within his jurisdiction. When the duke interfered in a peremptory fashion and insisted that the appointment should be made at his instance, the son refused to accept his authority, especially as his father's nominee was Philip de Croy, one of a family already over-dominant in the Burgundian court. At least, that was Charles's opinion. Therefore, when he obeyed his father's commands to bring his *ordonnance*, or household list, to the duke's oratory, he unhesitatingly carried the document which contained the name of Antoine Raulin, Sire d'Émeries, in place of Philip de Croy.

The duke was very angry at this apparent contempt for his expressed wishes. Indignantly he threw the lists into the fire with the words, "Now look to your *ordonnances* for you will need new ones."[1]

There was evidently a succession of violent scenes in which the duchess tried to stand between her husband and son. But Philip was beside himself with wrath and refused to listen to a word from her or from the dauphin, who also endeavoured to mediate.[2]

Finally, the irate duke lost all control of himself, ordered a horse, and rode out alone into the forest of Soignies. When he became calmer it was dark and he found himself far from the beaten tracks, in the midst of underbrush through which he could not ride. He dismounted and wandered on foot for hours in the January night until smoke guided him to a charcoal burner, who conducted him to the more friendly shelter of a forester's hut. In the morning he made his way to Genappe.

Meantime, in the palace, consternation reigned. Search parties seeking their sovereign were out all night. No one, however, was in such a state of dismay as the dauphin, who declared that he would be counted at fault when family dissensions followed so soon on his arrival. Delighted he was, therefore, to act as mediator between father and

[1] Chastellain (iii., 233) says that he heard the story from the clerk of the chapel, sole witness of this family quarrel. The duke was so angry that it was hideous to see him.

[2] La Marche, ii., 418; Du Clercq, ii., 237; Chastellain, iii., 230, etc. In the last the narrative is more elaborate. The author dwells much on the danger to the young countess in her delicate state of health.

son after the duke was in a sufficiently pacified state to listen to reason. Charles betook himself to Dendermonde for a time until the duke was ready to see him.[1] His young wife made the most of her expectations to soften her father-in-law's resentment, and between her entreaties and those of the guest, proud to show his tact and his gratitude, the quarrel was at last smoothed over.

There was one marked difference between this family dispute and the breach between the French king and the dauphin. In the latter case no feeling was involved. In the former, the son was really deeply wounded by what he deemed lack of parental affection for his interests. At the same time he was shocked by the bitter words and was, for the moment, so filled with contrition that he was eager to make any concession agreeable to the duke. He dismissed two of his servants,[2] suspected by his father of fomenting trouble between them, and he showed himself in general very willing to placate paternal displeasure.

Reconciliation between duke and duchess was

[1] "Thus there was much coming and going: and it was ordered by Monseigneur le Dauphin that Monseigneur de Ravestein and the king-at-arms of the Toison d'Or should go to Dendermonde to learn the wishes of the Count of Charolais and his intentions, of which I am entitled to speak for I was despatched several times to Brussels in behalf of my said Seigneur of Charolais, to ask the advice of the Chancellor Raulin as to the best method of conducting the present affair"—(La Marche, ii., 419.)

[2] La Marche, ii., 420. One of these, Guillaume Biche, went to France and La Marche says that he himself often went to him to obtain valuable information.

more difficult. Isabella resented Philip's reproaches for her sympathy with Charles. She said she had stepped between the two men because she had feared lest the duke might injure his son in his wrath.[1] This was in answer to the Marshal of Burgundy when he was telling her of Philip's displeasure. She concluded her dignified defence with an expression of her utter loneliness. Stranger in a strange land she had no one belonging to her but her son.

She was certainly present at the baptism of her grandchild, but shortly afterwards she retired to a convent of the Grey Sisters, founded by herself, and rarely returned to the world or took part in its ceremonies during the remainder of her life.

The quarrel, too, left its scar upon Charles. It is not probable that he had much personal liking for the guest upon whom his father heaped courtesies and solicitous care. On one occasion, when the two young men were hunting they were separated by chance. When Charles returned alone to the palace, the duke was full of reproaches at his son's careless desertion of the guest in his charge. Again the court was organised into search parties and there was no rest until the dauphin was discovered some leagues from Brussels.[2] Here, also, it is an easy presumption that the Count of Charolais was a trifle sulky over his father's preoccupation in regard to the prince.

The transient character of the dauphin's sojourn in his cousin's domains soon changed. In

[1] La Marche, ii., 418.   [2] Du Clercq, ii., 239.

the summer of 1457, when news came that Dauphiné had submitted to Charles VII., when the successive embassies despatched by Philip to the king had all proved fruitless in their conciliatory efforts, Philip proceeded to make more permanent arrangements for the fugitive's comfort.

"Now, Monseigneur, since the king has been pleased to deprive you of Dauphiné . . . you are to-day lord and prince without land. But, nevertheless, you shall not be without a country, for all that I have is yours and I place it within your hand without reserving aught except my life and that of my wife. Pray take heart. If God does not abandon me I will never abandon you."[1]

The duke made good his words by giving his guest the estate of Genappe, of which Louis took possession at the end of July. Then as a further step to make things pleasant for the exile, Philip sent for Charlotte of Savoy who had remained under her father's care ever since the formal marriage in 1451. She was now eighteen.

It was an agreeable spot, this estate at Genappe. Louis's favourite amusement of the chase was easy of access. "The court is at present at Louvain," wrote a courtier [2] on July 1st, "and Monseigneur the Dauphin likes it very much, for there is good hunting and falconry and a great number of rabbits within and without the city." With killing

[1] Chastellain, iii., 308.
[2] Du Fresne de Beaucourt, vi., 123. Thierry de Vébry to the Count de Vaudemart.

of every kind at his service, what greater solace could a homeless prince expect?

From Louvain to Genappe is no great distance, and the sum of 1200 livres, furnished by Philip for the dauphin's journey to his new abode, seemed a large provision. The pension then settled on him was 36,000 livres, and when the dauphiness arrived 1000 livres a month were provided for her private purse.[1]

Pleasant was existence in this château. There was no dearth of company to throng around the prince in exile, and the dauphin allowed no prejudice of mere likes and dislikes, no consideration of duty towards his host to hamper him in making useful friends. A word here and a word there, aptly thrown in at a time when Philip's anger had exasperated, when Charles had failed to conciliate, were very potent in intimating to many a Burgundian servant that there might come a time when a new king across the border might better appreciate their real value than their present or future sovereign.

Hunting was a favourite amusement, but the dauphin did not confine his invitations to sportsmen. The easy accessibility of the little court attracted men of science and of letters as well as others capable of making the time pass agreeably. When there was nothing else on foot, it is said that the company amused themselves by telling stories, each in turn, and out of their tales grew the collec-

[1] Du Fresne de Beaucourt, vi., 123.

tion of the *Cent Nouvelles Nouvelles*,[1] named in imitation of Boccaccio's *Cento Novelle*.

The first printed edition of this collection was issued in Paris, in 1486, by Antoine Verard, who thus admonishes the gentle reader: "Note that whenever *Monseigneur* is referred to, Monseigneur the Dauphin must be understood, who has since succeeded to the crown and is King Louis. Then he was in the land of the Duke of Burgundy." Another editor asserts that *Monseigneur* is evidently the Duke of Burgundy and not Louis, and later authorities decide that Anthony de la Sale wrote the whole collection in imitation of Boccaccio, and that the names of the narrators were as imaginative or rather as editorial as the rest of the volume.

If this be true, it may be inferred that the author would have given an appearance of verisimilitude to his fiction by mentioning the actual habitués of the dauphin's court. The name of the Count of Charolais does not appear at all. The duke tells three or more stories according to the interpretation given to *Monseigneur*. With three exceptions the tales are very coarse, nor does their wit atone for their licentiousness. Possibly Charles held himself aloof from the kind of talk they suggest. All reports make him rigid in standards of morality not observed by his fellows. That he had little to do with the court is certain, whatever his reason.

[1] *Les Cent Nouvelles Nouvelles*, ed. A. J. V. Le Roux. The stories are, as a rule, only retold tales.

Louis did not confine himself to the estate assigned him. There were various court visits to the Flemish towns where he was afforded excellent opportunities for seeing the wealth of the burghers and their status in the world of commerce.

Ghent was very anxious to have the duke bring his guest within her gates and give her an opportunity of displaying her regret for the past unpleasantness. "In his goodness," Philip at last yielded to their entreaties to make them a visit himself, but he decided not to take the prince or the count with him.[1] He was either afraid for their safety or else he did not care to bring a future French king into relation with citizens who might find it convenient to remember his suzerainty in order to ignore the wishes of their sovereign duke.[2]

Eastertide, 1458, was finally appointed for this state visit of reconciliation. The duke took the precaution to send scouts ahead to ascertain that the late rebels were sincere in their contrition, and that there was no danger of anarchist agitations. The report was brought back that all was calm and that joyful preparations were making to show appreciation of Philip's kindness.

[1] "The spectacle was not witnessed by Count Charolais nor by Louis the Dauphin, nor by the Lord of Croy, whom for certain reasons he was unwilling to take with him." (Meyer, p. 322.)

[2] Kervyn, *Hist. de Flandre*, v., 23. At this time Philip was ignoring a peremptory summons to appear before the Parliament of Paris.

On April 22d, the duke slept at l'Écluse, and on the 23d he was gaily escorted into the city by knights and gentlemen summoned from Holland, Hainaut, and Flanders, "but neither clerks nor priests were in his train." As a further assurance to him of their peaceful intention, the citizens actually lifted the city gates off their hinges so as to leave open exits.

Once within the walls, the duke found the whole community, who had shown intelligent and sturdy determination not to endure arbitrary tyranny, ready to weave themselves into a frenzy of biblical and classical parable whose one purpose was to prove how evil had been their ways. A pompous procession sang *Te Deum* as the duke rode in, and the first "mystery" that met his eyes within the gates was a wonderful representation of Abraham sacrificing Isaac, while the legend "All that the Lord commanded we will do," was meant not to refer to the Hebrew's fidelity to Jehovah, but to the Ghenters' perfect submission to Philip. A young girl stood ready to greet him with the words of Solomon, "I have found one my soul loves."[1]

Farther on there were various emblems all designed to compare Philip now to Cæsar, now to Pompey, now to Nebuchadnezzar. The most humiliating spectacle was that of a man dressed in a lion's skin, thus personifying the Lion of Flan-

---
[1] Meyer, p. 321.
All the legends were in Latin. *Inveni quem diligit anima mea.*

ders, leading Philip's horse by the bridle. "*Vive Bourgogne* is now our cry," was symbolised in every vehicle which the rhetoricians could invent.

Not altogether explicable is this extreme self-abnegation. Civic prosperity must have returned in four years or there would have been no money for the outlay. Apparently, Philip's countenance was worth more to them than their pride.

The birth and death of two children at Genappe gave the duke new reasons for showering ostentatious favours on his guest, and furnished the dauphin with suitable occasion for addressing his own father, who answered him in kind.

The following is one of the fair-phrased epistles [1]:
The King to the Dauphin, 1459.

"Very dear and much loved son:

"We have received the letters that you wrote us making mention that on July 27 our dear and much loved daughter, the dauphiness, was delivered of a fine boy, for which we have been and are very joyous, and it seems to me that the more God our Creator grants you favour, by so much the more you ought to praise and thank Him and refrain from angering Him, and in all things fulfil His commandments.

"Given at Compiègne, Aug. 7th.
"Charles."

During these five years, Charles was more or less aloof from the courts of his father and of their guest. He spent part of the time in Holland and part at Le Quesnoy with his young wife. The

[1] Du Fresne de Beaucourt, vi., 267.

The Count and the Dauphin

Count of St. Pol was one of his intimate friends, and a friend who managed to make many insinuations about the duke's treatment of his son and infatuation about the Croys whom Charles hated with increasing fervency.

There is a story that Charles went from Le Quesnoy to his father's court to demand a formal audience from the duke in order to lodge his protest against the Croys. Evidently relations were strained when such a degree of ceremony was needed between father and son.

Gerard Ourré was commissioned to set forth the count's grievances, and he was in the midst of his carefully prepared statement when the duke interrupted him with the curt observation: "Have a care to say nothing but the truth and understand, it will be necessary to prove every assertion." The orator was discomfited, stammered on for a few moments, and then excused himself from completing his harangue. There were only a few nobles present and all were surprised at this embarrassment, as Gerard passed for a clever man. Then, seeing that his deputy was too much frightened to proceed, Charles took up the thread of his discourse. In a firm voice he continued the list of accusations against the Croys, only to be cut short in his turn. Peremptory was the duke in his command to his son to be silent and never again to refer to the subject. Then, turning to Croy, Philip added "see to it that my son is satisfied with you," and withdrew from the audience chamber.

Croy addressed Charles and endeavoured to be conciliatory. "When you have repaired the ill you have wrought I will remember the good you have done," was the count's only reply. He took leave of his father with an outward show of love and respect and returned to his wife at Le Quesnoy, escorted, indeed, by Croy out of the gates of Brussels, but with no better understanding between them.

St. Pol found good ground to work on. He inflamed the count's discontent and his distrust of the duke's favourite until Charles despatched him to Bourges on a confidential mission to ascertain what Charles VII. would do for the heir of Burgundy should he decide to take refuge in the French court.[1]

At the first interview "I was not present," states the unknown reporter, but on succeeding occasions this man heard for himself that the king was ready to show hospitality to the Count of Charolais who "has no ill intentions against his father. All he wants to do is to separate him from the people who govern him badly."

The conferences were held in the lodgings of Odet d'Aydie. Among those present was Dammartin and the matter was discussed in its various aspects. Jehan Bureau and the anonymous witness were charged with drawing up a report of the discussion. When this was presented to the king it did not seem to him good. He doubted the good

[1] Report of an eye-witness. (Duclos, v., 195.)

faith of the count's message. He had been assured that it was all a fiction especially designed by the Sieur de Burgundy.

Certain general promises were made in spite of this royal distrust, quite natural under the circumstances. If he decided to espouse the cause of Henry VI., the Count of Charolais should be given a command. It was evident that the count was by no means ready to go to all lengths, for St. Pol states in one of his conferences with the "late king" that Charles of Burgundy had assured him that for two realms such as his he would not do a deed of villainy.

Nothing came of this talk. It would have been a singular state of affairs had the heirs of France and Burgundy thus changed places in their fathers' courts. Spying and counterspying there were between the courts to a great extent and rumours in number. A certain Italian writes to the Duke of Milan as follows, on March 23, 1461, after he had been at Genappe and at Brussels: [1]

"M. de Croy has given me clearly to understand that the reconciliation of the dauphin with the King of France would not be with the approval of the Duke of Burgundy. Nevertheless the prince laments that since he received the dauphin into his states, and treated him as his future sovereign, he has incurred the implacable hatred of the king added to his ancient grievances. On the other hand, the affairs of England, on whose issue depends war or peace for the

[1] Du Fresne de Beaucourt, vi., 326.

duke, being still in suspense, it did not seem to him honest to make advances to the king at this moment.

"M. de Croy thinks that the dauphin does not seem to have carried into this affair the circumspection and reflection befitting a prince of his quality. He has maintained towards the duke the most complete silence on the affair of Genoa, and the proposition concerning Italy. Croy does not think there is anything in it, but if the thing were so it ought not to be secret. He does not believe that peace will be made between the dauphin and his father, and mentioned that his brother was on the embassy from duke to king, in order, I suppose, to probe the matter to the bottom.

"The dauphin it seems has been out of humour with the Duke of Burgundy on account of the lukewarmness shown for his interests by the ambassador sent by this prince to the Duke of Savoy.

"The silent agreement which reigns between the dauphin and Monsg. de Charolais is one of the causes which has chilled this great love between the dauphin and the duke which existed at the beginning.

"Moreover, the dauphin having spent largely, especially in almsgiving without considering his purse finds himself very hard pressed. He has only two thousand ducats a month from the Duke of Burgundy and that seems to force him into peace with the king. The duke expects nothing during the king's lifetime.

"Everything makes me want to wait here for the arrival of news from England. It is expected daily, good or bad the last play must be made. The duke fears a descent on Calais, and for this reason is going to a town called St. Omer. Under pretext of cele-

PHILIP THE GOOD AND CHARLES THE BOLD
FROM A CONTEMPORARY SKETCH IN MS.

brating there the fête of the Toison d'Or he has ordered all his escort to be armed."

For a long time before his final illness the death of Charles VII. was anticipated. When it came it was a dolorous end.[1] At Genappe, the dauphin had been making his preparations for the wished-for event in many ways, all in exact opposition to his father's policy. In Italy and in Spain he sided with the opponents of Charles VII. In England, his sympathies were all for the House of York because his father was favourable to Henry of Lancaster and Margaret of Anjou. He learned with satisfaction of the success of Edward IV., and was more than willing to see him invade France. With certain princes of Germany he entertained relations shrouded in mystery, while his father's own agents disclosed secrets to him from time to time.

In his exile he kept reminding official bodies at Paris that he was heir to the throne. As dauphin he claimed the right to give orders to the *parlement* at Grenoble. There is no actual proof that he had a hand in the conspiracies which troubled the last year of his father's reign, but it is certain that he managed to win to himself a party within the royal circle.

Certain councillors, fearful of their own fate, did not hesitate to suggest that Louis should be disinherited and his brother Charles put in his stead, but this Charles VII. would not accept. He

[1] Lavisse, ivii., 321.

kept hoping for Louis's submission. The latter, however, had no idea of this. He was sure that his father would not live to grow old. A trouble in his leg threatened to be cancerous. In July, there was a growth in his mouth. He died July 22nd, convinced that his son had poisoned him.

After July 17th constant bulletins from the king's bedside came to Louis. Genappe was too far and the anxious son moved to Avesnes in order to receive his messages more speedily. Our chronicler Chastellain [1] begins his story of Louis's accession as follows:

"Since I am not English but French, I who am neither Spanish nor Italian but French, I have written of two Frenchmen, the one king, the other duke. I have written of their works and their quarrels and of the favour and glories which God has given them in their time.

. . . .

"Kings die, reigns vanish but virtue alone and meritorious works serve man on his bier and gain him eternal glory. O you Frenchmen, see the cause and the end in my labours!"

The guest who had displayed so much humility and thankfulness when he arrived, who had deprecated honours to his high birth and desired to offer all the courtesies, departed from the residence so generously given him for five years in a very cavalier manner.

"Now the king left the duke's territories without

[1] IV., 21.

having taken leave nor said adieu to the Countess of Charolais,[1] although he was in her neighbourhood, and he left behind him the queen, his wife. The said queen had neither hackneys nor vehicles with which to follow her husband. Therefore, the king ordered her to borrow the hackneys of the countess and chariots, too. Heartily did the countess accede to this request in spite of the fact that the thing seemed to her rather strange that a noble king, and one who had received so much honour and service from the House of Burgundy and had promised to recognise it when the hour came, should thus depart thence without saying a word. However, in spite of all, the countess would gladly have given the queen the hackneys as a gift if they had been asked, and she sent them to her by one of her equerries named Corneille de la Barre, together with chariots and waggons. And thus the queen left the country just as her husband had done without saying a word either to the duke or the countess, and Corneille went with her on foot to bring back the hackneys when the queen had arrived at the place of her desire."

Philip had difficulty in persuading his quondam guest to show outward respect to his father's memory. The duke clad himself and his suite in deep mourning before setting out to join Louis at Avesnes, whither representatives from the University of Paris and from all parts of the realm had flocked to greet their new sovereign.

It was a great concourse that marched from Avesnes as escort to the uncrowned king. Philip

[1] Chastellain, iv., 45.

was magnificent in his appointments as he entered Rheims, and behind him came his son,

"the Count of Charolais who, equally with his noble company of knights and squires, attracted hearts and eyes in admiration of his rich array wherein cloth of gold and jewelry, velvet and embroidery were lavishly displayed. And the count had ten pages and twenty-six archers, and this whole company numbered three hundred horse."[1]

This was a Thursday after dinner. Louis had waited at St. Thierry. On the actual day of the coronation, preliminaries absorbed so much time that the long cavalcade did not enter Rheims until seven o'clock. The king passed his night in a very pious and prayerful manner, taking no repose until 5 A.M. While his suite were occupied at their toilets he slipped off alone to church.

Finally all was ready for the grand ceremony. Very magnificent were the duke's robes and ermine when, as chief among the peers, he escorted his late guest to be consecrated king, and very devout and simple was Louis. After the consecration, the king and his friends listened to an address from the Bishop of Tournay, in which he described in Latin the dauphin's sojourn in the Netherlands.

The Duke of Burgundy was the hero of the occasion. He felt that all future power was in his hands and that Louis XI. could never do enough

[1] Chastellain was not present, but he says of Philip's suite (iv., 47): "From what I have been told and what I have seen in writing, it was a wonderful thing and its like had never been seen in this kingdom."

The Count and the Dauphin 105

to repay him for his wonderful hospitality. And for a time Louis was quite ready to foster this belief. When they entered Paris, the peer so far outshone the sovereign that there was general astonishment.[1] Moreover, whatever the latter did have was a gift. The very plate used on the royal table was a ducal present.[2]

Louis took great pains to preserve an attitude of grateful humility. When he met the *parlement* of Paris, he asked the duke's advice about its reformation. It was to Philip that all the petitioners flocked. But Louis was conscious, too, that there would be a morrow in Burgundy, and he took care to be friendly with the count even while he was flattering the duke. For this purpose he found Guillaume de Biche a very useful go-between.[3] This was one of the retainers dismissed in 1457 by Charles at his father's request. He had then passed into Louis's service. This man quickly insinuated himself into the king's graces, was admitted to his chamber at all hours, and walked arm in arm with the returned exile through Paris.

The Burgundian exile had learned the mysteries of the city well in his four years' residence. Louis found him an amusing companion and skilfully managed to flatter the count by his favour towards the man whom he had liked.

---

[1] "And I, myself, assert this for I was there and saw all the nobles" (Chastellain, iv., 52).

[2] When return presents were distributed to the nobles Philip received a lion, Charles a pelican.

[3] Chastellain, iv., 115.

For six weeks Philip remained in the capital and astonished the Parisians with the fêtes he offered. Equally astonished were they with their new monarch. Louis was thirty-eight and not attractive in person. His eyes were piercing but his visage was made plain by a disproportionate nose. His legs were thin and misshapen, his gait uncertain. He dressed very simply, wearing an old pilgrim's hat, ornamented by a leaden saint. As he rode into Abbeville in company with Philip, the simple folk who had never seen the king were greatly amazed at his appearance and said quite loud, "Benedicite! Is that a king of France, the greatest king in the world? All together his horse and dress are not worth twenty francs." [1]

From the beginning of his reign, Louis XI. never lived very long in any one place. He did not like the Louvre as a dwelling and had the palace of the Tournelles arranged for him. Touraine became by preference his residence, where he lived alternately at Amboise and in his new château at Plessis-lès-Tours. But his sojourns were always brief. He wanted to know everything, and he wandered everywhere to see France and to seek knowledge. His letters, his accounts, the chroniclers, the despatches of the Italian ambassador, show him on a perpetual journey.

He would set out at break of day with five or six intimates dressed in grey cloth like pilgrims;

[1] Lavisse, iv{ii}., 325

The Count and the Dauphin

archers and baggage followed at a distance. He would forbid any one to follow him, and often ordered the gates of the city he had left to be closed, or a bridge to be broken behind him. Ambassadors ordered to see him without fail, sometimes had to cross France to obtain an interview, at least if their object was something in which he was not much interested. Then he would often grant them an audience in some miserable little peasant hut.

In the cities where he stopped he would lodge with a burgomaster or some functionary. To avoid harangues and receptions he would often arrive unannounced through a little alley. If forced to accept an *entrée* he stipulated that it should not be marked with magnificence. There never was a prince who so disliked ceremonies, balls, banquets, and tourneys. At his court young people were bored to death. He never ordered festivals except for some visitor; his pleasures were those of a simple private gentleman. He liked to dine out of his palace. Cagnola relates with surprise that he had seen the king dine after mass in a tavern on the market-place at Tours. He invited small nobles and bourgeois to dine with him. He was intimate, too, with bourgeois women, and indulged in gross pleasantries, speaking to and of women without reserve, sparing neither sister, mother, nor queen.

Yet it was a sombre court. "Farewell dames,

citizens, demoiselles, feasts, dances, jousts, and tournaments; farewell fair and gracious maids, mundane pleasures, joys, and games," says Martial d'Auvergne. Pompous magnificence may have reminded Louis unpleasantly of his visit to Burgundy.

CHAPTER VI

THE WAR OF PUBLIC WEAL

1464-1465

THE era of good feeling between Louis XI. and his Burgundian kinsmen was of short duration, and no wonder. The rich rewards confidently expected as fitting recompense for five years' kindness more than cousinly, towards a penniless refugee were not forthcoming.

The king was lavish in fine words, and not chary in certain ostentatious recognition towards his late host, but the fairly munificent pension, together with the charge of Normandy settled upon the Count of Charolais, proved only a periodical reminder of promises as regularly unfulfilled on each recurring quarter day, while the post of confidential adviser to the inexperienced monarch, which Philip had intended to occupy, remained empty.

Louis put perfect trust in no one but turned now to one counsellor, now to another, and used such fragments of advice as pleased his whim and paid no further heed to the giver.

Not long after Louis's coronation there occurred that change in Philip's bodily constitution that comes to all active men sooner or later. His health began to give way, his energies relaxed, and matters that had been of paramount importance throughout his career were allowed to slip into the background of his desires. In the famous treaty of 1435, no article was rated at greater importance than that which placed the towns on the Somme in Philip's hands, subject to a redemption of two hundred thousand gold crowns. Whether Charles VII. had actually pledged himself that the mortgage should hold at least during Philip's life does not seem assured, but that any sum would be insufficient to induce the duke to release them unless his intellect were somewhat deadened, is clear.

In 1462, when he recovered from a sharp attack, possibly the result of his indulgence in the pleasures of the table during the prolonged festivities at Paris, he did not regain his previous vigour. This was the time, by the way, when opportunity was afforded his courtiers to prove that devotion to their seigneur outweighed personal vanity. When his head was shaved by order of the court physician, more than five hundred nobles sacrificed their own locks so that their becoming curls might not remind their chief of his own bald head. The sacrifice was not always voluntary, adds an informant.[1] Philip forced compliance with this new fashion upon all who seemed reluctant to be unnecessarily shorn of what beauty was theirs by nature's gift. This servility may have consoled

---

[1] La Marche, ii., 227. Peter von Hagenbach was the chamberlain to enforce this.

Philip for the deprivation of his hair. In his depressed condition any solace was acceptable.

It was just when the duke was in this enfeebled state that Louis, through the mediation of the Croys, pushed forward his proposition to redeem the towns and Philip agreed, possibly relying upon the chance that it would be no easy matter for the French king to wring the required sum from his impoverished land. Philip's assent was, however, promptly clinched by a cash payment of half the amount [1]; the remainder followed.

Amiens, Abbeville, and the other towns, valuable bulwarks for the Netherland provinces, fine nurseries for the human material requisite for Burgundian armies, rich tax payers as they were, all tumbled into the outstretched hands of the duke's wily rival.

The transaction was hurried through and completed before a rumour of its progress came to the ear of the interested heir. Charles was in Holland sulking and indignant. He had expected good results from his tender devotion during his father's acute illness, a devotion shared by Isabella of Portugal who hastened to her husband's bedside from her convent seclusion when Philip was in need of her ministrations. But, in his convalescence, Philip renewed his friendship for the Croys

[1] The receipt for this half payment was signed October 8, 1462. (Comines, *Mémoires*, Lenglet du Fresnoy edition, ii., 392–403.)

whom Charles continued to distrust with bitterness that varied in its intensity, but which never vanished from his consciousness. The young man felt misjudged, misused, and ever suspicious that personal danger to himself lurked in the air of his father's court.

The various rumours of plots against his life may not all have been baseless. At last, one of own cousins, the Count of Nevers, was accused of having recourse to diabolic means of doing away with the duke's legitimate heir.[1] Three little waxen images were found in his house, and it was alleged that he practised various magic arts withal in order to win the favour of the duke and of the French king, and still worse to cause Charles to waste away with a mysterious sickness. The accusations were sufficient to make Nevers resign all his offices in his kinsman's court and retire, post-haste, to France. Had he been wholly innocent he would have demanded trial at the hands of his peers of the Golden Fleece as behooved one of the order. But he withdrew undefended, and left his tattered reputation fluttering raggedly in the breeze of gossip.

Charles stayed in Holland aloof from the ducal court until a fresh incident drove him thither to give vent to his indignation. Only three days had Philip de Commines been page to Duke Philip, then resident at Lille, when an embassy headed by Morvilliers, Chancellor of France, was

[1] Du Clercq, iii., 236; Comines–Lenglet, ii., 393.

The War of Public Weal

given audience in the presence of the Burgundian court, including the Count of Charolais. The future historian,[1] then nineteen years old, was keenly alive to all that passed on that November fifth, 1464. Morvilliers used very bitter terms in his assertion that Charles had illegally stopped a little French ship of war and arrested a certain bastard of Rubempré on the false charge that his errand in Holland, where the incident occurred, was to seize and carry off Charles himself. Moreover, one knight of Burgundy, Sir Olivier de La Marche had caused this tale to be bruited everywhere,

"especially at Bruges whither strangers of all nations resort. This had hurt Louis deeply, and he now demanded through his chancellor that Duke Philip should send this same Sir Olivier de La Marche prisoner to Paris, there to be punished as the case required. Whereupon, Duke Philip answered that the said Sir Olivier was steward of his house, born in the County of Burgundy and in no respect subject to the Crown of France."

Philip added that if his servant had wrought ill to the king's honour he, the duke, would see to his punishment. As to the bastard of Rubempré, true it was that he had been apprehended in Holland,[2] but there was adequate ground for his arrest as his behaviour had been strange, at least

[1] Commines, *Mémoires* i., ch. i. In the above passages Dannett's translation is followed for the racy English.
[2] Commines says at The Hague; Meyer makes it Gorcum.

so thought the Count of Charolais. Philip added that if his son were suspicious

"he took it not of him for he was never so, but of his mother who had been the most jealous lady that ever lived. But notwithstanding" [quoth he] "that myself never were supicious, yet if I had been in my son's place at the same time that this bastard of Rubempré haunted those coasts I would surely have caused him to be apprehended as my son did."

In conclusion, Philip promised to deliver up Rubempré to the king were his innocence satisfactorily proven.

Morvilliers then resumed his discourse, enlarging upon the treacherous designs of Francis, Duke of Brittany, with whom Charles had lately sworn brotherhood at the very moment when he was the honoured guest of King Louis at Tours. During this discussion the Count of Charolais became very restive. Finally he could no longer endure Morvilliers's indirect slurs, and

"made offer eftsoon to answer, being marvellously out of patience to hear such reproachful speeches used of his friend and confederate. But Morvilliers cut him off, saying: 'My Lord of Charolais, I am not come of ambassage to you, but to my Lord your father.' The said earl besought his father divers times to give him leave to answer, who in the end said unto him: 'I have answered for thee as methinketh the father should answer for the son, notwithstanding if thou have so great desire to speak bethink thyself to-day and to-morrow speak and spare not.' "

The War of Public Weal

Then Morvilliers to his former speech added that he could not imagine what had moved the earl to enter into the league with the Duke of Brittany unless it were because of a pension the king had once given him together with the government of Normandy and afterwards taken from him.

In regard to Rubempré, Commines adds to his story Charles's own statement given on the morrow:

"Notwithstanding, I think nothing was ever proved against him, though I confess the presumption to have been great. Five years after I myself saw him delivered out of prison." This from Commines. La Marche is less detailed in his record[1] of the Rubempré incident:

"The bastard was put in prison and the Count of Charolais sent me to Hesdin to the duke to inform him of the arrest and its cause. The good duke heard my report kindly like a wise prince. In truth he at once suspected that the craft of the King of France lurked at the bottom of the affair. Shortly afterwards the duke left Hesdin and returned to his own land, which did not please the King of France who despatched thither a great embassy with the Count d'Eu at the head. Demands were made that I should be delivered to him to be punished as he would, because he claimed that I had been the cause of the arrest of the bastard of Rubempré and also of the duke's departure from Hesdin without saying adieu to the King of France, but the good duke, moderate in all his actions, replied that I was his

[1] III., 3.

subject and his servitor, and that if the king or any one else had a grievance against me he would investigate it. The matter was finally smoothed over [adds La Marche], and Louis evinced a readiness to conciliate his offended cousin."

In spite of La Marche, the matter proved to be one not easily disposed of by soft phrases flung into the breach. Charles obeyed his father and prepared in advance his defence to the chancellor. When he had finished his own statement about Rubempré, he proceeded to the point of his friendship with the Duke of Brittany, declaring that it was right and proper and that if King Louis knew what was to the advantage of the French sovereign, he would be glad to see his nobles welded together as a bulwark to his throne. As to his pension, he had never received but one quarter, nine thousand francs. He had made no suit for the remainder nor for the government of Normandy. So long as he enjoyed the favour and good will of his father he had no need to crave favour of any man.

"I think verily had it not been for the reverence he bore to his said father who was there present" continues the observant page, "and to whom he addressed his speech that he would have used much bitterer terms. In the end, Duke Philip very wisely and humbly besought the king not lightly to conceive an evil opinion of him or his son but to continue his favour towards them. Then the banquet was brought in and the ambassadors took their leave. As they passed out Charles stood apart from his father and said to the archbishop of Narbonne, who brought up the rear of the little company:

"'Recommend me very humbly to the good grace of the king. Tell him he has had me scolded here by the chancellor but that he shall repent it before a year is past.'" His message was duly delivered and to this incident Commines attributes momentous results.

Exasperated at the nonchalant manner in which Louis's ambassadors treated him, indignant at the injury to his heritage by the redemption of the towns on the Somme, and further, already alienated from his royal cousin through the long series of petty occasions where the different natures of the two young men clashed, in this year 1464, Charles was certainly more than ready to enter into an open contest with the French monarch. It was not long before the opportunity came for him to do so with a certain éclat.

In the early years of his own freedom, before he learned wisdom, Louis XI. had planted many seeds of enmity which brought forth a plentiful crop, and the fruit was an open conspiracy among the nobles of the land.

One of the causes of loosening feudal ties was the gradual growth of the body of standing troops instituted in 1439 by Charles VII. These, in the regular pay of the crown, gave the king a guarantee of support without the aid of his nobles. By the date of Louis's accession, certain ducal houses besides that of Burgundy had grown very independent within their own boundaries: Orleans, Anjou, Bourbon, not to speak of Brittany.[1] Now the efforts to curtail the prerogatives of these petty sovereigns, begun by Charles VII., were steady and persistent in the new reign. They had no longer the power of coining money, of levying troops, or of imposing taxes, while the judicial authority of the crown had been extended little by little over France. Then their privileges were further attacked by Louis's restrictions of the chase.

It was the accumulation of these invasions of local authority, added to a real disbelief in the king's ability, that led to a formation of a league among the nobles, designed to check the centralisation policy of the monarch, a League of Public Weal to form a bulwark against the tyrannical encroachments of their liege lord.

Not to follow the steps of the growth of this coalition, it is sufficient for the thread of this narrative to say that it comprised all the great French nobles, the princes of the blood as well as others. Men whom Louis had flattered as well as those whom he had slighted alike fell from his standards, distrustful of his ability to withstand organised opposition, and they threw in their lot with the protestors so as not to miss their share of the spoil.

[1] Lavisse ivii., 336.

The Count of Charolais, as already mentioned, was in a mood when his ears were eagerly open to overtures from Louis's critics. The redemption of the towns on the Somme he was unable to prevent, but the affair left him very sore. Shortly after its completion, the count did, indeed, succeed in depriving the Croys of their ascendency over the Duke of Burgundy, but when that long desired victory was attained, the towns had one and all accepted their transfer and were under French sovereignty. When the count joined the league, the hope of ultimate restoration was undoubtedly prominent among the motives for his own course of action, though his intimacy with the chief leader of the revolt, the Duke of Brittany, might easily have led to the same result.

Towards Francis of Brittany, Louis XI. had been especially wanting in tact during the first months of his reign. The king treated him as a vassal of France, while the duke held that he and his forbears owed simple homage to the crown, not dependence. Therefore, in order to resist being subordinated, the Duke of Brittany resolved not to leave his estates except in a suitable manner. His messages to the king were sent in all ceremony, he rendered proper homage, declared his readiness to serve him as a kinsman and as a vassal for certain territories, but demanded freedom to exercise his hereditary rights and to enjoy his hereditary dignities.[1]

[1] Chastellain, v., i, etc.

"Rude and strange" were the terms employed by the king in response to these statements, and then he proceeded to encroach still farther on the duke's seigniorial rights by attempts to dispose of the hands of Breton heiresses in unequal marriages, and to arrogate to himself other rights—all sufficient provocation to justify Francis of Brittany in becoming one of the chiefs in the league. Very delightful is Chastellain's colloquy with himself [1] as to the difficulty of maintaining perfect impartiality in discussing the cause of this Franco-Burgundian war, but unfortunately the result of his patient efforts is lost.

Olivier de La Marche and Philip de Commines, however, were both present in the Burgundian army and their stories are preserved. La Marche had reason to remember the first actual engagement between the royal and invading forces at Montl'héry, "because on that day I was made knight." He does not say, as does Commines, that this battle was against the king's desire. Louis had hoped to avoid any use of arms and to coerce his rebellious nobles into quiescence by other methods. Not that they characterised themselves as rebellious, far from it. Clear and definite was their statement that in their obligation

"to give order to the estate, the police and the government of the kingdom, the princes of the blood as chief supports of the crown, by whose advice and

[1] V., 11.

not by that of others, the business of the king and of the state ought to be directed, are ready to risk their persons and their property, and in this laudable endeavour all virtuous citizens ought to aid." [1]

Thus wrote Charles to the citizens of Amiens, and the words were typical of similar appeals made in every quarter of the realm by the various feudal chiefs to their respective subjects. In truth this war, ostentatiously called that of the Public Weal, was but a struggle on the part of the great nobles for local sovereignty. The weal demanded was home rule for the feudal chiefs. The War of Public Weal was a fierce protest against monarchical authority, against concentration. A king indeed, but a king in leading strings was the ideal of the peers.

Thus matters stood in June, 1465. Louis almost alone, deserted by his brother the Duke of Berry, and his nobles banded together in apparent unity, hedged in by their pompous and self-righteous assertions that all their thoughts were for the poor oppressed people whose burdens needed lightening. Of all the great vassals, Gaston de Foix was the single one loyal to the king.

[1] Letter of the Count of Charolais to the citizens of Amiens. (*Collection de Documents inédits sur l'histoire de France.*) "Mélanges," ii., 317. In this collection taken from MS. in the Bibl. Nat. there are many letters private and public about these events.

The part of the great duke fell entirely to the share of the Count of Charolais. A small force was levied for him within the Netherlands, and he started for Paris where he hoped to meet contingents from the two Burgundies and his brother peers of France with their own troops. His men were good individually but they had not been trained to act as one, and there was no coherence between the different companies.

July, 1465, found Charles at St. Denis, the appointed rendezvous. He was first in the field. While he awaited his allies, his little army became restive at the situation in which they found themselves, fifty leagues from Burgundian territory with no stronghold as their base. It was urged again and again upon the count that his first consideration ought to be his men's safety. His allies had failed him. He should retreat. " I have crossed the Oise and the Marne and I will cross the Seine if I have but a single page to follow me," was the leader's firm reply to these demands.

The leaguers were slow to keep their pledges, and Charles decided that it was his mission to prevent Louis from entering his capital, to which he was advancing with great rapidity from the south. To carry out this purpose Charles disregarded all protests, crossed the Seine at St. Cloud, and made his way to the little village of Longjumeau, whither he was preceded by the Count of St. Pol, commanding one division of the Burgundian army. Montl'héry was a village still

The War of Public Weal

farther to the south, and here it was that La Marche and other gentlemen were knighted. This ceremony was evidently part of the count's endeavour to encourage his followers—all unwilling to risk an engagement before the arrival of the allies.

To the king it was of infinite advantage that no delay should occur. Nevertheless, it was Charles who opened active hostilities on July 15th, with soldiers who had not broken their fast that day. Armed since early dawn, wearied by a forced march with a July sun beating down upon their heads, their movements hampered by standing wheat and rye, the men were at a tremendous disadvantage when they were led to the attack. It was a hot assault. No quarter was given, many fled. At length, Louis found himself abandoned by all save his body-guard. Pressed against the hill that bounded the grain fields, the king at last retreated up its slope into a castle on its summit.

Charles rode impetuously after the retreating royalists. Separated from his men, he fell among the royal guard at the gate of the castle. There was a vehement assault resisted as vehemently by his meagre escort. Several fell and Charles himself received a sword wound on his neck where his armour had slipped. Recognised by the French, he might have been taken or slain in his resistance, when the Bastard of Burgundy rode in and rescued him. Very desperate seemed

the count's condition. When night fell, no one
knew where lay the advantage. The fugitives
spread rumours that the king was dead and that
Charles was in possession, others carried the
reverse statements as they rode headlong to the
nearest safety. It was a rout on both sides with
no credit to either leader. But in the darkness
of the night, the king managed to slip out of his
retreat and march quietly towards the greater
security of Paris.

It was a very shadowy victory that Charles
proudly claimed. All through the night of July
15th, the Burgundians were discussing whether
to flee or to risk further fighting against the odds
all recognised. Daybreak found the council in
session when a peasant brought tidings that the
foe had departed. The fires in sight only covered
their retreat. To be sure that same foe had
taken Burgundian baggage with them to Paris.
But what of that? The Burgundians held the
battlefield and they made the best of it.

On July 16th, Louis supped with the military
governor of Paris and "moved the company,
nobles and ladies, to sympathetic tears by his
touching description of the perils he had met and
escaped." Charles, meanwhile, effected a junction
with his belated allies, Francis of Brittany and
Charles of France, the Duke of Berry, at Étampes.
Thither too, came the dukes of Bourbon and of
Lorraine, but none of these leaguers could claim
any share in the battle of Montl'héry.

BATTLE OF MONTL'HÉRY, JULY 16, 1465
(COMINES, ED. LENGLET DU FRESNOY, I.)

While these peers perfected their plans to force their chief into redressing the wrongs of the poor people, the king was showing a very pleasant side of his character to the Parisian citizens. In response to a petition that he should take advice on the conduct of his administration, he declared his perfect willingness to add to his council six burgesses, six members of *parlement*, and the same number from the university. Besides this concession, he relieved the weight of the imposts and hastened to restore certain financial franchises to the Church, to the university, and to various individuals. Three weeks were consumed in establishing friendly relations in this all important city, and then the king departed for Normandy to levy troops and to collect provisions for a siege.[1] There was need for this last for the allies had moved up to the immediate vicinity of Paris.

Before the king's return to his capital on August 28th, a formidable array was encamped at Charenton and its neighbourhood. More formidable, however, they were in numbers than in strength. Like all confederated bodies there was inherent weakness, for there was no leader whom all would be willing to obey. The Duke of Berry, heir presumptive to the throne, was the only one among the peers whose birth might have commanded the needful authority, but he had

[1] Since its recovery from the English, there had been no duke in Normandy. It was thus the one province open to the king.

not sufficient personal character to assert his position. So the confederates remained a loose aggregation of small armies. The longer they remained in camp the weaker they grew, the more disintegrated. A pitched battle might have been a great advantage to these gallant defenders of the Public Weal of France and that was the last desire of their antagonist.

Many skirmishes took place between the Parisians and the leaguers, but no engagement. Once, indeed, there were hurried preparations on the part of the Burgundians to repulse an attack, of whose imminence they were warned by a page before break of day, one misty morning. Yes, there was no doubt. The pickets could see the erect spears and furled banners of the enemy all ready to advance upon the unwary camp. Quick were the preparations. There were no laggards. The Duke of Calabria was more quickly armed than even the Count of Charolais. He came to a spot where a number of Burgundians, the count's own household stood, by the standard. Among them was Commines [1] and he heard the duke say: "We now have our desire, for the king is issued forth with his whole force and marches towards us as our scouts report. Wherefore let us determine to play the men. So soon as they be out of the town we will enter and measure with the long ell." By these words he

[1] I., ch. xi. His vivacious story of the siege should be read in detail.

The War of Public Weal

meant that the soldiers would speedily have a chance to use their pikes as yard sticks to measure out their share of the booty. False prophet was the duke that time! When the daylight grew stronger, the upright spears and furled banners of the advancing foe proved to be a mass of thistles looming large in the magnifying morning mist ! The princes took their disappointment philosophically, enjoyed early mass, and then had their breakfast.

The young Commines is surprised that Paris and her environs were rich enough to feed so many men. Gradually the aspect of affairs changed. Negotiating back and forth became more frequent. The disintegration of the allies became more and more evident. Louis XI. bided his time and then took the extraordinary resolution to go in person to the camp at Charenton to visit his cousin of Burgundy. With a very few attendants, practically unguarded, he went down the Seine. His coming had been heralded and the Count of Charolais stood ready to receive him, with the Count of St. Pol at his side. "Brother, do you pledge me safety?" (for the count's first wife was sister of Louis) to which the count responded: "Yes, as one brother to another." [1]

Nothing could have been more genial than was the king. He assured Charles that he loved a man who kept his word beyond anything.

[1] I., ch. xii.

Veracity was his passion. Charles had kept the promise he had sent by the archbishop of Narbonne, and now he knew in very truth that he was a gentleman and true to the blood of France. Further, he disavowed the insolence of his chancellor towards Charles, and repeated that his cousin had been justified in resenting it. "You have kept your promise and that long before the day."[1]

Then in a friendly promenade, Louis gave an opportunity to Charles and St. Pol to state, informally, the terms on which they would withdraw from their hostile footing, and count the weal restored to the oppressed public whose sorrows had moved them to a confederation.

Distasteful as was every item to Louis, he accepted the requisition of those who felt that they were in a position to dictate, and after a little more parleying at later dates, the treaty of Conflans was duly arranged. It was none too soon for the allies. They could hardly have held together many days longer in the midst of the jealousies rife in their camps.

The king paused at nothing. To his brother he gave Normandy, to Charles of Burgundy the towns on the Somme with guarantee of possession for his lifetime, while the Count of St. Pol was made Constable of France.

Boulogne and Guienne, too, were ceded to Charles, lesser places and pensions to the other

[1] Commines, I., ch. xii.

LOUIS XI. WITH THE PRINCES AND SEIGNEURS OF THE WAR OF PUBLIC WEAL
TAKEN FROM CONTEMPORANEOUS MINIATURE IN ABBEY OF ST. GERMAIN DES PRÉS
(COMINES-LENGLET, II., FRONTISPIECE)

confederates. The contest ended with complete victory for the allies who were left with the proud consciousness that they had set a definite limit to royal pretensions, at least, on paper.

After the treaty was signed, the king showed no resentment at his defeat but urged his cousin to amuse himself a while in Paris before returning home. Charles was rash, but he had not the temerity to trust himself so far. Pleading a promise to his father to enter no city gate until on paternal soil, he declined the invitation and soon returned to the Netherlands, where his own household had suffered change. During his absence, the Countess of Charolais had died and been buried at Antwerp. Charles is repeatedly lauded for his perfect faithfulness to his wife, but her death seems to have made singularly little ripple on the surface of his life. The chroniclers touch on the event very casually, laying more stress on the opportunity it gave Louis XI. to offer his daughter Anne as her successor, than on the event itself.[1]

[1] La Marche, iii., p. 27.

CHAPTER VII

LIEGE AND ITS FATE

1465-1467

"WHEN we have finished here we shall make a fine beginning against those villains the Liegeois." Thus wrote the count's secretary on October 18th.[1] Charles had no desire to rest on the laurels won before Paris. To another city he now turned his attention, to Liege which owed nothing whatsoever to Burgundy.

Before the days when the buried treasures of the soil filled the air with smoke, the valley where Liege lies was a lovely spot.[2] Tradition tells how, in the sixth century, Monulphe, Bishop of Tongres, as he made a progress through his diocese was attracted by the beauties of the site where a few hovels then clustered near the Meuse. After looking down from the heights to the river's banks for a brief space, the bishop turned to his followers and said, as if uttering a prophecy:

[1] *Doc. inédits sur l'hist. de France.* "Mélanges," ii., 398.

[2] Polain, *Récits historiques sur l'ancien pays de Liège*, 1, etc.

"Here is a place created by God for the salvation of many faithful souls. One day a prosperous city shall flourish here. Here I will build a chapel." Dedicated to Cosmo and Damian, the promised chapel became a shrine which attracted many pilgrims who returned to their various homes with glowing tales of the beautiful and fertile valley. Little by little others came who did not leave, and by the seventh century when Bishop Lambert sat in the see of Tongres, Liege was a small town.

An active and loving shepherd was this Lambert. He gave himself no rest but travelled continually from one church to another in his diocese to look after the needs of his flock. He was a fearless prelate, too, and his words of well-deserved rebuke to the Frankish Pepin for a lawless deed excited the wrath of a certain noble, accessory to the act. Trouble ensued and Lambert was slain as he knelt before the altar in Monulphe's chapel at Liege. Absorbed in prayer the pious man did not hear the servants' calls, "Holy Lambert, Holy Lambert come to our aid," words that later became a war-cry when the bishop was exalted into the patron saint of the town.

Not until the thirteenth century, however, when the episcopal see was finally established at Liege, was Lambert's successor virtual lay overlord of the region as well as Bishop of Liege. Monulphe's little chapel had given way to a mighty church dedicated to the canonised Bishop Lambert. The ecclesiastical state became almost autonomous, the episcopal authority being restricted without the walls only by the distant emperor and still more distant pope. Within the walls, the same authority had by no means a perfectly free hand. There were certain features in the constitution of Liege which differentiated it from its sister towns in the Netherlands.

Municipal affairs were conducted in a singularly democratic manner. There was no distinction between the greater and lesser gilds, and, within these organisations, the franchise was given to the most ignorant apprentice had he only fulfilled the simple condition of attaining his fifteenth year. Moreover, the naturalisation laws were very easy. Newcomers were speedily transformed into citizens and enjoyed eligibility to office as well as the franchise. The tenure of office being for one year only, there was opportunity for frequent participation in public affairs, an opportunity not neglected by the community.[1]

The bishop was, of course, not one of the civic officers chosen by this liberal franchise. He was elected by the chapter of St. Lambert, subject to papal and imperial ratification for the two spheres of his jurisdiction. But in the exercise of his function there were many restrictions to his free administration, which papal and imperial sanction together were unable to remove.

A bishop-prince of Liege could make no change

[1] See Kirk, *Charles the Bold*, i., 329.

Liege and Its Fate 133

in the laws without the consent of the estates, and he could administer justice only by means of the regular tribunals. Every edict had to be countersigned. When there was an issue between overlord and people, the question was submitted to the *schepens* or superior judges who, before they gave their opinion, consulted the various charters which had been granted from time to time, and which were not allowed to become dead letters. A permanent committee of the three orders supervised the executive and the administration of the laws. These "twenty-two" received an appeal from the meanest citizen, and the Liege proverb "In his own home the poor man is king," was very near the possible truth.

Yet the wheels of government were by no means perfect in their running. Many were the conflicts between the different members of the state, and broils, with the character of civil war in miniature, were of frequent occurrence. The submergence of the aristocratic element, the nobles, destroyed a natural balance of power between the bishop-prince and the people. The commons exerted power beyond their intelligence. Annual elections, party contests headed by rival demagogues kept the capital, and, to a lesser extent, the smaller towns of the little state in continuous commotion.[1]

[1] Jacques de Hemricourt suggested four chief points of difficulty in Liege government:

1. The size of the council—two hundred, where twenty would do.

The ecclesiastical origin of the community was evident at all points of daily life. The cathedral of St. Lambert was the pride of the city. Its chapter, consisting of sixty canons, took the place held by the aristocratic element in the other towns.

In the cathedral, the holy standard of St. Lambert was suspended. At the outbreak of war this was taken down and carried to the door by the clergy in solemn procession. There it was unfurled and delivered to the commander of the civic militia mounted on a snow-white steed. When he received the precious charge he swore to defend it with his life.

One object of popular veneration was this standard, another was the *perron*, an emblem of the civic organisation. This was a pillar of gilded bronze, its top representing a pineapple surmounted by a cross. This stood on a pedestal in the centre of the square where was the *violet* or city hall. In front of the perron were proclaimed all the ordinances issued by the magistrates, or the decrees adopted by the people in general assembly. On these occasions the tocsin was rung, the deans of the gilds would hasten out with their banners and plant them near the perron as rallying points for the various gild

---

2. The equal voice granted to all gilds without regard to size, when all were assembled by the council to vote on a matter.

3. Extension of franchise to youths of fifteen.

4. Facile naturalisation laws.

(*See* Kirk, i., 325.)

members who poured out from forge, work-shop, and factory until the square was filled.

There were two powerful weapons whereby the bishop-prince might enforce his will in opposition to that of his subjects did the latter become too obstreperous. He could suspend the court of the *schepens*, and he could pronounce an interdict of the Church which caused the cessation of all priestly functions. When this interdict was in action, civil suits between burghers could be adjudged by the municipal magistrates, but no criminals could be arrested or tried. The elementary principles of an organised society were thrown into confusion. Still worse confusion resulted from the bishop's last resort as prince of the Church. An interdict caused the church bells to be silent, the church doors to be closed. The celebration of the rites of baptism, of marriage, of burial ceased.[1] The fear of such cessation was potent in its restraint, unless the populace were too far enraged to be moved by any consideration.

While the Burgundian dukes extended their sway over one portion of Netherland territory after another, this little dominion maintained its complete independence of them. The fact that its princes were elective protected it from lapsing through heritage to the duke who had been so neatly proven heir to his divers childless kinsfolk. It was a rich little vineyard without his pale.

[1] In many cases when the interdict was imposed, it is probable that it was only partially operative.

They were clever people those Liegeois. Their Walloon language is a species of French with many peculiarities showing Frankish admixture.[1] The race was probably a mixed one too, but its acquired characteristics made a very different person from a Hollander, a Frisian, or a Fleming, though there was a certain resemblance to the latter.

In 1465, not yet exploited were the wonderful resources of coal and minerals which now glow above and below the furnace fires until, from a distance, Liege looks like a very Inferno. But the people were industrious and energetic in their crafts. It was a country of skilled workmen. The city of Liege is accredited with one hundred thousand inhabitants at this epoch, and the numbers reported slain in the various battles in which the town was involved run into the thousands.[2]

In 1456, Philip of Burgundy, encouraged by his

[1] See Victor Hugo, *Le Rhin*, i. The Walloon dialect varies greatly between the towns. Here are a few words of the "Prodigal Son" as they are written in Liege, Huy, and Lille:

LIEGE. Jésus lizi d'ha co: In homme aveut deux fis. Li pus jone dérit à s'père : père dinnez-m' con qui m' dent riv' ni di vosse bin; et l'pere lezi partagea s' bin.

HUY. Jésus l'zi d'ha co: Eun homme avut deux fis. Li peus jone dérit a s'père etc.

LILLE. Jesus leu dit incore: un homme avot deux garchens. L' pus jeune dit à sin père-mon père donez me ch que j'dor recouvre d'vo bien; et l'père leu-z-a doné a chacun leu parchen. See also *Doc. inédits concernant l'hist. de la Belgique*, ii., 238, for comment on Scott's treatment of the language.

[2] The numbers are probably exaggerated. To-day it contains about two hundred thousand.

success in the diocese of Utrecht, obtained a certain ascendency over the affairs of Liege by interfering in the election of a bishop. There was no natural vacancy at the moment. John of Heinsberg was the incumbent, a very pleasant prelate with conciliatory ways. He loved amusement and gay society, pleasures more easily obtainable in Philip's court than in his own, and his agreeable host found means of persuading him to resign all the cares of his see. Then the enterprising duke proceeded to place his own nephew, Louis of Bourbon, upon the vacant episcopal throne.

This nephew was an eighteen-year-old student at the University of Louvain, destitute of a single qualification for the office proposed. Nevertheless, all difficulties, technical and general were ignored, and a papal dispensation enabled the candidate even to dispense with the formality of taking orders. Attired in scarlet with a feathered Burgundian cap on his head, Louis made his entry into his future capital and was duly enthroned as bishop-prince in spite of his manifest unfitness for the place.

Nor did he prove a pleasant surprise to his people, better than the promise of his youth, as some reckless princes have done. On the contrary, ignorant, sensuous, extortionate, he was soon at drawn swords with his subjects. After a time he withdrew to Huy where he indulged in gross pleasures while he attempted to check the rebellious citizens of his capital by trying some of the measures of coercion used by his predecessors as a last resort.

Liege was lashed into a state of fury. Matters dragged on for a long time. The people appealed to Cologne, to the papal legate, to the pope, and to the "pope better informed," but no redress was given. Philip continued to protect the bishop, and none dared put themselves in opposition to him. Finally, the people turned to Louis XI. for aid. Their appeal was heard and the king's agent arrived in the city just as one of the bishop's interdicts was about to be enforced, an interdict, too, endorsed by a papal bull, threatening the usual anathema if the provisions were not obeyed.

It was the moment for a demagogue and one appeared in the person of Raes de la Rivière, lord of Heers. On July 5, 1465, there was to be unbroken silence in all sacred edifices. Heers and his followers proclaimed that every priest who refused to chant should be thrown into the river. Mass was said under those unpeaceful and unspiritual conditions, and the presence of the French envoys gave new heart to the bishop's opponents. A treaty was signed between the Liegeois and Louis; wherein mutual pledges were made that no peace should be concluded with Burgundy in which both parties were not included. It was a solemn pledge but it did not hamper Louis when he signed the treaty of Conflans whose articles contained not a single reference to the Liegeois.

Meanwhile, it chanced that the first report of the battle of Montl'héry reaching Liege gave the victory to Louis, a report that spurred on the Liegeois to carry their acts of open hostility to their neighbour, still farther afield. The other towns of the Church state were infected by an anti-Burgundian sentiment. In Dinant this feeling was high, and there was, moreover, a manifestation of special animosity against the Count of Charolais. A rabble marched out of the city to the walls of Bouvignes, a town of Namur, loyal to Burgundy, carrying a stuffed figure with a cow-bell round its neck. Certain well-known emblems of Burgundy on a tattered mantle showed that this represented Charles of Burgundy. With rude words the crowd declared that they were going to hang the effigy as his master, the King of France, had already hanged Count Charles in reality. Further, they said that he was no count at all, but the son of their old bishop, Heinsberg. They went so far as to suspend the effigy on a gallows and then riddled it with arrows and left it dangling like a scarecrow in sight of the citizens of Bouvignes.[1]

The actual contents of the treaty made at Conflans did not reach Liege until messages from Louis had assured them that he had been mindful of their interests in making his own terms, assurances, however, coupled with advice to make peace with their good friend the duke. But there speedily came later information that the only

[1] Du Clercq, iv., 203.

mention of Liege in the new treaty was an apology that Louis had ever made friends in that city!

The rebels lost heart at once. Without the king, they had no confidence in their own efforts. Envoys were despatched to Philip who refused to answer their humble requests for pardon until his son could decide what punishment the principality deserved. Nor was much delay to be anticipated before an answer would be forthcoming. Charles hastened to Liege direct from Paris, not pausing even to greet his father. By the third week of January, he was encamped between St. Trond and Tongres, where a fresh deputation from Liege found him. These envoys, between eighty and a hundred, were well armed chiefly because they feared attacks from their anti-peace fellow-citizens.[1]

They found Charles flushed by his recent achievement of bringing King Louis to his way of thinking. His army, too, was a stronger body than when it left the Netherlands. The troops were more skilled from their experience and elated at what they counted their success; more capable, too, of acting as one body under the guidance of a resolute leader, now inclined to despise councils with free discussion. The count's quick temper had gained him weight but it had made him feared. The slightest breach of discipline brought a thunder-cloud on his face. If we may believe one

[1] Du Clercq, iv., 249.

Liege and Its Fate

authority,[1] he himself was often so lacking in discipline that he would strike an officer with a baton, and once at least, he killed a soldier with his own hand.

His audience with the envoys resulted in a treaty, of which certain articles were so harsh that the messengers were insulted when the report was made in Liege. Only eleven out of thirty-two gilds voted to accept all the articles. A certain noble on pleasant terms with the count offered to carry the unpopular document back to him to ask for a modification of the harsh terms.

By this time the weather was severe. Charles's troops were in need of repose, and it seemed prudent to avoid hostility if possible. Charles revoked the objectionable clauses in consideration of an increase of the war indemnity. With this change the treaty was accepted, and a Piteous Peace it was indeed for the proud folk of Liege. Instead of owing allegiance to emperor and to pope alone as free imperial citizens, they agreed to recognise the Burgundian dukes as hereditary protectors of Liege.

When it was desired, Burgundian troops could march freely across the territory. Burgundian coins were declared valid at Burgundian values. No Liege fortresses were to menace Burgundian marches, and unqualified obedience was pledged to the new overlords. The same terms were

[1] Du Clercq, iv., 239–262.

conceded to all the rebel towns alike except to Dinant. The story of the personal insult to himself and his mother had reached the count's ears and he was not inclined to ignore the circumstance. His further action was, however, deferred.

January 24, 1466, is the final date of the treaty[1] and, after its conclusion, Charles ordered a review of his forces, a review that almost culminated in a pitched battle between army and citizens of St. Trond, and then on January 31st, the count returned to Brussels where there was a great display of Burgundian etiquette before the duke embraced his victorious son.

Piteous as was the peace for Liege and the province at large, still more piteous was the lot of Dinant which alone was excluded from the participation in the treaty. Her fate remained uncertain for months. Other affairs occupied the Count of Charolais until late in the summer of 1466. Time had quickly proven that Louis, well freed from the allies pressing up to the gates of Paris, was in very different temper from Louis ill at ease under their strenuous demands. Not only had he withdrawn his promises in regard to the duchy conferred on his brother, but he had begun taking other measures, ostensibly to prepare against a possible English invasion, which alarmed his cousin of Burgundy for the

[1] Gachard, *Doc. inéd.*, ii., 285, 322. For letters and negotiations anterior to this peace see p. 197 *et seq.*

Liege and Its Fate

undisturbed possession of his recently recovered towns on the Somme.

Excited by the rumours of Louis's purposes, Charles despatched the following letter from Namur[1]:

"MONSEIGNEUR:

"I recommend myself very humbly to your good grace and beg to inform you, Monseigneur, that recently I have been advised of something very surprising to me, Moreover, I am now put beyond doubt considering the source of my information. It is with much regret that I communicate it to you when I remember all the good words you have given to me this year, orally and in writing. Monseigneur, it is evident that there has been some agreement between your people and the English, and that the matter has been so well worked that you have consented, as I have heard, to yield them the land of Caux, Rouen, and the connecting villages, and to aid them in withholding Abbeville and the county of Ponthieu, and further, to cement with them certain alliances against me and my country in making them large offers greatly to my prejudice and, in order to complete the whole, they are to come to Dieppe.

"Monseigneur, you may dispose of your own as you wish: but, Monseigneur, in regard to what concerns me, it seems to me that you would do better to leave my property in my hand than to be the instrument of putting it into the hands of the English or of any foreign nation. For this reason I entreat you, Monseigneur, that if such overtures or greater ones have

[1] Duclos, v., 236.

been opened by your people that you will not commit yourself to them in any manner but will insist on their cessation, and that you will do this in a way that I may always have cause to remain your very humble servant as I desire to do with all my heart. Above all, write to me your good pleasure, and I implore you, Monseigneur, if there be any service that I can render you, I am the one who would wish to employ all that God has given me [to do it]. Written at Namur, August 16th.

"Your very humble and obedient subject,
"CHARLES."

Then the count proceeded to Dinant to inflict the punishment that the culprits had, to his mind, too long escaped.

Commines calls this a strong and rich town, superior even to Liege.[1] A comparison of the two sites shows, however, that this statement could hardly have been true at any time. Dinant lies in a narrow space between the Meuse and high land. A lofty rock at one end of the town dominating the river is crowned by a fortress most picturesque in appearance. It is difficult to estimate how many inhabitants there actually were in the place in 1466, but there is no doubt as to their energy and character. As mentioned before, the artisans had acquired a high degree of skill in their specialty, and their brass work was renowned far and wide. Pots and pans and other utensils were known as *Dinanderies*.

[1] Book II., ch. i. To-day there are only about eight thousand inhabitants.

Liege and Its Fate

The traffic in them was so important that Dinant had had her own commercial relations with England for a long period. Her merchants enjoyed the same privileges in London as the members of the Hanseatic League, and an English company was held in high respect at Dinant.[1] The brass-founders' gild ranked at Dinant as the drapers at Louvain, and the weavers at Ghent. As a "great gild they formed a middle class between the lower gilds and the *bourgeois*," the merchants and richer folk.[2] In municipal matters each of these three classes had a separate vote.

As it happened, Dinant had not been very ready to open hostilities against the House of Burgundy though she was equally critical of Louis of Bourbon in his episcopal misrule. It was undoubtedly her rivalry with Bouvignes of Namur that brought her into the strife. That neighbour had taunted her rival to exasperation, and the fact that it was safe under the Duke of Burgundy and backed by him as Count of Namur, had brought a Burgundian element into the local contest.

The incidents of the insult to Charles and the aspersion on his mother's reputation undoubtedly were due to an irresponsible rabble rather than to any action that could properly be attributed to the leading men. Further, it really seems probable that the weight attached to the insulting

[1] In addition to Commines and Du Clercq *see also* Kirk, i., 385, for quotations from Borgnet and others.
[2] Gachard, *Doc. inéd.*, i., 213, *et passim*.

act never occurred to the respectable burghers until they heard of it from others, so insignificant were the participants in it.

As soon as it was realised that serious consequences might result from reckless folly, the authorities were quite ready to separate themselves from the event, and to arrest the culprits as common malefactors. Once, indeed, the prisoners were temporarily rescued by their friends, and it seemed to Burgundian sympathisers a suspicious circumstance that this happened just at a moment when there was renewed hope for help from Louis XI. When convinced that such hopes were vain, the magistrates became seriously alarmed and ready to go to any lengths to avert Burgundian vengeance. Finally the following letter was despatched to the Duke of Burgundy[1]:

"The poor, humble and obedient servants and subjects of the most reverend father in God, Louis of Bourbon, Bishop of Liege, and your petty neighbours and borderers, the burgomaster's council and folk of Dinant, humbly declare that it has come to their knowledge that the wrath of your grace has been aroused against the town on account of certain ill words spoken by some of the inhabitants thereof, in contempt of your honourable person. The city is as displeased about these words as it is possible to be, and far from wishing to excuse the culprits has arrested as many as could be found and now holds them in durance awaiting any punishment your *grace* may decree. As heartily and as lovingly as possible do

[1] Gachard, *Doc. inéd.*, ii., 350.

Liege and Its Fate

your petitioners beseech your grace to permit your anger to be appeased, holding the people of Dinant exonerated, and resting satisfied with the punishment of the guilty, inasmuch as the people are bitterly grieved on account of the insults and have, as before stated, arrested the culprits."

With further apologies for any failure of duty towards the Duke of Burgundy, the petitioners humbly begged to be granted the same terms that Liege and the other towns had received. March 31st is the date of this humble document. Months of doubt followed before the terrible experience of August proved the futility of their pleas, to which the ducal family refused to listen, so deep was their sense of personal aggrievement. Long as it was since the duchess had taken part in public affairs, she, too, had a word to say here. And she, too, was implacable against the town where any citizen had dared accuse her of infidelity to her husband and to the Church whose interests were more to her than anything in the world except her son.[1]

The petition was as unheeded as were all the representations of the would-be mediators. Again Dinant turned in desperation to Louis XI. and with assurances that after God his royal majesty

[1] Est falme commune que tres haute princesse la ducesse de Bourgogne, à cause desdictes injures at conclut telle hayne sur cestedite ville de Dinant qu'elle a juré comme on dist que s'il li devoit couster tout son vaellant, fera ruynner cestedite ville en mettant toutes personnes à l'espée. (Gachard, *Doc. inéd.*, ii., 222.)

was their only hope, besought him from mere charity and pity to persuade his cousin of Burgundy to forgive them. Apparently Louis took no notice of this appeal. Dinant's last hope was that her fellow-communes of Liege would refuse to ratify the treaty unless she, too, were included. The sole concession, obtained by their envoys to Charles in the winter, had been a short truce afterwards extended to May, 1466.

During that summer the critical position of the little town was well known. Some sympathisers offered aid but it was aid that there was possible danger in accepting. Many of the outlaws from Liege, who had been expressly excluded from the terms of the peace, had joined the ranks of a certain free lance company called "The Companions of the Green Tent," as their only shelter was the interlaced branches of the forest. To Dinant came this band to aid in her defence.[1] At one time it seemed as though a peaceful accommodation might be reached but it fell through. Not yet were the citizens ready to surrender their charters—"Franchises,—to the rescue," was a frequent cry and no treaty was made.

Philip, long inactive, resolved to assist at the reduction of this place in person. Too feeble to ride, he was carried to the Meuse in a litter, and arrived at Namur on August 14th. Then attended by a small escort only, he proceeded to Bouvignes, a splendid vantage point whence he

[1] Gachard, *Doc. inéd.*, ii., 337, *et passim*.

Liege and Its Fate

could command a view of the scene of his son's intended operations. As the crisis became imminent there were a few further efforts to effect a reconciliation. When these failed, the town prepared to meet the worst.[1] Stories gravely related by Du Clercq[2] represent the people of Dinant goaded to actual fury of resistance.

By August 17th, the Burgundian troops made their appearance, winding down to the river. Conspicuous among the standards—and nobles from all Philip's dominions were in evidence—was the banner of the Count of Charolais, displaying St. George slaying the dragon.

On Tuesday, August 19th, Dinant was invested and the siege began. Within the walls the most turbulent element had gained complete control of affairs. All thought of prudence was thrown to the winds. From the walls they hurled words at the foe:

"Is your old doll of a duke tired of life that you have brought him here to perish?[3] Your Count Charlotel is a green sprout. Bid him go fight the King of France at Montl'héry. If he waits for the noble Louis or the Liegeois he will have to take to his heels," etc.

It was a heavy siege and the town was riddled

---

[1] Du Clercq, iv., 273.

[2] He says messengers were put to death without regard to their sacred office, even a little child being torn limb from limb. Priests were thrown into the river for refusing to say mass, and the situation was strained to the last degree.

[3] *Qui a mandé ce vieil monnart vostre duc*, etc.

with cannon-balls but there was no assault. By the sixth day the magistrates determined to send their keys to the Count of Charolais and beg for mercy. The captain of the great gild of coppersmiths, Jean de Guérin, tried to encourage the faint-hearted to protest openly against this procedure. Seizing the city colours he declared: "I will trust to no humane sentiment. I am ready to carry this flag to the breach and to live or die with you. If you surrender, I will quit the town before the foe enter it." It was too late, the capitulation was made.

When the keys were brought to Charles he remembered that he was not yet duke and ordered them presented to his father in his stead, and to his half-brother Anthony was entrusted the task of formally accepting the surrender.

It was late in the evening when the Bastard of Burgundy marched in. At first he held the incoming troops well under control, but the stores of wine were easy to reach, and by the morning there were wild scenes of disorder. When Charles arrived, however, on the morrow, Tuesday, just a week after the beginning of the siege, lawlessness was checked with a strong hand. Any ill treatment of women was peculiarly repugnant to him, and he did not hesitate to execute the sternest justice upon offenders.[1]

His entry into the fallen town was made with all the wonted Burgundian pomp. Nothing in the

[1] Du Clercq, iv., 278.

ANTHONY OF BURGUNDY
AFTER HANS MEMLING. DRESDEN GALLERY

Liege and Its Fate

proceedings occurred in a headlong or passionate manner. A council of war was held and the proceedings decided upon. The cruelty that was exercised was used in deliberate punishment, not in savage lawlessness. The personal insults to his mother and to himself rankled in the count's mind. As one author remarks [1] with undoubted reason, it is not likely that any of those responsible for the insult were among those punished. After the siege, "pitiable it was to see, for the innocent suffered and the guilty escaped."

Certain rich citizens bought their lives with large sums, others *were sold as slaves*,[2] or were hanged or beheaded, or were thrown into the Meuse.[3] In the monasteries, life was conceded to the inmates but that was all. All their property was confiscated. The Count of St. Pol, now Constable of France, tried to intercede for the citizens with Philip who remained at Bouvignes, but to no result. It might have been chance or it might have been intentional that at last flames completed the work of destruction. The abode of Adolph of Cleves, at the corner of Nôtre Dame, was found to be on fire at about one o'clock in the morning of Thursday, August 28th.

That Charles was responsible for this conflagra-

[1] De Ram, *Documents relatifs aux troubles du pays de Liége*, "Henricus de Merica," p. 159.

[2] Vel vendebantur in servos. See De Ram *et passim* for documents.

[3] It seems to be well attested that the prisoners were tied together and drowned.

tion Du Clercq thinks is incredible.[1] He would certainly have saved all ecclesiastical property which was almost completely consumed. Indeed, Charles gave orders to extinguish the flames as soon as they were discovered, but every one was so occupied with saving his own portion of booty that nothing was accomplished and the town-hall caught fire and the church of Nôtre Dame. From the latter some ornaments and treasures were saved and the bones of Ste. Perpète, with other holy relics, were rescued by Charles himself at risk to his own life.

"It was never known how the fire originated. Some say it was due to a defective flue. To my mind," [concludes the pious historian],[2] "it was the Divine Will that Dinant should be destroyed on account of the pride and ill deeds of the people. I trust to God who knows all. The duke's people alone lost more than a hundred thousand crowns' value."

Cy fust Dinant, "Dinant was," is the sum of his description, four days after the conflagration.[3]

On September 1st, Philip, who had remained at Bouvignes while all this passed under the direction of Charles, took boat and sailed down to Namur. It was almost a triumph,—that trip that proved one of the last ever made by the proud duke—and the procession on the river and the

[1] Du Clercq, iv., 280.

[2] *Ibid.*, 281.

[3] In 1472, a new church was erected "on the spot formerly called Dinant" and after that, little by little, the town came to life. (Gachard, *Analectes Belgiques*, 318, etc.).

Liege and Its Fate

entry into Namur were closed by a humble embassy from Liege in regard to certain points of their peace.

Du Clercq gravely relates, by the way, that the Count of St. Pol's men had had no part in the plunder of Dinant. This was hard on the poor fellows. Therefore, Philip turned over to their mercies, as a compensation for this deprivation, the little town of Tuin, which had been rebellious and then submitted. Tuin accepted its fate, submitted to St. Pol, and then compounded the right of pillage for a round sum of money. Moreover, they promised to lay low their gates and their walls and those of St. Trond. In this way, it is said that the constable made ten thousand Rhenish florins. Still both he and his men felt ill-compensated for the loss of the booty of Dinant.

Charles continued a kind of harassing warfare on the various towns of Liege territory. The people of Liege themselves seem to have varied in their humour towards Charles, sometimes being very humble in their petitions for peace and again very insolent. As a rule, this conduct seems to be traceable to their hope of Louis's support. On September 7th, there was one pitched battle where victory decided the final terms of the general peace, and after various skirmishes and submissions, Charles disbanded his troops for the winter and joined his father at Brussels.

CHAPTER VIII

THE NEW DUKE

1467

THE Good Duke's journey to Bouvignes where he witnessed the manner in which his authority was vindicated was his last effort. In the early summer following, on Friday, June 10th, Philip, then at Bruges, was taken ill and died on the following Monday, June 13th, between nine and ten in the evening.[1] Charles was summoned on the Sunday, and it seemed as though his horse's hoofs hardly struck the pavement as he rode, so swift was his course on the way to Bruges.

When he reached the house where his father lay dying, he was told that speech had already ceased, but that there was still life. The count threw himself on his knees by the bedside, weeping in all tenderness, and implored a paternal benediction and pardon for all wherein he had offended his father. Near the duke stood his confessor who begged the dying man to make a sign if he could

[1] Du Clercq, iv., 302 *et seq.* Erasmus was born in this year, 1467.

The New Duke

still understand what was said to him. On this admonition and in reply to his son's prayers, Philip turned his eyes to Charles, looked at him and pressed the hand which was laid upon his own, but further token was beyond his strength. The count stayed by his side until he breathed his last.

Thus ended the life of a man who had been a striking figure in Europe for forty years. His most fervent dream, indeed, had never been fulfilled. All his pompous vows to wrest the Holy Land from the invading Turks had proved vain. Many years had passed since he had had military success of any kind, and even in his earlier life his successes had been owing to diplomacy and to a happy conjunction of circumstances rather than to skilful generalship. He possessed pre-eminently the power of personality.

When Duke John of Burgundy fell on the bridge at Montereau and Philip came into his heritage, Henry V. of England was in the full flush of his prosperity, standing triumphant over England and France, and in a position to make good his claim with three stalwart brothers to back him. All these young men had died prematurely. Their only descendant was Henry VI., and that meagre and wretched representative of the ambitious Henry V. had had no spark of the character of his father and uncles. The one vigorous element in his life was his wife, Margaret of Anjou, who diligently exerted herself to keep her husband on his throne. In vain were her efforts. By 1467, Edward of York was on that throne. Gone, too, was Charles VII., whose father's acts had clouded his early, whose son darkened his latter years.

Out of his group of contemporaries, Duke Philip alone had marched steadily to every desired goal. His epitaph gave a fairly accurate list of his achievements in doggerel verses:

"John was born of Philip, child of good King John.
To that John, I, Philip, was born his eldest son.
Flanders, Artois, and Burgundy his will bequeathed to me
Therein to follow him and rule them legally.
With Holland, Zealand, Hainaut, my own realm greater grew.
Luxemburg, Brabant, Namur soon were added too.
The Liegeois and the German my lawful rights defied,
By force of right and arms they have been pacified.
At one single time against me were maintained
French, English, German forces,—nothing have they gained.
Against King Charles the Seventh, I warred in great array.
From me he begged a peace and king was from that day!
The mighty conflicts that I fought in all are numbered seven.
Not once was I defeated. To God the praise be given.
Time and time again Liege and Ghent revolted,
But I put them down. I would not be insulted.
In Barrois and Lorraine, King René warred upon me.
Of Sicily erst king, captivity soon won he.

The New Duke

Louis, son of Charles, depressed and refugee,
From me received his crown. Five years my guest was he.
Edward, Duke of York, fled, wretched, to my land;
That now he 's England's king is due my aid and hand.
To defend the Church, which is the House Divine,
The Golden Fleece was founded, that great order mine.
Christian faith to succour in vigour and in strength,
My galleys sailed the sea in all its dreary length.
In later days I planned and most sincerely meant
To take the field myself, but Death did that prevent.
When Eugene the Pope by the council was disdained,
Through my control alone as Pope was he retained.
In 1467, Time my goal has set.
When I am seventy-one, I pay Dame Nature's debt.
With father and grandfather, I now lie buried here.
As in life I ever was their equal and their peer.
Good Jesu was my guide in every word and deed,
Beseech him every one that Heaven be my meed!"

The territories thus named, that passed to the new duke, covered a goodly space of earth. Had Philip not slacked his ambition at a critical time, undoubtedly he could have left a royal rather than a ducal crown to his son. He did not so will it, and, moreover, in a way he had receded from his independence as he had accepted feudal obligations towards Louis XI. which he never had towards Charles VII.

Lured by the hope of becoming prime adviser of the French king, he had emphasised his position as first peer of France. Thus it was as Duke of Burgundy *par excellence* that Philip died, as the typical peer whose luxury and magnificence far surpassed the state possible to his acknowledged liege. To his son was bequeathed the task of attempting to turn that ducal state into state royal, and of establishing a realm which should hold the balance of power between France and Germany.

There was no doubt in Charles's mind as to which was the greater, the cleverer, the more powerful of the two, Louis the king and Charles the duke. Had not the former been a beggarly suppliant at his father's gates, as dauphin? As king, had he not been forced to yield at the gates of his own capital to every demand made by Charles, standing as the comscientious representative of the public welfare of France?

Had not Louis befriended the contumelious neighbour of Charles, only to learn that his Burgundian cousin could and would deal summarily with all protests against his authority among the lesser folk on Netherland territory?

The Croys made an attempt to gain the new duke's friendship, as appears from this letter to Duke Charles:

"Our very excellent lord, we have heard that it has pleased Our Lord to take to Himself and to withdraw from the world the good Duke Philip, our beloved lord and father, prince of glorious memory, august duke, most Christian champion of the faith, patron and pattern of the virtues and honours of Christianity, and the dread of infidel lands. By his valorous deeds, he has won an immortal name among living men, and deserves to our mind to find grace before the merciful bounty of God whom we implore to pardon his faults.

"Alas! our most doughty seigneur, thus dolorous death shows what is to be expected by all mortals. How many lands, how many nobles, how many peoples, how many treasures, and how many powers would have been ready to prevent what has come to pass, and how many prayers would have risen to God could He have prevented this death! . . .

"Death is inevitable, and the death of the good is the end of all evils and the beginning of all benefits, but still your loss and ours cannot pass without affliction. Nevertheless, our most puissant lord, when we consider that we are not left orphans, and that you, his only son, remain to fill his place, this is a cause for comfort.

. . . .

"We implore you to be pleased to count us your loyal subjects and very humble servitors and to permit us to go to you, to thus declare ourselves, etc.

"A. DE CROY,
"J. DE CROY."

At the time of the duke's death, Olivier de La Marche was in England, whither he had accompanied the Bastard of Burgundy on a mission to King Edward.[1] Right royally had the latter received the embassy.

"Clad in purple, the gaiter on his leg and a great baton in his hand, he seemed, indeed, a personage

[1] II., 49.

worthy of being king, for he was a fine prince with a grand manner. A count held the sword in front of him, and around his throne were from twenty to twenty-five old councillors, white-haired and looking like senators gathered together to advise their master."

Thus appeared Edward on the occasion of a tourney given in honour of the embassy which La Marche proceeds to describe in detail. The Bastard of Burgundy, wearing the Burgundian coat-of-arms with a bar sinister, made a fine record for himself.

After the tournament he invited the ladies to a Sunday dinner,

"especially the Queen and her sisters and made great preparations therefor and then we departed, Thomas de Loreille, Bailiff of Caux, and I to go to Brittany to accomplish our embassy. We arrived at Pleume and were obliged to await wind and boats to go into Brittany. While there, came the news that the Duke of Burgundy was dead. You may believe how great was the bastard's mourning when he heard of his father's death, and how the nobility who were with him mourned too. Their pleasures were melted into tears and lamentations for he died like a prince in all valour.

"In his life he accomplished two things to the full. One was he died as the richest prince of his time, for he left four hundred thousand crowns of gold cash, seventy-two thousand marks of silver plate, without counting rich tapestries, rings, gold dishes garnished with precious stones, a large and well equipped library, and rich furniture. For the second, he died as the most liberal duke of his time. He married his nieces at his own expense; he bore the whole cost of great wars several times. At his own expense, he refitted the church and chapel at Jerusalem. He gave ten thousand crowns to build the tower of Burgundy at Rhodes; . . . No one went from him who was not well recompensed. The state he maintained was almost royal. For five years he supported Monseigneur the Dauphin, and was a prince so renowned that all the world spoke well of him."

The Bastard of Burgundy took leave of the English court and hastened to Bruges to join his brother, the Count of Charolais, who received him warmly. "Henceforth," explains Olivier, "when I mention the said count I will call him the Duke of Burgundy as is reasonable."

Solemnly was the prince's body carried into the church of St. Donat in Bruges, there to repose until it could be taken to Burgundy to be buried at Dijon with his ancestors. La Marche dismisses the funeral with a brief phrase as he was not himself present at Bruges, being busied in Brittany. There was a memorial service there, the finest he ever saw. The arms of Burgundy were inserted in the chapel decorations, not merely pinned on,[1] a fact that impressed the chronicler. No nobles, not even those from Flanders, were permitted to put on mourning. The Duke of Brittany declared that none but him was worthy of the honour for so high a prince.

[1] "Non par armes attachées à espingles."

"So he alone wore mourning. At the end of the service I went to thank him for the reverence he had shown the House of Burgundy, and he responded that he had only done his duty. Then I finished my business as quickly as I could and crossed the sea again and returned to my new master."

In his treatise on the eminent deeds of the Duke of Burgundy,[1] Chastellain recounts, more at length than La Marche, all that his great master had accomplished. Then he proceeds to describe the duke as he knew him.

He was medium in height, rather slight but straight as a rush, strong in hip and in arm, his figure well-knit. His neck was admirably proportioned to his body, his hand and foot were slender, he had more bone than flesh, but his veins were full-blooded. Like all his ancestors, his face was long, as was his nose, his forehead high. His complexion was brunette, his hair brownish, soft, and straight, his beard and eyebrows the same colour, but the former curly, the latter were bushy and inclined to stand up like horns when he was angry. His mouth was well-proportioned, his lips full and high-coloured; his eyes were grey, sometimes arrogant but usually amiable in expression. His personality corresponded perfectly to his appearance. His countenance showed his character, and his character was a witness to the truth of his physiognomy. Nothing was contradictory, perfect was the

[1] *Œuvres*, vii., 213.

harmony between the inner and the outer man, between the nobility of thought and the simple dignity, well-poised and graceful. Among the great ones of this earth, he was like a star in heaven. Every line proclaimed "I am a prince and a man unique."

It was for his bearing rather than his beauty that he commanded universal admiration. In a stable he would have looked like an image in a temple. In a hall he was the decoration. Wherever his body was, there, too, was his spirit, ready for the demands of the hour. He was singularly joyous and nicely tempered in speech with so much personal magnetism that he could mollify any enemy if he could only meet him face to face. His dress was always rich and appropriate. He was skilful in horsemanship, in archery, and in tennis, but his chief amusement was the chase. He liked to linger at the table and demanded good serving but was really moderate in his tastes, as often he neglected pheasant for a bit of Mayence ham or salted beef. Oaths and abuse were never heard from him. To all alike his speech was courteous even when there was nothing to be gained.

"Never, I assert, did falsehood pass his lips, his mouth was equal to his seal and his spoken word to his written. Loyal as fine gold and whole as an egg." Chastellain repeats himself somewhat in the profusion of his eulogy, but such are the main points of his characterisation. Then he proceeds to some qualifications:

"In order to avoid the charge of flattery, I acknowledge that he had faults. None is perfect except God. Often he was very careless in administration, and he neglected questions of justice, of finance, and of commerce in a way that may redound to the injury of his house. The excuse urged is that it was his deputies who were at fault. The answer to that is that he trusted too much to deputies and should not be excused for his confidence. A ruler ought to understand his business himself.

"Also he had the vices of the flesh. He pleased his heart at the desire of his eyes. At the desire of his heart he multiplied his pleasures. His wishes were easy to attain. What he wanted was offered freely. He neglected the virtuous and holy lady his wife, a Christian saint, chaste and charitable. For this I offer no excuse. To God I leave the cause.

"Another fault was that he was not wise in his treatment of his nobles. Especially in his old age he often preferred the less worthy, the less capable advisers. The answer to this charge is that, as his health failed, whoever was by his side obtained ascendency over him and succeeded in keeping the others at a distance. Ergo, theirs is the malice and the excuse is to the princely invalid. In his solitude even valets used their power, as is not wonderful.

"He went late to mass and often out of hours. Sometimes he had it celebrated at two o'clock or even three, and in so doing he exceeded all Christian observance. For this there is no excuse that I dare allege. I leave it to the judgment of God. He had, indeed, obtained dispensation from the pope for causes which he explained, *and he only* is responsible. God alone can judge about him.

"It would be a dreadful shame if his soul suffered for this neglect in lifetime. Earth would not suffice to deplore, nor the nature of man to lament the perdition of such a soul and of such a prince. Hell is not worthy of him nor good enough to lodge him. O God, who rescued Trajan from Hades for a single virtuous act, do not suffer this man to descend therein!"

Having thus tried his best to give a vivid description of the father's personality, while acknowledging that he is not sure of the fate of his soul, the chronicler decides that it would be an excellent moment to paint the son, too, for all time, in view of his mortality. "I will use the past tense so that my words may be good for always."

Duke Charles was shorter and stouter than Duke Philip, but well formed, strong in arm and thigh. His shoulders were rather thick-set and a trifle stooping, but his body was well adapted to activity. The contour of his face was rounder than that of his father, his complexion brunette. His eyes were black and laughing, angelically clear. When he was sunk in thought it seemed as though his father looked out of them. Like his father's mouth was his, full and red. His nose was pronounced, his beard brown, and his hair black. His forehead was fine, his neck white and well set, though always bent as he walked. He certainly was not as straight as Philip, but nevertheless he was a fine prince with a fair outer man.

When he began to speak he often found difficulty in expressing himself, but once started his speech became fluent, even eloquent. His voice was fine and clear, but he could not sing, although he had studied the technique and was fond of music. In conversation he was more logical than his father, but very tenacious of his own opinion and vehement in its expression, although, at the bottom, he was just to all men.

In council he was keen, subtle, and ready. He listened to others' arguments judicially and gave them due weight before his own concluded the discussion. He was attentive to his own business to a fault, for he was rather more industrious than became a prince. Economical of his own time, he demanded conscience of his subordinates and worked them very hard. He was fond of his servants and fairly affable, though occasionally sharp in his words. His memory was long and his anger dangerous. As a rule, good sense swayed him, but being naturally impetuous there was often a struggle between impulse and reason.

He was a God-fearing prince, was devoted to the Virgin Mary, rigid in his fasts, lavish in charity. He was determined to avoid death and to hold on to his own, tooth and nail, and was his father's peer in valour. Like his father, he dressed richly; unlike him, he cared more for silver than for jewels. He lived more chastely than is usual to princes and was always master of himself. He drank little wine, though he liked it, because he found that it engendered fever in him. His only beverage was water just coloured with wine. He was inclined to no indulgence or wantonness. "At the hour in which I write his taste for hard labour is excessive, but in other respects his good sense has dominated him, at least thus far. It is to be hoped that as his reign grows older he will curb his over-strenuous industry."

As to the duke's sympathies, Chastellain regrets that circumstances have turned him towards England. Naturally he belonged to the French, and it was a pity that the machinations of the king, "whose crooked ways are well known to God, have forced him into self-defence. Yet on his forehead he wears the fleur-de-lys."

Chastellain acknowledges that Charles is accused of avarice, but defends him on the ground that he has been driven into collecting a large army. "A penny in the chest is worth three in the purse of another." "To take precautions in advance is a way to save honour and property," prudently adds the historian, who evidently flourishes his maxims to strengthen his own appreciation of the duke's economy, which, quite as evidently, is not pleasing to him. "I have seen him the very opposite of miserly, open-handed and liberal, rejoicing in largesse. When he came into his seigniory his nature did not change." It was simply the exigencies of his critical position that forced him to restrain his natural propensities and thus to gain the undeserved reputation for parsimony.

It was also said that he was a very hard taskmaster, but as a matter of fact he demanded nothing of his soldiers that he was not ready to undertake himself. Like a true duke, he was his own commander, drew up his own troops himself in battle array, and then passed from one end of the line to the other, encouraging the men individually with cheery words, promising them glory and profit, and pledging himself to share their dangers. In victory he was restrained and showed more mercy than cruelty.

After expatiating on the points where Charles was like his father—conventional princely qualities—Chastellain adds: "In some respects they differed. The one was cold and the other boiling with ardour; the one slow and prone to delay, the other strenuous in his promptness; the elder negligent of his own concerns, the younger diligent and alert. They differed in the amount of time consumed at meals and in the number of guests whom they entertained. They differed more or less in their voluptuousness and in their expenditures and in the way in which they took solace and amusement." But in all other respects, "in life they marched side by side as equals and if it please God He will be their conductor in glory everlasting" is the final assurance of their eulogist.

Yet, lavish as the Burgundian poet is in his adjectives about his patron, there is considerable discrimination between his summaries of the two dukes. It is very evident that from his accession

The New Duke

Charles was less of a favourite than his father. While endeavouring to be as complimentary as possible, distrust of his capacities creeps out between the lines. Chastellain died in 1475, and thus never saw Charles's final disaster. But the violence of his character had inspired lack of confidence in his power of achievement, a violence that made people dislike him as Philip with all his faults was never disliked.

CHAPTER IX

THE UNJOYOUS ENTRY

1467

AFTER the dauphin was crowned at Rheims, he was monarch over all his domains. Charles of Burgundy, on the other hand, had a series of ceremonies to perform before he was properly invested with the various titles worn by his father. Each duchy, countship, seigniory had to be taken in turn. Ghent was the first capital visited. Then he had to exchange pledges of fidelity with his Flemish subjects before receiving recognition as Count of Flanders.

According to the custom of his predecessors, Charles stayed at the little village of Swynaerde, near Ghent, the night before he made his "joyous entry" into that city. It had chanced that the day selected by Charles for the event was St. Lievin's Day and a favourite holiday of the workers of Ghent. The saint's bones, enclosed conveniently in a portable shrine, rested in the cathedral church, whence they were carried once a year by the fifty-two gilds in solemn procession to the little village of Houthem, where the blessed

The Unjoyous Entry

saint had suffered martyrdom in the seventh century. All day and all night the saint's devotees, the Fools of St. Lievin, as they were called, remained at this spot. Merry did the festival become as the hours wore on, for good cheer was carried thither as well as the sacred shrine.

Now the magistrates were a little apprehensive about the rival claims of the new count of Flanders and the old saint of Ghent. They knew that they could not cut short the time-honoured celebration for the sake of the sovereign's inauguration, so they decided to prolong the former, and directed that the saint should leave town on Saturday and not return until Monday. This left Sunday free for the young count's entry. It probably seemed a very convenient conjunction of events to the city fathers, because the more turbulent portion of the citizens was sure to follow the saint.

Accordingly, Charles made a very quiet and dignified entrance,[1] having paused at the gates to listen to the fair words of Master Mathys de Groothuse as he extolled the virtues of the late Count of Flanders, and requested God to receive the present one, when he, too, was forced to leave earth, as graciously as Ghent was receiving him that day. All passed well; oaths of fealty were duly taken and given at the church of St. John the Baptist. Charles himself pulled the bell rope according to the ancient Flemish custom, and the Count of

[1] Gachard, *Doc. inéd.*, i., 210, etc.

Flanders was in possession. This all took place in the morning of June 28th. At the close of the ceremonies Charles withdrew to his hotel and the magistrates to their dwellings.

The devotees of St. Lievin prolonged their holiday until Monday afternoon. It was five o'clock [1] when the revellers returned to Ghent. Many of the saint's followers were, by that time, more or less under the influence of the contents of the casks which had formed part of the outward-bound burden. The protracted holiday-making had its natural sequence. There was, however, too much method in the next proceedings for it to be attributed wholly to emotional inebriety.

The procession passed through the city gate and entered a narrow street near the corn market, where stood a little house used as headquarters for the collection of the *cueillotte*, a tax on every article brought into the city for sale, and one particularly obnoxious to the people. Suddenly a cry was raised and echoed from rank to rank of St. Lievin's escort, "Down with the *cueillotte*."

Then with the ingenious humour of a Celtic crowd, quick to take a fantastic advantage of a situation, a second cry was heard: "St. Lievin must go through the house. Lievin is a saint who never turns aside from his route."

Delightful thought, followed by speedy action. Axes were produced and wielded to good effect.

[1] Some authorities make this five A. M., but the *Rapport* is probably correct.

The Unjoyous Entry

Down came the miniature customs-house in a flash. Little pieces of the ruin were elevated on sticks and carried by some of the rabble as standards with the cry "I have it—I have it." As they marched the procession was constantly augmented and the cries become more decidedly revolutionary: "Kill, kill these craven spoilers of God and of the world.[1] Where are they? Let us seek them out and slay them in their houses, those who have flourished at our pitiable expense."

This was rank rebellion. Even under cover of St. Lievin's mantle, resistance to regularly instituted customs could hardly be described by any other name. Excited by their own temerity, the crowd now surged on to the great market-place in front of the Hôtel de Ville, where the Friday market is held, instead of returning the saint promptly to his safe abiding-place as was meet.

There the lawless deeds—lawless to the duke's mind certainly—became more audacious. Counterparts of the very banners whose prohibition had been part of the sentence in 1453 were unfurled,[2] and their possession alone proved insurrectionary premeditation on the part of the gild leaders. Ghent was in open revolt, and the young duke in their midst felt it was an open insult to him as sovereign count.

His messenger failed to return from the market-

---

[1] Chastellain, v., 260 *et passim*.

[2] So say some historians. But it seems probable that the drapery of St. Lievin's shrine was hastily used as a flag.

place. His master became impatient and followed him to the scene of action with a small escort. As they drew near, the crowd thickened and hedged them in. The nobles became alarmed and urged the duke to return, but cries from the crowd promised safety to his person. To the steps of the Hôtel de Ville rode the duke, his face dark, menacing with suppressed wrath.[1]

As he dismounted, he turned towards a man whom he thought he saw egging on a disturbance and struck him with his riding whip, saying, "I know you." The man was quick enough to realise the value of the duke's violence at that moment and cried, "Strike again," but the Seigneur Groothuse, who had already tried to check Charles's anger and to curb the popular turbulence, exclaimed, "For the love of God do not strike again!" The wiser burgher at once understood the unstable temper of the mob, which had been fairly civil to the duke up to this moment. There were ugly murmurs to be heard that the blow would cost him dear.

"Indeed," says the courtly Chastellain, "the mischief was so imminent that God alone averted it, and there was not an archer or noble or man so full of assurance that he did not tremble with fear, nor one who would not have preferred to be in India for his own safety. Especially were they in terror for their young prince, who, they thought, was exposed to a dolorous death."

[1] Chastellain, v., ch. 7, etc.

The Unjoyous Entry

It was Groothuse alone who averted disaster:

"Do you not see that your life and ours hang on a silken thread? Do you think you can coerce a rabble like this by threats and hard words—a rabble who at this moment do not value you more than the least of us? They are beside themselves, they have neither reason nor understanding.[1] . . . If you are ready to die, I am not, except in spite of myself. You must try quite a different method—appease them by sweetness and save your house and your life.

"What could you do alone? How the gods would laugh! Your courage is out of place here unless it enables you to calm yourself and give an example to those poor sheep, wretched misled people whom you must soothe. Go down in God's name. [They were within the town hall.] Show yourself and you will make an impression by your good sense and all will go well."

To this eminently sound advice the young duke yielded. He appeared on a balcony or on the upper steps of the town hall and stood ready to harangue his unruly and turbulent subjects. A moment sufficed to still the turmoil and the silence showed a readiness to hear him speak.

Charles was not perfectly at ease in Flemish, but he was wise enough to use that tongue. One trait of the Ghenters was respect for the person of their overlord. When that overlord showed any disposition to meet them half-way the response

[1] These are Chastellain's words to be sure, but the sober *Rapport* is similar in purport.

was usually immediate. So it was now. The crowd which had been attending to St. Lievin, and not to the duke's joyous entry, suddenly remembered that his welcome had been strangely ignored. Their grumblings changed to greetings. "Take heart, Monseigneur. Have no fear. For you we will live and die and none shall be so audacious as to harm you. If there be evil fellows with no bump of reverence, endure it for the moment. Later you shall be avenged. No time now for fear."

This sounded better. Charles was sufficiently appeased to address the crowd as "My children," and to assure them that if they would but meet him in peaceful conference, their grievances should be redressed. "Welcome, welcome! we are indeed your children and recognise your goodness."

Then Groothuse followed with a longer speech than was possible either to Charles's Flemish or to his mood. This address was equally well received, and matters were in train for the appointment of a conference between popular representatives and the new Count of Flanders, when suddenly a tall, rude fellow climbed up to the balcony from the square. Using an iron gauntlet as a gavel to strike on the wall, he commanded attention and turned gravely to address the audience as though he were on the accredited list of speakers:

"My brothers, down there assembled to set your complaints before your prince, your first wish—is

The Unjoyous Entry

it not?—is to punish the ill governors of this town and those who have defrauded you and him alike." "Yes, yes," was the quick answer of the fickle crowd.—"You desire the suppression of the *cueillotte*, do you not?"—"Yes, yes."—"You want all your gates opened again, your banners restored, and your privileges reinforced as of yore?"—"Yes, yes." The self-appointed envoy turned calmly to Charles and said:

"Monseigneur, this is what the citizens have come together to ask you. This is your task. I have said it in their behalf, and, as you hear, they make my words their own."

Noteworthy is Chastellain's pious and horrified ejaculation over the extraordinary insolence of this big villain, who thus audaciously associated himself with his betters: "O glorious Majesty of God, think of such an outrageous and intolerable piece of villainy being committed before the eyes of a prince! For a low man to venture to come and stand side by side with such a gentleman as our seigneur, and to proffer words inimical to his authority—words the poorest noble in the world would hardly have endured! And yet it was necessary for this noble prince to endure and to tolerate it for the moment, and needful that he should let pass as a pleasantry what was enough to kill him with grief."

Groothuse's answer to the man was mild. Evidently he did not think it was a safe moment to exasperate the mob: "'My friend, there was no necessity of your intruding up here, a place reserved for the prince and his nobles. From below, you could have been heard and Monseigneur could have answered you as well there as here. He requires no advocate to make him content his people. You are a strange master. Get down. Go down below and keep to your mates. Monseigneur will do right by every one.'

"Off went the rascal and I do not know what became of him. The duke and his nobles were simply struck dumb by the scamp's outrage and his impudent daring."

The sober report[1] is less detailed and elaborate, but the thread is the same. Monseigneur, having returned to his hotel, sent Monseigneur de la Groothuse, Jean Petitpas, and Richard Utenhove back to the market to invite the people to put their grievances in writing. A draft was made and carried to the duke. After he had examined it and discussed it with his council, he sent Monseigneur de la Groothuse back to the market-place to tell the people that he wanted to sleep on the proposition and would give his answer at an early hour on the morrow. All through the night the people remained in arms on the market-place. At about eight o'clock on June 30th Groothuse returned, thanked the people in the count's name for having kept such good watch, and was answered by cries of "*À bas la cueillotte.*"

Then he assured them that all was pardoned and

[1] Gachard, *Doc. inéd.*, i., 212.

The Unjoyous Entry

that they should obtain what they had asked in the draft. Only he requested them to appoint a committee of six to present their demands to Monseigneur and then to go home. This they did. St. Lievin was restored to the church and his followers betook themselves to the gates specified in the treaty of Gaveren. These they broke down, and also destroyed another house where was a tax collector's office.

"The report of these events carried to Monseigneur did not have a good effect upon his spirit. On the morrow Monseigneur quitted the city." The members of the corporation with the two deans and the popular committee of six having obtained audience before his departure, Groothuse acted as spokesman: "We implore you in all humility to pardon us for the insult you have suffered, and to sign the paper presented. The bad have had more authority than the good, which could not be prevented, but we know truly that if the draft is not signed they will kill us."

It is evident in all this story that the municipal authorities were frightened to death and that Charles allowed himself to be restrained to an extraordinary extent considering the undoubted provocation. His reasons for conciliatory measures were two, and literally were his ducats and his daughter. He had with him all the portable treasure and ready money that his father had had at Bruges, a large treasure and one on which he counted for his immediate military operations—

operations very important to the position as a European power which he ardently desired to attain.

Still more important was the fact that his young daughter, Mary, now eleven years old, was living in Ghent, to a certain degree the ward of the city. If the unruly majority should realise their strength what easier for them than to seize the treasure and hold the daughter as hostage, until her father had acceded to every demand, and until democracy was triumphant not only in Ghent but in the neighbouring cities?

Charles simply did not dare attempt further coercion of the democratic spirit until he was beyond the walls. It is evident that he was completely taken by surprise at Ghent's attitude towards him, as the city had always professed great personal attachment to him. But there was a difference between being heir and sovereign. The agreement was signed, with a mental reservation on the part of the Duke of Burgundy. He only intended to keep his pledge until he could see his way clear to make terms better to his liking.

On Tuesday, June 30th, Charles left Ghent, taking his daughter and his treasure away, but a safe shelter for both was not easy to find. The duke's anticipations of the effect of Ghent's actions upon her neighbours were quickly proved to be no idle fears. There were revolts of more or less importance at Mechlin, at Antwerp, at Brussels, and other places. Moreover, there was serious discussion in the estates assembled at Louvain as to whether Charles should be acknowledged as Duke of Brabant, or whether the claims of his cousin, the Count of Nevers, should be considered as heir to Philip's predecessor, for the late duke's title had never been considered perfect.

Louis XI. seized the opportunity to urge the pretensions of the latter, and there were many reasons to recommend him, in the estimation of the Brabanters, who saw advantage in having a sovereign exclusively their own, instead of one with the widespread geographical interests of the Burgundian family. The final decision was, however, for Charles; a notice of the resolution of the deputies was sent to him at Mechlin, and he made his formal "entry" into Louvain, where he received homage from the nobles, the good cities, and the university.

The various insurgent manifestations were promptly quelled one after another, but, with a nature that neither forgot nor forgave, the duke was strongly impressed by them as personal insults. He blamed Ghent for their occurrence and deeply resented every one. Throughout Philip's whole career he remembered the localised tenure of his titles and the fact that they were not perfectly incontestable. For his own advantage he often found a conciliatory attitude the best policy. Charles considered all his rights heaven-born. Questioning his authority was rank rebellion. That he had accepted advice in regard to

Ghent, and had been ruled by expediency for the nonce, did not mitigate his intense bitterness.

In another town that gave him serious trouble at this time, nothing led him to curb the severity of his measures. Though only a "protector," not an overlord, when he suppressed a rebellion in Liege he rigorously exacted the most complete and humiliating penalties. The city charters were abrogated, all privileges were forfeited. As an unprotected village must Liege stand henceforth, walls and fortifications rased to the ground.

"The perron on the market-place of the said town shall be taken down, and then Monseigneur the duke shall treat it according to his pleasure. The city may not remake the said perron, nor replace another like it in the market-place or elsewhere in the city. Nor shall the said perron appear in the coat-of-arms of Liege."[1]

This was a terrible indignity for the city and a clear proof of their fear of their bishop's friend.

The episode impressed the citizens of Ghent with the duke's power, and made the more timorous anxious to erase the event of 1467 from his mind. The peace party finally prevailed in their arguments, but the scene of abnegation and self-humiliation crowning their apology was not enacted until eighteen months after the events apologised for, when the new duke had still further proven his metal.

[1] Gachard. *Doc. inéd.*, ii., 462, "*Instrument notarié.*"

CHAPTER X

THE DUKE'S MARRIAGE

1468

FOR many months before Philip's death there had been negotiations concerning Charles's marriage with Margaret of York. Always feeling a closer bond with his mother than with his father, Charles's sympathy had ever been towards the Lancastrian party in England, the family to whom Isabella of Portugal was closely related. Only the necessity for making a strong alliance against Louis XI. turned him to seek a bride from the House of York. It was on this business that La Marche and the great Bastard were engaged when Philip's death interrupted the discussion, which Charles did not immediately resume on his own behalf.

Pending the final decision in regard to this important indication of his international policy, the duke busied himself with the adjustment of his court, there being many points in which he did not intend to follow his father's usage.[1] Philip's lavishness, without too close a query as to the disposition of every penny, was naturally very agreeable to his courtiers. There was a liberal air about his households. It was easy to come and

[1] Chastellain, v., 570.

go, and it was pleasant to have the handling of money and the giving of orders—orders which were fulfilled and richly paid without haggling. Charles had other notions. He was willing to pay, but he wanted to be sure of an adequate return. How he started in on his administration with reform ideas is delightfully told by Chastellain.[1]

One of his first measures when he was finally established at Brussels was to secure more speedy execution of justice. He appointed a new provost, "a dangerous varlet of low estate, but excellently fitted to carry out perilous work." Then he determined to settle petty civil suits himself, as there were many which had dragged on for a long time. In order to do this and to receive complaints from poor people, he arranged to give audience three times a week, Monday, Wednesday, and Friday, after dinner. On these occasions he required the attendance of all his nobles, seated before him on benches, each according to his rank. Excuses were not pleasantly accepted, so that few places were empty. Charles himself was elevated on a high throne covered with cloth of gold, whence he pompously pronounced judgments and heard and answered petitions, a process that sometimes lasted two or three hours and was exceedingly tiresome to the onlookers.

"In outer appearance it seemed a magnificent course of action and very praiseworthy. But in

[1] V., 576.

my time I have never heard of nor seen like action taken by prince or king, nor any proceedings in the least similar.

"When the duke went through the city from place to place and from church to church, it was wonderful how much state and order was maintained and what a grand escort he had. Never a knight so old or so young who dared absent himself and never a squire was bold enough to squeeze himself into the knights' places."

At the levee, the same rigid ceremony was observed. Every one had to wait his turn in his proper room—the squires in the first, the knights in the second, and so on. All left the palace together to go to mass. As soon as the offering was made all the nobles were free to dine, but they were obliged to report themselves to the duke immediately after his repast. Any failure caused the forfeiture of the fee for the day. It was all very orderly and very dull.

Thus Charles of Burgundy felt that he was lawgiver, paternal guide, philosopher, and friend to his people. From time to time he delivered harangues to his court, veritable sermons. He obtained hearing, but certainly did not win popularity. The adulatory phrases used as mere conventionalities seemed to have actually turned his head. And those stock phrases were very grandiloquent. There is no doubt that such comparisons were used as Chastellain puts into the mouths of the first deputation from Ghent to ask pardon for the sins committed at the dolorous unjoyous entry into the Flemish capital.[1]

"My very excellent seigneur, when you who hold double place, place of God and place of man, and have in yourself the double nature by office and commission in divine estate, and as your noble discretion knows and is cognisant, like God the Father, Creator, of all offences committed against you, and who may be appeased by tears and by weeping as He permits Himself to be softened by contrition, entreaties, etc., and resumes His natural benignity by forgetting things past [etc.]. . . . Alas, what kindness did He use toward Adam, His first offender, upon whom through his son Seth He poured the oil of pity in five thousand future years, and then to Cain the first born of mother He postponed vengeance for his crime for ten generations etc. What did he do in Abraham's time, when He sent word to Lot that if there were ten righteous men in Sodom and Gomorrah He would remit the judgment on the two cities? In Ghent," etc.[2]

[1] This deputation was composed of representatives from "all the city in its entirety in three chief members — the bourgeois and nobles, the fifty-two *métiers*, and the weavers who possess twelve different places in the city entirely for themselves and in their control." The formal apology was made later. (Chastellain, v., 291.)

[2] *Ibid* 306. By letters patent given on July 28, 1467, Duke Charles pardoned the Ghenters and confirmed the privileges which he had conceded to them, but he exacted that a deputation from the three members [*Trois membres*] of the city should come to Brussels to beg pardon on their knees, bareheaded, ungirded, for all the disorder of St. Lievin. This act of submission took place probably not until January, 1469, though August 8, 1468, is also mentioned as the date.

The Duke's Marriage

In the chancellor's answer to this plea, the duke's consent to grant forgiveness to Ghent is again compared to God's own mercy. The divine attributes were referred to again and again, not only on the pages of contemporaneous chroniclers who may be accused of desiring ducal patronage, but also in sober state papers.

There was one antidote to this homage universally offered to Charles wherever there was no rebellion against him. One of the rules of the Order of the Golden Fleece was that all alike should be subject to criticism by their fellows. In May, 1468, at Bruges, Charles held an assembly of the Order, the first over which he had presided. It was a fitting opportunity for the knights to express their sentiments. When it came to his turn to be reviewed, Charles listened quietly to the representations that his conduct fell short of the ideals of chivalry because he was too economical, too industrious, too strenuous, and not sufficiently cognisant of the merits of his faithful subjects of high degrees.[1]

In these plaints, respectful as they are, there is perhaps a note of regret for the lavish and amusing good cheer of the late duke's times. Charles was undoubtedly husbanding his resources at this period. The vision of wide dominions was already in his dreams, and he was prudent enough to begin his preparations. And prudence is not a popular quality. Still his courtiers were not

[1] *Hist. de l'Ordre*, etc., p. 511.

quite bereft of the gorgeous and spectacular entertainments to which the "good duke" had accustomed them. Soon after the assembly of the Order, the alliance between Duke Charles and Margaret of York was celebrated at Bruges. Our Burgundian Chastellain is not pleased with this marriage. That Charles inclined towards England at all was due to the French king, whom both he and his father had found untrustworthy. Again, had there been any other eligible *partie* in England Charles would never have allied himself with King Edward when all his sympathies were with the blood of Lancaster. But when King Louis forsook his cousin Margaret of Anjou, whose woes should have commanded pity, simply for the purpose of undermining the Duke of Burgundy, the latter felt it wise to make Edward his friend.

"That it was sore against his inclination he confessed to one who later revealed it to me, but he decided that it was better to injure another rather than be down-trodden and injured himself.[1]

"For a long time there had been little love lost between him and the king. The monarch feared the pride and haughtiness of his subject, and the subject feared the strength and profound subtilty of the king who wanted, he thought, to get him under the whip. And all this, alas, was the result of that cursed War of Public Weal cooked up by the French against their own king. When Charles was deeply involved in it he was deserted by the others and the whole weight of the burden fell on his shoulders, so

[1] Chastellain, v., 342.

CHARLES, DUKE OF BURGUNDY, PRESIDING OVER A CHAPTER OF THE
GOLDEN FLEECE

FROM CONTEMPORANEOUS MINIATURE REPRODUCED IN LENGLET DU FRESNOY EDITION OF
COMINES

The Duke's Marriage

that he alone was blamed by the king, and he alone was forced to look to his own safety and comfort. It is a pity when such things occur in a realm and among kinsfolk."

Louis was busied with his own affairs in Touraine when news came to him that the marriage was to take place immediately. "If he mourned, it is not marvellous when I myself mourn it for the future result. But the king used all kinds of machinations to break off the alliance. . . . God suffered two young proud princes to try their strength each at his will, often in ways that would have been incompatible in common affairs."

The fullest account of the wedding is given by La Marche, an eyewitness of the event [1]:

"Gilles du Mas, maître d'hôtel du Duc de Bretagne—to you I recommend myself. I have collected here roughly according to my stupid understanding what I saw of the said festival, to send it to you, beseeching you as earnestly as I can to advise me of the noble states and high deeds in your quarter . . . as becomes two friends of one rank and calling in two fraternal, allied and friendly houses.

"My lady and her company arrived at l'Écluse on a Saturday, June 25th, and on the morrow Madame the Duchess of Burgundy, mother of the duke, Mlle. of Burgundy and various other ladies and demoiselles visited Madame Margaret[2] and only

[1] III., 101. Evidently this was composed for a separate work and then incorporated into the memoirs.

[2] There is a beautiful portrait of her in MS. 9275 in the Bibliothèque de Burgogne. *See* also Wavrin, *Anchiennes Croniques d'Engleterre*, ii., 368.

stayed till dinner. The duchess was greatly pleased with her prospective daughter-in-law and could not say enough of her character and her virtues. There remained with Dame Margaret, on the part of the duchess, the Charnys, Messire Jehan de Rubempré and various other ladies and gentlemen to act the hosts to the strange ladies and gentlemen who had crossed from England with the bride. The Count and Countess de Charny met Madame as she disembarked and never budged from her side until she had arrived at Bruges.

"The day after the duchess's visit, Monseigneur of Burgundy made his way to l'Écluse with a small escort and entered the château at the rear. After supper, accompanied only by six or seven knights of the Order, he went very secretly to the hôtel of Dame Margaret, who had been warned of his intention, and was attended by the most important members of her suite, such as the Seigneur d'Escalles, the king's brother.

"At his arrival when they saw each other the greetings were very ceremonious and then the two sat down on one bench and chatted comfortably together for some time. After some conversation, the Bishop of Salisbury, according to a prearranged plan of his own, kneeled before the two and made complimentary speeches. He was followed by M. de Charny, who spoke as follows:

"' Monseigneur, you have found what you desired and since God has brought this noble lady to port in safety and to your desire, it seems to me that you should not depart without proving the affection you bear her, and that you ought to be betrothed now at this moment and give her your troth.'

The Duke's Marriage

"Monseigneur answered that it did not depend upon him. Then the bishop spoke to Margaret and asked her what she thought. She answered that it was just for this and nothing else that the king of England had sent her over and she was quite ready to fulfil the king's command. Whereupon the bishop took their hands and betrothed them. Then Monseigneur departed and returned on the morrow to Bruges.

"Dame Margaret remained at l'Écluse until the following Saturday and was again visited by Monseigneur. On Saturday the boats were richly decorated to conduct my lady to Damme, where she was received very honourably according to the capacity of that little town. On the morrow, the 3rd of July, Monseigneur the duke set out with a small escort between four and five o'clock in the morning, and went to Damme, where he found Madame quite ready to receive him as all had been prearranged, and Monseigneur wedded her as was suitable, and the nuptial benediction was duly pronounced by the Bishop of Salisbury. After the mass, Charles returned to his hôtel at Bruges, and you may believe that during the progress of the other ceremonies he slept as if he were to be on watch on the following night.

"Immediately after, Adolph of Cleves, John of Luxemburg, John of Nassau, and others returned to Damme and paid their homage to the new duchess, and then my lady entered a horse litter, beautifully draped with cloth of gold. She was clad in white cloth of gold made like a wedding garment as was proper. On her hair rested a crown and her other jewels were appropriate and sumptuous. Her English ladies followed her on thirteen hackneys, two close by her litter and the others behind. Five chariots followed the thirteen hackneys, the Duchess of Norfolk, the most beautiful woman in England, being in the first. In this array Madame proceeded to Bruges and entered at the gate called Ste. Croix."

There were too many names to be enumerated, but La Marche cannot forbear mentioning a noble Zealander, Adrian of Borselen, Seigneur of Breda, who had six horses covered with cloth of gold, jewelry, and silk.

"I mention him for two reasons [he explains[1]]: first, that he was the most brilliant in the procession, and the second is that by the will of God he died on the Wednesday from a trouble in his leg, which was a pity and much regretted by the nobility.

"The procession from Ste. Croix to the palace was magnificent, with all the dignitaries in their order. So costly were the dresses of the ducal household that Charles expended more than forty thousand francs for cloth of silk and of wool alone.

"Prominent in this stately procession were the nations or foreign merchants in this order: Venetians, Florentines—at the head of the latter marched Thomas Portinari, banker and councillor of the duke at the same time that he was chief of their nation and therefore dressed in their garb; Spaniards; Genoese—these latter showed a mystery, a beautiful girl on horseback guarded by St. George from the dragon.— Then came the Osterlings, 108 on horseback, followed by six pages, all clad in violet.

[1] III., 108.

The Duke's Marriage

"Gay, too, was Bruges and the streets were all decorated with cloth of gold and silk and tapestries. As to the theatrical representations I can remember at least ten. There were Adam and Eve, Cleopatra married to King Alexander, and various others.

"The reception at the palace was very formal. The dowager duchess herself received her daughter-in-law from the litter and escorted her by the hand to her chamber, and for the present we will leave the ladies and the knighthood and turn to the arrangement of the hôtel.

"In regard to the service, Mme. the new duchess was served *d'eschançon et d'escuyer tranchant et de pannetier*. All English, all knights and gentlemen of great houses, and the chief steward cried 'Knights to table,' and then they went to the buffet to get the food, and around the buffet marched all the relations of Monseigneur, all the knights of the Order and of great houses. And for that day Mme. the duchess the mother declined to be served *à couvert* but left the honour to her daughter-in-law as was right.

"After dinner the ladies retired to their rooms for a little rest and there were some changes of dress. Then they all mounted their chariots and hackneys and issued forth on the streets in great triumph and wonderful were the jousts of the Tree of Gold. Several days of festivity followed when the usual pantomimes and shows were in evidence.

"Tuesday, the tenth and last day of the fête, the grand *salle* was arranged in the same state as on the wedding day itself, except the grand buffet which stood in the middle of the hall. This banquet, too, was a grand affair and concluded the festivities.

On the morrow, Wednesday, July 15th, Monseigneur departed for Holland on a pressing piece of business, and he took leave of the Duchess of Norfolk and the other lords and ladies of quality and gave them gifts each according to his rank. Thus ends the story of this noble festival, and for the present I know nothing worth writing you except that I am yours."

To this may be added the letter of one of the Paston family who was in Margaret's train.[1]

"John Paston the younger to Margaret Paston:

"To my ryght reverend and worchepfull Modyr Margaret Paston dwelling at Caster, be thys delyveryed in hast.

"Ryth reverend & worchepfull Modyr, I recommend me on to you as humbylly as I can thynk, desyryng most hertly to her of your welfare & hertsese whyche I pray God send you as hastyly as my hert can thynk. Ples yt you to wete that at the makyng of thys byll my brodyr & I & all our felawshep wer in good helle, blyssyd be God.

"As for the gydyn her in thys countre it is as worchepfull as all the world can devyse it, & ther wer never Englyshe men had so good cher owt of Inglong that ever I herd of.

"As for tydyngs her but if it be of the fest I can non send yow; savyng my Lady Margaret was maryed on Sonday last past at a town that is called Dame iij myle owt of Brugge at v of the clok in the morning; & sche was browt the same day to Bruggys to hyr dener; & ther sche was receyvyd as worchepfully as all the world cowd devyse as with presession with ladys and lordys best beseyn of eny pepell that ever

[1] *The Paston Letters*, ii., 317.

The Duke's Marriage

I sye or herd of. Many pagentys were pleyed in hyr way to Brugys to hyr welcoming, the best that ever I sye. And the same Sonday my Lord the Bastard took upon hym to answere xxiiij knyts & gentylmen within viij dayis at jostys of pese & when that they wer answered, they xxiiij & hymselve shold torney with other xxv the next day after, whyche is on Monday next comyng; & they that have jostyd with hym into thys day have been as rychly beseyn, & hymselfe also, as clothe of gold & sylk & sylvyr & goldsmith's werk might mak hem; for of syche ger & gold & perle & stonys they of the dukys coort neyther gentylmen nor gentylwomen they want non; for with owt that they have it by wyshys, by my trowthe, I herd nevyr of so gret plente as ther is.

. . . .

And as for the Dwkys coort, as of lords & ladys & gentylwomen knyts, sqwyers & gentylmen I hert never of non lyek to it save King Artourys cort. And by my trowthe I have no wyt nor remembrance to wryte to you half the worchep that is her; but that lakyth as it comyth to mynd I shall tell you when I come home whyche I trust to God shal not be long to; for we depart owt of Brygge homward on Twysday next comyng & all folk that cam with my lady of Burgoyn out of Ingland, except syche as shall abyd her styll with hyr whyche I wot well shall be but fewe.

"We depart the sooner for the Dwk hathe word that the Frenshe king is purposyd to mak wer upon hym hastyly & that he is with in iiij or v dayis jorney of Brugys & the Dwk rydeth on Twysday next comyng forward to met with hym. God geve hym good sped

& all hys; for by my trowthe they are the goodlyest felawshep that ever I cam among & best can behave themselves & most like gentlemen.

"Other tydyngs have we non her; but that the Duke of Somerset & all hys band departyd well beseyn out of Brugys a day befor that my Lady the Duchess cam thedyr & they sey her that he is to Queen Margaret that was & shal no more come her agen nor be holpyn by the Duke. No more; but I beseche you of your blessyng as lowly as I can, wyche I beseche you forget not to geve me everday onys. And, Modyr, I beseche you that ye wol be good mastras to my lytyll man & to se that he go to scole.

. . . .

Wreten at Bruggys the Friday next after Seynt Thomas.

"Your sone & humbyll servaunt,

"J. PASTON THE YOUNGER."

CHAPTER XI

THE MEETING AT PERONNE

1468

"MY brother, I beseech you in the name of our affection and of our alliance, come to my aid, come as speedily as you can, come without delay. Written by the own hand of your brother.

"FRANCIS."

Such were the concluding sentences of a fervent appeal from the Duke of Brittany that followed Charles into Holland, whither he had hastened after the completion of the nuptial festivities.

The titular Duke of Normandy found that his royal brother was in no wise inclined to fulfil the solemn pledges made at Conflans. His ally, Francis, Duke of Brittany, was plunged into terror lest the king should invade his duchy and punish him for his share in the proceedings that had led up to that compact.

It is in this year that Louis XI. begins to show his real astuteness. Very clever are his methods of freeing himself from the distasteful obligations assumed towards his brother. They had been easy to make when a hostile army was encamped at the gates of Paris. Then Normandy weighed lightly when balanced by the desire to separate the allies. That separation accomplished, the point of view changed. Relinquish Normandy, restored by the hand of heaven to its natural liege lord after its long retention by the English kings? Louis's intention gradually became plain and he proved that he was no longer in the isolated position in which the War for Public Weal had found him. He had won to himself many adherents, while the general tone towards Charles of Burgundy had changed.[1]

In April, 1468, the States-General of France assembled at Tours in response to royal writs issued in the preceding February.[2] The chancellor, Jouvençal, opened the session with a tedious, long-winded harangue calculated to weary rather than to illuminate the assembly. Then the king took the floor and delivered a telling speech. With trenchant and well chosen phrases he set forth the reasons why Normandy ought to be an intrinsic part of the French realm. The advantages of centralisation, the weakness of decentralisation, were skilfully drawn. The matter was one affecting the kingdom as a whole, in perpetuity; it was not for the temporal interests of the present incumbent

[1] *See* Lavisse iv[ii]., 356.

[2] The letters of convocation bear the date February 26, 1467, o.s. Tournay elected four deputies. By April 30th, they had returned home, and on May 2d they made a report. The items of expenditure are very exact. So hard had they ridden that a fine horse costing eleven crowns was used up and was sold for four crowns. M. Van der Broeck, archivist of Tournay, extracted various items from the register of the Council. *See* Kervyn's note. Chastellain, v., 387.

The Meeting at Peronne

of regal authority, who had only part therein for the brief space of his mortal journey. Louis's words are pathetic indeed, as he calls himself a sojourner in France, *en voyage* through life, as though the fact itself of his likeness to the rest of ephemeral mankind was novel to his audience. He reiterated the statement that the interests involved were theirs, not his.

It was a goodly body which listened to Louis. The greatest feudal lords, indeed, were not present, but many of the lesser nobility were, while sixty-four towns sent, all told, about 128 deputies. These hearers gave willing attention to the thesis that it was a burning shame for the French people to pay heavy taxes simply to restrain the insolent peers from rebelling against their sovereign—those noble scions of the royal stock whose bounden duty it was to protect the state and the head of the royal house.

What was the reason for their selfish insubordination? The root of the evil lay in the past, when extensive territories had been carelessly alienated, and their petty over-lords permitted to acquire too much independence of the crown, so that the monarchy was threatened with disruption. There was more to the same purpose and then the deputies deliberated on the answer to make to this speech from the throne. It was an answer to Louis's mind, an answer that showed the value of suggestion. Charles the Wise had thought that an estate yielding an income of twelve thousand livres was all-sufficient for a prince of the blood. Louis XI. was more generous. He was ready to allow his brother Charles a pension of sixty thousand livres. But as to the government of Normandy—why! no king, either from fraternal affection or from fear of war, was justified in committing that province to other hands than his own.

The States-General dissolved in perfect accord with the monarch, and a definite order was left in the king's hands, declaring that it was the judgment of the towns represented that concentration of power was necessary for the common welfare of France. Public opinion declared that national weakness would be inevitable if the feudatories were unbridled in their centrifugal tendencies. Above all, Normandy must be retained by the king. On no consideration should Louis leave it to his brother.[1]

Before the dissolution of the assembly there was some discussion as to the probable attitude of the great nobles in regard to this platform of centralisation. Very timid were the comments on Charles of Burgundy. Would he not perhaps be an excellent mediator between the lesser dukes and the king? Would it not be better to suspend action until his opinion was known, etc? But at large there was less reserve. The statements were emphatic. Naught but mischief had ever come to France from Burgundy. The present

[1] *See* Lavisse iv[ii]., 356.

The Meeting at Peronne

duke's father and grandfather had wrought all the ill that lay in their power. As for Charles, his illimitable greed was notorious. Let him rest content with his paternal heritage. Ghent and Bruges were his. Did he want Paris too? Let the king recover the towns on the Somme. Rightfully they were French. Louis made no scruple in pleading the invalidity of the treaty of Conflans, because it had been wrested from him by undue influence. And this royal sentiment was repeated here and there with growing conviction of its justice.

While Charles was occupied with the preparation for his wedding, Louis was engaged in levying troops and mobilising his forces, and these preparations continued throughout the summer of 1468. Naturally, news of this zeal directed against the dukes of Normandy and of Brittany followed the traveller in Holland.

Charles was in high dudgeon and wrote at once to the king, reminding him that these seigneurs were his allies, and demanding that nothing should be wrought to their detriment. Conscious that his remonstrance might be futile, and urged on by appeals from the dukes, Charles hastened to cut short his stay in Holland so that he might move nearer to the scene of Louis's activities. His purpose in going to the north had been twofold—to receive homage as Count of Holland and Zealand, and to use his new dignity to obtain large sums of money for which he saw immediate need if he were to hold Louis to the terms wrested from him.

In early July, Charles had crossed from Sluis in Flanders to Middelburg, and thence made his progress through the cities of Zealand, receiving homage as he went. Next he passed to The Hague, where the nobles and civic deputies of Holland met him and gave him their oaths of fealty on July 21st. Fifty-six towns[1] were represented and there were also deputies from eight bailiwicks and the islands of Texel and Wieringen. "It is noteworthy," comments a Dutch historian, "that the people's oath was given first. The older custom was that the count should give the first pledge while the people followed suit."

As soon as he was thus legally invested with sovereign power, Charles demanded a large *aide* from Holland and Zealand—480,000 crowns of fifteen stivers for himself; 32,000 crowns as pin money for his new consort; 16,000 crowns as donations for various servants, and 4800 crowns towards his travelling expenses. The total sum was 532,800 crowns. The share of Holland and West Friesland was 372,800 crowns, and of Zealand 16,000 crowns, to be paid within seven and a half years. In Holland, Haarlem paid the heaviest quota, 3549 crowns, and Schiedam the smallest, 350 crowns, while Dordrecht and the South Hol-

[1] Dordrecht was not among them. Her deputies held that it was illegal for them to go to The Hague. Some time later Charles received the oaths at Dordrecht. (Wagenaar, *Vaderlandsche Hist.*, iv., 101.)

The Meeting at Peronne 203

land villages were assessed at 39,200 crowns, and the remainder was divided among the other cities and villages.

There was considerable opposition to the assessments. In many cases the new imposts upon provisions pressed very heavily on the poor villagers. Having obtained promise of the grant, however, Charles left all further details in its regard to the local officials and returned to Brussels at the beginning of August to make his own preparation. For, by that time, Louis's intentions of evading the treaty of Conflans were plain, though there still fluttered a thin veil of friendship between the cousins. Gathering what forces he could mobilise, ordering them to meet him later, Charles moved westward and took up his quarters at Peronne on the river Somme.

Louis had been bold in his utterance to the States-General as to his perfect right to ignore the treaty of Conflans, to dispossess his brother, and to bring the great feudatories to terms. In the summer of 1468 he made advances towards accomplishing the last-named desideratum. Brittany was invaded by royal troops, but his victory was diplomatic rather than military, as Duke Francis peaceably consented to renounce his close alliances with Burgundy and England, nominally at least. Further, he agreed to urge Charles of France to submit his claims to Normandy to the arbitration of Nicholas of Calabria and the Constable St. Pol.[1]

[1] Treaty of Ancenis, September 10, 1468. *See* Lavisse, iv[ii].

Charles of Burgundy remained to be settled with on some different basis. And in regard to him Louis XI. took a resolve which terrified his friends and caused the world to wonder as to his sanity. All previous attempts at mediation having failed—St. Pol was among the many who tried—the king determined to be his own messenger to parley with his Burgundian cousin. It is curious how small was his measure of personal pride. He had been negligent of his personal safety at Conflans, but even then Charles had better reason to respect and protect him than in 1468, after Louis had manœuvred for three years in every direction to harass and undermine the young duke's power, and when, too, the latter was aware of half of the machinations and suspicious of more.

Yet Louis's famous visit to Peronne was no sudden hare-brained enterprise. There is much evidence that he nursed the project for many weeks without giving any intimation of his intentions. Nor was the situation as strange as it appears, looking backward.

Charles had doubtless made all preparations to combat Louis if need were, and had chosen Peronne for his headquarters with the express purpose of being able to watch France, and, at the same time, he had published abroad that his military preparations were solely for the purpose of

---

One of the results of the War of Public Weal was that St. Pol was appointed constable of France.

keeping his obligations to his allies. Now these obligations were momentarily removed by the action of those same allies. Francis of Brittany had entered into amicable relations with his sovereign, young Charles of France had accepted arbitration to settle the fraternal relations of the royal brothers, while the correspondence between Louis and Liege, was still unknown to the Duke of Burgundy. For the moment, the latter, therefore, had no definite quarrel with the French king. But he was not in the least anxious for an interview with him. Charles was as far as ever from understanding his cousin. Even without definite knowledge of Louis's efforts to make friends in the Netherlands, Charles suspected enough to turn his youthful distrust of the man's character into mature conviction that friendship between them was impossible. But he could not refuse the royal overtures. His letter of safe-conduct to his self-invited visitor bears the date of October 8th, and runs as follows:[1]

"MONSEIGNEUR:

"I commend myself to your good graces. Sire, if it be your desire to come to this city of Peronne in order that we may talk together, I swear and I promise you by my faith and on my honour that you may come, remain and return in safety to Chauny or Noyon, according to your pleasure and as often as it shall please you, freely and openly without any hindrance offered either to you or to any of your people by me

[1] The original is in the Mss. de Baluze, Paris, Bibl. Nat.; Lenglet, iii., 19.

or by any other for any cause that now exists or *that may hereafter arise.*"

Guillaume de Biche acted as confidential messenger between duke and king. He it was whom Charles had dismissed from his own service in 1456 at his father's instance. From that time on the man had been in Louis's household, deep in his secrets it was said, and certainly admitted to his privacy to an extraordinary degree. This letter was written by Charles in the presence of Biche, through whose hand it passed directly to the king.

By October, Louis was at Ham, prepared to move as soon as the safe-conduct arrived. No time was lost after its receipt. On Sunday, October 9th, the king started out, accompanied by the Bishop of Avranches, his confessor, by the Duke of Bourbon, Cardinal Balue, St. Pol, a few more nobles, and about eighty archers of the Scottish guard. As he rode towards Peronne, Philip of Crèvecœur, with two hundred lances, met him on the way to act as his escort to the presence of the duke, who awaited his guest on the banks of a stream a short distance out of Peronne.

St. Pol was the first of the royal party to meet the duke as herald of Louis's approach. Then Charles rode forward to greet the traveller. As he came within sight of his cousin, he bowed low to his saddle and was about to dismount when Louis, his head bared, prevented his action. Fervent were the kisses pressed by the kingly lips upon the

The Meeting at Peronne

duke's cheeks, while Louis's arm rested lovingly about the latter's neck. Then he turned graciously to the by-standing nobles and greeted them by name. But his cousinly affection was not yet satisfied. Again he embraced Charles and held him half as long as before in his arms. How pleasant he was and how full of confidence towards this trusted cousin of his!

The cavalcade fell into line again, with the two princes in the middle, and made a stately entry into Peronne at a little after mid-day.[1] The chief building then and the natural place to lodge a royal visitor was the castle. But it was in sorry repair, ill furnished, and affording less comfort than a neighbouring house belonging to a city official. Here rooms had been prepared for the king and a few of his suite, the others being quartered through the town. At the door Charles took his leave and Louis entered alone with Cardinal Balue and the attendants he had chosen to keep near him. These latter were nearly all of inferior birth, and were treated by their master with a familiarity very astonishing to the stately Burgundians.

Louis entered the room assigned for his use, walked to the window, and looked out into the street. The sight that met his view was most disquieting. A party of cavaliers were on the

[1] Commines and a letter to the magistrates of Ypres are the basis of this narrative. (Gachard, *Doc. inéd.*, i., 196.) There is, however, a mass of additional material both contemporaneous and commentating. *See also* Michelet, Lavisse, Kirk, etc. Chastellain's MS. is lost.

point of entering the castle. They were gentlemen just arrived from Burgundy with their lances, in response to a summons issued long before the present visit was anticipated. As he looked down on the troops, Louis recognised several men who had no cause to love him or to cherish his memory. There was, for instance, the queen's brother Philip de Bresse[1] who had led a party against Louis's own sister Yolande of Savoy. At a time of parley this Philip had trusted the sincerity of his brother-in-law's profession and had visited him to obtain his mediation. The king had violated both the specified safe-conduct and ambassadorial equity alike, and had thrown De Bresse into the citadel of Loches, where he suffered a long confinement before he succeeded in making his escape. He was a Burgundian in sympathy as well as in race. But with him on that October day Louis noticed various Frenchmen who had fallen under royal displeasure from one cause or another and had saved their liberty by flight, renouncing their allegiance to him for ever. Four there were in all who wore the cross of St. Andrew. Approaching Peronne as they had from the south, these new-comers had ridden in at the southern gates without intimation of this royal visitation extraordinary until they were almost face to face with guest and host. Their arrival was "a half of a quarter of an hour later than that of the king."

[1] *See* Lavisse, iv[ii]., 397.

The Meeting at Peronne

When Philip de Bresse and his friends learned what was going on, they hastened to the duke's chambers "to give him reverence." Monseigneur de Bresse was the spokesman in begging the duke that the three above named should be assured of their security notwithstanding the king's presence at Peronne,—of security such as he had pledged them in Burgundy and promised for the hour when they should arrive at his court. On their part they were ready to serve him towards all and against all. Which petition the duke granted orally. "The force conducted by the Marshal of Burgundy was encamped without the gates, and the said marshal spoke no ill of the king, nor did the others I have mentioned."[1]

It was, however, a situation in which apprehension was not confined to the men of lower station. To Louis, looking down from his window, there seemed dire menace in the mere presence of these persons who had heavy grievances against him, and the unfortified private house seemed slight protection against their possible vengeance. Here, Charles might disavow injury to him as something happening quite without his knowledge. On ducal soil the safest place was assuredly under shelter patently ducal. There, there would be no doubt of responsibility did misfortune happen.

Straightway the king sent a messenger to Charles asking for quarters within the castle. The

[1] Ludwig v. Diesbach. (*See* Kirk, i., 559.) The author was a page in Louis's train, who afterwards played a part in Swiss affairs.

request was granted and the uneasy guest passed through the massive portals between a double line of Burgundian men-at-arms. It was no cheerful, pleasant, palatial dwelling-place this little old castle of Peronne. So thick were the walls that vain had been all assaults against it.[1] Designed for a fortress rather than a residence, it had been repeatedly used as a prison, and the air of the whole was tainted by the dungeons under its walls, dungeons which had seen many unwilling lodgers. Five centuries earlier than this date, Charles the Simple had languished to death in one of the towers.

This change of arrangement, or rather the disquieting reason for the change, undoubtedly clouded the peacefulness of the occasion. Yet outward calm was preserved. Commines asserts that the two princes directed their people to behave amicably to each other and that the commands were scrupulously obeyed. For two or three days the desired conferences took place between Charles and Louis. The king's wishes were perfectly plain. He wanted Charles to forsake all other alliances and to pledge himself to support his feudal chief, first and foremost, from all attacks of his enemies. The Duke of Brittany had submitted to his liege. If the Duke of Burgundy would only accept terms equally satisfactory in their way, the pernicious alliance between the two would vanish, to the weal of French unity.

[1] It was never captured until Wellington took it in 1814.

PHILIP DE COMMINES

The Meeting at Peronne

Apparently the first discussion was heard by none except the Cardinal Balue and Guillaume de Biche. Charles was willing to pledge allegiance and to promise aid to his feudal chief, but under limitations that weakened the value of his words. Nothing could induce him to renounce alliance with other princes for mutual aid, did they need it. There was a second interview on the following day. Charles held tenaciously to his position. Then there came a sudden alteration in the situation, a strange dramatic shifting of the duke's point of view.

The city of Liege had submitted perforce to the behests of her imperious neighbour, but the citizens had never ceased to hope that his unwelcome "protection" might be dispensed with; that, by the aid of French troops, they might eventually wrest themselves free from the Burgundian incubus. In spite of all promises to Charles, secret negotiations between the anti-Burgundian party and Louis XI. had never ceased. The latter never refused to admit the importunate embassies to his presence. He was glad to keep in touch with the city even in its ruined condition. He sent envoys as well as received them, and Commines states definitely that, in making his plan to visit Peronne, the fact of a confidential commission recently despatched to Liege had wholly slipped the king's mind.

In that town the duke's lieutenant, Humbercourt, had been left to supervise the humiliating changes ordered. And the work of demolition was the only industry. Other ordinary business was at a standstill. For a period there was a sullen silence in the streets and the church bells were at rest. In April, a special legate from the pope arrived to see whether ecclesiastical affairs could not be put on a better footing.

It was about the same time that the States-General were meeting at Tours that, under the direction of this legate, Onofrio de Santa-Croce, the cathedral was purified with holy water, and Louis of Bourbon celebrated his very first mass, though he had been seated on the episcopal throne for twelve years. Then Onofrio tried to mediate between the city and the Duke of Burgundy. To Bruges he went to see Charles, and obtained permission to draft a project for the re-establishment of the civic government, to be submitted to the duke for approval.

If Onofrio thought he had reformed the bishop by forcing him into performing his priestly rites he soon learned his mistake. That ecclesiastic speedily disgusted his flock by his ill-timed festivities, and then forsook the city and sailed away to Maestricht in a gaily painted barge, with gay companions to pass the summer in frivolous amusements suited to his dissolute tastes. Such was the state of affairs when the report of Louis's extensive military preparations encouraged the Liegeois to hope that he was to take the field openly against the duke.

About the beginning of September, troops of forlorn and desperate exiles began to return to the city. They came, to be sure, with shouts of *Vive le Roi!* but, as a matter of fact, they seemed willing to make any accommodation for the sake of being permitted to remain. "Better any fate at home than to live like wild beasts with the recollection that we had once been men."

To make a long story short, Onofrio again endeavoured to rouse the bishop to a sense of his duty. Again he tried to make terms for the exiles and to re-establish a tenable condition. It was useless. Louis of Bourbon refused to approach nearer to Liege than Tongres, and declined to meet the advances of his despairing subjects. It was just at this moment that fresh emissaries arrived from Louis, despatched, as already stated, *before* Charles had consented to prolong the truce.

Excited by their presence the Liegeois once more roused themselves to action. A force of two thousand was gathered at Liege, and advanced by night upon Tongres — also without walls — surrounded the house where lay their bishop, and forced him to return to Liege. Violence there was and loss of life, but, as a matter of fact, the mob respected the person of their bishop and of Humbercourt the chief Burgundian official. This event happened on October 9th, the very day that Louis rode recklessly into Peronne.

On Wednesday, October 11th, the news of the fray reached Peronne, but news greatly exaggerated by rumour. Bishop, papal legate, and Burgundian lieutenant all had been ruthlessly murdered in the very presence of Louis's own envoys, who had aided and abetted the hideous crime! To follow the story of an eyewitness:[1]

"Some said that everyone was dead, others asserted the contrary, for such advertisments are never reported after one sort. At length others came who had seen certain canons slain and supposed the bishop [2] to be of the number, as well as the said seigneur de Humbercourt and all the rest. Further, they said that they had seen the king's ambassadors in the attacking company and mentioned them by name. All this was repeated to the duke, who forthwith believed it and fell into an extreme fury, saying that the king had come thither to abuse him, and gave commands to shut the gates of the castle and of the town, alleging a poor enough excuse, namely, that he did this on account of the disappearance of a little casket containing some good rings and money.

"The king finding himself confined in the castle, a small one at that, and having seen a force of archers standing before the gate, was terrified for his person—the more so that he was lodged in the neighbourhood of a tower where a certain Count de Vermandois had caused the death of one of his predecessors as king of France.[3] At that time, I was still with the duke

[1] Commines, ii., ch. vii.

[2] The bishop did indeed meet his death at the hands of the mob, but it was many years later.

[3] *Le roi . . . se voyait logé, rasibus d'une grosse tour ou un Comte de Vermandois fit mourir un sien prédécesseur Roy de France.* (Commines, ii., ch. vii.)

and served him as chamberlain, and had free access to his chamber when I would, for such was the usage in this household.

"The said duke, as soon as he saw the gates closed, ordered all to leave his presence and said to a few of us that stayed with him that the king had come on purpose to betray him, and that he himself had tried to avoid his coming with all his strength, and that the meeting had been against his taste. Then he proceeded to recount the news from Liege, how the king had pulled all the wires through his ambassadors, and how his people had been slain. He was fearfully excited against the king. I veritably believe that if at that hour he had found those to whom he could appeal ready to sympathise with him and to advise him to work the king some mischief, he would have done so, at the least he would have imprisoned him in the great tower.

"None were present when the words fell from the duke but myself and two grooms of the chamber, one of whom was named Charles de Visen, a native of Dijon, an honest fellow, in good credit with his master. We aggravated nothing, but sought to appease the duke as much as in us lay. Soon he tried the same phrases on others, and a report of them ran through the city and penetrated to the very apartment of the king, who was greatly terrified, as was everyone, because of the danger that they saw imminent, and because of the great difficulty in soothing a quarrel when it has commenced between such great princes. Assuredly they were blameworthy in failing to notify their absent servants of this projected meeting. Great inconveniences were bound to arise from this negligence."

Such is Commines's narrative. Eyewitness though he was, it must be remembered that when he wrote the account of this famous interview it was long after the event, and when his point of view was necessarily coloured by his service with Louis. Delightful, however, are the historian's own reflections that he intersperses with his plain narrative. To his mind the only period when it is safe for princes to meet is

"in their youth when their minds are bent on pleasure. Then they may amuse themselves together. But after they are come to man's estate and are desirous each of over-reaching the other, such interviews do but increase their mutual hatred, even if they incur no personal peril (which is well-nigh impossible). Far wiser is it for them to adjust their differences through sage and good servants as I have said at length elsewhere in these memoirs."

Then our chronicler proceeds to give numerous instances of disastrous royal interviews before returning to his subject and to Peronne:

"I was moved [he adds again at the beginning of his new chapter] to tell the princes my opinion of such meetings.[1] Thus the gates were closed and guarded and two or three days passed by. However, the Duke of Burgundy would not see the king, nor had Louis's servants entry to the castle except a few, and those only through the wicket. Nor did the duke see any of his people who had influence over him.

[1] *Mémoires*, ii., ch. ix.

"The first day there was consternation throughout the city. By the second day the duke was a little calmed down. He held a council meeting all day and the greater part of the night. The king appealed to every one who could possibly aid him. He was lavish in his promises and ordered fifteen thousand crowns to be given where it might count, but the officer in charge of the disbursement of this sum acquitted himself ill and retained a part, as the king learned later.

"The king was especially afraid of his former servants who had come with the army from Burgundy, as I mentioned above, men who were now in the service of the Duke of Normandy.

"Diverse were the opinions in the above-mentioned council-meeting. Some held that the safe-conduct accorded to the king protected him, seeing that he fairly observed the peace as it had been stated in writing. Others rudely urged his capture without further ceremony, while others again advised sending for his brother, the Duke of Normandy, and concluding with him a peace to the advantage of all the princes of France. They who gave this advice thought that in case it was adopted, the king should be restrained of his liberty. Further, it was against all precedent to free so great a seigneur when he had committed so grave an offence.

"This last argument so nearly prevailed that I saw a man booted and spurred ready to depart with a packet of letters addressed to Monseigneur of Normandy, being in Brittany, and stayed only for the Duke of Burgundy's letter. However, this came to naught. The king made overtures to leave as hostages the Duke of Bourbon, the cardinal, his brother, and the constable with a dozen others while he should be permitted to return to Compiègne after peace was concluded. He promised that the Liegeois should repair their mischief or he would declare himself their foe. The appointed hostages were profuse in their offers to immolate themselves, at least they were in public. I do not know whether they would have said the same things in private. I rather suspect not. And in truth, I believe that those who were left would never have returned.

"On the third night after the arrival of the news, the duke never undressed, but lay down two or three times on his bed, and then rose and walked up and down. Such was his way when he was troubled. I lay that night in his chamber and talked with him from time to time. In the morning his fury was greater than ever, his tone very menacing, and he seemed ready to go to any extreme.

"However, he finally brought himself to say that if the king would swear the peace and would accompany him to Liege to help avenge Monsgn. of Liege, his own kinsman, he would be satisfied. Then he suddenly betook himself to the king's chamber and expressed himself to that effect. The king had a friend [1] who warned him, assuring him that he should suffer no ill if he would concede these two points. Did he

---

[1] Undoubtedly Commines wishes it to be inferred that this was he. The main narrative followed here is Commines, whose memoirs remain, as Ste.-Beuve says, the definitive history of the times. There are the errors inevitable to any contemporary statement. Meyer, to be sure, says, apropos of an incident incorrectly reported, *Falsus in hoc ut in pluribus historicus.* Kervyn de Lettenhove three centuries later is also severe. *See*, too, "L'autorité historique de Ph. de Commynes," Mandrot, *Rev. Hist.*, 73.

do otherwise he ran grave risk, graver than he would ever incur again."

When the duke entered the royal presence his voice trembled, so agitated was he and on the verge of breaking into a passion. He assumed a reverential attitude, but rough were mien and word as he demanded whether the king would keep the treaty of peace as it had been drafted, and whether he was ready to swear to it. "Yes" was the king's response. In truth, nothing had been added to the agreement made before Paris, or at least little as far as the Duke of Burgundy was concerned. As regarded the Duke of Normandy, it was stipulated that if he would renounce that province he should have Champagne and Brie besides other neighbouring territories for his share.

Then the duke asked if the king would accompany him to avenge the outrage committed upon his cousin the bishop.

"To which demand the king gave assent as soon as the peace was sworn. He was quite satisfied to go to Liege and with a small or large escort, just as the duke preferred. This answer pleased the duke immensely. In was brought the treaty, out of the king's coffer was taken the piece of the true cross, the very one carried by Saint Charlemagne, called the Cross of Victory, and thereupon the two swore the peace.

"This was now October 14th. In a minute the bells pealed out their joy throughout Peronne and all men were glad. It hath pleased the king since to attribute the credit of this pacification to me."

There was undoubtedly an immense sense of relief in Peronne when this degree of accommodation was reached. The duke was unwilling, however, to have too much rejoicing in his domains until he had ascertained for himself the state of Liege. Among the letters despatched from Peronne this October 14th, was the following to the magistrates of Ypres:[1]

"Dear and well beloved friends, considering that we have to-day made peace and convention with Monseigneur the king, and that for this reason you might be inclined to let off fire-works and make other manifestations of joy, we hasten to advise you that . . . our pleasure is you shall not permit fireworks or assemblies in our town of Ypres on account of the said peace until we have subdued the people of Liege, and avenged the said outrage [described above]. This with God's aid we intend to do. We are on the point of departure with all our forces for Liege. Beloved, may our Lord protect you.

"Written in our castle of Peronne, October 14, 1468."

A certain G. Ruple conveyed his own impressions to the magistrates of Ypres, possibly managing to slip them under the same cover.[2]

"To-day, at about 10 o'clock, peace was concluded between the king and Monseigneur, and also between the king and the Duke of Berry. Here, bells are ringing and the *Te Deum* is sung. It is generally believed that Monseigneur will depart to-morrow. God de-

[1] Gachard, *Doc. inéd.*, i., 199. [2] *Ibid.*, 200.

The Meeting at Peronne

serves thanks for the result, for I assure you that last night the outlook was not clear."[1]

The king wrote as follows to his confidential lieutenant:

"PERONNE, October 14th.

" Monseigneur the grand master, you are already informed how there has been discussion in my council and that of my brother-in-law of Burgundy, as to the best manner of adjusting certain differences between him and me. It went so far that in order to arrive at a conclusion I came to this town of Peronne. Here we have busied ourselves with the requisitions passing between us, so that to-day we have, thanks to our Lord, in the presence of all the nobles of the blood, prelates and other great and notable personages in great numbers, both from my suite and from his, sworn peace solemnly on the true cross, and promised to aid, defend and succour each other for ever. Also on the same cross we have ratified the treaty of Arras with its corrections and other points which seemed productive of peace and amity.

"Immediately after this the Duke of Burgundy ordered thanksgivings in the churches of his lands, and in this town he has already had great solemnity. And because my brother of Burgundy has heard that the Liegeois have taken prisoner my cousin the bishop of Liege, whom he is determined to deliver as quickly as possible, he has besought me as a favour to him, and also because the bishop is my kinsman whom I ought to aid, to accompany him to Liege, not far from here. This I have agreed to, and have

---

[1] *Waer ic certiffiere dat het dezen nacht niet wel claer ghestaen heeft.*

chosen as my escort a portion of the troops under monseigneur the constable, in the hopes of a speedy return by the aid of God.

"And because it is for my weal and that of my subjects I write to you at once, because *I am sure* you will be pleased, and that you will order like solemnities. Moreover, monseigneur the grand master, as I lately wrote to you, pray as quickly as possible disband my *arrière ban* together with the free lances, and do every possible thing for the mass of poor folks; appoint well-to-do men as leaders in every bailiwick and district. Above all, see to it that they do not indulge in any new and startling conduct. That done, if you wish to come to Bohan, to be nearer me, I would be glad, so as to be able to provide for any further action that may arise. Written at Peronne October 14th.

"Loys
Meurin.

"To our dear and beloved cousin the Count of Dammartin, grand master of France."[1]

Dammartin thought that this letter was phrased for the purpose of passing Charles's censorship. He took the liberty of disregarding his master's orders; the troops were not disbanded, and he held himself in readiness to go to fetch the errant monarch if he did not return speedily from the enemy's country. His letter to the king and the unwritten additions delivered by his confidential messengers terrified his liege lest too much zeal

[1] *Lettres de Louis XI*, iii., 289. The king apparently never resented the part played by Dammartin when he was dauphin. His letters to him are very intimate.

The Meeting at Peronne

on his behalf in France might work him ill in Liege. A week later Louis writes again:

"Namur, Oct. 22nd.

"Monseigneur the Grand Master:

"I have received your letter by Sire du Bouchage. *Be assured that I make this journey to Liege under no constraint, and that I never took any journey with such good heart as I do this.* Since God and Our Lady have given me grace to be friends with Monseigneur of Burgundy, be sure that never shall our rabble over there take arms against me. Monseigneur the grand master, my friend, you have proved that you love me, and you have done me the greatest service that you can, and there is another service that you can do. The people of Monseigneur of Burgundy think that I mean to deceive them, and people there [in France] think that I am a prisoner. Distrust between the two would be my ruin.

"Monseigneur, as to the quarters of your men, you know what we planned, you and I, touching the action of Armagnac. It seems to me that you ought to send your people straight ahead in that direction and I will furnish you four or five captains as soon as I am out of this, and you can make what choice you will. M. the grand master, my friend, come, I beg you, to Laon and await me there. Send me a messenger the minute you arrive and I will let you have frequent news. Be assured that as soon as the Liegeois are subdued, on the morrow I will depart, for Monsg. of Burgundy is resolved to urge me to go as soon as he has finished his work at Liege, and he desires my return more than I do. François Dunois will tell you what good cheer we are making. Adieu, monseigneur, etc.

"Writ at Namur, Oct. 22nd.

"Louis
"Toussaint.

"To our dear and beloved cousin the Count of Dammartin, grand master of France."[1]

Letters of the same date to Rochefoucauld and others also declare that Louis goes most gladly with his dear brother of Burgundy and that the affair will not require much time. To Cardinal Balue he writes only a few words, telling him that the messenger will be more communicative.

Between Peronne and Namur did the party turn aside to visit the young Duchess of Burgundy, either at Hesdin or at Aire? Such is the conjecture of a learned Belgian editor, and he carries his surmise further in suggesting that in this brief sojourn was performed Chastellain's mystery of "The Peace of Peronne."[2] Perhaps these verses, if put in the mouths of Louis and Charles, may have pleased the princely spectators of the dramatic poem. Mutual admiration was the keynote of these flowery speeches while the other

[1] *Lettres*, iii., 295. (Toussaint is probably Toustain.)

[2] Kervyn ed., *Œuvres de Chastellain*, vii., xviii. *See* poem, *ibid.*, 423. The MS. in the Laurentian Library at Florence bears this line: "Here follows a mystery made because of the said peace of good intention in the thought that it would be observed by the parties." Hesdin is, however, a long way out of the route between Peronne and Namur, where the party was on October 14th. It would hardly seem possible for journey and visit in so brief a time.

The Meeting at Peronne

dramatis personæ expressed unstinted admiration for the wonderful deed accomplished by these two pure souls who have sworn peace when they might have brought dire war on their innocent subjects.

"Never did David, nor Ogier, nor Roland, that proud knight, nor the great Charlemagne, nor the proud Duke of Mayence, nor Mongleive, the heir, from whom issued noble fruit, nor King Arthur, nor Oliver, nor Rossillon, nor Charbonnier in their dozens of victories approach or touch with hand or foot the work I treat of."

. . . .

[The king speaks.]

"Charles, be assured that Louis will be the re-establisher and provider of all that touches your honour and peace between you and him. That he will ever be appreciator of you and avenger, a nourisher of joy and love in repairing all that my predecessor did.

[The duke speaks.]

"And Charles, who loves his honour as much as his soul, wishes nothing better than to serve you and this realm and to extol your house. For I know that is the reason why I have glory and reputation. Then if it please God and Our Lady, my body will keep from blame."

One stanza, indeed, uttered by Louis strikes a note of doubt: "Charles, so many debates may occur, so many incidents and accidents in our various actions, that a rupture may be dreaded."

Vehemently did the duke repudiate the bare possibility of a new breach between him and his liege. The whole is a pæan at a love feast. If the two together heard their counterfeits express such perfect fidelity, how Louis XI. must have laughed to himself behind his mask of forced courtesy! Charles, on the other hand, was quite capable of taking it all seriously, wholly unconscious that he had not cut the lion's claws for once and all.

CHAPTER XII

AN EASY VICTORY

1468

IT was in the midst of heavy rains that the journey was made to Namur and then on to the environs of Liege. Grim was the weather, befitting, in all probability, Charles's own mood. The king's escort was confined to very few besides the Scottish guard, but a body of three hundred troopers was permitted to follow him at a distance, while the faithful Dammartin across the border kept himself closely informed of every incident connected with the march that his scouts could gather, and in readiness to fall upon Burgundian possessions at a word of alarm, while he restrained his ardour for the moment in obedience to Louis's anxious command.

By the fourth week of October the Franco-Burgundian party were settled close to Liege in straggling camps, separated from each other by hills and uneven ground. Long was the discussion in council meeting as to the best mode of procedure. Liege was absolutely helpless in the face of this coalition. Wide breaches made her walls useless. Moats she had never possessed, for digging was well-nigh impossible on her rocky site covered by mud and slime from the overflow of the Meuse.

On account of this evident weakness, the king advised dismissing half the army as needless, advice that was not only rejected immediately but which excited Charles's doubts of the king's good faith. Over a week passed and feeble Liège continued obstinate, while each division of the army manœuvred to be first in the assault for the sake of the plunder. But advance was very difficult, for the soldiers were impeded in their movements by the slime. Wild were some of the night skirmishes over the uneven, slippery ground and amidst the little sheltering hills.

On one occasion, "a great many were hurt and among the rest the Prince of Orange (whom I had forgotten to name before), who behaved that day like a courageous gentleman, for he never moved foot off the place he first possessed. . . . The duke, too, did not lack in courage but he failed sometimes in order giving, and to say the truth, he behaved himself not so advisedly as many wished because of the king's presence."[1]

There is no doubt that Charles entertained increasingly sinister suspicions of his guest. He thought the king might either try to enter the city ahead of him and manage to placate his ancient allies by a specious explanation, or else he might succeed in effecting his escape without fulfilling his compact. At last Charles appointed Sunday, October 30th, for an assault. On the 29th, his own

[1] Commines, ii., ch. xi. It was not far from the place where another Prince of Orange tried to cross the Meuse exactly a hundred years later.

An Easy Victory

quarters were in a little suburb of mean, low houses, with rough ground and vineyards separating his camp from the city. Between his house and that of the king, both humble dwellings, was an old granary, occupied by a picked Burgundian force of three hundred men under special injunctions to keep close watch over the royal guest and see that he played no sudden trick. To further this purpose of espionage, they had made a breach in the walls with heavy blows of their picks.

The men were wearied with all their marching and skirmishing, and in order to have them in fighting trim on the morrow, Charles had ordered all alike to turn in and refresh themselves. The exhausted troops gladly obeyed this injunction. Charles was disarmed and sleeping, so, too, were Philip de Commines and the few attendants that lay within the narrow ducal chamber. Only a dozen pickets mounted guard in the room over Charles's little apartment, and kept their tired eyes open by playing at dice.

On that Saturday night when Charles was thus prudently gathering strength for the final tussle, the people of Liege also indulged in repose, counting on Sunday being a day of rest, that is, the major part of the burgher folk did within city limits. But another plan was on foot among some of the inhabitants of an outlying region. An attack on the Burgundian camp was planned by a band from Franchimont, a wild and wooded district, south of the episcopal see. The natives there had all the characteristics of mountaineers, although the heights of their rugged country reached only modest altitudes.[1]

These invaders were fortunate in obtaining as guides the owners of the very houses requisitioned for the lodgings of the two princes. Straight to their goal they progressed through paths quite unknown to the foe, and therefore unwatched. The highlanders made a mistake in not rushing headlong to the royal lodgings, where in the first confusion they might have accomplished their design upon the lives of Louis and of Charles or at least have taken the two prisoners. But a pause at a French nobleman's tent created a disturbance which roused the archers in the granary. The latter sallied out, to meet with a fierce counter-attack. In order to confuse them the mountaineers echoed the Burgundian cries, *Vive Bourgogne, vive le roy et tuez, tuez*, and they were not always immediately identified by their harsh Liege accent.

The highlanders were far outnumbered by the Burgundians, and it was only by dint of their desperate courage and by reason of the pitchy darkness and of the locality with its unknown roughness that the former inflicted the damage that they did.

Commines and his fellows helped the duke into his cuirass, and stood by his person, while the king's bodyguard of Scottish archers "proved

[1] The story of the "men of Franchimont" is questioned. Commines is the only authority for it.

An Easy Victory

themselves good fellows, who never budged from their master's feet and shot arrow upon arrow out into the darkness, wounding more Burgundians than Liegeois." The first to fall was Charles's own host, the guide of the marauders to his own cottage door. There were many more victims and no mercy. It was, indeed, an encounter characterised by the passions of war and the conditions of a mere burglarious attack on private houses.

Quaking with fear was the king. He thought that if the duke should now fail to make a complete conquest of Liege, his own fate would hang in the balance. At a hasty council meeting held that night, Charles was very doubtful as to the expediency of carrying out his proposed assault upon the city. Very distrustful of each other were the allies, a fact that caused Philip de Commines to comment,[1] "scarcely fifteen days had elapsed since these two had sworn a definitive peace and solemnly promised to support each other loyally. But confidence could not enter in any way."

Charles gave Louis permission to retire to Namur and wait until the duke had reduced the recalcitrant burghers once for all. Louis thought it wiser to keep close to Charles's own person until they parted company for ever, and the morrow found him in the duke's company as he marched on to Liege.

"My opinion is, [says Commines], that he would

[1] II., ch. xiii.

have been wise to depart that night. He could have done it for he had a hundred archers of his guard, various gentlemen of his household, and, near at hand, three hundred men-at-arms. Doubtless he was stayed by considerations of honour. He did not wish to be accused of cowardice."

Olivier de la Marche, also present as the princely pair entered Liege, heard the king say: "March on, my brother, for you are the luckiest prince alive." As they entered the gates, Louis shouted lustily, "*Vive Bourgogne*," to the infinite dismay of his former friends, the burghers of Liege.

The remainder of the history of that dire Sunday morning differs from that of other assaults only in harrowing details, and the extremity of the pitilessness and ferocity manifested by the conquerors. Charles had previously spared churches, and protected the helpless. Above all he had severely punished all ill treatment of respectable women. Little trace of this former restraint was to be seen on this occasion. The inhabitants were destroyed and banished by dozens. Those who fled from their homes leaving their untasted breakfasts to be eaten by the intruding soldiers, those who were scattered through the numerous churches, those who attempted to defend the breaches in the walls—all alike were treated without mercy.

The Cathedral of St. Lambert, Charles did endeavour to protect. "The duke himself went thither, and one man I saw him kill with his own

OLIVIER DE LA MARCHE
(FROM MS. REPRODUCED IN MÉM. COURONNÉS, ETC., PAR L'ACAD.
ROYALE DE BELGIQUE VOL. XLIX.)

An Easy Victory

hand, whereupon all the company departed and that particular church was not pillaged, but at the end the men who had taken refuge there were captured as well as the wealth of the church."

At about midday Charles joined Louis at the episcopal palace, where the latter had found apartments better suited to his rank than the rude huts that had sheltered him for the past few days. The king was in good spirits and enjoyed his dinner in spite of the unsavoury scenes that were still in progress about him. He manifested great joy in the successful assault, and was lavish in his praises of the duke's courage, taking care that his admiring phrases should be promptly reported to his cousin.[1] His one great preoccupation, however, was to return to his own realm.

After dinner the duke and he made good cheer together. "If the king had praised his works behind his back, still more loud was he in his open admiration. And the duke was pleased." No telling sign of friendship for Charles had Louis spared that day, so terrified was he lest some testimony from his ancient protégés might prove his ruin. "Let the word be Burgundy," he had cried to his followers when the attack began. "*Tuez, tuez, vive Bourgogne.*"

There is another contemporaneous historian who somewhat apologetically relates the following incident of this interview.[2] In this friendly

[1] Commines, ii., ch. xiii.

[2] Oudenbosch,*Veterum scriptorum*, etc. *Amplissima Collectio*, ed. E. Martene, iv. Rerum Leodiensim. Opus Adriani de

Sabbath day chat, Charles asked Louis how he ought to treat Liege when his soldiers had finished their work. No trace of kindliness towards his old friends was there in the king's answer.

"Once my father had a high tree near his house, inhabited by crows who had built their nests thereon and disturbed his repose by their chatter. He had the nests removed but the crows returned and built anew. Several times was this repeated. Then he had the tree cut down at the roots. After that my father slept quietly."

Four or five days passed before Louis dared press the question of his return home. The following note written in Italian, dated on the day of the assault, is significant of his state of mind:

Louis XI. to the Count de Foix

"Monseigneur the Prince:

"To-day my brother of Burgundy and I entered in great multitude and with force into this city of Liege, and because I have great desire to return, I advise you that on next Tuesday morning I will depart hence, and I will not cease riding without making any stops until I reach there.[1] I pray you to let me know what is to be done.

"Writ at Liege, October 30th.

"Loys
"De la Loere."

Veteri Busco, p. 1343. The writer acknowledges that the story is hearsay.

[1] "*Non cessero di cavalchare senza fare demoia alcuna. Lettres*, iii., 300.

An Easy Victory

Punctilious was Louis in his assurances to his host that if he could be of any further aid he hoped his cousin would command him. If there were, indeed, nothing, he thought his best plan would be to go to Paris and have the late treaty duly recorded and published to insure its validity. Charles grumbled a little, but finally agreed to speed his parting guest after the treaty had been again read aloud to the king so that he might dissent from any one of its articles or ever after hold his peace.

Quite ready was Louis to re-confirm everything sworn to at Peronne. Just as he was departing he put one more query: " 'If perchance my brother now in Brittany should be dissatisfied with the share I accord him out of love to you, what do you want me to do?' The duke answered abruptly and without thought: 'If he does not wish to take it, but if you content him otherwise, I will trust to you two.' From this question and answer arose great things as you shall hear later. So the king departed at his pleasure, and Mons. de Cordes and d'Émeries, Grand Bailiff of Hainaut escorted him out of ducal territory.''[1]

"O wonderful and memorable crime of this king of the French [declares a contemporaneous Liege sympathiser.][2] Scarcely anything so bad can be found in ancient annals or in modern history. What could be

[1] Commines, ii., ch. xiv.
[2] *"O præclarum et memorabile facinus hujus regis Francorum."*

more stupid or more perfidious, or a better instance of infamy than for a king who had incited a people to arms against the Burgundians to act thus for the sake of his own safety? Not once but many times had he pledged them his faith, offering them defence and assistance against the same Burgundians. And now when they are overwhelmed and confounded by this Burgundian duke, this king actually co-operates with their foe, to their damage, wears that foe's insignia and dares to hide himself behind those emblems, and assist to destroy those to whom he himself had furnished aid and subsidies with pledges of good faith! I am ashamed to commit this to writing, and to hand it down to posterity, knowing that it will seem incredible to many. But it is so notorious throughout France and is confirmed by so many adequate witnesses who have seen and heard these things that no room is left for doubt of their veracity except to one desiring to ignore the truth." [1]

November 2d is the date of Louis's departure. It needs no stretch of the imagination to believe the words of his little Swiss page, Diesbach, when he says that on reaching French soil Louis dismounted and kissed the ground in a paroxysm of joy that he was his own man again.[2] Devoutly, too, he gave thanks to God for helping him in his need. Still this joy was concealed under euphemistic phrases in his correspondence. On No-

[1] Basin, *Histoire des règnes de Charles VII. et de Louis XI.*, Quicherat ed., ii., 204. This also appears in *Excerpta ex Amelgardi. De gestis Ludovici XI.*, cap. xxiii. Martene's *Amplissima Collectio*, iv., 740 *et seq.*

[2] Quoted in Kirk, i., 606, note.

vember 5th, he wrote again to the Duke of Milan from Beaumont:

"We went in person with the duke against the Liegeois, on account of their rebellion and offence, and the city being reduced by force to the power of the duke, we have left him in some part of Liege as we were anxious to return to our kingdom of France."

In January, 1469, Guillaume Toustain, the brother of the faithful secretary Aloysius Toustain, who had written several of Louis's letters from Liege, goes to Pavia to finish his studies, and Louis writes to the Duke of Milan asking him to assure his protégé a pleasant reception in the university.

The ratification of the treaty took place duly at Paris on Saturday, November 19th, and the king also sternly forbade the circulation of any "paintings, rondels, ballads, songs, or defamatory pamphlets" about Charles.[1] The same informant tells us that loquacious birds were put under a ban.

"And on the same day in behalf of the king, and by virtue of his commission addressed to a young man of Paris named Henry Perdriel, all the magpies, jays, and *chouettes*, caged or otherwise, were taken in charge, and a record was made of all the places where the said birds were taken and also all that they knew how to say, like *larron, paillart*, etc., *va hors, va! Perrette donnes moi à boire*, and various other phrases that they had been taught."

Abbé le Grand thinks that "Perrette" was

[1] Jean de Roye, *Chronique Scandaleuse*, ed. Mandrot, i., 220.

meant for Peronne instead of a mistress of Louis of that name. But this conjecture seems the only basis for the very deep-rooted tradition that *Peronne* was a word Louis could not bear to have uttered.

"In the way of justice there is nothing going on here, [wrote one Anthony de Loisey from Liege to the president of Burgundy], except every day they hang and draw such Liegeois as are found or have been taken prisoners and have no money to ransom themselves. The city is well plundered, nothing remains but rubbish. For example I have not been able to find a sheet of paper fit for writing to you, but with all my pains could get nothing but some leaves from an old book."[1]

Charles decided that nothing should be left standing except churches and ecclesiastical buildings. On November 9th, before the final fires were lit, he departed from the wretched town and went down the left bank of the Meuse to an abbey on the river, where he paused for the night. Four leagues distant from the city was this place, and from it were plainly visible the flames of the burning buildings on that grim St. Hubert's Day—a day when Liege had been wont to give vent to merriment.

"From all the dangers that had encompassed him, Charles escaped with his life, simply because his hour had not yet struck, and because he was God's chosen instrument to punish the sinning city," is the verdict of one chronicler who does

[1] Comines-Lenglet, iii., 83.

An Easy Victory

not spare his fellow-Liegeois for their follies while he profoundly pities their fate.[1]

Out of the many contemporaneous accounts a portion of a private letter from the duke's cup-bearer to his sister is added:[2]

"Very dear sister, with a very good heart I recommend myself to you and to all my good friends, men and women in our parts, not forgetting my *beaux-pères*, Martin Stephen and Dan Gauthier. Pray know that, thanks to God, I and all my people are safe and sound. As to my horses, one was wounded and another is sick in the hands of the marshals at Namur, and the others are thin enough and have no grain to eat except hay. The weather, has, indeed, been enough to strike a chill to the hearts of men and horses. Since we left Burgundy there have not been three fine days in succession and we are in a worse state than wolves.

"You already know how we passed through Lorraine and Ratellois without troubling about Salesart or other French captains, nor the other Lorrainers either, although they were under orders to attack us, and were no more afraid of us than we of them. As we approached the territory of Hainaut, M. the duke sent Messire Pierre de Harquantbault[3] to us to show us what road to take. He told us that the duke had made a treaty with the king, who had visited him, news that filled us with astonishment. . . .

[1] Johannes de Los, *Chronicon*, p. 60. *Quia hora nendum venerat.* De Ram, "Troubles du pays de Liége."

[2] Commynes-Dupont, *Preuves*, iii., 242. Letter of Jehan de Mazilles to his sister.

[3] Hagenbach, later Governor of Alsace.

After skirmishing for several days we reached the faubourgs of Liege and remained there three of four days under arms, with no sleep and little food, and our horses standing in the rain with no shelter but the trees. While we were thus lodged, the king and the duke with a fair escort arrived and took up their quarters in certain houses near the faubourg. [. . . Constant firing was interchanged for several days. Sallies were essayed and men were slain.]

"Finally a direct attack was made on the king and Monseigneur and there were more of their people than ours and that night Monseigneur was in great danger. The following Sunday at 9 A.M. we began the assault in three separate quarters. It was a fine thing, to see the men-at-arms march on the walls of the said city, some climbing and others scaling them with ladders. The standards of monseigneur the marshal and monsgn. de Renty who had been stationed together in the faubourgs, were the first within the said city which contained at that moment sixteen to eighteen thousand combatants. who were surprised when they saw their walls scaled.

"In a moment we entered crying 'Burgundy' and 'city gained.' Ever so many of their people were slain and drowned in their flight. We flew to reach the market-place and the church of St. Lambert where a number of prisoners were taken and thrown into the water. Our ensign stood in the midst of the fray on the market-place, in the hopes that they would rally for a combat but they rallied only to flee. While we held our position on the square several were created knights. . . . All the churches—more than four hundred—were pillaged and plundered. It is rumoured that they will be burnt together with the rest of the city. Piteous it is to see what ill is wrought. . . . [The king] stayed in the city with Monseigneur two or three days. Then he departed, it is said for Brussels to await my said lord. It is a great thing to have seen the puissance of my master, *which is great enough to defeat an emperor*. I believe the Burgundians will shortly return to Burgundy.

"I paid my respects to my said lord, who received me very well. At present I am listed [1] among those whose term is almost expired and I am ready to follow him wherever he wishes until my service is out, which will be soon. I would have written before had I had any one to send it by. Pray write me about yourself by the first comer. Praying our Lord, beloved sister, to keep you. Written in Liege, November 8, 1468.

"JEHAN DE MAZILLES."

This sober letter and other accounts by reliable witnesses agree as to the terrible havoc wrought in the city by the assault on October 30th and by determined and systematic measures of destruction, both during Charles's ten days' sojourn for the express purpose of completing the punishment and after his departure. Yet the result assuredly fell short of the intention. The destruction was not complete as was that of Dinant. Vitality remained, apart from the ecclesiastical nucleus intentionally preserved by the duke.

Having watched the tongues of flame lap the

[1] *Conté aux escros.* This word strictly applies to the prisoners on a jailer's list—evidently used in jest.

unfortunate city, Charles turned with his army towards Franchimont, that rugged hill country which had proved a nest of hardy and persistent antagonists to Burgundian pretensions. Jehan de Mazilles is in close attendance and gives further details of the pitiless fashion in which Charles carried out his purpose of leaving no seed of resistance to germinate. Four nights and three days they sojourned in a certain little village while there was a hard frost and where, without unarming, they "slept under the trees and drank water." Meantime a small party was despatched by the duke to attack the stronghold of Franchimont. The despairing Liegeois who had taken refuge there abandoned it, and it was taken by assault. A few more days and the duke was assured that Liege and her people were shorn of their strength. When the remnant of survivors began to creep back to the city and tried to recover what was left of their property, many were the questions to be settled. Lawsuits succeeded to turmoils and lingered on for years.

In the lordly manner of conquerors Charles, too, demanded reimbursement for his trouble in bending these free citizens to his illegal will. The reinstated bishop wanted his rents and legal perquisites, all difficult to collect, and many were the ponderous documents that passed on the subject. How justly pained sounds Charles's remonstrance on the default of payment of taxes to his friend, the city's lord!

An Easy Victory

" Therefore [he writes,] in consideration of these things, taking into account the terror of our departure to Brussels last January, we decide, my brother and I, that the payment of both *gabelle* and poll tax must be forced, and that we cannot permit the retarding of such taxes under any colour or pretence. At the request of our brother and cousin we order the inhabitants of the said territories to pay both *gabelle* and poll tax, all that is due from the time it was imposed and for the time to come, under penalty of the confiscation of their goods and their persons."

It was the old story of bricks without straw—taxes and rents for property ruthlessly destroyed were so easy. To this extent of tyranny had Duke Philip never gone, and undoubtedly the treatment of Liege was a step towards Charles's final disaster. So much hatred was excited against him that his adherents fell off one by one when his luck began to fail him.

No omen of misfortune was to be seen at this time, however. That month of November saw him master absolute wherever he was and he used his power autocratically. At Huy, he had a number of prisoners executed. At Louvain, at Brussels, he gave fresh examples of his relentlessness as an overlord.

CHAPTER XIII

A NEW ACQUISITION

1469–1473

THIS successful expedition against Liege carried Charles of Burgundy to the very crest of his prosperity. His self-esteem was moreover gratified by the regard shown to him at home and abroad. A man who could force a royal neighbour into playing the pitiful rôle enacted by Louis XI. at Peronne was assuredly a man to be respected if not loved. And messages of admiration and respect couched in various terms were despatched from many quarters to the duke as soon as he was at Brussels to receive them.

Ghent had long since made apologies for the sorry reception accorded to their incoming Count of Flanders in 1467, but Charles had postponed the formal *amende* until a convenient moment of leisure. January 15, 1469, was finally appointed for this ceremony and the occasion was utilised to show the duke's grandeur, the city's humiliation, to as many people as possible who might spread the report far and wide.

It was a Sunday. Out in the courtyard of the palace the snow was thick on the ground where a group of Ghent burghers cooled their heels for an hour and a half, awaiting a summons to the ducal

A New Acquisition

presence. There, too, where every one could see those emblems of the artisans' corporate strength, fluttered fifty-two banners unfurled before the deans of the Ghentish *métiers*.[1]

Within, the great hall of the palace showed a splendid setting for a brilliant assembly. The most famous Burgundian tapestries hung on the walls. Episodes from the careers of Alexander, of Hannibal, and of other notable ancients formed the background for the duke and his nobles, knights of the Golden Fleece, in festal array. As spectators, too, there were all the envoys and ambassadors then present in Brussels from "France, England, Hungary, Bohemia, Naples, Aragon, Sicily, Cyprus, Norway, Poland, Denmark, Russia, Livornia, Prussia, Austria, Milan, Lombardy, and other places."

Charles himself was installed grandly on a kind of throne, and to his feet Olivier de la Marche conducted the civic procession of penitents. Before this pompous gathering, after a statement of the city's sin and sorrow, the precious charter called the Grand Privilege of Ghent was solemnly read aloud, and then cut up into little pieces with a pen-knife. Next followed a recitation of the penalties imposed upon, and accepted by, the citizens (closing of the gates, etc)., and then the paternal Count of Flanders, duly mollified, pronounced the fault forgiven with the benediction,

---

[1] Gachard, *Doc. inéd.*, i., 204–209. "Relation de l'assemblée solennelle tenue à Bruxelles le 15 Jan., 1469."

"By virtue of this submission and by keeping your promises and being good children, you shall enjoy our grace and we will be a good prince." "May our Saviour Jesus Christ confirm and preserve this peace to the end of this century," is the pious ejaculation with which the *Relation* closes.

Among the witnesses of the above scene, when the independent citizens of Ghent meekly posed as the duke's children, were envoys from George Podiebrad, ex-king of Bohemia. Lately deposed by the pope, he was seeking some favourable ally who might help him to recover his realm. He had conceived a plan for a coalition between Bohemia, Poland, Austria, and Hungary to present a solid rampart against the Turks, and strong enough to dictate to emperor and pope. He was ready for intrigue with any power and had approached Louis XI. and Matthias Corvinus, King of Hungary, before turning to Charles of Burgundy.[1]

Meantime, the Emperor Frederic tried to knit links with this same Matthias by suggesting that he might be the next emperor, assuring him that he could count on the support of the electors of Mayence, of Trèves, and of Saxony. He himself was world-weary and was anxious to exchange his imperial cares for the repose of the Church could he only find a safe guardian for his son,

[1] See Toutey, *Charles le Téméraire et la ligue de Constance*, p. 7.

A New Acquisition

Maximilian, and a desirable successor for himself. Would not Matthias consider the two offices?

Potent arguments like these induced Matthias not only to turn his back on Podiebrad, but to accept that deposed monarch's crown which the Bohemian nobles offered him May 3,1469. Then he proceeded to ally himself with Frederic, elector palatine, and with the elector of Bavaria. This was the moment when the ex-king of Bohemia made renewed offers of friendly alliance to Charles of Burgundy. In his name the Sire de Stein brought the draft of a treaty of amity to Charles which contained the provision that Podiebrad should support the election of Charles as King of the Romans, in consideration of the sum of two hundred thousand florins (Rhenish).[1]

This modest sum was to secure not only Podiebrad's own vote but his "influence" with the Archbishop of Mayence, the Elector of Saxony and the Margrave of Brandenburg.[2] While Podiebrad thus dangled the ultimate hopes of the imperial crown before the duke's eyes, he over-estimated his credulity. As a matter of fact the royal exile had no "influence" at all with the first named elector, and the last, too, showed no disposition whatsoever to serve his unstable policy. Both were content to advise Emperor Frederic. The sole result of the empty

[1] See the text given in Comines-Lenglet, iii., 116. Charles is characterised as *ducem strenuum in armis ac justitiæ præcipium zelatorem*.

[2] See Toutey, p. 8; also Lavisse, iv[ii]., 371.

overtures was to increase Charles's own sense of importance.

Another negotiation which sought him unasked had, however, a material influence on the course of events, and must be touched on in some detail. Sigismund of Austria—first duke then archduke, —Count of Tyrol, cousin of the Emperor Frederic, was a member of the House of Habsburg. In 1449, he had married Eleanor of Scotland, and became brother-in-law of Louis during the term of the dauphin's first marriage. An indolent, extravagant prince, he was greatly dominated by his courtiers. His heritage as Count of Tyrol included certain territories lying far from his capital, Innsbruck. Certain portions of Upper Alsace, lands on both sides of the Rhine, Thurgau, Argau in Switzerland, Breisgau, and some other seigniories in the Black Forest were under his sway.

These particular domains were so remote from Innsbruck that the authority of the hereditary overlord had long been eluded. The nobles pillaged the land near their castles very much at their own sweet will. The harassed burghers appealed to the Alsatian Décapole,[1] and again to the free Swiss cantons for protection, and sometimes obtained more than they wanted.

Mulhouse was seriously affected by these lawless depredations. To her, Berne promised aid in a twenty-five years' alliance signed in 1466, and

[1] Thus was named the assembly of ten Alsatian towns from Strasburg to Basel, organised into a half independent confederation by the Emperor Charles IV.

at Berne's insistance the cowardly nobles restrained their license. But when the city attempted to extend its authority Sigismund interfered. Having no army, however, he could not recover Waldshut, which the Swiss claimed a right to annex, except by offering ten thousand florins for the town's ransom. Poor in cash as he was in men, he had, however, no means to pay this ransom and begged aid in every direction. Moreover, he feared further aggressions from the cantons, which were growing more daring. What man in Europe was better able to teach them a lesson than Charles, the destroyer of Liege, the stern curber of undue liberty in Flanders? Was he not the very person to tame insolent Swiss cowherds?

In the course of the year 1468, Sigismund made known to Charles his desire for a bargain, intimating that in case of the duke's refusal, he would carry his wares to Louis XI. At that moment, Charles was busied with Liege and showed no interest in Sigismund's proposition. The latter tried to see Louis XI. personally in accordance with his imperial cousin's advice that an interview might be more effective than a letter.

It did not prove a propitious time, however; Louis was deeply engaged with Burgundy and he was not disposed to take any steps that might estrange the Swiss—and any espousal of Sigismund's interests might alienate them. He did not even permit an opening to be made, but stopped Sigismund's approach to him by a message that he would not for a moment entertain a suggestion inimical to those dear friends of his in the cantons—a sentiment that quickly found its way to Switzerland.

Thus stayed in his effort to win Louis's ear, Sigismund decided that he would make another essay towards a Burgundian alliance, this time face to face with the duke. On to Flanders he journeyed and found Charles in the midst of the ostentatious magnificence already described. Ordinary affairs of life were conducted with a splendour hardly attained by the emperor in the most pompous functions of his court. Sigismund was absolutely dazzled by the evidence of easy prosperity. The fact that a maiden was the duke's sole heiress led the Austrian to conceive the not unnatural idea that this attractive Burgundian wealth might be turned into the impoverished imperial coffers by a marriage between Mary of Burgundy and Maximilian, the emperor's son.

The visitor not only thought of this possibility, but he immediately broached it to Charles. The bait was swallowed. As to the main proposition which Sigismund had come expressly to make, that, too, was not rejected. The duke perceived that the transfer of the Rhenish lands to his jurisdiction might militate to his advantage. A passage would be opened towards the south for his troops without the need of demanding permission from any reluctant neighbour. The risk of trouble with the Swiss did not affect him when weighing the

MARY OF BURGUNDY
FROM CONTEMPORANEOUS MINIATURE REPRODUCED IN BARANTE, "LES DUCS DE BOURGOGNE"

A New Acquisition

advantages of Sigismund's proffer, a proffer which he finally decided to accept. Probably he found his guest a pleasant party to a bargain, for not only did he broach the tempting alliance between Mary and Maximilian, but he, too, seems to have hinted that the title of "King of the Romans" might be added to the long list of appellations already signed by Charles.[1] As Sigismund was richer in kin, if not in coin, than the feeble Podiebrad, Charles gave serious heed to the suggestion which fell incidentally from his guest's lips, in the course of the long conversations held at Bruges.

Certain precautions were taken to protect Charles from being dragged into Swiss complications against his will, and then in May, 1469, the treaty of St. Omer was signed,[2] wherein the Duke of Burgundy accorded his protection to Sigismund of Austria and received from him all his seigniorial rights within certain specified territories.

The most important part of this cession comprised Upper Alsace and the county of Ferrette, but there were also many other fragments of territory and rights of seigniory involved, besides lordship over various Rhenish cities, such as Rheinfelden, Saeckingen, Lauffenburg, Waldshut and Brisac. This last named town commanded the route eastward, as Waldshut that to the south-

[1] Toutey, p. 11.
[2] See "Fontes Rerum Austriacarum" Chmel, J., *Urkunden zur Geschichte von Osterreich*, etc., II², 223 *et passim*. One document, p. 229, has *Marz* as a misprint for *Mai*.

east, and Thann the highway through the Vosges region.

Fifty thousand florins was the price for the property and the claims transferred from Sigismund to Charles. Ten thousand were to be paid at once, in order to ransom Waldshut from the Swiss. The remainder was due on September 24th. On his part, Sigismund specifically recognised the duke's right to redeem all domains nominally his but mortgaged for the time being, certain estates or seignorial rights having been thus alienated for 150 years.

This territorial transfer was not a sale. It was a mortgage, but a mortgage with possession to the mortgagee and further restricted by the provision that there could be no redemption unless the mortgager could repay at Besançon the whole loan plus all the outlay made by the mortgagee up to that date. Instalment payments were expressly ruled out. The entire sum intact was made obligatory. Therefore the danger of speedy redemption did not disquiet Charles. He knew the man he had to deal with. Sigismund's lack of foresight and his prodigality were notorious. There was faint chance that he could ever command the amount in question. Accordingly, Charles was fairly justified in counting the mortgaged territory as annexed to Burgundy in perpetuity.

Sigismund pocketed his florins eagerly. Nothing could have been more welcome to him. But this relief from the pressure of his pecuniary embarrass-

A New Acquisition

ment did not inspire him with love for the man who held his lost lands. His sentiments towards Charles were very similar to those of an heir towards a usurer who has helped him in a temporary strait by mulcting him of his natural rights.

As for the emperor, when this transfer of territory was an accomplished fact, he began to take fright at the consequences. He did not like this intrusion of a powerful French peer into the imperial circle.[1] At the same time he was ready to make him share responsibility in any further difficulties that might arise between Sigismund and the Swiss.

The least skilful of prophets could have foreseen difficulties for Charles on his own account, both foreign and domestic. His own relations with the Swiss had always been friendly enough, but he had never before been so near a neighbour, while, within the Rhine lands, it was an open question whether the bartered inhabitants were to enjoy or regret their new tie with Burgundy. The importance of their sentiments was a matter of as supreme indifference to Charles as was danger from the Confederation. Neither conciliation nor diplomacy was in his thoughts. He had no conception of the intricacies of the situation. He counted the landgraviate as definitely his by the treaty of St. Omer as Brabant by heritage or Liege by conquest.

[1] Charles was, to be sure, already within that circle for some of his Netherland provinces, but his feudal obligations there were very shadowy.

The need of a kindly policy towards the little valley towns—a policy that might have won their allegiance—never occurred to him. They were his property and Peter von Hagenbach was, in course of time, made lieutenant-governor in his behalf.

Apart from all personal considerations of enmity and amity of natives and neighbours, the territory of Upper Alsace and the county of Ferrette, delivered from needy Austria to rich Burgundy, like a coat pawned by a poor student, was held under very complex and singular conditions.[1] The status of the bargain between Sigismund and Charles was in point of fact something between pawn and sale, according to the point of view. Sigismund fully intended to redeem it, while Charles did not admit that possibility as remotely contingent. Nor was that the only peculiarity. The itemised list of the ceded territories as given in the treaty was far from telling the facts of the possessions passing to Sigismund's proxy.

In the first place the Austrian seigniories were not compact. They were scattered here and there in the midst of lands ruled by others, as the Bishop of Strasburg, the Abbé of St. Blaise in the Black Forest, the count Palatine, the citizens of Basel and of Mulhouse, and others.

[1] See Toutey, Lavisse, etc., and above all a valuable article by L. Stouff, entitled "Les Possessions Bourguignonnes dans la vallée du Rhin sous Charles le Téméraire," *Annales de l'Est*, vol. 18. This article is the result of a careful examination of the reports made by Poinsot and Pellet, Charles's commissioners.

The existent variety in the extent and nature of Austrian title was extraordinary. Nearly every possible combination of dismembered prerogative and actual tenure had resulted from the long series of ducal compositions. In some localities a toll or a quit-rent was the sole cession, and again a toll or a prerogative was almost the only residue remaining to the ostensible overlord, while all his former property or transferable birthright privileges were lodged in various hands on divers tenures. There were cases in which the mortgagee—noble, burgher, or municipal corporation—had taken the exact place of the Austrian duke and in so doing had become the vassal of his debtor, stripped of all vested interest but his sovereignty. For in these bargains wherein elements of the Roman contract and feudal customs were curiously blended, two classes of rights had been invariably reserved by the ducal mortgagers:

(1) Monopolies, regal in nature, such as assured free circulation on the highways, the old Roman roads, all jurisdiction of passports and travellers' protection.

(2) The suzerainty. This comprised the power to confer fiefs, of requisition of military service, of requesting *aids* and admission to strongholds, cities, or castles, *le droit de forteresse jurable et rendable*.

In these regards the compact between Charles and Sigismund differed from all previous covenants not only in degree, but in kind. The Duke of

Burgundy entered into the *sovereign* as well as into the mangled, maimed, and curtailed proprietary rights of the hereditary over-lord.

In his assumption of this involved and doubtful property, Charles laid heavy responsibilities on his shoulders. The actual price of fifty thousand gold florins paid to Sigismund was a mere fraction of the pecuniary obligations incurred, while the weight of care was difficult to gauge. He succeeded to princes weak, frivolous, prodigal, whose misrule had long been a curse to the land. The incursions of the Swiss, the repeated descents of the Rhine nobles from their crag-lodged strongholds to pillage and destroy, terrified merchants and plunged peaceful labourers into misery.

Through hatred of the absentee Austrians, the neighbouring cities repeatedly became the accomplices of these brigands, affording them asylums for refitting and free passage when they were laden with evident booty.

In all departments of finance and administration disorder prevailed. The chief officials, castellans and councillors, enjoyed high salaries for neglected duties. The castles were in wretched repair and there were insufficient troops to guard the roads. There was no dependence upon the receipts nominally to be expected. In the sub-mortgaged lands, the lords simply levied what they could, without the slightest responsibility for the order of the domain; they did not hesitate to charge their suzerain for repairs never made, confident that no one would verify their declaration.

In the territories of the immediate domain, the Austrian dukes and their officials had no notion of the rigid system maintained in Burgundy. Only here and there can little memoranda be found and these are confused and obscure. There is a dearth of accurate records like those voluminous registers of outlays kept by Burgundian receivers, registers so rich in detail that they are more valuable for the historian than any chronicle.

Exact appraisal of the resources of these *pays de par de là* was very difficult. Between 1469 and 1473 there were three efforts to obtain reliable information by means of as many successive commissions despatched to the Rhine valley by the Duke of Burgundy.

Envoys drew up minutes of their observations in addition to their official reports and all were preserved in the archives. As these were written from testimony gathered on the spot, such as the accounts of the receivers now lost, etc., there is real value in the documents.

The first commission in behalf of Burgundy was composed of two Germans and three Walloons. One of the former was Peter von Hagenbach, who won no enviable reputation in the later exercise of his office as lieutenant-governor of the annexed region, to which he was shortly afterwards appointed. This first commission entered into formal possession in Charles's name and instituted some desired reforms immediately, such as policing the highways, etc.

The second commission made its visit in 1471. It consisted of Jean Pellet, treasurer of Vesoul, and Jean Poinsot, procureur-general of Amont.

The third commission (1473) was under the auspices of Monseigneur Coutault, master of accounts at Dijon. He carried with him the report of his predecessors and made his additions thereto.

Charles's directions to Poinsot and Pellet (June 13, 1471) were vague and general. They were "to see the conduct of his affairs" (*voir la conduite de ses affaires*). The important point was to find out how much revenue could be obtained. As the duke's plan of expansion grew larger he had need of all his resources.

The reports were eminently discouraging. Outlay was needed everywhere—income was small. As the chances of peculation diminished, the castellans deserted their posts and left the castles to decay. The Burgundian commission of 1471 found the difficulties of their exploration increased by two items. Charles had not advanced an allowance for their expenses and they were anxious to be back at Vesoul by Michaelmas, the date of the change in municipal offices and of appropriations for the year. It was in hopes of receiving advance moneys that they delayed in starting, but the approaching election and coming winter finally decided them to set out, pay their

A New Acquisition

own expenses, and complete the business as rapidly as they could in a fortnight.

The summary of this report of 1471 was that there was little present prospect that Charles would be able to reimburse himself for his necessary expenses. An undue portion of authority and of revenue was legally lodged in alien hands. Charles was possessed of germs of rights rather than of actual rights. The earlier creditors of Austria held all the best mortgages with their attendant emoluments. The immediate profits accruing to the Duke of Burgundy fell far short of the minimum necessary to disburse to keep his government, his strongholds, his highways in repair. Very disturbed were the good treasurer of Vesoul and the procureur-general of Amont at this state of affairs, and distressed at the prospect of the ampler receipts from Burgundy being required to relieve the pressing necessities of the poor territories *de par de là*.

To avoid this contingency, the commissioners recommended the duke to redeem all the existing mortgages great and small. It would cost 140,000 florins, but the revenue would at once increase with the new security which would immediately follow under firm Burgundian rule. Sole master, Charles could then enforce obedience from nobles and cities and better conditions would be inaugurated.

Evidently this rational advice was not taken, for it is repeated by Coutault in 1473. Redemption of the mortgages, "if your affairs can afford it," is the counsel given by the chamber of accounts at Dijon, though this sage board adds that they were well aware that in the previous month Monseigneur could not put his hands on a hundred florins to redeem one wretched little *gagerie*. The native coffers of the region did not suffice to settle the salaries of the officers in charge.

Such then was the new acquisition of Charles after four years of his administration. Peter von Hagenbach, his deputy in charge of this unremunerative territory, is a character painted in the darkest colours by all historians. It is more than probable that his unpopular efforts to make bricks without straw were largely responsible for his unenviable reputation. Ground between the upper and lower millstones of Charles's clamours for revenues and popular clamours that the people had nothing wherewith to pay, Hagenbach developed into a taskmaster of the hardest and most unpitying type, who made himself thoroughly hated by the people he was set to rule.

It must be remembered that there was no cleft in nationality or in language between governor and governed. He was not a foreigner set over them. He was one of them raised to a high position. There was then no French element in Lower Alsace. It was then German pure and simple.

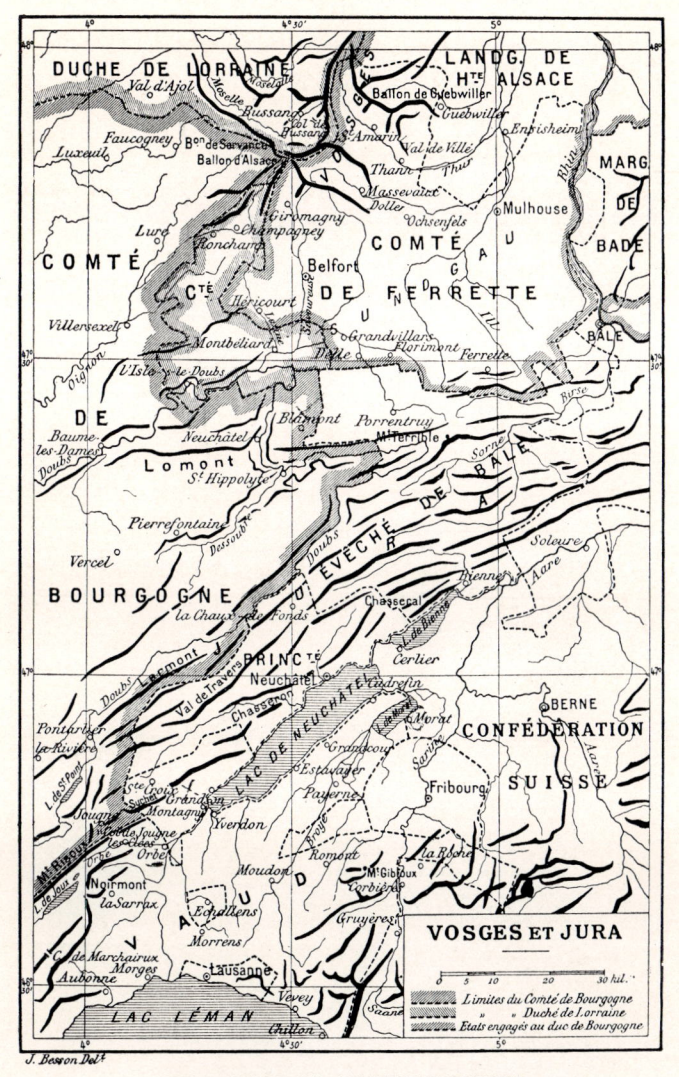

UPPER ALSACE AND ADJACENT TERRITORY
BY PERMISSION OF HACHETTE, 1902

CHAPTER XIV

ENGLISH AFFAIRS

1470–1471

IN order to follow out the extension of Burgundian jurisdiction in one direction, the course of events in the duke's life has been anticipated a little. The thread of the story now returns to 1469, when Charles and Sigismund separated at St. Omer both well pleased with their bargain. Charles tarried for a time at Ghent and Bruges and then proceeded to Zealand and Holland, where his sojourn had been interrupted in 1468 by his alarm about French duplicity. In the glow caused by his past achievements, his present reputation, and future prospects, Charles of Burgundy was in a mood to prove to his subjects his excellence as a paternal ruler. Wherever he paused on his journey easy access was permitted to his presence and he was lavish in the time given to receiving petitions from the humblest plaintiff. The following gruesome incident is an illustration of the summary methods attributed to him.[1]

Shortly before the ducal visit to Middelburg, the governor, a man of noble birth, a knight, fell in

[1] Meyer is the earliest historian to tell this story and it is vouched for by no existing contemporary evidence.

love with a married woman who indignantly repudiated his advances. In revenge the governor had the husband arrested on a charge of high treason. The wife, left without a protector, continued obdurate to the knight until the alternative of her husband's release or his death was offered her as the reward for accepting the governor's base suit or as the penalty of her refusal. She chose to redeem the prisoner. Having paid the price she went to the prison and was led to her husband truly, but he lay dead and in his coffin!

When the Duke of Burgundy was once within the Zealand capital, this injured woman hastened to throw herself at his feet, a petitioner for justice. He heard her complaint and straightway summoned the ex-governor to his presence. The accused confessed that he had been carried away by his adoration for the woman, reminded Charles of his long and faithful devotion to the late duke and to himself, and offered any possible reparation for his crime. The duke ordered him to marry his victim. The widow was horrified at the suggestion, but was forced by her family to accept it. After the nuptial benediction, the knight again appeared before Charles to assure him that the plaintiff was satisfied. "She, yes," replied the duke coldly, "but not I." He remanded the bridegroom to prison, had him shriven and executed all within an hour. Then the bride was summoned and shown her second husband in his coffin as she had seen her first, and on the same spot. "It was a penalty

English Affairs

that hit the innocent as well as the guilty, for the plaintiff died from the double shock."

The duke, satisfied with his rigour, went on to Holland. Everywhere he evinced himself equally uncompromising towards the nobles, amiable and considerate towards the lower classes and humble folk. Various other stories related about him at this epoch are difficult to accept as authentic, for the main detail has appeared at other times under different guises. Wandering tales seem to alight, like birds of passage, on successive people in lands and epochs widely apart, mere hallmarks of certain characteristics re-embodied.

The Hague was the duke's headquarters during two months, and there also he held open court and gave audience to many embassies in the midst of his administrative work pertaining to Holland and its nearest neighbours. He took measures to recover what he claimed had been usurped by Utrecht, and he initiated proceedings to make good the title of Lord of Friesland, that will-o'-the wisp to successive Counts of Holland and never acknowledged by the Frisians. In efforts to weld together the various provinces the months passed, until a new turn of foreign events began to absorb the duke's whole attention.

The details of English politics with all the reasons for revolution and counter-revolution involved in the complicated civil disorders, the Wars of the Roses, affected Charles's policy but they can only be suggested in his biography. It must be remembered that the modern impression of English stability and French fickleness in political institutions, an impression casting reflections direct and indirect upon literature as well as history, is based on the changes in France from 1789 down to the fourth quarter of the nineteenth century. Quite the reverse is the earlier tradition based on the kaleidoscopic shifts familiar to several generations of observers in the fifteenth century[1]; stable and firm felt the French as they heard the tidings of the brief triumphs of belligerent factions across the Channel.

Since 1461, Henry VI. of the House of Lancaster had been a passive prisoner, while Margaret of Anjou had exhausted herself in efforts to win adherents at home and abroad for her captive husband and her exiled son.[2] In 1463, she had received some aid, some encouragement from Philip of Burgundy, although he had recognised Edward IV. as king and although, too, his personal sympathies were Yorkish rather than Lancastrian.

It was Charles who escorted the errant lady into Lille, but later the duke himself entertained her munificently. The poverty-stricken exile prob-

[1] From Henry VI.–Henry VII. the English throne was twice lost and twice regained by each of the rival Houses of York and Lancaster. Thirteen pitched battles were fought between Englishmen on English soil. Three out of four kings died by violence. Eighty persons connected with the blood royal were executed or assassinated.

[2] Ramsay, *Lancaster and York*, ii., 232 *et seq.;* Oman, *Hundred Years' War* and *Warwick, the King-maker*, are followed here in addition to Kirk, Lavisse, etc.

ably found the accompanying ducal gifts more to the immediate purpose than the ducal feasts. Two thousand gold crowns were bestowed upon herself, a hundred upon each of her ladies, while various Lancastrian nobles were tided over hard times by useful sums of money.

Pleasant though the recognition was, however, the pecuniary assistance was quite insufficient to accomplish Margaret's purpose. For nine years Edward IV. sat on his throne and no serious efforts were made to dislodge him. As he never forgot his mother's lineage, the sympathies of Charles of Burgundy were with the exiles, and Queen Margaret may have counted confidently on that sympathy proving valuable for her son as soon as Charles himself had a free hand. But when he came into his heritage, his marriage with Margaret of York put a definite end to those hopes. The new duke thereby declared his acceptance of the king whom the Earl of Warwick had seated upon the English throne. Then came clashing of wills between that king and his too powerful subject-adviser.[1] To punish his unruly royal protégé, Warwick turned his attention to the Duke of Clarence, brother and heir presumptive to Edward IV. A marriage was planned between this possible future monarch and the earl's eldest daughter and then quickly celebrated

[1] That the king chose his wife without the earl's knowledge or consent has been accepted as the chief cause, and again denied by various authorities.

at Calais without the king's knowledge (July, 1469).

In the same summer occurred a rising in Yorkshire, possibly instigated by Warwick.[1] The malcontents, sixty thousand strong, declared that the king was giving ear to base counsellors and must be coerced into better ways. An attempt to suppress this revolt by the royal troops resulted in a pitched battle where Earl Rivers, the father of Elizabeth Woodville, the young queen, was taken prisoner and beheaded.

Edward, baffled, finally turned for aid to Warwick. Over the Channel hastened the earl and his new son-in-law, levied troops, met the king at Olney, and—Edward found himself if not exactly a prisoner, at least under restraint. Two sovereigns—both without power even over their own actions,—such was the situation in England at the end of 1469, when Charles of Burgundy was self-complacently regarding Louis XI. as a foe convinced of his own inferiority.

A menacing letter from this redoubtable ducal brother-in-law was probably the reason why Edward IV. was set at liberty, and why a reconciliation was patched up between him and his councillor, with full pardon for Warwick's adherents. But it was short-lived. A fresh outbreak in March, 1470, made another change. Warwick and Clarence sided with the rebels, the king was victorious, and his unfaithful friend and brother were

[1] See Oman's *Warwick*, p. 185.

English Affairs

again forced to flee under a shower of menaces hurled after them.

"But, and He [Clarence] or Richart Erle of Warrewyk our Rebell and Traytour come into oure seid Land we woll . . . that ye doo Hym and Theym to be arrested . . . He that Taketh and Bryngeth unto Us either of theym, he shal have for his Reward C.*l* of Land in Yerely Value to Hym and to his Heyres or Mil. *Lib* in Redy money at his election."[1]

Such was the proclamation issued on March 22d by the king himself at York.

Between Edward and Charles a new link had just been forged in the chain of friendship. The Order of the Garter is thus acknowledged by the duke:

"We have to-day received from our much honoured seigneur and brother, the king of England, his Order of the Garter together with the mantle and other ornaments and things appertaining to the said Order and have . . . taken the oath according to the statutes of the Order.

"Done in our city of Ghent under our Grand Seal, February 4, 1469 [O. S.]."[2]

Now it was in consideration of needs that might arise in the near future, following on the trail of these wide-reaching English convulsions, that Charles felt it necessary to make preparations for

[1] Rymer, *Fœdera*, xi., 654; negotiations had been going on for about a year.
[2] *Ibid.*, 651.

a strong military defence calculated to suit any emergency. Louis XI. had a permanent force at his command. He had made the beginning of the French standing army, the nucleus of one of those bodies that have ever since urged each other on to expensive growth from opposite sides of European frontiers. What one monarch possessed that must his near neighbour have.

Feudal service, volunteer militia, paid mercenaries, were all alike unstable bulwarks for a nation. Nation as yet Charles had not, but he wanted to be betimes with his bulwarks. This was why he issued an ordinance for the levy of a thousand lances, amounting to five thousand combatants, to be paid with regular wages and kept ready at call under officers of his own appointment. The ducal treasury could not stand the whole expense. To meet the deficit, Charles asked from his Netherland Estates an annual subsidy of 120,000 crowns for three years. Power to impose taxes he had none. A request to each individual province was all the requisition that he could make.

In this case, most of the provinces approached had acceded to the demand, when the Estates of Flanders convened at Lille. Here the Chancellor of Burgundy expounded to them the grounds of the demand, and then the session was changed to Bruges, where they debated on the merits of the request, urged on further by explanatory letters from Charles. Finally, a deputation was appointed by the Estates to go over to Ghent and

English Affairs

present a *Remonstrance* to their impatient sovereign beggar.

Three points were set forth. The deputies objected to this grant being asked only from the lands *de par de ça*—the Netherlands and not from the Burgundies. Secondly, they wished a definite assessment imposed on each province. Thirdly, they desired a declaration that the fiefs and arrière-fiefs already bound to furnish troops should be exempt from share in this tax. The remonstrance was courtly in tone. Written in French, the concluding phrases were in Latin and suggested that nothing was more becoming a prince than clemency, especially towards his subjects.[1]

Vigorous and emphatic was the prince's response.[2] How could Burgundy furnish money? It is a poor land. It takes after France.[3] But its men make a third of the army. They are the Burgundian contribution. As to an assessment, what is the use unless the tax is surely to be paid? Only out of malice is this idle point suggested.

"You act as you have always done—you Flemings. Neither to my father nor to me have you ever been liberal. What you have granted—sometimes more than our request—has always been given so tardily as to prove the lack of good will. Your Flemish

[1] "Quia nihil est quod ita relucet in principe sicut clemencia et maxime circa domesticos et subditos."

[2] Gachard, *Doc. inéd.*, i., 216. The editor thinks that the speech was preserved in the register of Ypres just as it was delivered, untouched by chroniclers.

[3] *Il sent la France.*

skulls are hard and thick and you cling to your stubborn and perverse opinions. . . . I am half of France and half of Portugal and I know how to meet such heads as yours, ay and *will* do it. You have always either hated or despised your prince—if powerful you hated, if weak you despised. I prefer your hatred to your contempt. Not for your privileges or anything else will I permit myself to be trampled on—and I have the power to prevent such trampling."

Laying stress on the extreme modesty of his demand, whose purpose mainly was for defence of Flanders, the duke proceeded to berate his visitors soundly for their presumptuous haggling, declaring that as to the fiefs and arrière-fiefs he would see to it that no double burdens were borne.

"And when you shall have determined to accord my request,—which you will assuredly do (and I do not mean to burden you further unless I am forced to it),—send some of your deputies after me to Lille or St. Omer, and there, with my chancellor and my council, I will determine the apportionment and we will speak also of other matters touching my province of Flanders."

It was this vehement oratory—and this vehemence was repeated on many occasions—that did more to alienate Charles from his hereditary subjects than his actual demands. There is little doubt that his period of residence in their midst brought with it hatred rather than liking. No political error of his serves to explain the Flemish attitude towards the duke as does his method of address, the gratuitous contempt displayed towards burghers whose purses were needed for his game. The *aide* was granted, indeed, but it was levied with sullen reluctance.

What cause Charles had to make his preparations, what were the proceedings of the English exiles may be seen from the following letters to his mother and to the town of Ypres. The first is probably in answer to her questionings; the second is a specimen of the epistles showered upon the border towns.

" TO MY VERY REDOUBTABLE LADY AND MOTHER,
    MADAME THE DUCHESS, AT AIRE:

"May it please you to know that in regard to what the Sgr. de Crèvecœur has written you about the king's proclamations that he intends to maintain his treaties and promises to me, etc., and has no desire to sustain the Earl of Warwick, and wishes my subjects to be reimbursed for the damages inflicted by him and his, assuredly, my Lady and Mother, the contrary has been and is well known before the said publications and after. The Earl of Warwick is my foe and could not, according to the treaty existing between the king and me, be received in Normandy or elsewhere in the realm . . . [complaints about the procedure have been sent to king and parliament and councillors, without redress, etc.] What is more, the Admiral of France has sent thither a spy under pretext of carrying a letter to Sgr. de la Groothuse, which man was charged to spy upon my ships and by means of a caravel named the *Brunette*, sent for this purpose by the admiral, to cut the cables to set them adrift and founder—or to capture certain ships with such captains, knights, and gentlemen as he could find, and myself, too, if they were able.

"Furthermore, the said spy was charged to spy on my towns, etc., and those of the caravel called the *Brunette* were charged, if they failed in taking my ships, or in cutting their cables, to set fire to them —all in direct conflict with the terms of the treaties, and procedures that the king would never have tolerated had he had the slightest intention of maintaining his word . . . [Charles does not consider Groothuse to blame at all, etc.][1]

Letter from Charles of Burgundy to the Magistrates of Ypres, June 10, 1470

"DEAR FRIENDS:

"It has come to your knowledge how after the Duke of Clarence and the Earl of Warwick were expelled from England on account of their sedition and their ill deeds, they have declared themselves both by words and deeds of aggression our enemies, and on *Vendredi absolut*[2] went so far as to capture by fraud ships and property belonging to our subjects, and have further done damage whenever opportunity presented itself.

"In order to repel them we have ordered them to be attacked on the sea. Moreover, at the same time we were advised that the same Clarence and Warwick and their people, after they were routed at sea by the

---

[1] Middleburg, the 3d of June, 1470. "Madame's sign manual" on the copy is dated June 6th. (Plancher, *Histoire générale et particulière de Bourgogne*, etc., iv., cclxxi).

[2] Good Friday, April 20th.

troops of my honoured lord and brother, Edward, King of England, retreated to the marches of Normandy and were honourably received at Honfleur by the Admiral of France with all which they had saved from the raid on our subjects after the defeat.

"All this was direct infringement of the treaties lately made between Monseigneur the king and myself. Therefore, we wrote at once to Monsgr. the king begging him not to favour or aid the said Clarence and Warwick in his land of Normandy or elsewhere in his realm, nor to permit them to sell or distribute the property of our subjects, and to show his will by publishing such prohibitions throughout Normandy and elsewhere where need is.

"Also we wrote to the court of parliament at Paris, and to the council of my said seigneur at Rouen. The answer was that the king meant to keep the treaty between him and us and had ordered his subjects in Normandy not to retain the property belonging to our subjects . . . but we have since learned that, notwithstanding, this same property has been distributed and ransoms have been negotiated in the sight and knowledge of the Admiral of France and his officers.

"Moreover, it is perfectly evident that by means of the aid furnished by the king to the said Clarence and Warwick, the latter are enabled to continue the war on our subjects and not on the English, it being understood that they who were banished from England are not strong enough to return by the force of arms but must do so by friendship and favour. . . . On account of the above and other depredations, we shall attack the said Warwick and Clarence on the sea as pirates, and all who aid them as is needful for the protection of our lands and subjects. "Written at Middelburg in Zealand, June 20, 1470."[1]

"Tell Monsieur de Warwick that the king will assist him to recover England either with the help of Queen Margaret or by whatever other means he may propose. . . . Only let him communicate his desires in this respect as speedily as possible and the king will lay aside all other affairs for the purpose of accomplishing it,"

wrote the complaisant King of France in his directions to the confidential messenger sent to discuss matters with the English earl.[2]

But that was not his language towards his cousin of Burgundy, whom he assured that there should be no infringement of their treaty, and that it was greatly to his royal displeasure that Flemish property captured at sea in defiance of that treaty should be sold in French market-places. There is a hot correspondence,[3] that is, it is hot on the side of Charles, while Louis's phrases are smoothly surprised at there being any cause for dissatisfaction. The circumstances shall be investigated, his cousin satisfied, etc. One letter from the duke to two of Louis's council is emphatic in its expressions of doubt as to the good faith of these royal statements:

"ARCHBISHOP AND YOU ADMIRAL:

"The vessels which you assure me are destined by

---

[1] Gachard, *Doc. inéd.*, i., 226.
[2] Comines–Lenglet., "Preuves," iii., 124. Written at Amboise, May, 12, 1470.   [3] Plancher, iv., cclxi., etc.

the king for an attack on England have attempted nothing except against my subjects; but, by St. George, if some redress be not seen to, I will take the matter into my own hands without waiting for your motions, tardy and dilatory as they are."[1]

Reprisals were made accordingly, and the innocent French merchants, coming peaceably to the fair at Antwerp, suffered confiscation of their private property, while the duke felt fully justified in stationing his fleet off the coast of Normandy to guard the Channel. Philip de Commines was one of the company who went at the duke's behest to Calais to urge the governor, Wenlock, to be faithful to King Edward, and to give no shelter to the rebellious earl and his protégé Clarence.[2]

Louis feared an outbreak of hostilities at an inconvenient moment. He temporised. To Warwick, he denied a personal interview, but at the same time he sent him a confidential emissary, Sr. du Plessis, to whom he wrote as follows:

"Monsieur du Plessis, you know the desire I have for Warwick's return to England, as well because I wish to see him get the better of his enemies—or that at least through him the realm of England may be embroiled—as to avoid the questions which have arisen out of his sojourn here. . . . For you know that these Bretons and Burgundians have no other aim than to find a pretext for rupturing peace

[1] Duke Charles to the Council of the King at Rouen, May 29th. (Plancher, iv., cclxix.)
[2] *Mémoires*, iii., ch. iv.

and reopening the war, which I do not wish to see commenced under this colour. . . . Wherefore I pray you take pains, you and others there, to induce Mons. de Warwick to depart by all arguments possible. Pray use the sweetest methods that you can, so that he shall not suspect that we are thinking of anything else but his personal advantage."[1]

To gain time was Louis's ardent wish at that moment. The envoys sent by Louis to placate the duke's resentment at the incidents in connection with the Warwick affair, and to assure him that Louis meant well by him and his subjects, found Charles holding high state at St. Omer. When they were admitted to audience, the duke was discovered sitting on a lofty throne, five feet above floor level, "higher than was the wont of king or emperor to sit." His hat remained on his head as the representatives of his feudal overlord bowed to him and he acknowledged their obeisance by a slight nod and a gesture permitting them to rise.

Hugonet, a member of the ducal council, answered their address with a prosy speech. Burgundian officials revelled in grandiloquent phrases—which this time bored Charles. He cut short the harangue impatiently, took the floor himself, and made a statement of the injuries he had suffered. Louis had promised to be his friend, but he was aiding the foe of the duke's brother. The envoys repeated their sovereign's offers of

[1] Duclos, "Preuves," v., 296.

redress. Charles declared that redress was impossible. Pained, very pained were the French envoys to think that a petty dispute could not be settled amicably. "The king desires to avoid friction. He offers you friendship, peace, and redress for every wrong. It will not be his fault if trouble ensue. Monseigneur, the king and you have a judge who is above you both."

The insinuation that it was he who was ready to break the peace infuriated Charles. He started to his feet, his eyes flashing with fire. "Among us Portuguese there is a custom that when our friends become friends to our foes we send them to the hundred thousand devils of hell."[1] "A piece of bad taste to send by implication a king of France to a hundred thousand devils," comments the suave Chastellain, aghast at this impolite, emphatic, though indirect reference to Louis XI.

Equally aghast were the Burgundian courtiers present at this occasion. After all, they, too, were French by nature. To wreck the new-made peace for the sake of the English alliance, which had never been really popular among them, that seemed an act of rash unwisdom.

"A murmur went the rounds of the ducal suite because their chief thus implied contempt for the name of France to which the duke belonged. Not going

[1] Chastellain, v., 453. These phrases are, to be sure, those of our literary and imaginative chronicler, but the substance is that of attested words from Charles. M. Petit-Dutaillis accepts it. (Lavisse, iv[ii]., 363.)

quite so far as to call himself English, though that was what his heart was, he boasted of his mother, ancient friend of England and enemy of France."

There were, indeed, times when the duke was more emphatic in asserting his English blood. Plancher cites a scrap of writing in his own hands which probably belonged to a letter to the magistrates and citizens of Calais, whom he addresses, "O you my friends."[1] While reiterating that he simply must defend his own state he adds, "By St. George who knows me to be a better Englishman and more anxious for the weal of England than you other English . . . [you] shall recognise that I am sprung from the blood of Lancaster," etc. His claims of kinship varied with the circumstances.

While he was so conscious of his own greatness, present and future, and of his own laudable intentions to do well by his subjects, it is quite possible, too, that Charles was puzzled more or less consciously by his failure to win popularity. For he was quite as unpopular with his courtiers as with his subjects. The former did not like the rigid court rules. There was no pleasure in sitting through audiences silent and stiff "as at a sermon," and exposed to personal reprimands from their chief if there were the slightest lapses from his standard of conduct. They did not know on what meat the duke was feeding his imagination,

[1] *See* Plancher, iv., cclxxxix.

an imagination that already saw him as Cæsar. Had he actually attained the loftier rank that he dreamed of, his premature arrogance might have been forgotten, but his pride of glory invisible to the world about him was undoubtedly a bar to his popularity during the years 1470–73.

Before this pompous scene passed at St. Omer, Louis had been relieved of anxiety in regard to the stability of his kingdom, and the dangers of an heir like his brother who might easily be used as a tool by some clever faction opposed to the ruling monarch. On June 10th, a son was born to him, afterwards Charles VIII. of France. Complaisant still were his words to his Burgundian cousin, but the moment was drawing near when his efforts to circumvent him were no longer secret.

The embassy returned home. Possibly their report of the duke's passionate words goaded the king into discarding his mask of friendship. At any rate, his next steps were unequivocal in showing which side of the fresh English quarrel he meant to espouse. Margaret of Anjou hated the Earl of Warwick, not only because he had unseated her husband but because he had doubted her fidelity to that husband. Nevertheless, under Louis's persuasions, she consented to forget her past wrongs and to stake her future hopes on fraternising with him on a basis of common hate for Edward IV. The alliance was to be sealed by the marriage of young Edward of Lancaster, the prince whose very legitimacy Warwick had questioned, with the earl's younger daughter. It was a singular union to be accepted by the parents, separated as they had been by the wall of insults interchanged during more than a decade of bitter enmity.

Louis brought his cousin to this step of concession. She saw her seventeen-year-old son betrothed to the sixteen-year-old Anne Neville, and later she herself swore reconciliation to Warwick on a piece of the true cross in St. Mary's Church at Angers (August 4, 1470).

"Monsieur du Plessis [wrote Louis XI. on July 25th], I have sent you Messire Ivon du Fou, to put the affairs of Monsieur de Warwick in surety, and I order him to make such arrangements that the people of the said M. de Warwick will suffer no necessity until he is there. To-day we have made the marriage of the Queen of England and of him, and hope tomorrow to have all in readiness to depart."[1]

[1] "Aujourd'hui avons fait le mariage de la reine d'Angleterre et de lui." Undoubtedly a half jocose way of stating the alliance of the children. The following item occurs in the King's accounts for December, 1470: "à maistre Jehan le prestre, la somme de xxvii l. x s.t pour vingt escus d'or à lui donnée par le roy, pour le restituer de semblable somme que, par l'ordonnance d'icellui seigneur, il avait baillée du sien au vicaire de Bayeux auquel icellui seigneur en a fait don en faveur de ce qu' il estait venu espouser le prince de Galles à la fille du Comte de Warwick." This was a betrothal, not the actual marriage. In August, Louis was still asking for a dispensation. (Wavrin, Dupont ed., iii., 41, note. See also *Lettres de Louis XI.*, iv., 131.)

MEDAL OF CHARLES, DUKE OF BURGUNDY
(FROM BARANTE)

Meanwhile, the king kept agents in all the Somme towns, insinuating opposition to the duke, and reminding the citizens that they were French at heart. His ambassadors passed in and out of the Burgundian court, saying many things in secret besides those they said in public. Plenty there were that wished for war, remarks the observant Commines. Nobles like St. Pol and others could not maintain the same state in peace as in war, and state they loved. In time of war four hundred lances attended the constable, and he had a large allowance to maintain them from which he reaped many a profitable commission besides the fees of his office and his other emoluments. " Moreover," adds Commines, " the nobles were accustomed to say among themselves that if there were no battles without, there would be quarrels within the realm."

The matter of the grants to Charles of France had been settled to his royal brother's liking, not to that of his Burgundian ally. Champagne and Brie, so cheerfully promised at Peronne, were withdrawn and Guienne substituted. When Normandy had been exchanged for Champagne and Brie, as it was arranged at Peronne, Charles of Burgundy approved the change as he thought it assured him an obedient friend as neighbour.[1] The second change, Guienne instead of Champagne and Brie, was quite a different thing.

[1] A group of smaller seigniories was also involved, Quercy, Périgord, La Rochelle, etc. *See* letter-patent, (Comines–Lenglet, "Preuves," iii., 97.)

Guienne bordered the Bay of Biscay far away from Burgundy. Naturally, Charles was not content. Then, too, it looked as though he had lost a useful friend as well as a neighbour, for the new Duke of Guienne was formally reconciled to his brother and took oath that his fraternal devotion to his monarch should never again waver.

Long before Charles was completely convinced that Louis was not going to maintain the humble attitude assumed at Peronne and Liege, he became very suspicious that intrigues were on foot against him. "He hastened to Hesdin where he entered into jealousy of his servants" says Commines. That he was assured that there were reasons for his apprehensions appears in an epistle circulated as an open letter,[1] to various cities, wherein he makes a detailed statement of the plots against his life by one Jehan d'Arson and Baldwin, son of Duke Philip.

Sorry return was this from one recognised as Bastard of Burgundy and brought up in the ducal household. Further, one Jehan de Chassa, Charles's own chamberlain, had taken French leave of the duke's service and made his way to the king in his castle of Amboise, where he had been pleasantly received and promised rich reward when he had "executed his damnable designs against our person."

Messengers sent by this Chassa to Baldwin in Charles's court at St. Omer were arrested as sus-

[1] Duclos, "Preuves" v., 302.

OMAN, CHARLES W. C. *Warwick the Kingmaker.* 1890.

ONUFRIUS DE SANCTA CROCE, Bishop of Tricaria. *Mémoire sur les affaires de Liege* (1468). (Ed., S. Bormans.) (Brussels, 1885.)

OUDENBOSCH. *Veterum scriptorum et monumentorum, historicorum,* etc. *Rerum Leodiensius. Opus Adriani de vetere Buseo,* 1343. See Marténe.

PICQUÉ, CAMILLE. *Mémoire sur Philippe de Commines.* (Brussels, 1864.) Mém. couronnés par l'acad. royale de Belgique, vol. xvi.

PIOT, G. J. C., Ed. *Chronycke van Nederlandt*—1565. *Vlaamsche Kronijk*—1598. *Collection des chroniques belges.* (Brussels, 1836–.)

PIRENNE, HENRI. *Histoire de Belgique.* 2 vols. (Brussels, 1903.)

PIRENNE, HENRI. *Bibliographie de l'histoire de Belgique : catalogue méthodique et chronologique des sources et des ouvrages principaux relatifs à l'histoire de tous les Pays-Bas jusqu' en 1598.* (Brussels, 1902.)

PLANCHER, URBAIN. *Histoire générale et particulière de Bourgogne avec des notes et les preuves justificatives,* etc. 4 vols. (Dijon, 1739.)

POICTIERS, ALIENOR DE. *Les honneurs de la cour.* (In Sainte-Palaye, *Mémoires sur l'ancienne chevalerie,* vol. 2, pp. 171–267.) (Paris, 1781.)

POLAIN, M. L. *Récits historiques sur l'ancien pays de Liège.* 4th ed. (Brussels, 1866.)

PUTNAM, RUTH. *A Mediæval Princess.* (New York, 1904.)

RAM, P. F. X. DE. *Documents relatifs aux troubles du pays de Liège sous les princes-évêques Louis de Bourbon et Jean de Horne.* 1 vol. (Brussels, 1844.)

RAMSAY, SIR JAMES H. *Lancaster and York, a Century of English History* (A.D., 1399–1485). 2 vols. (Oxford, 1892.)

REIFFENBERG, BARON F. A. DE. *Essai sur les enfants naturels de Philippe de Bourgogne.*

REIFFENBERG, BARON F. A. DE. *Histoire de l'Ordre de la Toison d'Or.* (Brussels, 1830.)

REIFFENBERG, BARON F. A. DE. *Mémoire sur le sejour de Louis XI. aux Pays-Bas.* Nouveaux mém. de l'acad. royale. 1829.

REIFFENBERG, BARON F. A. DE. *De l'état de la population,*

etc., *dans les Pays-Bas pendant le XV⁰ et le XVI⁰ siècle*. Mem. de l'acad. royale in 4°. (Brussels, 1822.)

[Also editor of various works.]

RODT, EMANUEL VON. *Die Feldzüge Karls des Kühnen*. 2 vols. (Schaffhausen, 1843.)

ROLAND, P. AUBERT. *La guerre de René II. contre Charles le Hardi*. (Luxembourg, 1742.)

ROYE, JEAN DE. *Chronique scandaleuse*. [A journal of the years 1460–1483.] (Ed. Bernard de Mandrot.) 2 vols. (Paris, 1894–96.)

RUHL, GUSTAVE. *L'expedition des Franchimontoir en 1468*. Soc. d'art et d'histoire de Liège, ix. (Liege, 1895.)

RYMER, THOMAS. *Fœdera, conventiones, litteræ et cujuscumque generis acta publica inter reges Angliæ et alios quosvis reges*, etc. 20 vols. Vol. xi. (London, 1704–1716.)

SCHELLHASE, K. "Zur Trierer Zusammenkunft im Jahre 1473." In *Deutsche Zeitschrift für Geschichtswissenschaft*. Band VI. (Freiburg, 1891.)

SELDEN, JOHN. *Titles of Honor*. 3d ed. (London, 1672.)

SNOY, RENIER (Snoyus Reinerus). *De rebus Batavicis*. (Frankfurt, 1620.) In fol.

STEIN, H. "*Olivier de la Marche historien, poete et diplomate Bourgogne*." In mén couronné etc., par l'acad. royale vol. xlix. (Brussels, 1888.)

STOUFF, LOUIS. *Les comtes de Bourgogne et leurs villes domaniales*. (Paris, 1899.)

STOUFF, LOUIS. "Les possessions bourguignonnes dans la vallée du Rhin sous Charles le téméraire." *Annales de l'est*. Vols. xvii.–xviii. (Paris, 1903.)

TOUTEY, E. *Charles le téméraire et la ligue de Constance*. (Paris, 1902.)

VANDER MAELEN, PH. *Dictionnaire géographique de la province de Liège*. (Brussels, 1831.)

WAGENAAR, JAN. *Vaderlandsche Historie*. 21 vols. (Amsterdam, 1749–1759.)

WAVRIN, JEHAN DE (living 1465–1471). *Anchiennes croniques de Engleterre*. (Ed. Mlle. Dupont.) 3 vols. (Paris, 1858–63.)

Even Commines shows that it is not surprising that there was unanimity[1] in the declaration that according to God and his conscience in all honour and justice the king was released from those treaties, and the way was paved for an invasion into Picardy as soon as possible.

Charles's public accusations of plots against him did not go unanswered. Jehan de Chassa promptly issued a rejoinder:

"As Charles, soi-disant Duke of Burgundy, has sent to divers places letters signed by himself and his secretary, Jehan le Gros, written at Hesdin, December 13th, falsely charging me with plotting against his life with Baldwin, Bastard of Burgundy, and Jehan d'Arson, I, considering that it is matter touching my honour, feel bound to reply. . . . By God and by my soul I declare that these charges against me made by Charles of Burgundy are false and disloyal lies."[2]

Baldwin, too, expressed righteous indignation at the slur on his character, but he remained in the French court as did many others who had formerly served Charles.

Meanwhile, the Earl of Warwick, having left his daughter in the hands of Margaret of Anjou, openly aided by Louis, sailed back to England in September. But there had been one further change of base of which the earl was still unconscious. His

[1] *See* Lavisse iv[ii]., 364. He states that the king named all the deputies that the towns were to appoint.
[2] Duclos, "Preuves," v., 307.

picious, and that circumstance frightened Baldwin and caused him to take to his heels, leaving his retinue, his horses, and his baggage behind. He dreaded lest he might be attainted and convicted of treason, and therefore he took shelter with the king.

"Saved from this conspiracy by the goodness and clemency of God, we inform you of the events so that you may render thanks by public processions, solemn masses, sermons, and prayers, beseeching Him devoutly and from the heart that He will always guard and defend our person, our lands, seigniories, and subjects from such plots.

"May God protect you, dear subjects. Written in our castle of Hesdin, December 13, 1470.

"CHARLES.
"LE GROS."

It was not long before Charles had less reason to fear French "subtleties." At an assembly of notables[1] convened at Tours at the end of 1470, Louis dropped the mask of friendship worn uneasily for just two years, and made an open brief of his grievances against the duke.

His case was cited with a luxury of detail more or less authentic. The interview at Peronne was a simple trap conceived by Balue and the Duke of Burgundy. The treaties of 1465 and 1468, both obtained by undue pressure, had not been respected by Charles, etc. The assembly was obedient to suggestion. It was a packed house.

[1] Comines–Lenglet, "Preuves," iii., 68; Lavisse, iv[ii]., 364.

elder son-in-law had not rejoiced in the Warwick-Lancaster alliance. It brought young Prince Edward to the fore, and bereft the Duke of Clarence—long ready to replace Edward of York—of any immediate prospects. Therefore he was inclined to accept offers of a reconciliation tendered him by King Edward.

Despite his secret change of heart, Clarence sailed with Warwick and joined with him in the proclamations scattered over England, declaring that the exiles were returning to "set right and justice to their places, and to reduce and redeem for ever the realm from its thraldom." Never a mention of either Edward IV. or Henry VI. Perhaps it was as convenient to see which way the wind blew and to put in a name accordingly.

On landing, however, "King Henry VI." was raised as a cry. In Nottinghamshire, where Edward lay, not a word was heard for York. There was no conflict. Edward felt that Fate had turned against him and off he rode to Lyme with a small following, took ship, and made for Holland. It was stormy, pirates from the Hanseatic towns gave chase, and glad was Edward to take shelter at Alkmaar where De la Groothuse, Governor of Holland, welcomed him in the name of the duke.[1] Edward was quite destitute. He had nothing with which to pay his fare across the Channel but a gown lined with marten's fur, and as for his train, never so poor a company was seen.

[1] Commines, iii., ch. v.

Eleven days later, Warwick was master of all England and official business was transacted in the name of Henry VI., "limp and helpless on his throne as a sack of wool." He was a mere shadow and pretence and what was done in his name was done without his will or knowledge.

Charles of Burgundy did not hasten to greet his unbidden guest. He would rather have heard that his brother-in-law were dead, but he bade Groothuse show him every courtesy and supply him with necessaries and five hundred crowns a month for luxuries. After a time, and perhaps informed by weather prophets that the Lancastrian wind blowing over in England was but a fickle breeze, he consented to forget his hereditary sympathies.

"The same day that the duke received news of the king's arrival in Holland, I was come from Calais to Boulogne (where the duke then lay) ignorant of the event and of the king's flight.[1] The duke was first advised that he was dead, which did not trouble him much for he loved the Lancaster line far better than that of York. Besides he had with him the Dukes of Exeter and of Somerset and divers others of King Henry's faction, by which means he thought himself assured of peace with the line of Lancaster. But he feared the Earl of Warwick, neither knew he how to content him that was to come to him, I mean King Edward, whose sister he had married and who was also brother-in-arms, for the king wore the Golden Fleece and the duke the Garter.

"Straightway then the duke sent me back to Calais

[1] Commines, iii., ch. vi.

English Affairs

accompanied by a gentleman or two of this new faction of Henry, and gave me instructions how to deal with this new world, urging me to go because it was important for him to be well served in the matter.[1] I went as far as Tournehem, a castle near to Guisnes, and then dared not proceed because I found people fleeing for fear of the English who were devastating the country. . . . Never before had I needed a safe-conduct for the English are very honourable. All this seemed very strange to me for I had never seen these mutations in the world."

Commines was uncertain as to what he had better do and wanted instructions. "The duke sent me a ring from his finger, bidding me go forward with the promise that if I were taken prisoner he would redeem me." New surprises met the envoy at Calais. None of the well-known faces were to be seen. "Further, upon the gate of my lodgings and the very door of my chamber were a hundred white crosses and rhymes signifying that the King of France and Earl of Warwick were one—all of which seemed strange to me." Well received was Commines and entertained at dinner. It was told at table how within a quarter of an hour after the arrival of news from England every man wore this livery (the ragged staff of Warwick), so speedy and sudden was the change. "This is the first time that I ever knew how little stable are these mundane affairs."

[1] *See* instructions given to him for this mission, Wavrin-Dupont, iii., 271.

"In all communications that passed between them and me, I repeated that King Edward was dead, of which fact I said I was well assured, notwithstanding that I knew the contrary, adding further that though it were not so, yet was the league between the Duke of Burgundy and the king and realm of England such that this accident could not infringe it—whomever they would acknowledge as king him would we recognise. . . . Thus it was agreed that the league should remain firm and inviolate between us and the king and realm of England save that for Edward we named Henry."

Commines explains further that the wool trade was what made amity with England necessary to Flanders and Holland, "which is the principal cause that moved the merchants to labour earnestly for peace."

Charles made vague promises to his uninvited guest, declaring ostentatiously that his blood was Lancastrian. Nevertheless he finally consented to an interview with him of York, in spite of the remonstrances of the Lancastrians, Somerset and Exeter. "The duke could not tell whom to please and either party he feared to displease. But in the end, because sharp war was upon him face to face, he inclined to the English dukes, accepting their promises against the Earl of Warwick, their ancient enemy." King Edward, "who was on the spot and very ill at ease," was quieted by secret assurances that the duke was obliged to dissimulate. "Seeing that he could not keep

English Affairs

the king but that he was bound to return to England and fearing for divers considerations altogether to discontent him, Charles pretended that he could not aid the king and forbade his subjects to enter his service." Privately, however, he gave him fifty thousand florins of St. Andrew's cross, and had two or three ships fitted out at Vere in Zealand, a harbour where all nations were received. Besides this he secretly hired fourteen well appointed ships of the Easterlings, which promised to serve him till he landed in England and for fifteen days after, "great aid considering the times."

King Edward departed out of Flanders in the year 1471, when the Duke of Burgundy went to wrest Amiens and St. Quentin back from the king.[1] "The said duke thought now howsoever the world went in England he could not speed amiss because he had friends on both sides."[2]

Edward's adventures in England proved that he had not lost his hold there. Warwick's extraordinary brief success was but a flash in the pan. London opened her gates and then the pitched battle at Barnet gave a final verdict between the rival Houses which England accepted. This battle was fought on April 14th, when the thick fog and the like speech of the two bodies caused hopeless confusion. Many friends slew each other unwittingly, and among the slain was the indefatigable,

[1] Commines, iii., ch. vii.
[2] As soon as Edward and his English exiles sailed, Charles published a proclamation forbidding his subjects to aid him.

energetic Warwick who had hoped to play with his royal puppets. Only forty-four was he and worthy of a better and more statesmanlike career.

On that same day Margaret of Anjou and her son landed at Weymouth. Hearing of Warwick's death, they tried to reach Wales but were intercepted and forced to fight at Tewkesbury. Here the young prince, too, met his death. To Edward's direct command is attributed the murder of the unfortunate Henry VI. in the Tower, which happened at about the same time. The desolated Margaret of Anjou lingered five years under restraint in England before she was ransomed by King Louis.

"Sir John Paston to Margaret Paston. Wreten at London the Thorysdaye in Esterne weke, 1471.

"God hathe schewyd Hym selffe marvelouslye lyke Hym that made all and can undoo agayn whare Hym lyst." [1]

Charles of Burgundy could now pride himself on his foresight. His brother of the two Orders was himself again.

"The very day on which this fight happened [says Commines] the Duke of Burgundy, being before Amiens, received letters from the duchess his wife, that the King of England was not at all satisfied with him, that he had given his aid grudgingly and as if for very little cause he would have deserted him. To speak plainly there never was great friendship between

[1] *Letters*, iii., 4.

them afterwards. Yet the Duke of Burgundy seemed to be extremely pleased at this news and published it everywhere."

A transaction of his own of this time, the duke did not publish. It was a procedure perhaps justified by these wonderful "mutations in the world" which impressed Commines as strange and terrible. The Duke of Burgundy caused a legal document to be drawn up attesting his own heirship to Henry VI. of England, and filed the same in the Abbey of St. Bertin with all due formality. If there came more "mutations" in the world whose very existence was a new experience to Philip de Commines, Charles was ready to interpose his own plank in the new structure.

In the archives of the House of Croy in the château of Beaumont, rests this document, which was duly signed by Charles on November 3, 1471, in his own hand "so that greater faith" be given to the statement that no one was truer heir to the Lancaster House than Charles of Burgundy.[1] Two canons attested the instrument as notaries, and the witnesses were Hugonet, Humbercourt, and Bladet.

---

[1] *See* Gachard, *Études et Notices historiques concernant l'histoire des Pays-Bas*, ii., 343, en approuvant et emologant toutes les choses deseurdittes et chascune d'icelles et a fin que plus grant foy soit adjoustée à tout ce que cy desus est escript, avant signé ce présent instrument de nostre propre main et le fait sceller de nostre seau en signe de vérité, l'an et jour desusdit. [This in French, the body in Latin.]

"Charles."

It was expressly stipulated that if there were any delay in the duke's entering upon his English inheritance—which devolved to him through his mother,—a delay caused by motives of public utility of Christendom, and of the House of Burgundy, this should not prejudice his rights or those of his successors. A mere deferring of assuring the titles, etc., brought no prejudice to his rights. His delay ended in his death and Edward IV. never had to combat this claim of the brother-in-law who had helped him, though grudgingly, to regain his throne.

CHAPTER XV

NEGOTIATIONS AND TREACHERY

1471

ALL work had ceased at Paris for three days by the king's command, while praise was chanted to God, to the Virgin, and to all saints male and female, for the victory won by Henry of Lancaster, in 1470, over the base usurper Edward de la Marche. From Amboise, Louis made a special pilgrimage to Notre Dame de Celles at Poitiers to breathe in pious solitude his own prayers of thanksgiving for the happy event. The battle of Tewkesbury stemmed the course of this abundant stream of gratitude, and there were other thanksgivings.[1]

In the spring of 1471, Edward IV. was dating complacent letters from Canterbury to his good friends at Bruges,[2] acknowledging their valuable assistance, and to his brother Charles,[3] recognising his part in restoring Britain's rightful sovereign to his throne. To his sister, the Duchess of Burgundy, the returned exile gave substantial proof of his

[1] *Journal de Jean de Roye*, i., 258.
[2] Commynes-Dupont, iii., 202.
[3] Plancher, iv., cccvi., May 28th.

gratitude in the shape of privileges in wool manufacture and trade.[1]

Like one of the alternating figures in a Swiss weather vane the King of England had swung out into the open, pointing triumphantly to fair weather over his head, while Louis was forced back into solitary impotence. He seemed singularly isolated. His English friends were gone, his nobles were again forming a hostile camp around Charles of France, now Duke of Guienne, who had forgotten his late protestations of fraternal devotion, and there were many indications that the Anglo-Burgundian alliance might prove as serious a peril to France as it had in times gone by but not wholly forgotten.

The two most important of the disputed towns on the Somme were, however, in Louis's possession, and Charles of Burgundy, ready to reduce Amiens by siege on March 10, 1471, consented to stay his proceedings by striking a truce which was renewed in July. This afforded a valuable respite to the king, and he busied himself in energetic efforts to detach his brother from the group of malcontents. Various disquieting rumours about the prince's marriage projects caused his royal brother deep anxiety, and induced him to despatch a special envoy to Guienne. To that envoy Louis wrote as follows [2]:

[1] Rymer, *Fœdera*, xi., 735. *Pro Ducissa Burgundiæ super Lana claccanda*.
[2] *Lettres de Louis XI.*, iv., 256.

"Monseigneur du Bouchage:

"Guiot du Chesney[1] has brought me despatches from Monsg. de Guienne and Mons. de Lescun and has, further, mentioned three points to me: First, in behalf of Mme. de Savoy,[2] . . . second, in regard to M. d'Ursé . . . third, touching the mission of Mons. de Lescun to marry Monsg. of Guienne to the daughter of Monsg. de Foix. . . . The Ursé matter I will leave to you, and will agree to what you determine upon. On the spot you will be a better judge of what I ought to say and what would be advantageous to me, than I can here.

"In regard to the third point, the Foix marriage, you know what a misfortune it would be to me. Use all your five senses to prevent it. I am told that my brother does not really like the idea, and it has occurred to me that Mons. de Lescun has brought him to consent in order to further the marriage of the duchess,[3] so that in taking the sister, the duke will be relieved of this sum, a condition that would please him greatly because he has nothing to pay it with. I would prefer to pay both it and all the accompanying claims and then be through with it. In effect, I beg you make him agree to another [bride] before you leave, and do not be in any hurry to come to me. If this Aragon affair[4]

[1] One of Guienne's retinue who, later, passed to Louis's service.

[2] Louis's sister Yolande.

[3] The Duke of Brittany had married the third daughter of the Count de Foix.

[4] This was an allusion to a proposed marriage between Guienne and Jeanne, reputed daughter of Henry IV. of Castile. Vaesen cannot explain the use of Aragon. Various documents relating to this negotiation are given. (Comines–Lenglet, iii., 156.)

can be arranged you will place me in Paradise.

"*Item.* I have thought that Monsg. de Foix would not approve this Aragon girl, because he himself has some hopes of the kingdom of Aragon through his wife. If Monsg. of Guienne were advised of this, I believe it would help along our case.

"*Item.* It seems to me that you have a splendid opportunity to be very frank with my brother. For he has informed me through this man that the duke [of Brittany] has paid no attention to the representations made him in my behalf, through Corguilleray, and since my brother himself confides this to me, you have an opportunity to assure him that I thank him, and that I never cherish him so highly as when he tells me the truth, and that I now recognise that he does not desire to deceive me, since he does not spare the duke [of Brittany] and that, since he sees him opposed to me, he should return the seal that you know of and refuse to take his sister [Eleanor de Foix, the sister of the Duchess of Brittany], or to enter into any other league.

"If he will choose a wife quite above suspicion, as long as I live I will harbour no misgiving of him and he shall be as puissant in all the realm of France as I myself, as long as I live. In short, Mons. du Bouchage my friend, if you can gain this point, you will place me in Paradise. Stay where you are until Monseigneur de Lescun has arrived, and a good piece afterwards, even if you have to play the invalid, and before you depart put our affair in surety if you can, I implore you. And may God, Monseigneur du Bouchage my friend, to whom I pray, and may Nostre Dame de Behuart aid your negotiations. The women[1]

[1]Vaesen gives *femmes*, Duclos *filles*. The king was above all afraid that his brother might marry Mary of Burgundy.

of Mme. de Burgundy have all been ill with the *mal chault*, and it is reported that the daughter is seriously afflicted and bloated. Some say that she is already dead. I am not sure of the death but I am quite certain of the malady.

"Written at Lannoy, Aug. 18th.
"LOYS.
"TILHART."

That the king's professed confidence in his brother did not remove all suspicions of that young man's steadfastness from his mind is shown by the following letter, written two days later than the above, to Lorenzo de' Medici:

"Dear and beloved cousin, we have learned that our brother of Guienne has sent to Rome to ask a dispensation from the oath he swore to us, of which we send you a duplicate. Since you are a great favourite with our Holy Father pray use your influence with his Holiness so that our brother may not obtain his dispensation, and that his messenger may not be able to do any negotiating. In this you will do us a singular and agreeable pleasure which we will recognise in the future as we have in the past on fitting occasion. . . .

"Written at St. Michel sur Loire, August 20th.
"LOYS."

Louis does not seem to have taken his own doubts as to the very existence of Mary of Burgundy very seriously. While he was infinitely anxious to prevent her alliance with his brother, he made overtures to betroth her to his baby son, while he reminded her father in touching phrases that he, Louis, was Mary's loving godfather and hence exactly the person to be her father-in-law.

The winter of 1471–72 was filled with attempts to make terms between the king and the duke before the termination of the truce. The king was very hopeful of attaining this good result, and sweetly trustful of the duke's pacific and friendly intentions. He sternly refused to listen to suggestions that Charles meant to play him false and was very definite in his expressions of confidence. The following epistle to his envoys at the duke's court was an excellent document to fall by chance into Burgundian hands [1]:

"To Monsieur de Craon and Pierre d'Oriole:

"My cousin and monseigneur the general, I received your letters this evening at the hostelry of Montbazon where I came because I have not yet dared to go to Amboise.[2] When I imparted to you the doubts that I had heard, it was not with the purpose of delaying you in completing your business but only to advise you of the dangers that were in the air. And to free you from all doubts I assure you, that if Monseigneur of Burgundy is willing to confirm, by writing or verbally, the terms which we arranged at Orleans[3], I wish you to accept it and to clinch the matter and I am quite determined to trust to it. As

[1] *Lettres de Louis XI.*, iv., 286.

[2] There was a pestilence raging at Amboise.

[3] At Orleans, in the last days of October and the first of November, there was a conference wherein the king apparently promised to restore St. Quentin and Amiens to Charles, if he would renounce his alliance with the dukes of Brittany and Guienne and would betroth his daughter to the dauphin.

Negotiations and Treachery

to your suspicion that he may wish to make the chief promises in private letters without putting it in a formal shape, you know that I agreed to it by a pronotary, and when I have once accepted a thing I never withdraw my decision.

"My cousin and you monseigneur the general, see to it that Monseigneur of Burgundy gives you adequate assurance of the letters that he is to issue. When I once have the letter such as we agreed upon and he is bound, I do not doubt that he will keep faith. If my life were at stake, I am resolved to trust him. Do not send me any more of your suspicions for I assure you that my greatest worldly desire is that the matter be finished, since he has given verbal assurance that he wishes me well. You write that the pronotary told you that I was negotiating in every direction. By my faith, I have no ambassador but you, and by the words that Monseigneur of Burgundy said to you you can easily solve the question, for he has only offered you what he mentioned before when the matters were discussed. It looks to me as though they were not free from traitors since they have Abbé de Begars and Master Ythier Marchant.[1]

"A herald of the King of England came here on his way to Monsg. of Burgundy, who asked for a safe conduct to send a messenger to me for this truce. Since your departure the council thought I ought not to give any pass for more than forty days except to merchants. If it please God and Our Lady that you may conclude your mission, I assure you that as long

[1] Ythier Marchant negotiated the proposed marriage between Guienne and Mary of Burgundy. He had received "signed and sealed blanks" from the two princes in order to enable him to hasten matters. (*Lettres de Louis XI.*, iv., 289.)

as I live I will have no embassy either large or small without immediately informing Monsg. of Burgundy and I will only answer as if through him. I assure you that until I hear from you whether Monsg. of Burgundy decides to conclude this treaty or not as we agreed together, I will make no agreement with any creature in the world and of that you may assure him.

"Written at Montbazon, December 11th (1471).
"Loys."

At the same time Louis did not neglect friendly intercourse with the towns he proposed to cede.

"To the inhabitants of Amiens in behalf of the king:
"Dear and beloved, we have heard reports at length from Amiens and we are well content with you. . . . Give credence to all my messengers say. We thank you heartily for all that you and your deputies have done in our cause."

At the Burgundian court the duke's friends thought that he would play the part of wisdom did he keep an army within call, and refrain from implicitly trusting the king's promises. There was, moreover, an impression abroad that the latter was not in a position to be very formidable.

"Once [says Commines][1] I was present when the Seigneur d'Ursé [envoy from the Duke of Guienne] was talking in this wise and urging the duke to mobilise his forces with all diligence. The duke called me to a window and said, 'Here is the Seigneur

[1] III., ch. viii.

d'Ursé urging me to make my army as big as possible, and tells me that we would do well for the realm. Do you think that I should wage a war of benefit if I should lead my troops thither?' Smiling I answered that I thought not and he uttered these words: 'I love the welfare of France more than Mons. d' Ursé imagines, for instead of the one king that there is I would fain see six.'"

The animus of this expression is clear. It implies a wish to see the duke's friends, the French nobles, exalted, Burgundy at the head, until the titular monarch had no more power than half a dozen of his peers. Yet Commines states in unequivocal terms that Charles's next moves were to disregard his friendship for the peers, to discard their alliance, and to sign a treaty with Louis whose terms were wholly to his own advantage and implied complete desertion of the allied interest.

"This peace did the Duke of Burgundy swear and I was present[1] and to it swore the Seigneur de Craon and the Chancellor of France[2] in behalf of the king. When they departed they advised the duke not to disband his army but to increase it, so that the king their master might be the more inclined to cede promptly the two places mentioned above. They took with them Simon de Quingey to witness the king's oath and confirmation of his ambassadors' work. The king delayed this confirmation for several

[1] "Cette paix jura le Duc de Bourgogne et y estois présent."
[2] The king's envoys who had spent the winter in the Burgundian court. *See* letter to them in December.

days. Meanwhile occurred the death of his brother, the Duke of Guienne . . . shortly afterwards the said Simon returned, dismissed by the king with very meagre phrases and without any oath being taken. The duke felt mocked and insulted by this treatment and was very indignant about it."

This story involves so serious a charge against Charles of Burgundy that the fact of his setting his signature to the treaty has been indignantly denied. Certain authorities impugn the historian's truthfulness rather than accept the duke's betrayal of his friends. It is true that only a few months later than this negotiation, Commines himself forsook the duke's service for the king's, a change of base that might well throw suspicion on his estimate of his deserted master.

Yet it must be remembered that he does not gloss over Louis's actions, even though he had an admiration for the success of his political methods, methods which Commines believed to be essential in dealing with national affairs. In many respects he gives more credit to the duke than to the king even while he prefers the cleverer chief. That there is no documentary evidence of such a treaty is mere negative evidence and of little importance.

The fact seems fairly clear that Charles of Burgundy was at a parting of the ways, in character as in action. His natural bent was to tell the

[1] *See* Kervyn, *Bulletin de l'Académie royale de Belgique*, p. 256. *Also* Kirk, ii., 160; Commynes–Mandrot, i., 234.

truth and to adhere strictly to his given word. He felt that he owed it to his own dignity. He felt, too, that he was a person to command obedience to a promise whether pledged to him by king or commoner. In the years 1469–1472 several severe shocks had been dealt him. He had lost all faith in Louis, a faith that had really been founded on the duke's own self-esteem, on a conviction that the weak king must respect the redoubtable cousin of Burgundy.

The effect on Charles of his suspicions was to make him adopt the tools used by his rival, or at least to attempt to do so. At the moment of the negotiation of 1471–1472, the duke's preoccupation was to regain the towns on the Somme. That accomplished, it is not probable that he would have abandoned his friends, the French peers, whom he desired to see become petty monarchs each in his own territory. There seems no doubt that words were used with singular disregard of their meaning. It is surprising that time was wasted in concocting elaborate phrases that dropped into nothingness at the slightest touch.

In citing the above passage from Commines referring to the treaty, the close of the negotiations has been anticipated. Whether or not any draft of a treaty received the duke's signature, the king's yearning for peace ceased abruptly when his brother's death freed him from the dread of a dangerous alliance between Charles of France and Charles of Burgundy. As late as May 8th, he was still uncertain as to the decree of fate and wrote as follows to the Governor of Rousillon[1]:

"Keep cool for the present I implore you. If the Duke of Burgundy declares war against me, I will set out immediately for that quarter [Brittany], and in a week we will finish the matter. On the other hand, if peace be made we shall have everything without a blow or without any risk of restoration. However, if you can get hold of anything by negotiating and manœuvring, why do it. As to the artillery, it is close by you, and when it is time, and I shall have heard from my ambassador, you shall have it at once."

Ten days later he is more hopeful.[2]

"Since my last letter to you I have had news that Monsieur de Guienne is dying and that there is no remedy for his case. One of the most confidential persons about him has advised me by a special messenger that he does not believe he will be alive a fortnight hence. . . . The person who gave me this information is the monk who repeated his Hours with M. de G[uienne.] I am much abashed at this and have crossed myself from head to foot.

"Written at Moutils-lès-Tours, May 18th."

This prognostic was correct. In less than a fortnight the Duke of Guienne lay dead, and the heavy suspicion rested upon his royal brother of having done more than acquiesce in the decree of fate. Whether or not there was any truth in this charge the king was certainly not heartbroken by

[1] Louis to the Vicomte de la Bellière, *Lettres*, etc., iv., 319.
[2] Louis to Dammartin, *Ibid.*, 325. *Mars* was written first and then replaced by *Mai*.

Negotiations and Treachery

the loss. Indeed, the event interested him less than the question of making the best use of the remainder of his truce with Charles. The following letters to Dammartin and the Duke of Milan belong to this time.

"Thank you for the pains you have taken but pray, as speedily as you can, come here to draw up your ordinance for we only have a fortnight more of the truce. I have sent the artillery and soldiers to Angers. Monsg. the grand master, strengthen Odet's forces, do not let one man go, and see to it that the seneschal of Guienne enrols sufficient to fill his company. Then if there are more at large, form them into a body and send them to me and I will find them a captain and pay all those who are willing to stay.

"As to him,[1] make him talk on the way and learn whether he would like to enter into an agreement in his brother's name, and work it so that the duke will leave the Burgundian in the lurch at all points for ever, and make a good treaty, as you will know how, for I do not believe that the Seigneur de Lescun left here for any other reason than to attempt to make an arrangement of some kind.

"Now monseigneur the grand master, you are wiser than I and will know how to act far better than I can instruct you, but, above all, I implore you come in all haste for without you we cannot make an ordinance.

"Written at Xaintes, May 28th.

"Loys."[2]

[1] Odet d'Aydie, younger brother of the Seigneur de Lescun.
[2] *Lettres*, XI., iv., 328. Louis to Dammartin, 1472.

"AMBOISE, June 7th.

"Loys, by the grace of God, King of France. Beloved brother and cousin, we have received the letters you have written making mention, as you have heard, that in the truce lately concluded between us and the Duke of Burgundy up to April 1st next coming, which will be the year 1473, the Duke of Burgundy has mentioned you as his ally, which you do not like because you never asked the Duke of Burgundy to do so, and you do not know whether he made this statement on the advice of the Venetian ambassador who is with him.

"Therefore, and because you do not mean to enter into alliance or understanding with the Duke of Burgundy but wish to remain our confederate and ally and have sworn to that effect before notaries, and sealed your oath with your seal . . . that you are no ally of the Duke of Burgundy and that you renounce and repudiate his nomination as such . . . also you may be certain that on our part we are determined to maintain all friendship between us and you . . . and if we make any treaty in the future we will expressly include you in it and never will do otherwise."[1]

"Monseigneur the grand master, I am advised how while the truce is still in being, the Duke of Burgundy has taken Nesle and slain all whom he found within. I must be avenged for this. I wished you to know so that if you can find means to do him a like injury in his country you will do it there and anywhere that you can without sparing anything. I have good hopes that God will aid in avenging us,

[1] *Lettres*, iv., 331. Louis to the Duke of Milan.

considering the murders for which he is responsible within the church and elsewhere, and because by virtue of the terms of their surrender [they thought] they had saved their lives.

"Done at Angers, June 19th.

"P. S.—If the said place had been destroyed and rased as I ordered this never would have happened. Therefore, see to it that all such places be rased to the ground, for if this be not done the people will be ruined and there will be an increase of dishonour and damage to me."[1]

One fact stated by Louis in this letter was true. Charles of Burgundy broke the truce when it had but two weeks to run, and thus put himself in the wrong. The death of Guienne made him wild with anger. Apparently he had not believed in the imminence of the danger, although he had been constantly informed of the progress of the prince's illness. But to his mind, it was the hand of Louis, not the judgment of God, that ended the life of the prince.

"On the morrow, which was about May 15, 1472, so far as I remember [says Commines] came letters from Simon de Quingey, the duke's ambassador to the king, announcing the death of the Duke of Guienne and that the king had recovered the majority of his places. Messages from various localities followed headlong one on the other, and every one had a different story of the death.

[1] *Lettres*, etc., v., 4. Louis to Dammartin. *See also* Duclos, v., 331. There are slight discrepancies between the two texts, but the differences do not affect the narrative.

"The duke being in despair at the death, at the instigation of other people as much concerned as himself, wrote letters full of bitter accusations against the king to several towns—an action that profited little for nothing was done about it.[1] . . . In this violent passion the duke proceeded towards Nesle in Vermandois, and commenced a kind of warfare such as he had never used before, burning and destroying wherever he passed."

It is interesting to note how smoothly Commines sails by the capital charges against the king. He neither accepts nor denies the king's crime, while frankly admitting that Guienne's decease was an

[1] Odet d'Aydie, whom Louis had hoped to have converted to his cause, was the man to spread the charge against Louis broadcast over the land. The truth of the death is not proven. Frequent mentions of Guienne's condition occur through the letters of the winter '71–72. The story was that the poison, administered subtly by the king's orders, caused the illness of both the prince and his mistress, Mme. de Thouan. She died after two months of suffering, December 14th, while he resisted the poison longer, though his health was completely shattered and his months of longer life were unutterably wretched and painful, a constant torture until death mercifully released him in May. Accusations of poisoning are often repeated in history. In this case, there was certainly a wide-spread belief in Louis's guilt. In his manifestos, (Lenglet, ii., 198) Charles declares that the king's tools in compassing his brother's death were a friar, Jourdain Favre, and Henri de la Roche, esquire of his kitchen.

The story told by Brantôme (*Œuvres Complètes* de Pierre de Bourdeille, Seigneur de Brantôme, ii., 329. "Grands Capitaines François." There is nothing too severe for Brantôme to say about Louis XI.) is very detailed. A fool passed to Louis's service from that of the dead prince. While this man was attending his new master in the church

opportune circumstance for Louis. He apologises for mentioning any evil report of either king or duke, but urges his duty as historian to tell the truth without palliation.

Nesle was a little place on a tributary of the Somme which refused the duke's summons to surrender, sent to it on June 10th. It seems possible that there was a misunderstanding between the citizens and the garrison which resulted in the slaughter of the Burgundian heralds. Whereupon, the exasperated soldiers rushed headlong upon the ill-defended burghers and wreaked a terrible vengeance on the town.

When the duke arrived on the spot, the carnage

of Notre Dame de Cléry, he heard him make this prayer to the Virgin: "Ah! my good Lady, my little mistress, my great friend in whom I have always put my trust, I pray thee be a suppliant to God in my behalf, be my advocate with Him so that He may pardon me for the death of my brother whom I had poisoned by this wicked Abbé of St. John. I confess it to thee as to my good patron and mistress. But what was to be done? He was a torment to my realm. Get me pardoned and I know well what I will give thee."

Brantôme tells further that the fool, using the privilege of free speech accorded to his class, talked about Guienne's death at dinner in public and after that day was never seen again. On the other hand, the young duke's will was all to his brother's favour. Louis was made executor and legatee, "and if we have ever offended our beloved brother," dictated the dying man, "we implore him to pardon us as we with *débonnaire* affection pardon him." Mandrot, editor of Commynes (1901), i., 230, considers the whole story a malicious fabrication of Odet d'Aydie, and other authorities refer the cause to disease. The very date of the death varies from May 12th to May 24th.

was over, but he was unreproving as he inspected the gruesome result. Into the great church itself he rode, and his horse's hoofs sank through the blood lying inches deep on the floor. The desecrated building was full of dead—men, women, and children—but the duke's only comment as he looked about was, "Here is a fine sight. Verily I have good butchers with me," and he crossed himself piously.

"Those who were taken alive were hanged, except some few suffered to escape by the compassionate common soldiers. Quite a number had their hands chopped off. I dislike to mention this cruelty but I was on the spot and needs must give some account of it."[1]

The story of the duke's treatment of the innocent little town of Nesle is painted in colours quite as lurid as the king's murder of his brother. There is some ground for the denunciations of Charles, but the gravest accusation, that the duke promised clemency to the citizens on surrender and then basely broke his word, does not deserve credence. He was in a state of exasperation and the horrors were committed in passion, not in cold blood.[2]

[1] Commines, iii., ch. ix.

[2] There is a curious document in existence (see *Bulletins de L'Hist. de France*, 1833–34) dated fifty years after the event. It is the deposition of several old people who had been just old enough to remember that awful experience of their youth. Fifty years of repetition gave time for the growth of the story.

BURGUNDIAN STANDARD PRESERVED AT BEAUVAIS
AFTER THE DRAWING BY WILLEMIN

It is delightful to note the king's virtuous indignation at his cousin's proceedings, coupled with his regrets that he himself had not destroyed the town.

With the terrible report of the events at Nesle flying before his advance guard, Charles went on towards Normandy. Roye he gained easily, and then, passing by Compiègne where "Monseigneur the grand master" had intrenched himself, and Amiens with the good burghers whom Louis delighted to honour, he marched on until he reached Beauvais, an old town on the Thérain. Some of the garrison from the fallen Roye had taken refuge there, but the place was weak in its defences, not even having its usual garrison or cannon, as it happened.

Disappointed in his first expectation of picking the town like a cherry, Charles sat down before it. The siege that followed won a reputation beyond the warrant of its real importance from the extraordinary tenacity and energy of the people in their own defence. Every missile that the ingenuity of man or woman could imagine was used to drive back the besiegers when the town was finally invested.

From June 27th to July 9th Charles waited, then an assault was ordered. Charles laughed at the idea of any serious resistance. "He asked some of his people whether they thought the citizens would wait for the assault. It was answered yes, considering their number even if they had nothing before them but a hedge."[1] He took

[1] Commines, iii., ch. x.

this as a joke and said, "To-morrow you will not find a person." He thought that there would be a simple repetition of his experience at Dinant and Liege, and that the garrison would simply succumb in terror. When the Burgundians rushed at the walls their reception showed not only that every point had a defender, but also that those same defenders were provided with huge stones, pots of boiling water, burning torches—all most unpleasant things when thrown in the faces of men trying to scale a wall. Three hours were sufficient to prove to the assailants the difficulty of the task. Twelve hundred were slain and maimed, and the strength of the place was proven.

Charles was not inclined to relinquish his scheme, but the weather came to the aid of the besieged. Heavy rains forced the troops to change camp. More men were lost in skirmishes and mimic assaults, losses that Charles could ill afford at the moment. Finally at the end of three fruitless weeks, the siege was raised and the Burgundians marched on to try to redeem their reputation in Normandy. Had Beauvais fallen, it would have been possible to relieve the Duke of Brittany, against whom Louis had marched with all his forces and whom he had enveloped as in a net. This reverse was the first serious rebuff that had happened to Charles, and it marked a turn in his fortunes.

Louis fully appreciated the enormous advantage

to himself, and was not stinting in his reward to the plucky little town. Privileges and a reduction of taxes were bestowed on Beauvais. An annual procession was inaugurated in which women were to have precedence as a special recognition of their services with boiling water and other irregular weapons, while a special gift was bestowed on one particular girl, Jeanne Laisné, who had wrested a Burgundian standard from a soldier just as he was about to plant it on the wall. Not only was she endowed from the royal purse, but she and her husband and their descendants were declared tax free for ever.[1]

Charles to the Duke of Brittany

"My good brother, I recommend myself to you with good heart. I rather hoped to be able to march through Rouen, but the whole strength of the foe was on the frontier, where was the *grand master, of whose loyalty I have not the least doubt*, so that the project could not be effected. I do not know what will happen. Realising this, I have given subject for thought elsewhere and I have pitched my camp between Rouen and Neufchâtel, intending, however, to return speedily. If not I will exploit the war in another quarter more injurious to the enemy, and I will exert myself to keep them from your route. My Burgundians and Luxemburgers have done bravely in Champagne. I know, too, that you have done well on

[1] Legend makes it that Jeanne Laisné, called *Fouquet*, chopped off the hands of the standard-bearer with a hatchet. Hence her name was changed to *La Hachette*, and she is represented with a hatchet.

your part, for which I rejoice. I have burned the territory of Caux in a fashion so that it will not injure you, nor us, nor others, and I will not lay down arms without you, as I am certain you will not without me. I will pursue the work commenced by your advice at the pleasure of Our Lord, may He give you good and long life with a fruitful victory.

"Written at my camp near Boscise, September 4th.

"Your loyal brother,

"CHARLES."[1]

The duke's course was marked by waste and devastation from the walls of Rouen to those of Dieppe, but nothing was gained from this desolation. By September, keen anxiety about his territories led him to fear staying so far from his own boundaries, and he decided to return. Through Picardy he marched eastward burning and laying waste as before.

Hardly had he turned towards the Netherlands, when Louis marched into Brittany against his weakest foe. There was no fighting, but Francis found it wise to accept a truce. Odet d'Aydie, who had ridden in hot haste to Brittany, scattering from his saddle dire accusations of fratricide against Louis—this same Odet became silenced and took service with the king.[2] When reconcilations were effected, most kind to the returning ally or servant did Louis always show himself.

[1] Barante, vii., 333.
[2] *See* Lavisse, iv[ii.], 368.

On November 3d, a truce was struck between Louis and Charles, which, later, was renewed for a year. But never again did the two men come into actual conflict with each other, though they were on the eve of doing so in 1475.

The period of the great coalitions among the nobles was at an end. Charles of France was dead and so, too, were others who were strong enough to work the king ill. The Duke of Brittany showed no more energy. When again within his own territories, Charles of Burgundy became absorbed in other projects which he wished to perfect before he again measured steel with Louis.

> "The Duke of Berry, he is dead,
> Brittany doth nod his head,
> Burgundy doth sulky sit,
> While Louis works with every wit."[1]

Such was the tenor of a doggerel verse sung in France, a verse that probably never came to Charles's ears—though Louis might have listened to it cheerfully.

Infinitely disastrous were the events of that summer to Charles of Burgundy. Not only had he lost in allies, not only had he squandered life and money uselessly in his reckless expedition over the north of France, but his own retinue was

---

[1] "Berri est mort,
Bretagne dort,
Bourgogne hongne,
Le Roy besogne."

Le Roux de Lincy, *Chants historiques et populaires du temps de Louis XI*.

diminished and weakened by the men whom Louis had succeeded in luring from his service. The loss that Charles suffered was not only for the time but for posterity. Among those convinced that there was more scope for men of talent in France than in Burgundy was that clever observer of humanity who had been at Charles's side for eight years. In August of 1472, Philip de Commines took French leave of his master and betook himself to Louis, who evidently was not surprised at his advent.

The historian's own words in regard to this change of base are laconic: "About this time I entered the king's service (and it was the year 1472), who had received the majority of the servitors of his brother the Duke of Guienne. And he was then at Pont de Cé."[1] This passing from one lord to another happened on the night between the 7th and 8th of August, when the Burgundian army lay near Eu.

The suddenness of the departure was probably due to the duke's discovery of his servant's intentions not yet wholly ripe, and those intentions had undoubtedly been formed at Orleans, in 1471, when Commines made a secret journey to the king. On his way back to Burgundy, he deposited a large sum of money at Tours. Evidently he did not dare put this under his own name, or claim it when it was confiscated as the

[1] Commines also mentions here "the confessor of the Duke of Guienne and a knight to whom is imputed the death of the Duke of Guienne." (iii., ch. xi.)

Negotiations and Treachery 317

property of a notorious adherent of Louis's foe.[1]

When the fugitive reached the French court, however, he was amply recompensed for all his losses.[2] For, naturally, at his flight, all his Burgundian estates were abandoned.[3] It was at six o'clock on the morning of August 8th that the deed was signed whereby the duke transferred to the Seigneur de Quiévrain all the rights appertaining to Philip de Commines, "which rights together with all the property of whatever kind have escheated to us by virtue of confiscation because he has to-day, the date of this document, departed from our obedience and gone as a fugitive to the party opposed to us."[4]

There are various surmises as to the cause of this precipitate departure. Not improbable is the suggestion that Charles often overstepped the bounds of courtesy towards his followers. Once, so runs one story, he found the historian sleeping on his bed where he had flung himself while awaiting

[1] Kirk (ii., 156) thinks that this confiscation was only Louis's way of prodding him up to act.

[2] Dupont (Commynes, iii., xxxvi). The fugitive did not enter immediately into his new possessions. The king's gift of the principality of Talmont, dated October, 1472, was not registered in *Parlement* until December 13, 1473, and in the court of records May 2, 1474. Prince of Talmont did Commines become at last, and as such he married Helen de Chambes, January 27, 1473.

[3] It is strange that La Marche does not mention this defection.

[4] See document quoted by Gachard, *Études et Notices*, etc. ii., 344. The original is in the Croy family archives preserved in the château of Beaumont.

his master. Charles pulled off one of his boots "to give him more ease" and struck him in the face with it. In derision the courtiers called Commines *tête bottée*, and their mocking sank deep into his soul.

Contemporary writers make little of the chronicler's defection. These crossings from the peer's to the king's camp were accepted occurrences. But by Charles they were not accepted. There is a vindictive look about the hour when he disposes of his late confidant's possessions, only explicable by intense indignation not itemised in the deed approved by the court of Mons.[1]

More loyal was that other chronicler, Olivier de la Marche, though to him, also, came intimations that he would find a pleasant welcome at the French court. He, too, had opportunities galore to make links with Louis. The accounts teem with references to his secret missions here and there, and with mention of the rewards paid, all carefully itemised. So zealous was this messenger on his master's commissions, that his hackneys were ruined by his fast riding and had to be sold for petty sums. The keen eye of Louis XI. was not blind to the quality of La Marche's services, and he thought that they, too, might be diverted to his use.[2]

[1] *See also* Comines–Lenglet, i., xcj., for discussion of this event. He asserts that the court of Burgundy was too corrupt for honest men to endure it.

[2] *See* Stein. *Étude*, etc., *sur Olivier de la Marche*. (Mém. Couronnés) xlix.

CHAPTER XVI

GUELDERS

1473

THE affairs of the little duchy of Guelders were among the matters urgently demanding the attention of the Duke of Burgundy at the close of his campaign in France. The circumstances of the long-standing quarrel between Duke Arnold and his unscrupulous son Adolf were a scandal throughout Europe. In 1463, a seeming reconciliation of the parties had not only been effected but celebrated in the town of Grave by a pleasant family festival, from whose gaieties the elder duke, fatigued, retired at an early hour. Scarcely was he in bed, when he was aroused rudely, and carried off half clad to a dungeon in the castle of Buren, by the order of his son, who superintended the abduction in person and then became duke regnant. For over six years the old man languished in prison, actually taunted, from time to time, it is said, by Duke Adolf himself.

Indignant remonstrances against this conduct were heard from various quarters, and were all alike unheeded by the young duke until Charles of Burgundy interfered and ordered him to bring his father to his presence, and to submit the dis-

"Monsieur du Bouchage, Guillaume de Thouars has told me that Messire Olivier de la Marche is willing to enter my service and I am afraid that there may be some deception. However, there is nothing that I would like better than to have the said Sieur de Cimay, as you know. Therefore, pray find out how the matter stands, and if you see that it is in good earnest work for it with all diligence. Whatever you pledge I will hold to. Advise me of everything.

"Written at Cléry, October 16th [1472].
"To our beloved and faithful councillor and chancellor, Sire du Bouchage."[1]

But La Marche was not tempted, and was rewarded for his fidelity by high office in a duchy which, shortly after these events, was "annexed" to his master's domain.

[1] Letter of Louis XI. in Bibl. Nat.; *Ibid.*, p. 179.

pute to his arbitration. Charles was too near and too powerful a neighbour to be disregarded, and his peremptory invitation was accepted. Pending the decision, the two dukes were forced to be guests in his court, under a strict surveillance which amounted to an arrest.

The first suggestion made by Charles was for a compromise between father and son. "Let Duke Arnold retain the nominal sovereignty in Guelders, actual possession of one town, and a fair income, while to Adolf be ceded the full power of administration." The latter was emphatic in his refusal to consider the proposition. "Rather would I prefer to see my father thrown into a well and to follow him thither than to agree to such terms. He has been sovereign duke for forty-four years; it is my turn now to reign." Arnold thought it would be a simple feat to fight out the dispute. "I saw them both several times in the duke's apartment and in the council chamber when they pleaded, each his own cause. I saw the old man offer a gage of battle to his son."[1] The senior belonged to the disappearing age of chivalry. A trial of arms seemed to him an easy and knightly fashion of ending his differences with his importunate heir.

No settlement was effected before the French expedition, but Charles was not disposed to let the matter slip from his control, and when he proceeded to Amiens, the two dukes, still under

[1] Commines, iv., ch. i.

restraint, were obliged to follow in his train. At a leisure moment Charles intended to force them to accept his arbitration as final. Before that moment arrived, the more agile of the two plaintiffs, Adolf, succeeded in eluding surveillance and escaping from the camp at Wailly. He made his way successfully to Namur disguised as a Franciscan monk. Then, at the ferry, he gave a florin when a penny would have sufficed. The liberality, inconsistent with his assumed rôle, aroused suspicion and led to the detection of his rank and identity. He was stayed in his flight and imprisoned in the castle of Namur to await a decision on his case by his self-constituted judge. This was not pronounced until the summer of 1473.

By that time, Charles was resolved on another course of action than that of adjusting a family dispute in the capacity of puissant, impartial, and friendly neighbour. Adolf's behaviour towards his father had been extraordinarily brutal and outrageous. Public comment had been excited to a wide degree. It was not an affair to be dealt with lightly by Duke Charles. The young Duchess of Guelders was Catharine of Bourbon, sister to the late Duchess of Burgundy, and Adolf himself was chevalier of the Golden Fleece. In consideration of these links of family and knightly brotherhood, Charles desired that the case should be tried with all formality.

On May 3, 1473, an assembly of the Order was

ARNOULD.
Duc de Gueldres,
Mort au Mois d'Aougt 1472.

ARNOLD, DUKE OF GUELDERS
(FROM THE ENGRAVING BY PINSSIO, AFTER THE DRAWING BY J. ROBERT)

Guelders

held at Valenciennes,[1] and the knights were asked to pass upon the conduct of their delinquent fellow, who was permitted to present his own brief through an attorney, but was detained in his own person at Namur. The innocence or guilt of his prisoner was no longer the chief point of interest as far as the Duke of Burgundy was concerned. The latter had made an excellent bargain on his own behalf with the moribund Duke of Guelders, who had signed (December, 1472) a document wherein he sold to Charles all his administrative rights in Guelders and Zutphen for

[1] *Hist. de l'Ordre*, etc., p. 64. One of the places to be filled at this session was that of Frank van Borselen, the widower of Jacqueline, Countess of Holland. Thus the last faint trace of the ancient family disappeared. It is expressly stated in the minutes of the session that Adolf of Guelders was asked to nominate candidates from his prison, but he would not do it. Striking is Charles's remark on the nomination of the son of the King of Naples. Considering that the Order was already decorated and honoured by four kings, very excellent, he judged it more *à propos* to distribute the five empty collars within his own states. Nevertheless the infant was elected, as was also Engelbert of Nassau.

Various members are criticised as permitted by the rules of the Order. There was reproach for Anthony the Bastard for taking a gift of 20,000 crowns from Louis XI. Payable as it was in terms, it savoured of a pension. Had Henry van Borselen done all he could to prevent Warwick's landing in England? etc.

Among the minor pieces of business discussed was the disposition of the scarlet mantles now discarded by the chevaliers. It was decided after deliberation that they should be sold and the proceeds applied to the purchase of tapestries for the chapel of Dijon, and the treasurer was deputed to see about it. Perhaps it was in this connection that the discussion turned on the wide-spread use, or rather

ninety-two thousand florins,[1] in consideration of Arnold's enjoying a life interest in half of the revenue of his ancient duchy. That clause soon lost its significance. The old man's life ceased in March, 1473, and, by virtue of the contract, Charles proposed to enter into full possession of his estates, setting aside not only Adolf, whom he was ready to pronounce an outlawed criminal, quite beyond the pale of society, but that Adolf's innocent eight-year-old heir, Charles, whose hereditary claims had also been ignored by his grandfather.

Before the knights of the Order as a final court, were rehearsed all the circumstances of the old family quarrel and of the late commercial transaction. Their verdict was the one desired by their chief. It was proven to their entire satisfaction that Arnold's sale of the duchy of Guelders and Zutphen was a legitimate proceeding, and that the deed executed by him was a perfect and valid instrument, whereby Charles of Burgundy was duly empowered to enjoy all the revenues of, and to exert authority in, his new duchy at his pleasure. As to Duke Adolf, he was condemned by this tribunal of his peers to life imprisonment

---

abuse of gold and velvet. It tended to depreciate the Order and the state of chivalry. But the sovereign thought it best to defer this point until his return from his proposed journey to Guelders. Lengthy, too, were the discussions upon the exact usage in respect to wearing the collar and insignia of the Order.

[1] The first sum named was three hundred thousand.

as punishment for his unfilial and unjustifiable cruelty towards Arnold, late Duke of Guelders.

Adolf's protests were stifled by his prison bars, but the people of Guelders were by no means disposed to accept unquestioned this deed of transfer, made when the two parties to the conveyance were in very unequal conditions of freedom. In order to convince them of the justice of his pretensions, Charles levied a force almost as efficient as his army of the preceding summer, and fell upon Guelders. A truce, a triple compact with France and England, had recently been renewed, so that for the moment his hands were free from complications, an event commented upon by Sir John Paston, as follows:

"April 16, 1473, CANTERBURY.

"As for tydings ther was a truce taken at Brusslys about the xxvi day off March last, betwyn the Duke of Burgoyn and the Frense Kings inbassators and Master William Atclyff ffor the king heer, whiche is a pese be londe and be water tyll the ffyrst daye off Apryll nowe next comyng betweyn Fraunce and Ingeland, and also the Dukys londes. God holde it ffor ever."

The writer had recently been in Charles's court. Writing from Calais in February, he says:

"As ffor tydyngs heer ther bee but few saff that the Duke of Burgoyen and my Lady hys wyffe fareth well. I was with them on Thorysdaye last past at Gaunt."[1]

[1] *The Paston Letters*, iii., 79.

The Duke of Burgundy was not the only pretender to the vacated sovereignty of Guelders. The Duke of Juliers was also inclined to urge his cause, were Adolf's family to be set aside. At the sight of Burgundian puissance, however, he was ready to be convinced, and accepted 24,000 florins for his acquiescence in the righteousness of the accession. Several of the cities manifested opposition to Charles, but yielded one after another. In Nimwegen—long hostile to Duke Arnold—there was a determined effort to support little Charles of Guelders who, with his sister, was in that city. The child made a pretty show on his little pony, and there were many declarations of devotion to his cause as he was put forward to excite sympathy. For three weeks, the town held out in his name. The resistance to the Burgundian troops was sturdy. When the gates gave way before their attacks the burghers defended the broken walls. Six hundred English archers were repulsed from an assault with such sudden energy that they left their banners sticking in the very breaches they thought they had won, fine prizes for the triumphant citizens. But the game was unequal, and the combatants, convinced that discretion was the better part of valour, at last accepted the Duke of Cleves as a mediator with their would-be sovereign.

On July 19th, a long civic procession headed by the burgomasters, wearing neither hats nor shoes, marched to the Duke of Burgundy with a

Guelders

prayer for pardon on their lips. The leaders of the opposition to his accession were delivered over to the mercy of the victor. The garrison were accorded their lives and a tax was imposed on the city to indemnify the duke for his needless trouble, and Guelders was added *de facto* to the list of Burgundian ducal titles. In the various state papers presently issued by the new ruler, the mention of the circumstance of his accession to the sovereignty was simple and straightforward, as in a certain document appointing Olivier de la Marche to be treasurer. The patent bears the date of August 18th and was one of the earliest issued by Charles in this new capacity.

"As by the death of the late Messire Arnold, in his life Duke of Guelderland, these counties and duchy have lapsed to me, and by the same token the offices of the land have escheated to our disposition, and among others the office of master of the moneys of those countships . . . using the rights, etc., escheated to me, and in consideration of the good and agreeable services already rendered and continually rendered by our knight, etc., Olivier de la Marche, having full confidence in his sense, loyalty, probity, and good diligence—for these causes and others we entrust the office of master and overseer of moneys of the land of Guelders to him, with all the rights, duties, and privileges thereto pertaining. In testimony of this we have set our seal to these papers. Done in our city of Nimwegen, August 18, 1473. Thus signed by M. le duc."

On the back of this document was written:

"To-day, November 3, 1473, Messire Olivier de la Marche . . . took the oath of office of master and overseer of the land and duchy of Guelders."[1]

The charge of the ducal children, Charles and Philippa, was entrusted to the duke who, in his turn, deputed Margaret of York to supervise their education. In a comparatively brief time agitation in behalf of the disinherited heir ceased, and imperial ratification alone was required to stamp the territory as a legal fraction of the Burgundian domains. Under the circumstances the minor heirs were the emperor's wards, and it was his express duty to look to their interests, but Frederic III. showed no disposition to assert himself as their champion. On the contrary, the embassy that arrived from his court on August 14th was charged with felicitations to his dear friend, Charles of Burgundy, for his acquisition, and with assurances that the requisite investiture into his dignities should be given by his imperial hand at the duke's pleasure.[2]

Communication between Frederic and Charles had been intermittently frequent during the past three years, and one subject of their letters was probably a reason why Charles had been willing to abandon a losing game in France to give another bias to his thoughts. He was lured on by the

[1] See *Mémoires Couronnés*, xlix., 180.

[2] Toutey, p. 42; Lenglet, ii., 207. August 14th the Duke of Burgundy crossed the Rhine and made his way to Nimwegen where the ambassador of the emperor visited him.

bait of certain prospects, varying in their definite form indeed, but full of promise that he might be enabled, eventually, to confer with Louis XI. from a better vantage ground than his position as first peer of France. The story of these hopes now becomes the story of Charles of Burgundy.

When Sigismund of Austria completed his mortgage, in 1469, at St. Omer, and returned home, as already stated, he was fired with zeal to divert some of the dazzling Burgundian wealth into the empty imperial coffers. An alliance between Mary of Burgundy and the young Archduke Maximilian seemed to him the most advantageous matrimonial bargain possible for the emperor's heir. He urged it upon his cousin with all the eloquence he possessed, and was lavish in his offers to be mediator between him and his new friend Charles.

Frederic was impressed by Sigismund's enthusiastic exposition of the advantages of the match, and little time elapsed before his ambassador brought formal proposals to Charles for the alliance. The duke received the advances complacently and returned propositions significant of his personal ambitions. As early as May, 1470, his instructions to certain envoys sent to the intermediary, Sigismund, are plain. In unequivocal terms, his daughter's hand is made contingent on his own election as King of the Romans, that shadowy royalty which veiled the approach to the imperial throne.

"*Item*—And in regard to the said marriage, the ambassadors shall inform Monseigneur of Austria that, since his departure from Hesdin, certain people have talked to Monseigneur about this marriage and mentioned that, in return, the emperor would be willing to grant to Monseigneur the crown and the government of the Kingdom of the Romans, with the stipulation that Monseigneur, *arrived at the empire by the good pleasure of the emperor* or by his death, would, in his turn, procure the said crown of the Romans for his son-in-law. The result will be that the empire will be continued in the person of the emperor's son and his descendants.

"*Item*—They shall tell him about a meeting between the imperial and ducal ambassadors, at which meeting there was some talk of making a kingdom out of certain lands of Monseigneur and joining these to an *imperial* vicariate of all the lands and principalities lying along the Rhine."

In the following paragraphs of this instruction,[1] Charles directs his envoys to make it clear to Monseigneur of Austria (Sigismund) that the duke's interest in the plan does not spring from avarice or ambition. He is purely actuated by a yearning to employ his time and his strength for God's service and for the defence of the Faith, while still in his prime.

[1] This instruction, printed by Lenglet (iii., 238) from the Godefroy edition of Commines, has no date and has been referred to 1472. From internal evidence it seems fair to conclude that it belongs rather to 1470. The question of the marriage comes in at the end of the paper, the first part being devoted to Swiss affairs.

Guelders

Should the emperor refuse to approve the duke's nomination as King of the Romans, the ambassadors are instructed to say that they are not empowered to proceed with the marriage negotiations without first referring to their chief. They must ask leave to return with their report. If Sigismund should take it on himself to sound the emperor again about his sentiments, the envoys might await the result of his investigations. He was to be assured that while Charles was resolved to hold back until he was fully satisfied on this point, if it were once ceded, he would interpose no further delay in the celebration of the nuptials. He must know, however, just what power and revenue the emperor would attach to the proposed title. He was not willing to accept it without emoluments. His present financial burdens were already heavy, etc. The concluding items of the instructions had reference to the marriage settlements.

A kingdom of his own was not the duke's dream at this stage of Burgundo-Austrian negotiations. The title that Charles desired primarily was King of the Romans, one empty of substantial sovereign power, but rich with promise of the all-embracing imperial dignity. Significant is the intimation that after this preliminary title was conferred, its wearer would be glad to have Frederic step aside voluntarily. A resignation would be as efficient as death in making room for his appointed successor.

Frederic III. had, indeed, intimated occasionally that a life of meditation would suit his tastes better than the imperial throne, but he seems in no wise to have been tempted by the offer made by Charles to relieve him of his onerous duties, and then to pass on the office to his son. At any rate, the emperor rejected the opportunity to enjoy an irresponsible ease. His answer to the duke was that he did not exercise sufficient influence over his electors to ensure their accepting his nominee as successor to the *imperium*.

There was, however, one honour that lay wholly within his gift. If Charles desired higher rank, the emperor would be quite willing to erect his territories into a realm and to create him monarch of his own agglomerated possessions, welded into a new unity. This proposition wounded Charles keenly. He assured Sigismund[1] (January 15, 1471) that his nomination as King of the Romans would never have occurred to him spontaneously. He had been assured that it was a darling project of the emperor, and he had simply been willing to please him, etc. As to a kingdom of his own, he refused the proposition with actual disdain.

Then various suitors for the hand of Mary of Burgundy appeared on the scene successively. To Nicholas of Calabria, Duke of Lorraine, grandson of old King René of Anjou, she was formally betrothed.[2]

[1] Toutey, p. 36.   [2] Lenglet, iii., 192.

"My cousin, since it is the pleasure of my very redoubtable seigneur and father, I promise you that, you being alive, I will take none other than you and I promise to take you when God permits it." So wrote Mary with her own hand on June 13, 1472, at Mons. On December 3d, she declared all such pledges revoked as though they never had been made, and Nicholas, too, formally renounced his pretensions to her hand.

There were several moments when Charles of France had appeared to be very near acceptance as Mary's husband, and several other princes seemed eligible suitors. Doubtless her father found his daughter very valuable as a means of attracting friendship. Doubtless, too, as Commines says, he was not anxious to introduce any son-in-law into his family. His fortieth year was only completed in 1473, and he was by no means ready to range himself as an ancestor.

At successive times the negotiations between Charles and Frederic were ruptured only to be renewed on some slightly different basis. Threaded together they made a story fraught with interest for Louis XI., and one that, very probably, he had an opportunity to hear. Up to August, 1472, it is a safe inference that Philip de Commines was fully cognisant of the propositions and counter-propositions, the understandings and misunderstandings, the private letters of, as well as the interviews with, the accredited Austrian envoys that appeared at one Burgundian camp after another. Probably there was nothing more valuable in the store of learning carried by the astute historian from his first patron to his second than all this fund of confidential miscellany.

It seems a fair surmise that Louis XI. enjoyed immensely the delightful private view into his rival's dreams, the disappointments and rehabilitation of his shattered visions. The relation would have made him not only fully aware of the reasons why Charles was diverted from his hot pursuit of the Somme towns, but thoroughly informed as to the great obstacles lying in the path which the duke hoped to travel. Naturally, the king was quite willing to rest assured that ruin was inevitable. If his rival were disposed to wreck himself rashly on German shoals, the king was equally disposed to be an acquiescent onlooker and to spare his own powder.

On his part, Charles was wholly unconscious of the extent of his loss of prestige within the French realm in 1472. There had been other periods when the king had appeared triumphant over his aspiring nobles only to be again checked by their alliance. In the radical change undergone by the feudatories after Guienne's death and Brittany's reconciliation, there was, however, no opening left for the Duke of Burgundy's re-entry as a French political leader. It was this definitive cessation of his importance that Charles failed to recognise. Confident that his star was rising in the east he did not note the significance of its setting in the west. Thereupon the situation was,—Charles, believing that his plans were his own secret, *versus* Louis, fully advised of those plans and alert to all incidents of the past, present, and future in a fashion impossible to the duke in his absorbed contemplation of his own prospects, blocking the scope of his view.

With the emperor's congratulations at the duke's accession to Guelders, and his offers to invest him with the title, were coupled intimations that it was an opportune moment to resume consideration of an alliance between the Archduke Maximilian and Mary of Burgundy. The duke accepted the new overtures, and Rudolf de Soulz and Peter von Hagenbach proceeded to the Burgundian and Austrian courts respectively, as confidential envoys to discuss the marriage.[1]

Charles was far more gracious to De Soulz than he had been to the last imperial messenger, the Abbé de Casanova, who had restricted his proposals to Mary's fortunes and ignored her father's. The duke had no intention of permitting any conference to proceed on that line. He was explicit as to his requisitions. De Soulz was surprised by a gift of ten thousand florins, explained by the phrase, "because Monseigneur recognised the love and affection borne him by the said count." That was a simple retainer. Other benefits, offices, and estates were conferred, to take effect on the

[1] Toutey, p. 44; Chmel, *Monumenta Habsburgica*, 1, 3.

day when Monseigneur was named King of the Romans.

The instructions to Hagenbach were definite, covering the ground of those previously mentioned, issued in 1470. He was, however, especially enjoined to assure Frederic that the duke did not require his abdication. He would be content to step into the shoes naturally vacated by his death.

The final suggestion resulting from these parleyings was that an interview between the two principals would be far more satisfactory than any further interchange of messages. It was not only a propitious time for a conference, but it was necessary. The ceremony of investiture of the duke into his latest acquired fief made it evidently imperative that he should visit the emperor. And to preparations for that event, Charles turned his attention, now absolutely confident that the outcome must be to his satisfaction. He had as little comprehension of the character of the man with whom he was to deal as he had of Louis XI. The choice of a place caused some difficulty, each prince preferring a locality near his own frontier. Metz was selected and abandoned on account of an epidemic. Finally Trèves was appointed for the important occasion, and Frederic sent official invitations to the princes of the empire to follow him thither in October.

Before Charles arrived at the rendezvous, another event had occurred that had an import-

MARY OF BURGUNDY
(AFTER THE DESIGN BY C. LAPLANTE)

ant bearing on his fortunes. Nicholas, Duke of Lorraine, died (July 27th), leaving no direct heir. He had been relinquished as a son-in-law, but the geographical position of his duchy made the question of its sovereignty all important to Charles of Burgundy. If it could be under his own control, how convenient for the passage of his troops from Luxemburg to the south! The taste for duchies like many another can grow by what it feeds upon.

Prepared to set out for his journey to Trèves, Charles hastened his movements and proceeded to Metz with an escort so large that it had a formidable aspect to the city fathers. Whether they feared that their free city was too tempting a base for attack on Lorraine or not, the magistrates yet found it expedient to keep the Burgundian thousands without their walls. The emperor, too, was on his way to Trèves. Many of his suite were occupying quarters in Metz. Room might be found for Charles and his immediate retainers, indeed, but the troops must make themselves as comfortable as possible outside the gates. So said the burgomaster, and Charles was forced to yield and he made a splendid entry into the town under the prescribed conditions.

His own paraphernalia had been forwarded from Antwerp, so that there should be an abundance of plate, tapestry, etc., to grace his temporary quarters, and the forests of Luxemburg had been scoured to secure game for the banquets.

It was all very fine, but Charles was not in a humour to be pleased. He was annoyed about his troops; very probably he had intended leaving a portion at Metz, ready to be available in Lorraine if occasion offered. He cut short his stay in the town and marched on with his imposing escort to Trèves, whence he hoped to march out again a greater personage than any Duke of Burgundy had ever been.[1]

[1] Toutey, p. 46.

CHAPTER XVII

THE MEETING AT TRÈVES

1473

ON Wednesday, September 28th, Emperor Frederic made his entry into the old Roman city on the dancing Moselle. Two days later, the Duke of Burgundy arrived and was welcomed most pompously outside of Trèves, by his suzerain.

After the first greetings, ensued an argument about the etiquette proper for the occasion, an argument similar to those which had absorbed the punctilious in the Burgundian court, when the dauphin made his famous visit to Duke Philip. For thirty minutes, the emperor argued with his guest before feudal scruples were overcome and the vassal was induced to ride by his chief's side into the city.

The entry was a grand sight, and crowds thronged the streets, more curious about the duke than about the emperor. Charles was then in the very prime of life. His personality commanded attention, but there were some among the onlookers who found it more striking than attractive. One bystander thought that the very splendour of his dress, wherein cloth of gold and pearls played a part, only brought into high relief the severity of his features. His great black eyes, his proud and determined air failed to cast into oblivion a certain effect of insignificance given by his square figure, broad shoulders, excessively stout limbs, and legs rather bowed from continuous riding.[1]

There is, however, another word portrait of the duke as he looked in the year 1473, whose trend is more sympathetic.[2] "His stature was small and nervous, his complexion pale, hair dark chestnut, eyes black and brilliant, his presence majestic but stern. He was high-spirited, magnanimous, courageous, intrepid, and impetuous. Capable of action, he lacked nothing but prudence to attain success."

From the two descriptions emerges a fairly clear picture of an energetic man, somewhat undersized, and sometimes inclined to assert his dignity in a fashion that did not quite comport with his physical characteristics. The conviction that he was a very important personage with greater importance awaiting him, and his total lack of a sense of humour, combined with his inability to feel the pulse of a situation, undoubt-

[1] This comment of the Strasburg chronicler, Trausch, is quoted by De Bussière in his *Histoire de la Ligue contre Charles le Téméraire*, p. 64. Kirk (ii., 222) points out that this contemporary had a peculiar hostility towards Charles.

[2] Guillaume Faret or Farrel. His *Hist. de René II.* is lost. This citation from it is found in *La Guerre de René II. contre Charles le Hardi*, by P. Aubert Roland.

CHARLES THE BOLD
IDEALISED BY RUBENS. IN THE IMPERIAL GALLERY AT VIENNA
BY PERMISSION OF J. J. LÖWY, VIENNA

edly affected his bearing and made it seem more pompous.

The emperor was not an heroic figure in appearance any more than he was in the records of his reign, distinguished for being the feeblest as well as the longest in the annals of the empire. He was indolent, timid, irresolute, and incapable. His features and manners were vulgar, his intellect sluggish. Peasant-like in his petty economies, he was shrewder at a bargain than in wielding his imperial sceptre. At Trèves he was accompanied by his son, the Archduke Maximilian, a fairly intelligent youth of eighteen, very ready to be fascinated by his proposed father-in-law, who was a striking contrast to his own languid and irresolute father, in energy and strenuous love of action.

As the two princes rode together into the city, Charles's accoutrements attracted all eyes. The polished steel of his armour shone like silver. Over it hung a short mantle actually embroidered with diamonds and other precious stones to the value of two hundred thousand gold crowns. His velvet hat, graciously held in his hand out of compliment to the emperor, was ornamented with a diamond whose price no man could tell. Before him walked a page carrying his helmet studded with gems, while his magnificent black steed was heavily weighted down with its rich caparisons.

Frederic III., very simple in his ordinary dress,

had exerted himself to appear well to his great vassal. His robe of cloth of gold was fine, though it may have looked something like a luxurious dressing-gown, as it was made after the Turkish fashion and bordered with pearls. The emperor was lame in one foot, injured, so ran the tradition, by his habit of kicking, not his servants, but innocent doors that chanced to impede his way.

The Archduke Maximilian, gay in crimson and silver, walked by the side of an Ottoman prince, prisoner of war, and converted to Christianity by the pope himself. And then there was a host of nobles, great and small. Among them were Engelbert of Nassau[1] and the representative of the House of Orange-Châlons, whose titles were destined to be united in one person within the next half-century.

The magnificence remained unrivalled in the history of royal conferences. The very troopers wore habits of cloth of gold over their steel, while their embroidered saddle-cloths were fringed with silver bells. Surpassing all others, were the heralds-at-arms of the various individual states which acknowledged Charles as their sovereign, seigneur, count, or duke as the case might be. They preceded their liege lord, clad in their distinctive armorial coats, ablaze with colour. Before them were the trumpeters in white and

[1] He had been made knight of the Golden Fleece at the May meeting. From this time on some member of the Nassau family was prominent in Burgundian affairs.

blue, their very instruments silvered, while first of all rode one hundred golden haired boys, "an angel throng."

It was so difficult to decide as to the requisite etiquette of escort, that the emperor and duke agreed to separate on the fairly neutral ground of the market-place. Each proceeded with his own suite to his lodgings, Frederic to the archbishop's palace, and Charles to the abbey of St. Maximin, which had conferred on him, some years previously, the honorary title of "Protector." His army was quartered within and without the city. Two days for repose and then the first official interview took place, which is described as follows, by an unknown correspondent, evidently in the ducal suite:[1]

"Yesterday, which was Sunday, Monseigneur waited upon the emperor and escorted him to his own lodging which is in the abbey of St. Maximin. My said lord was clad in ducal array except for his hat. The emperor wore a rich robe of cloth of gold of cramoisy, and his son was in a robe of green damask. As to their people, both suites were very brave, jewelry and cloth of gold being as common as satin or taffeta. Monseigneur received the emperor in a little chamber decorated with hangings from Holland that many recognised.

"The emperor made the Bishop of Mayence his mouthpiece to describe the stress of Christianity and to urge Charles to lend his assistance. Having list-

[1] Gachard, *Doc. inédits*, i., 232. Letter from Trèves, October 4, 1473.

ened to this address, Monseigneur requested the emperor to please come into a larger place where more people could hear his answer. Accordingly they entered a hall decorated with the tapestry of Alexander, while the very ceiling was covered with cloth of gold. There was a dais whereon stood a double row of seats. Benches and steps were spread over with tapestry wrought with my lord's arms. Thither came the emperor and mounted the dais with difficulty. . . . Mons., the chancellor, clad in velvet over velvet cramoisy, first pronounced a discourse in beautiful Latin as a response to what had been said by the seigneur of Mayence. Then, showing how the affairs of my said lord were affected by the king, he began with an account of the king's reception by Monseigneur, whom God absolve [evidently the late duke], in his own residence, and he continued down to the present day, dilating upon the great benefits, services, and honour by him [Louis] received in the domains of Burgundy, and the extortions he had made since and desires to make. Never a word was forgotten, but all was well stated, especially the case of M. de Guienne.[1] Finally, Monseigneur declared that if his lands were in security, there was nothing he would like better than to give aid to Christianity.

"After this statement, which was marvellously honest, the emperor arose from the throne, wine and spices were brought, and then Monseigneur escorted the emperor to his quarters with grand display of torches. This is the outline of what hap-

[1] About this time Louis XI. made strenuous efforts to unravel the mystery of his brother's death. (Letter to the chancellor of Brittany, *Lettres de Louis XI.*, v., 190.)

pened on October 4th, in the said year lxxiii. And as to the future, next Thursday the emperor will dine where Monseigneur lodges, *et là fera les grants du roy*,[1] and there will be novelties. In regard to the fashion of the said emperor and his estate, he is a very fine prince and attractive, very robust, very human, and benign. I do not know with whom to compare his figure better than Monseigneur de Croy, as he was eight or ten years ago, except that his flesh is whiter than that of the Sr. de Croy. The emperor has seven or eight hundred horse as an escort, but the major part of the nobles present come from this locality. In regard to Monseigneur's departure, there is no news, and they make great cheer—this is all for this time."

The German scholars in the imperial party listened most attentively to the style of the Netherlander's speech as well as to his subject-matter. "More abundant in vocabulary than elegant in Latinity," was their comment, a fault they considered marking all French Latin. The audience found time to note the style for the subject of the address did not interest them greatly. The least observant onlooker knew that the main purpose of this interview was not the plan of a Turkish campaign, though Frederic appointed a committee to discuss that, whose members, Burgundian and German in equal numbers, were instructed to study the Eastern

[1] Gachard could not explain this phrase. It might easily refer to the desired investiture.

question while emperor and duke were absorbed in other matters.[1] In their very first session, this committee decided that the chief obstacle to a Turkish expedition was the Franco-Burgundian quarrel. This point was also raised by Charles in his first conference with Frederic. No campaign was feasible until the European powers were ready to act in concert. Louis XI. was aiding and abetting the heathen by being a disturbing element which rendered this desired unity impossible. So Frederic appointed a fresh commission to discuss European peace. And this insolvable problem was a convenient blind for other discussions.

On October 5th, a Burgundian fête gave new occasion for a display of wealth; "vulgar ostentation," sneered the less opulent German nobles who tried to show that their pride was not wounded by the sharp contrasts between imperial habits and those of a mere duke. On their side, the Burgundians remarked that it was a pity to waste good things on boors so little accustomed to elegantly equipped apartments that they used silken bedspreads to polish up their boots!

A running commentary of international criticism, fine feasts, ostensible negotiations about projects that probably no one expected would come to pass, and an undercurrent, persistent and mandatory, of demands emphatically made on one side, feebly accepted by the other while the

[1] Chmel, *Mon. Habs.*, i., lxxvii., 50, 51: Toutey, p. 50.

two principals were together, and petulantly disliked by the emperor as soon as he was alone again —such was the course of the conference.

Frederic III. had one simple desire—to marry his son to the Burgundian heiress. Charles desired many things, some of which are clear and others obscure. The very fact that the emperor did not at once refuse his demands, gave him confidence that all were obtainable. Very probably he hoped to overawe his feudal chief by a display of his resources, and by showing the high esteem in which he was held by all nations. There at Trèves, embassies came to him from England, from various Italian and German states, and from Hungary.

On October 15th, a treaty was signed that made the new Duke of Lorraine virtually a vassal to Charles, an important step towards Burgundian expansion. There was time and to spare for these many comings and goings during the eight weeks of the sojourn at Trèves, and the duke was not idle. That his own business hung fire, he thought was due to the machinations of Louis XI. He had no desire to prolong his visit, for he was well aware of the risk involved in keeping his troops in Trèves.[1] At first the magnificence of his equipage had amused the quiet old town, but little by little, in spite of the duke's strict discipline, the presence of idle soldiers became very onerous. Charles did not hesitate to hang on the

[1] Toutey, p. 53.

nearest tree a man caught in an illicit act, but much lawlessness passed without his knowledge. Provisions became very dear; there was some danger of an epidemic due to the unsanitary conditions of the place, ill fitted to harbour so many strangers. The precautions instituted by the Roman founders in regard to their water supply had long since fallen into disuse.

Weary of delays, the duke demanded a definite answer from the emperor as to the proposed kingdom, the matrimonial alliance, and his own status. Frederic appeared about to acquiesce, and then substituted vague promises for present assent to the demands. But when Charles, indignant, broke off negotiations on October 31st, and began to prepare for immediate departure, Frederic became anxious, renewed his overtures, and a new conference took place, in which he consented to fulfil the duke's wishes, with the proviso the sanction of his election should be obtained.

Charles promised to go against the Turk in person, and to place a thousand men at Frederic's disposal, so soon as all points at issue between him and Louis XI. were settled, and provided that his estates were erected into a kingdom, which should also comprise the bishoprics of Liege, Utrecht, Toul, Verdun, and the duchies of Lorraine, Savoy, and Cleves. This realm was to be a fief of the empire like Hungary, Bohemia, and Poland, and transmissible by heredity in the male and female line—a necessary recognition of a

The Meeting at Trèves 349

woman's right, approved by both parties, for Mary of Burgundy was to marry Maximilian.

Electoral confirmation alone was wanting, and in regard to that there was much voluminous correspondence and much shuffling of responsibility. The electors of Mayence and of Trèves were the only ones present to speak for themselves, and they declared that the matter ought to be referred to a full conclave of the electoral college.[1] Let the candidate for royalty await the decision of the next diet, appointed for November at Augsburg.

Never loth to delay, the emperor proposed this solution to Charles, who replied haughtily that if his request were not complied with he would join Louis XI. in a league hostile to the empire. This was on November 6th. The Archbishop of Trèves then suggested that if the question could not wait for a diet, at least the electors should be summoned, especially the elector of Brandenburg, whom he knew to be influential with the emperor, and who was a leader in the anti-Burgundian and anti-Bohemian German party. This seemed fair, but the emperor suddenly put on a show of authority and declared, with an injured air, that he was perfectly free to act on his own initiative without confirmation. In the interests of Christianity and of the empire he

[1] Toutey bases this statement on three letters (October 30, 31, and November 7, 1473) written by the envoys of the elector of Brandenburg, Ludwig von Eyb and Hertnid von Stein.

would appoint Charles of Burgundy chief of the crusade, and he would crown him king.

The organised opposition to his plan came to the duke's ears and made him very angry. Yet, at the same time, he had no desire to dispense with electoral consent. Possibly he felt that the imperial staff alone was too feeble to conjure his kingdom into permanent existence. It was finally decided that Frederic III. should display his power to the extent of investing Charles at once with the duchy of Guelders, while the more important investiture should be postponed.

Very imposing was the ceremony enacted in the market-place. Frederic was exalted upon a high platform ascended by a flight of steps. Charles, clad in complete steel but bareheaded and unattended, rode slowly around the platform three times, "which they say was the custom in such solemnities of investiture," adds an eye-witness,[1] as though he considered the ceremony somewhat archaic. Then the candidate dismounted, received the mantle of the empire from an attendant, and slowly ascended the steps to the emperor's feet, while a new escutcheon, displaying the insignia of the freshly acquired fiefs, quartered on the Burgundian arms, was carried before him. Kneeling at the emperor's feet, the duke laid

[1] Basin, *Histoire des règnes de Charles VII. et de Louis XI.*, ii., 323. Between Nov. 6th and this ceremony there had been new ruptures. Hugonet had gone back and forth many times between the chiefs and " all the world had wondered."

MAXIMILIAN OF AUSTRIA, MEDAL

The Meeting at Trèves

two fingers on his sword hilt and repeated the oath of fealty and service in low but distinct tones. Other rites followed, and then Charles was proclaimed Duke of Guelders.

Thus one object of the conference was attained, and all the world thought it was only a question of time when the greater investiture would be celebrated. Charles's star was in the ascendant. There seemed no limit to the power he had acquired over his suzerain, who apparently graciously nodded assent to his requests, while the duke, too, withdrawing from his alliance with the King of Hungary, appeared very conciliatory in all doubtful issues. At the same time, his confidence in Frederic was by no means perfect.

"The emperor is acting with perfect imperial authority and thinks that no one has a right to dispute it, nevertheless the duke yearns for the sanction of the electors and is set upon obtaining it."[1] The tone taken by Charles was that of humble ignorance. "Little instructed as I am in imperial German law, I am anxious to have your opinion on the legal ability of the emperor to erect a kingdom." On November 8th, in the evening, the electors present in Trèves declared that they were not exactly sure about the imperial authority, but they were sure that it was not their duty to discuss the legal attributes of imperial puissance.

[1] Albert of Brandenburg to the Duke of Saxony. (Muller, *Reichstag Theatrum*, p. 598.)

Under these circumstances what remained to hinder the attainment of Charles's desire? The emperor consented, and the only people who could have stayed his consent expressly stated that his was the final word, not theirs. It was easy for onlookers to conclude not only that the coronation was certain but that it was done.

"Know that our lord the emperor has made the Duke of Burgundy a king of the lands hereafter mentioned and has assured the royal title to him and his heirs, male and female; all the territories that he holds from the empire together with Guelderland lately conquered, and the land of Lorraine, lately lapsed to the empire in fief, besides the duchy of Burgundy that formerly was held from the crown of France; also the bishoprics of Liege, Utrecht, Dolen, and others belonging to the empire, besides a few seigniories, also imperial fiefs. All this, royalty and principalities, he receives from a Roman emperor."

So wrote Albert of Brandenburg on November 13th, trusting to the word of an envoy who had left matters in so advanced a state when he departed from Trèves that he felt safe in concluding that achievement had been reached.[1]

Various letters from the citizens of Berne, too, were filled with rumours from Trèves. Most extraordinary is one of November 29th, intended to go the rounds of the Swiss confederacy, containing *exact details of the coronation of Charles*

[1] Toutey, p. 57.

The Meeting at Trèves

as it had taken place five days previously. The boundaries of the new kingdom were specified.[1] Venice, in hot haste to please the monarch, had instantly shown exceptional honour to the Burgundian resident. How exact it all sounded! Yet there was no truth in it.

The vacillating emperor was affected by the attitude of his suite, and by their varying representations. There is no actual proof of French interference, but French agents had been seen in the city, and might have had private audiences with the emperor. Gradually, relations changed between Charles and Frederic. There was a cloud, not dissipated by a three days' fête given by the duke (November 19th–22d), evidently in farewell. Was Charles too exigeant with his demands, too chary of his daughter? Probably.

On November 23d, instead of a definitive treaty a simple convention was signed, postponing the coronation until February. Emperor and regal candidate were to meet again at Besançon, Cologne, or Basel. In the interval, Charles was to come to a satisfactory understanding with the electors and obtain their official endorsement for the imperial grant.

November 25th was appointed, *not* for the regal investiture, but for Frederic's departure. On the evening of the 24th, he gave audience to his councillors and princes. The electors present were urged by the Burgundians to give their own

[1] Toutey, p. 60, note.

conditional approval at least, and to consent to a reduction of the military obligations to be incurred by Charles. It was a crisis, however, where nobody wished to pledge anything definitely. There was an evident disposition to await some further issue before final action.

The leave-taking between the bargain makers was expected to be as pompous as had been the entry into Trèves. It was far into the night of November 24th when the audience broke up. Little rest was there for the imperial suite, for when the tardy November sun arose above the eastern horizon, its rays met Frederic sailing down the Moselle. Not only had no imperial adieux been uttered, but no imperial debts had been settled. This was the news that was awaiting Charles when he awoke. Baffled he was, but not in his hope of being a king that day. No, only in his expectation of a stately pageant.[1] In all haste he sent Peter von Hagenbach to ride more swiftly along the bank than the boat could sail, so as to overtake the traveller and urge him to wait for a few more words on divers topics. In one account it is reported that Frederic, though annoyed at the interruption, still assented to Hagenbach's request. No sooner was the latter away, however, than he changed his mind and continued his course.

[1] In this account, differing from the current tradition, Toutey has followed Bachmann's conclusions (*Deutsche Reichsgeschichte*, ii., 435).

The Meeting at Trèves

Rumour was busy in regard to this strange exit of the emperor from the scene. The general belief among contemporaries was that it was on the eve of the intended coronation that Frederic turned his back on the scene. Take first the words of Thomas Basin, whose statement that he was in the very midst of the events can hardly be doubted:[1]

"But alas how easily and instantly human desires change, and how fragile are the alliances and friendships of men, especially of princes, which are not joined and confirmed by the glue of Christ . . . as the sacred Psalm sings, 'Put not your trust in princes nor in the sons of men in whom there is no safety.' Suddenly, forsooth, when they were thought to be harmonious in charity, benevolence, and friendship, when they offered each other such splendid entertainment, when they feasted together in regal luxury in all unity and friendship, when all things, as has been said, needed for the magnificence of such a great honour were made ready and prepared, so that on the third day should occur the celebration of that regal dignity [*fastigii*], and the [*provectio*] promotion of a new king and the erection of a new kingdom or the restoration and renovation of an ancient one, now obsolete from antiquity, were expected by all with great attention;—something occurred, I do not know what; hesitation or suspicion, fancied or justified, unexpectedly affected the emperor . . . and embarking on his ship in the very early morning he sailed down the river Moselle to the Rhine. And thus was frustrated

[1] Basin, ii., 325.

the hope of the duke and of all the Burgundians who believed that he was to be elevated to a king. In a moment this hope was extinguished like a candle.

"We were present there in the city of Trèves, attached to the suite of neither prince, not serving or pretending to serve either of them. But we ascertained nothing either then or later, although we made many inquiries, about the cause of this sudden departure and we are still ignorant of the truth. When the day broke after the emperor's departure, and the duke was informed of the fact, he was also assured that the vessel in which the emperor sailed was opposite the monastery of St. Mary Blessed to the Martyrs. So he sent messengers hastily to beg the emperor to stay for a very brief interview with the duke, assuring him that the very least delay possible should occur if he did the favour. But no attention was paid to the signals from the shore and the course was continued."

The bishop wrote these words some time after the event. There are other accounts preserved, actual letters written within a few days or weeks of November 25th, wherein is evinced similar ignorance of what had actually passed. The following gives several suggestions of difficulties not mentioned elsewhere. A certain Balthasar Cesner, secretary, writes to Master Johannes Gelthauss and others in Frankfort, from Cologne, on December 6th.[1] He was attached to the im-

[1] Preserved in the municipal archives in Frankfort (nr. 5808 or ch. lit. clausa c. sig in verso impr.). This is published by Karl Schellhass in *Deutsche Zeitschrift für Geschichtewissenschaft*, (1891) pp. 80–85. The language is a queer mixture of German and Latin.

The Meeting at Trèves

perial service, and possibly was one of the few attendants on Frederic in the hasty journey from Trèves. After touching on Cologne affairs he proceeds:

"I must inform your excellencies how the Duke of Burgundy came with all pomp for his coronation as king of the kingdom of Burgundy and Friesland with twenty-six standards besides a magnificent sceptre and crown. He also wished to take his duchy and territories in Savoy[1] and Guelders and others in fief from him [the emperor] and not from the empire.[2] This and other extraordinary demands his imperial grace did not wish to grant, and on that account he has broken off the interview and gone away. Everything was prepared for the coronation, the chair for the taking.[3] It is said that he is to be crowned in Aix. It may be hoped not [*non speratur*]. You can understand me as well as your faithful servant.

"Dear Master Hans I hope that you will not laugh at me. I can please my gracious lord and be worthy of praise if you will only trust me.

"Despatched from Cologne on St. Nicholas Day itself.

"To the Jurisconsult Master Johannes Gelthauss, Distinguished advocate, master, preceptor of the city of Frankfort."

The two kingdoms are also mentioned by Snoy:

[1] Charles asked on October 23d, through his chancellor, for investiture into Savoy. (Note by Schellhass.)

[2] Under this head is meant Lorraine, which he alleged had lapsed to the emperor at the death of Nicholas of Calabria.

[3] This means the throne from which Charles was to step down to receive the fief.

"Two realms, namely Burgundy and Frisia; in the second, Holland, Zealand, Guelders, Brabant, Limburg, Namur, Hainaut, and the dioceses of Liege, Cambray, and Utrecht; in the first, Burgundy, Luxemburg, Artois, Flanders, and three bishoprics."

The chronicler adds that this plan was discussed in secret conference.[1]

Again the rumour that the final straw that broke the emperor's resolution was the duke's desire to take Savoy and Guelders from his hand alone, is suggestive. On the duke's part, this wish might indicate an attempt to separate a portion of territory from the empire in a way to deceive his contemporaries into thinking that his kingdom was an imperial fief, while, in reality, it was an independent realm, as he or his successors could declare at a convenient moment. But this seems at variance with his attested desire for electoral support.

It was a curious tangle and never fully un-

---

[1] "Loquitur etiam ferunt de regnis Frisiæ et Burgundiæ sibi constituendes quæ audissimis auribus accepta visus non tam negare imperator quam dissimulare.

"Nam et ad eam [majestatem regiam] aspirare et ditiones suas velle in duo regna partiri visue Burgundiæ et Frisiæ: in hoc Hollandia, Zelandia, Gelria, Brabantia, Limburgum, Namureum, Hannonia et dioceses Leodiensis, Cameracensis et Trajectina: altero Burgundia, Luxemburgum, Arthesia, Flandria, ecclesiæque cathedrales Sadunensis, Tullensis Verdunensis essent." (P. 1131.)

Renier Snoy was born the year of Charles's death, so that his statement is tradition but founded on what he might have heard from eye-witnesses.

ravelled. Yet, considering the emperor's personal characteristics, his last action does not seem inexplicable. As his visitor showed the intensity of his will, Frederic became restive. Phlegmatic, obstinate, yet conscious of his own weakness, personal conflicts with a nature equally obstinate and much more vigorous were exceedingly unpleasant. The collision made him writhe uneasily and prefer to slip out of his embarrassment as quietly as he could.

The proposed leave-taking was to be very magnificent, and the magnificence again was significant of Burgundian wealth. Whether the duke would surely keep his pledge of sharing that wealth with the archduke if the emperor went so far that he could not draw back, was a consideration that undoubtedly may have affected Frederic. Had Mary of Burgundy accompanied her father, had the wedding of the daughter and investiture of the new king been planned for the same day, had the promises been exchanged simultaneously, the leave-taking might have passed, indeed, as a third ceremonial in all stateliness.

If Frederic doubted the surety of his bargain, it is not surprising. It was notorious how the duke had played fast and loose with his daughter's hand, withdrawing it from the grasp of a suitor as the greater advantages of another alliance were presented to him, or as the mere disadvantage of any marriage at all became unpleasantly near. Vigorous man of forty that he was,

Charles had no personal desire to see a son-in-law, *in propria persona*, waiting for his shoes—a fact perfectly patent to the emperor, as it was to the rest of the world.

The task of making the imperial adieux was entrusted to the imperial chamberlain, Ulrich von Montfort, who duly presented his master's formal excuses to the duke, on the morning of November 25th. "Important and urgent affairs had necessitated his presence elsewhere. The arrangement discussed between them was not broken but simply postponed until a more convenient occasion rendered its execution possible," etc.

The Strasburg chronicles report that Charles was in a towering rage on receiving this communication. He clinched his fists, ground his teeth, and kicked the furniture about the room in which he had locked himself up.[1] But by the time these words were penned, these authors were better informed than Charles about the ultimate result of the emperor's intentions. The duke may have been angry, but he certainly controlled himself sufficiently to give several audiences in the course of the day—to envoys from Lorraine among others—and was ready to take his own departure by evening, not doubting that the crown and sceptre, carefully packed with the mountain of his valuable treasure, would assuredly fulfil their destiny in the near future. Trèves was

[1] Chmel, i., 49–51; Toutey, p. 59.

left to its pristine repose, and Charles was the last man to realise that in its silence were entombed for ever his chances of wearing the prematurely prepared insignia.

CHAPTER XVIII

COLOGNE, LORRAINE, AND ALSACE

1473-1474

LATE as it was in November, the weather was still very mild, and as the emperor and duke travelled in opposite directions, neither the former as he went down to Cologne, nor the latter as he passed up the valley of the Moselle to that of the Ell, was hindered by autumn storms. The summer of 1473 had been marked by unprecedented heat and a prolonged drouth.[1] Forest fires raged unchecked on account of the dearth of water and, for the same reason, the mills stood still. The grape crops, indeed, were prodigious, but the vintage was not profitable because the wine had a tendency to sour. Gentle rains in September prepared the ground for an untimely fertility. Trees blossomed and, though some fruits withered prematurely, cherries actually ripened. Thus the Rhinelands presented a pleasant appearance as Charles rode to Lorraine.

His first pause was at Thionville in Luxemburg, where he stayed about a fortnight and received

[1] De Roye, p. 105.

Cologne, Lorraine, and Alsace 363

ambassadors from Hungary, Poland, Venice, England, Denmark, Brittany, Ferrara, the Palatinate, and Cologne.[1] The result of his conference with the last named was a declaration on the duke's part which seriously affected his later career. The condition of Cologne must be touched on as an essential part of this narrative.

The late Duke of Burgundy had attempted to pursue a line of policy in regard to the ecclesiastical elections in the diocese of Cologne that had succeeded in Liege and in Utrecht. In 1463, he had tried to force the chapter to elect his candidate. They had refused to follow his leading, but their own choice, Robert, brother of the elector-palatine, did not prove a congenial chief, and the new prelate turned to Philip for aid when he found his chapter disposed to restrict both his revenues and his temporal authority. Later, in 1467, as the audacity of his opponents increased, the archbishop appealed to his brother, the elector, and to Charles of Burgundy. The latter was busy in France, but he wrote a sententious letter to Cologne, exhorting both chapter and city to be obedient to their chosen spiritual and lay lord. This intervention was resented. The breach wid-

[1] He also issued administrative orders. It was at this time that he instituted a high court of justice and a chamber of accounts at Mechlin, both designed to serve for all the Netherland provinces. This measure was bitterly resented by the local authorities. (Fredericq. *Le rôle politique et social des ducs de Bourgogne*, p. 183.)

ened between Robert and his people, culminating in actual hostilities. The chapter took possession of the town of Neuss, accepted Hermann of Hesse as their protector, and sent an embassy to Rome to state their grievances. The elector aided his brother and the belligerent parties grew in strength.

The city of Cologne wavered for a space, undecided which cause to espouse, and finally chose the chapter's side, signing a five years' alliance with that body, which had officially renounced allegiance to Robert, pending the judgment of pope and emperor on the dissension. Such was the state of affairs when Charles entered into possession of Guelders and manifested a disposition to interest himself in Cologne. He informed the chapter that he was greatly displeased with their contumely. To Cologne he said, "Be neutral," but the burghers showed so little inclination to heed his neighbourly advice that he tried harsher measures and permitted Cologne merchants to be molested in his domains.

In 1473, all hostilities were suspended in the hopes of imperial intervention.[1] While Charles was still in Guelders, Robert paid him a visit, held long conferences with him, and probably received promises of future aid, for he had an air of arrogance when he returned from the interview. During the sojourn of duke and emperor at Trèves, a papal legate, the Bishop of Fossom-

[1] Letters are preserved in the Cologne archives. (Toutey, p. 64.)

brone, arrived from Rome with plenary powers to settle Cologne affairs, and his measures were endorsed by Charles in a letter from Trèves.

For a time Frederic III. seemed inclined to refrain from interference, then something influenced him in another direction. When he arrived at Cologne in November, he received a warm welcome and costly gifts, which he repaid by conferring a mass of privileges on his "good city,"—cheap and easy benefits,—but he did not prove an efficient arbitrator, simply postponing any decision from day to day, though he was begged to settle all difficulties before Charles should attempt to relieve him of the trouble.

True, Charles was detained elsewhere. But he no longer felt the need of conciliating the emperor, and at Thionville, on December 11, 1473, he issued a manifesto declaring that his friend Robert was entirely in the right, his opponents in the wrong.[1] As these latter defied papal legate and arbitrator duly authorised to settle the points of dispute, he, Charles of Burgundy, would constitute himself defender of the insulted archbishop. At the same time, he despatched Étienne de Lavin to check the encroachments of the insolent rebels. The declaration emboldened Robert to defy the emperor's summons to meet him and the papal legate. They both declared that they would take measures to bring him to obedience, but Frederic did not wish to tarry longer at Cologne. In

[1] Toutey, p. 66. This document is in the Cologne archives.

January he took his departure, having directed Hermann of Hesse to protect that see against all aggression.

Apparently, at that time, in spite of the manifesto, there was no formal treaty between Charles and Robert, but there are two drafts for such a treaty in existence,[1] wherein the former pledged himself to force chapter, nobles, and city to submission, in consideration of the sum of 200,000 florins, while the archbishop gave permission to his ally to garrison all strongholds, including Cologne. Pending his autumn sojourn in the upper Rhinelands, Charles had, therefore, plans regarding Cologne definitely in mind.

Lorraine

This duchy was even more interesting to Charles than Cologne, and there were many matters in its regard which demanded his urgent attention in 1473. It, too, was a pleasant territory, and conveniently adjacent to Burgundian lands. A natural means of annexation had been considered by Charles in the proposed marriage between Nicholas, Duke of Lorraine, and Mary of Burgundy. When that project was abandoned to suit Charles's pleasure, he retained the friendship of his rejected son-in-law until the latter's death in the spring of 1473. So unexpected was this event, that

[1] *See* Toutey, p. 66. These are printed in Lacomblet, *Urkunden*, iv., 468, 470.

there was the usual suspicion of poisoning, and this crime, too, was charged to the account of Louis XI., apparently without foundation. Certainly that monarch reaped no immediate advantage from the death, for the family to whom the succession passed was more friendly to Burgundy than to France.

The heir to the childless Nicholas was his aunt Yolande of Anjou, daughter of old King René of Anjou, sister to the unfortunate Margaret, late Queen of England, and widow of the Duke of Vaudemont. The council of Lorraine lost no time in acknowledging Yolande as their duchess. She hastened to Nancy, the capital, with her son René, aged twenty-two, where they were received hospitably, and then Yolande formally abdicated in favour of the young man, who was duly accepted as Duke of Lorraine.

Now there was a large party of Burgundian sympathisers in Nancy, and it was probably owing to their pressure that very strong links were at once forged between Charles and the new sovereign of the duchy. The apprehension lest the former should protect the land as he had the heritage of his namesake, little Charles of Guelders, was expressed by the timorous, but their counsels were overweighted, and, on October 15th, René accepted a treaty whose terms were very favourable to Burgundy. In exchange for being "protector,"—an office that the emperor had already been asked to change into suzerainty,—René cemented an alliance, offensive and defensive, with Charles, giving the latter full permission to march his forces across Lorraine. Further, he pledged himself to appoint as officials in all important places on the route "men bound by oath to the Duke of Burgundy." Yes, more, these were discharged from fidelity to René in case he abandoned Burgundian interests.

Yolande of Vaudemont endorsed these articles by adding her signature to that of her son. Charles feared, however, that the provisions might not be adhered to by the Lorrainers—so humiliating were the terms—and exacted in addition the signatures of the chief nobles. On November 18th, seventy-four of these gentlemen attested their approval of an act that practically delivered their land to a stranger,—evidence that they doubted the ability of their hereditary chief, and preferred Burgundy to France.

There is a story that Charles tried other methods than diplomacy, before he got the better of the young duke in this bargain, that he actually had him stolen away from the castle of Joinville where he was staying with his mother.[1] Louis promptly came forward and arrested a nephew of the emperor, a student in the University of Paris, and kept him as a hostage until the release of René. Rumour, too, asserts that there was a

[1] Jean de Roye is the only contemporary to tell this story. Both Toutey and Kirk reject it. (*See* Toutey, p. 76; Kirk, ii., 271.)

Cologne, Lorraine, and Alsace 369

treaty of Joinville, wherein René asserted his friendship with Louis, which was intermitted by his relations with Charles, to be resumed later. That also seems to be improbable. The formal alliance with Louis did not come then, though the king took immediate care to build up a party in his behalf in Lorraine, and to keep himself informed of the progress of the new régime.

From Thionville, Charles journeyed on to Nancy, where he was welcomed by his protégé, outside the city walls, and the two rode in together as the duke and the emperor had entered Trèves. Charles had been so long keeping up a show of obsequiousness which he did not feel that, undoubtedly, he enjoyed again being the first personage.[1] He refused, however, to accept the young man's hospitality, and spent the two days of his sojourn in the house of a certain Malhortie, where he felt more at ease in his conferences with Lorrainers willing to proceed further to the disadvantage of their new sovereign.

The ally certainly became more exigeant. In various towns on the Moselle, Épinal, Charmes, Dompaire, etc., the Lorraine soldiers were replaced by Burgundians. This immediate and arrogant use of the rights he had wrested from the Duke of Lorraine alienated many who had been warm for Burgundy. René himself admired Charles as Maximilian had done. The strong man exercised a fascination over both youths,

[1] Toutey's suggestion.

but the duke did not turn this admiration into real friendship, underestimating the character of his protégé. His measures, too, were taken without the slightest consideration for local feeling. Garrison after garrison was installed and commanded to obey his officers alone, while the soldiers were allowed to levy their own rations, equivalent to raids on a friendly country. As always, the agglomeration of mercenary companies was difficult to control. The duke did not succeed in having those remote from his jurisdiction kept in due restraint. Complaints began to pour into his headquarters. Public sentiment shifted day by day. The Burgundian became the personification of a public foe. Before Charles proceeded on his way to Alsace, René had begun to lose his admiration and it was not long before he impatiently awaited an opportunity to break with his too doughty protector.

Alsace

During the four years that Charles had delayed in coming to look at the result of the bargain of 1469 in the Rhine valley, his lieutenant, Peter von Hagenbach, had given the inhabitants reason to regret the easy-going absentee Austrian seigneurs. Much had been done, undoubtedly, in restraining the lawlessness of the robber barons. The roads were well policed, and safety was assured to travellers. "I spy," was the motto

Cologne, Lorraine, and Alsace 371

blazoned on the livery of the forces led by Hagenbach up and down the land, until he had unearthed lurking vagabonds. It was acknowledged that gold and silver could be carried openly from place to place, and that night journeys were as safe as day. Still, this advantageous change had not won popularity for the man who wrought it. Perhaps the people thought it less burdensome to make their own little bargains with highwaymen or petty nobles,[1] a law unto themselves, than to meet the rigorous requisitions of the Burgundian tax collector.

It was the country that had profited most by the new administration. The small towns had long enjoyed great independence, and had shown ability in managing their own affairs. They wanted no interference. Not liked by those whom he had really protected, Hagenbach was absolutely hated by the burghers who felt his iron hand, without acknowledging that its pressure had more good than evil in it.

Then there were the neighbours to be considered. The Swiss had hated Sigismund and all Austrians, and had been prepared to prefer Burgundy as a power in the Rhinelands. But Hagenbach took no pains to win their friendship. His insolent fashion of referring to them as "fellows" or "rascals," added to acts of aggression, unchecked if not condoned by him, aroused bitter dislike

[1] All sons inherited their father's title, so that there were many landless lords.

to him in the confederated cantons,[1] and in their allies, Berne, Mulhouse, etc. By 1473, there was a growing sentiment in Helvetia that they would be happier if Austria had her own again, while the uneasiness in the cities that stood alone had greatly increased.

Within Hagenbach's immediate jurisdiction, the opposition to his measures took a definite form long before the duke's arrival there. The various commissioners sent by Charles to inspect the quality of his bargain had all agreed in an urgent recommendation to the duke to redeem, at the earliest possible moment, all the troublesome mortgages honeycombing his authority. Hagenbach, too, was fully convinced of the necessity for this measure, but he was not provided with sufficient money to accomplish it.

In the spring of 1473, therefore, he resolved to lay a new tax on wine. This impost, called the "Bad Penny," was bitterly resented for two reasons. The burden was oppressive to the vintners and it was an illegal measure, as no sanction had been given by the local estates. Three towns, Thann, Ensisheim, and Brisac, declared that they were determined to refuse payment.

Hagenbach marched a force into the Engelburg, a stronghold dominating Thann, bombarded the town, and took it easily. Thirty citizens were

[1] At this period there were eight in the confederation, which was a loose structure in which each member preserved her individuality.

Cologne, Lorraine, and Alsace 373

condemned to death as leaders in an iniquitous rebellion against the just orders of their lawful governor. Some of these, indeed, were pardoned, though their estates were confiscated, but five or six were publicly executed, and their bodies hung exposed to view on the market-place, as a hideous object-lesson of the cost of resisting Burgundian orders.

One execution sufficed to render Ensisheim submissive, but Brisac proved more obstinate. The magistrates there did not resort to force. They declared there was no need, for they were fully protected by the article in the treaty of St. Omer, which forbade arbitrary imposition of any tax on the part of the suzerain. Their determined refusal made the lieutenant consent to refer the question to the Duke of Burgundy, and messengers were despatched to Trèves to represent the respective grievances of governor and governed. The collection of the tax was postponed until Charles could examine the situation.

A determined effort to bring the independent town of Mulhouse under Burgundian sway was another act of 1473, fanning opposition to a white heat that forged organised resistance to any extension of Burgundian authority. For three years, Hagenbach had endeavoured to convince the burghers of that imperial city that they would be wise to accept the duke's protection and have their debts paid. The latter were, indeed, oppressive, but there was fear lest "protection" might be more so, and conference after conference failed to produce the acquiescence desired by Hagenbach.

In 1473, that zealous servant of Burgundy declared that if the burghers persisted in their refusal he would resort to force. Their reply was that Mulhouse could not take such an important step without consulting her friends, the Swiss. "Are the cantons going to help you pay your debts?" was the sneering comment of Hagenbach. "Mulhouse is a bad weed in a rose garden, a plant that must be extirpated. Its submission would make a charming pleasure ground out of the Sundgau, Alsace, and Breisgau. The duke knew no city which he would prefer to Mulhouse for a sojourn," were his further statements.[1]

Two days were given to the town council for an answer. Hagenbach remarked that it was useless to think that time could be gained until the mortgaged territories should return to Austria. "Far from planning redemption, Duke Sigismund is now preparing to cede to *Charles le téméraire* as much again of his domain and vassals." Still Mulhouse was not convinced that the only course open to her was to let Charles pay her debts and receive her homage. No answer was forthcoming in the two days, but ready scribes had prepared many copies of Hagenbach's letter, which were

[1] *See* Toutey, p. 82, who quotes from the *Cartulaire de Mulhouse*, iv., *et passim*. This last furnishes the details for these passages.

Cologne, Lorraine, and Alsace

sent to all who might be interested in checking these proposals of Burgundy.

On February 24, 1473, a Swiss diet met at Lausanne and there the matter was weighed. Hagenbach's letter was shown to those who had not seen it, and methods of rescuing Mulhouse from her dilemma were carefully considered. Years ago a union had existed between the forest cantons and the Alsatian cities. There were propositions to renew this alliance so as to present a strong front to their Burgundian neighbour. The cantons had enough to do with their own affairs, but the result of the discussion was that, on March 14th, a ten-year Alsatian confederation was formed in imitation of the Swiss.

The chief members were Basel, Colmar, Mulhouse, Schlestadt, and two dioceses, and it is referred to as the *Basse-Union* or the Lower Union, the purposes being to guarantee mutually the rights of the contracting parties, to meet for discussion on various questions, and, specifically, to help Mulhouse pay her debts. A few days later, March 19th, there was a fresh proposition to make an alliance between this *Basse-Union* and the Swiss confederation. This required a *referendum*. Each Swiss delegate received a copy of the articles to take back to his constituents for their consideration. No bond between the confederation and the union was, however, in existence at the time when Charles was approaching Alsace. Various conciliatory measures on his part had somewhat lessened immediate opposition to him, but, nevertheless, there were frequent conferences about affairs. Diets were almost continuous and there were strenuous efforts to raise money to free Mulhouse from her hampering financial embarrassments.

Hagenbach had not followed up his threats of immediate war measures, but it was known that he had obtained imperial authorisation to assume the jurisdiction of Mulhouse, a step which her allies hoped to forestall by settling her debts. Strasburg offered to contribute six hundred florins, Berne and Soleure seven hundred, Basel four hundred, while Colmar, Schlestadt, Obernai, and Kaisersberg together hoped to raise another four hundred. A diet was called at Basel for December 11th, and Zürich and Lucerne were expected to enter into the union. The tidings of the duke's approach were undoubtedly a stimulus to these renewed efforts to make the league strong enough to withstand him. The sentiment expressed by the pious Knebel, "May God protect us from his mighty hand," voiced probably a wide-spread dread.

When Charles entered Alsace, his escort was large enough to inspire fear, but there was no opposition to his advance, though consultations, now at one city, now at another, were frequent. The duke paid little heed to their deliberations, under-estimating their importance, while he was gracious to any words of welcome offered to him.

Strasburg sent him greetings while he rested at Châtenois, and so did Colmar. The latter town expressed her willingness to receive him and an escort of one or two hundred, but was firm in her refusal to admit a larger force within her walls. By this precaution, Charles was baffled in his plot to gain possession of the town, and so passed on his way.

On Christmas eve, the traveller made a formal entry into Brisac, where a temporary court was established, and where audience was given to various embassies with the customary Burgundian pomp. Meanwhile the troops, forced to camp without the walls, were a burden to the land, and seem to have been more odious than usual to their unwilling hosts.

The citizens of Brisac offered homage on their knees and had their hopes raised high by their suzerain's pleasant greeting, but they failed to obtain the hoped-for assurance that the treaty of St. Omer should be observed in all respects. Among the envoys were many who undertook to remonstrate in a friendly fashion about the imposition of the "Bad Penny" tax on the Alsatians, and the over-severity of Hagenbach's administration. The cause of Mulhouse, too, was urged, notably by Berne. The representations of these last envoys were received most courteously. The duke rather thought that the city could be detached from the league, and therefore gave himself some trouble to establish friendly relations.

To Mulhouse, too, his tone was conciliatory. He wrote a pleasant letter to the town and despatched a councillor thither, who would, he assured them, arrange matters to their satisfaction. But an abortive *coup d'état* on the part of the Burgundians, which would have given them possession of Basel, destroyed the effect of these reassuring phrases. The burghers were warned in time, looked to their defences, and banished from their midst every individual suspected of Burgundian sympathies. Every newcomer was carefully scrutinised before he was admitted within the walls, and the Rhine was guarded most rigidly. The propriety of these precautions was soon proven.

Charles ordered a review at Ensisheim, the official capital of the landgraviate. Thither marched his troops from every quarter. Those from Säckingen, Lauffen, and Waldshut found their shortest route over the bridge at Basel, and there they appeared and begged to be allowed to cross. Their sincerity was doubted, and the least foothold on the city's territory was sternly refused then and a week later, when the request was renewed. The method of introducing friendly troops into a town and then seizing it by a sudden *coup de main* was what Charles had been suspected of plotting for Metz, and later for Colmar, and there seems to be no doubt that a third essay of this rather stupid stratagem was planned, only to fail again, and this time to be peculiarly disastrous in its reflex action.

Cologne, Lorraine, and Alsace 379

The review took place and the strength of the Burgundian mercenaries was duly displayed to the Alsatians, but no satisfactory assurances were given to Brisac and the other towns that their suzerain would restrict his measures of taxation and administration to the stipulations of the contract of St. Omer. On the contrary, when Charles passed on to Burgundy it was plain to all that he had *not* restricted the powers of his lieutenant in any respect, but rather had endorsed his general method of procedure.

One night was spent at Thann[1] and then the duke took his leave of the annexed region whose

---

[1] In this account Toutey's conclusions are accepted. There are discrepancies as to dates among the various chroniclers. The duke's itinerary as given in Comines-Lenglet (ii., 211) does not agree with that of Knebel and others. But the facts of the narrative are little affected by the variations. The following is the itinerary accepted by Toutey:

Dep. from Ensisheim	Jan.	8
Stay at Thann	"	9–10
Dep. from Belfort	"	11
Besançon	"	17
Auxonne, slept	"	18
Dijon, a	"	23
Dijon, d	Feb.	19, 1474
Auxonne, slept	"	20
Dôle	"	21–March 8
(Invested with the Franche Comté of Burgundy.)		
Besançon	March	12 or 15
Vesoul and Luxeuil	March	23–28
Lorraine	"	28
Luxemburg	Apr.	4–June 9
Easter fêtes	"	10
Fête of the Order of the Garter	"	23
Brussels	June	27

people had hoped so much from his visit to them. In mid-January he arrived at Besançon, his winter journeying being wonderfully easy in the unprecedentedly mild weather.

Hagenbach lost no time in proceeding to the levying of the impost now approved by the duke, who had at the same time expressly ordered that the people were to be treated mildly, and that summary punishment was to check all excesses on the part of the eight hundred Picards employed by Hagenbach to aid the tax collector. The governor, however, saw no further need for gentle treatment or for respect to privileges. In Brisac, municipal elections were arbitrarily set aside, and officers appointed by the governor. The corporation was curtailed of power, and the burghers were forced to prepare to march against Mulhouse.

Having accomplished his duty to his own satisfaction, Hagenbach proceeded to give himself some relaxation. His own marriage took place on January 24th, and he celebrated the occasion with great fêtes. It is of this period in Hagenbach's life that the stories of gross excess are told.[1] It seems as though, having once abandoned restraint towards the city, his personal passions, too, were permitted to run riot, and he spared no wife nor maid to whom he took a fancy.

As he had succeeded in impressing the "Bad

[1] Kirk considers that they are well founded and too indecent to repeat.

Penny" on the little independent landowners, he tried to extend it to the territory of the Bishop of Basel. Vehement was the opposition which was reported to the duke, who promptly ordered his lieutenant to restore the prisoners he had taken and to cease his aggressions. Charles was not ready to meet the Swiss, and was willing to defer an issue, but he was wholly ignorant of the real strength of the confederation. Hagenbach then proceeded to make a stronghold of Brisac and waited for further action.

CHAPTER XIX

THE FIRST REVERSES

1474–1475

"WHO is this that cometh, this that is glorious in his apparel, travelling in the greatness of his strength?" These words in Latin, on scrolls fluttering from the hands of living angels, met the eyes of Charles of Burgundy at his retarded arrival in Dijon. And the confident duke had no wish to disclaim the subtle flattery of the implied comparison between him and the subject of the words of the prophet.[1]

The traveller had slept at Périgny, about a league from the capital of Burgundy, so as to make the last stage of his journey thither in leisurely state. Unpropitious weather on Saturday, January 22d, the appointed day, made postponement of the ducal parade necessary, out of consideration for the precious hangings and costly ecclesiastical robes that were to grace the ceremonies of reception and investiture. Fortunately, Sunday, January 23d, dawned fair, and heralds

[1] Plancher, *Histoire générale et particulière de Bourgogne, avec des notes et des preuves justificatives*, iv., cccxxviii.

FORTIFIED CHURCH IN BURGUNDY
XVTH CENTURY

The First Reverses

rode through the city streets at an early hour, proclaiming the duke's gracious intention to make his entry on that day. Immediately, tapestries were spread and every one was alert with the last preparations.

Lavish was the display of biblical phrases, like that cited, which were planted along the ducal way and on a succession of stagings erected for various exhibits. On the great city square, the platform was capacious and many actors played out divers rôles. Here stood the scroll-bearing angels on either side of a living representation of Christ. In the background clustered three separate groups of people representing, respectively, the three Estates. Above their heads more inscriptions were to be read.[1] "All the nations desire to see the face of Solomon," "Behold him desired by all races," "Master, look on us, thy people," were among the legends.

The stately pageant, in which dignitaries, lay and ecclesiastical, from other parts of the duke's domains participated, proceeded past all these soothing insinuations that Charles of Burgundy resembled Solomon in more ways than one, to the church of St. Benigne. Here pledges of mu-

[1] Preparations for the duke's visit to Dijon had been set on foot almost immediately after Philip's death in 1467. One Frère Gilles had devoted many hours to searching the Scriptures for appropriate texts to figure in the reception. Every phrase indicating leonine strength was noted down. The good brother died before the anticipated event came to pass but the result of his patient labour was preserved.

tual fidelity were exchanged between the Burgundians and their ruler. The Abbé of Citeaux placed the ducal ring solemnly upon Charles's finger as a symbol, and he was invested with all the prerogatives of his predecessors.

From the church, the train wound its way to the Ste. Chapelle, past more stages decorated with more flowers of scriptural phrase such as "A lion which is strongest among beasts and turneth not away for any," "The lion hath roared, who will not fear?" "The righteous are as bold as a lion," etc.

Two days later, the concluding ceremonies of investiture were performed, and followed by a banquet. Charles was arrayed in royal robes, and his hat was in truth a crown, gorgeous with gold, pearls, and precious stones. After a repast, prelates, nobles, and civic deputies were convened in a room adjoining the dining-hall, where first they listened to a speech from the chancellor. When he had finished, the duke himself delivered an harangue wherein he expatiated on the splendours of the ancient kingdom of Burgundy. Wrongfully usurped by the French kings, it had been belittled into a duchy, a measure much to be regretted by the Burgundians. Then the speaker broke off abruptly with an ambiguous intimation "that he had in reserve certain things that none might know but himself."[1]

---

[1] *Dit qu'il avoit en soi des choses qui n'appartenoient de scavoir à nuls que à lui* (Plancher, *Preuves*, iv., cccxxxiii.).

What was the significance of these veiled allusions? It could not have been the simple scheme to erect a kingdom, because that was certainly known to many. Charles had, doubtless, an ostrich-like quality of mind which made him oblivious to the world's vision but even he could hardly have ignored the prevalence of the rumours regarding the interview of Trèves, rumours flying north, east, south, and west. Might not this suggestion of secrets yet untold have had reference to the ripening intentions of Edward IV. and himself to divide France between them?

When his own induction into his heritage was accomplished, Charles was ready to pay the last earthly tribute to his parents. A cortège had been coming slowly from Bruges bearing the bodies of Philip and Isabella to their final resting-place in the tomb at Dijon, to which they were at last consigned.[1]

A few weeks more Charles tarried in the city of his birth, and then went to Dôle where he was invested with the sovereignty of the Franche-Comté and confirmed the privileges. Thus after seven years of possession *de facto*, he first actually completed the formalities needful for the legal acquisition of his paternal heritage. The expansion of that heritage had been steady for over half a century. Every inch of territory that had

[1] Plancher, *Preuves*, iv., cccxxxiii. The document describing this ceremony gives February 28th as the date, but that is evidently an error and not accepted.

come under the shadow of the family's administration had remained there, quickly losing its ephemeral character, so that temporary holdings were regarded in the same light as the estates actually inherited. At least, Charles, sovereign duke, count, overlord, mortgagee, made no distinction in the natures of his tenures. But just as the last link was legally riveted in his own chain of lands, he was to learn that there were other points of view.

The statement is made and repeated, that the report of the duke's after-dinner speech at Dijon was a fresh factor in alarming the people in Alsace and Switzerland about his intentions, and making them hasten to shake off every tie that connected them with Charles and his ambitious projects of territorial expansion. As a matter of fact, there had been for months constant agitation in the councils of the Swiss Confederation and the Lower Union as to the next action.

Opposition to Sigismund had been long existent, antipathy to Austria was so deeply rooted that the idea of restoring that suzerainty in the Rhine valley was slow to gain adherents. Probably the arguments that came from France were what carried conviction. It was a time when Louis spared no expense to attain the end he desired, while he posed as a benevolent neutral.[2] His servants worked underground. Their open

[1] Toutey, p. 117.

[2] There are many records in the *Bibl. nat.* of the sums paid out to the Swiss at this time.

The First Reverses

work was very cautious. It was French envoys, however, who announced to the Swiss Diet, convened at Lucerne, that Sigismund was quite ready to come to an understanding in regard to an alliance and the redemption of his mortgaged lands.

That was on January 21, 1474, the very day when the mortgagee was preparing to ride into Dijon and read the agreeable assurances of his wisdom, strength, and puissance. Yet a month and Sigismund's envoys were seated on the official benches at the Basel diet, ranking with the delegates from the cantons and the emissaries from France. On March 27th, the diet met at Constance, and for three days a debate went on which resulted in the drafting of the *Ewige Richtung*, the *Réglement définitif*, a document which contained a definite resolution that the mortgaged lands were to be completely withdrawn from Burgundy, and all financial claims settled. This resolution was subscribed to by Sigismund and the Swiss cantons. Further, it was decided to ignore one or two of the stipulations made at St. Omer and to offer payment to Charles at Basel instead of Besançon.

Meantime that creditor, perfectly convinced in his own mind that the legends of his birthplace were correct in their rating of his character and his qualities, again crossed Lorraine and entered Luxemburg, where he celebrated Easter. It was shortly after that festival, on April 17th, that a letter from Sigismund was delivered to him announcing in rather casual and off-hand terms that he was now in a position to repay the loan of 1469, made on the security of those Rhinelands. Therefore the Austrian would hand over at Basel 80,000 florins, 40,000 the sum received by him, 10,000 paid in his behalf to the Swiss, and 30,000 which he understood that Charles had expended during his temporary incumbency,[1] and he, Sigismund, would resume the sovereignty in Alsace.

It was all very simple, at least Sigismund's wish was. The expressions employed in the paper were, however, so ambiguous, the language so involved, that Charles expended severe criticism on his cousin's style before he proceeded to answer his subject-matter. To that he replied that the bargain between him and Sigismund was none of his seeking. The latter had implored his protection from the Swiss, had begged relief in his financial straits. Touched by his petitions, Charles had acceded to his prayers and the lands had enjoyed security under Burgundian protection as they never had under Austrian. Charles had duly acquitted himself of his obligations, he had done nothing to forfeit his title. The conditions of redemption offered by Sigismund were not those expressly stipulated. If a commission were sent to Besançon, the duke would see to it that the merits of the case were properly examined.

"If, on the contrary, you shall adhere to the purpose

[1] Chmel, i., 92 *et seq.*

The First Reverses

you have declared, in violation of the terms of the contract and of your princely word, we shall make resistance, trusting with God's help that our ability in defence shall not prove inferior to what we have used to repulse the attacks of the Swiss—those attacks from which you sought and received our protection."

Before this letter reached its destination, the duke's deputy in the mortgaged lands had already found his resources wholly inadequate to maintain his master's authority. After Charles departed from Alsace, Hagenbach's increased insolence and abandonment of all the restraint that he had shown while awaiting the duke's visit soon became unbearable. The deliberations in Switzerland concerning their return to Austrian domination also naturally affected the Alsatians and made them bolder in resenting Hagenbach's aggressions.

Thann and Ensisheim were both firm in refusing admission to his garrisons. Brisac was in his hands already, and her fortifications held by mercenaries, but an order to the citizens to work, one and all, upon the defences, produced a sudden disturbance with very serious results. It was at Eastertide, and the command to desecrate a hallowed festival, one especially cherished in the Rhinelands, proved the final provocation to rebellion.

There is a black story in the Strasburg chronicle, moreover, that this misuse of Easter Day was not Hagenbach's real crime. He simply wished to get all combatants out of the city before butchering the inhabitants and his purpose was discovered in time. That charge does not, however, seem substantiated by other evidence. But there is no doubt that the citizens lashed themselves into a state of fury, fell upon the mercenaries, and killed many of them in spite of their own unarmed condition. Hagenbach, driven back into his lodgings, appeared at the window and offered various concessions, being actually humbled and intimidated by the unexpected turning of the submissive folk against him.

But the revolutionary spirit raged beyond the reach of conciliatory words. Some of the more intelligent burghers endeavoured to give a show of propriety to events, by promptly re-establishing their own ancient council, arbitrarily abolished by Hagenbach, while taking a new oath to the Duke of Burgundy, according to the formula of 1469. They also despatched envoys to the duke with explanations of their proceedings, stating further that it was Hagenbach's misrule alone to which protest was made; that they were not in revolt against Charles. The latter answered, "Send Hagenbach to me," but the provisional government, by the time they received this order, felt strong enough to disregard it and to continue to act on their own initiative.

Hagenbach was cast not only into prison but into irons. All fear of and respect for his authority was thrown to the winds, his offer of fourteen thousand florins as ransom being sternly refused.

The First Reverses

Deputations came from the confederation to congratulate the officials *de facto* and to promise aid. The next step gave the lie direct to the message sent to Charles upholding his authority while protesting against his lieutenant. Sigismund was urged to return to his own without further delay for legal formalities with his creditor. He assented. On April 30th, accordingly, the Austrian duke arrived in Brisac and picked up the reins of authority which he had joyfully dropped four years previously.

The rabble welcomed his coming with effusion, singing a ready parody of an Easter hymn:[1]

"Christ is arisen, the *landvogt* is in prison,
Let us all rejoice, Sigismund is our choice.
    Kyrie Eleison!
Had he not been snared, evil had it fared,
But now that he is ta'en, his craft is all in vain.
    Kyrie Eleison!"

Thus it was under Sigismund's auspices that the late governor was brought to trial. Instruments of torture sent from Basel were employed to make Hagenbach confess his crimes. But there was nothing to confess. As a matter of fact the charges against him were for well-known deeds the character of which depended on the point of view. What the Alsatians declared were infringements of their rights, the duke's deputy stoutly asserted were acts justified by the

[1] Kirk, ii., 488.

terms of the treaty. In regard to his private career the prisoner persisted in his statement that he was no worse than other men and that all his so-called victims had been willing and well rewarded for their submission to him.

On May 9th, the preliminaries were declared over and the trial began before a tribunal whose composition is not perfectly well known, but which certainly included delegates from the chief cities of the landgraviate, and from Strasburg, Basel, and Berne.[1]

The trial was practically lynch law in spite of the cloak of legality thrown over it. Charles alone was Hagenbach's principal and he alone was responsible for his lieutenant's acts. The intrinsic incompetence of the court was hotly urged by Jean Irma of Basel, Hagenbach's self-appointed advocate, but his defence was rejected. Public opinion insisted upon extreme measures, and the sentence of capital punishment was promptly followed by execution.

Petitions from the prisoner that he might die by the sword and be permitted to bequeath a portion of his property to the church of St. Étienne at Brisac were granted. The remainder of his wealth was confiscated by Sigismund, who had withdrawn to Fribourg during the progress of the trial. Even Hagenbach's bitterest foes acknowledged that the late governor made a dignified and Christian exit from the life he had not graced.

[1] Toutey, p. 141.

The First Reverses

Charles is said to have beaten well the messenger who brought him the news of this trial and execution, in the very presence of Sigismund who had not yet bought back his rights in the landgraviate, where he had appointed Oswald von Thierstein as governor, and where he was thus presuming to use sovereign power. This was not sufficient, however, to make the duke change his own plans. Stephen von Hagenbach was entrusted with the commission of punishing the Alsatians for his brother's ignominious deposition, and he did his task grimly. According to the Strasburg chronicler, this Hagenbach, at the north, and his colleague, the Count of Blamont, at the south, did not have more than six or eight thousand men apiece, but they left Hun-like reputations behind them. Devastation, slaughter, pillage in houses and churches, all in the name of the duke, contributed to the zeal with which the Austrian's return was ratified by popular acclamation, and with which the contingents sent to Alsace by the confederates were received.

Sigismund's letter to Charles is casual in tone and obscure in phraseology. A statement presented somewhat later to the emperor by the *Basse Union* is more precise in the justification offered for the events and in the grievances rehearsed.[1] That is, Sigismund treats the transaction as a purely financial one, naturally completed between him and his creditor by the offer to

[1] Text given by Toutey, *Pièces justificatives*, p. 442.

liquidate his debt. The plea made by the Alsatians and their friends is, that Charles had failed to keep his solemn engagements and that his appointed lieutenant had been peculiarly odious and had broken the laws of God and man, and that the mercenaries employed by him, the Burgundians, Lombardians, and their fellows, had pitilessly ravaged the county of Ferrette, the Sundgau, and the diocese of Basel. The charges are itemised.[1]

"All this, well-known to the Duke of Burgundy, has neither been checked nor punished by him. In consequence, our gracious Seigneur of Austria has been obliged to restore the land and people to his sovereignty and that of the House of Austria, which he has done with God's aid to prevent the complete annihilation and total destruction of land and people."

Charles did not hasten to Alsace to settle matters in person, but pursued his intention of reducing Cologne to the archbishop's control, undoubtedly thinking that the base which would then be open to the archbishop's protector on the lower Rhine would facilitate his operations in the upper valleys. Meanwhile the Emperor Frederic had emphatically declared that he alone was the Defender of the Diocese, and that the unholy alliance between Robert and Charles was a menace to the empire. His letters to Charles exhorted him to abandon the enterprise and to accept

[1] The details are very brutal and untranslatable.

mediation; those to the electors, princes, and cities of the empire urged them to defend Cologne against Burgundy until he himself arrived on the scene. There was a hot correspondence between all parties concerned, from which nothing resulted. Charles had various reasons for delay. There was trouble in other quarters of his domain. Flanders was in a state of ferment at his requisitions for money, and the Franche-Comté was on the point of making active resistance to the imposition of the *gabelle*.

In view of all these complications, Charles decided to prolong his truce with Louis XI., to May 1, 1475. That monarch was well pleased to continue to pursue his own plans under cover of neutrality. The determination of the anti-Burgundian coalition in Germany to keep Charles within the limits of his own estates was a pleasant sight to the French king, and he felt that he could afford to wait.

In June an edict was sent forth from Luxemburg, forbidding all owing allegiance to the Duke of Burgundy to have any commercial relations with the rebels of Cologne, or of Alsace, or with the cities of the *Basse Union*, and declaring the duke's intention to take the field at once, to reinstate the archbishop in his rightful see. This was a declaration of war and was speedily followed by the duke's advance to Maestricht, where he spent a few days in July, collecting a force which finally amounted to about twenty thousand men.

On the 29th he sat down before Neuss, which had again emphatically refused entry to him and his troops. Three days the duke gave himself for the reduction of the town, but there he remained encamped for nearly a whole year! Neuss was resolved to resist to the last extremity, while Bonn, Andernach, and Cologne contributed their assistance by worrying and harassing the besiegers to the best of their ability. It was a period when Charles seemed to have only one sure ally, and that was Edward of England, whose own plans were forming for a mighty enterprise—no less than a new invasion of France.

On July 25th, the very day that Charles was on his march up to Neuss, his envoys signed at London a treaty wherein the duke promised Edward six thousand men to aid him to "reconquer his realm of France." Nothing loth to dispose of his future chickens, Edward, in his turn, pledged himself to cede to Charles and his heirs, without any lien of vassalage, the duchy of Bar, the countships of Champagne, Nevers, Rethel, Eu, and Guise, all the towns on the Somme, and all the estates of the Count of St. Pol. Other territories of Charles were to be exempt from homage. Yes, and by June 1, 1475, Edward would land in France and set about his conquests. Nor were commercial interests forgotten; "to the duchess his sister (to the Flemings) is accorded permission to take from England wool, woollen goods, brass, lead, and to carry thither foreign merchandise."

The First Reverses

The year when Charles was waiting before the gates of Neuss was full of many abortive diplomatic efforts on the part of both the duke and Louis XI, and it was the latter who managed to save something even from broken bargains. The Swiss not only counted on his friendship, but were constantly encouraged by his money, which emboldened them to send a letter of open defiance to Charles: "We declare to your most serene highness and to all of your people, in behalf of ourselves and our friends, an honourable and an open war." To the herald who delivered this document Charles answered: "O Berne, Berne!"[1] He felt that he had been betrayed.

This was on October 26th. The defiance was followed by a descent of the mountaineers upon Alsace, which Charles had not yet released from his grasp. Stephen von Hagènbach prepared to defend Burgundian interests at Héricourt, a good strategic position on the tiny Luzine. Here, the Swiss were about to besiege him, when the Count of Blamont arrived with two bodies of Italian mercenaries, aggregating more than twelve thousand men, and attempted to draw off the besieging force. His plan failed—the tables were turned. It was the Burgundians who were fiercely attacked and who lost the day. Hagenbach was forced to surrender, obtaining honourable terms, however, and Sigismund put a garrison into Héricourt on November 16th.

[1] Toutey, p. 182.

This was a tremendous surprise to Charles. That cowherds could repulse his well-trained troops was a thought as bitter as it was unexpected. But he put aside all idea of punishing them for the moment, and continued to "reduce Neuss to the obedience of the good archbishop," and Hermann of Hesse continued to aid the town in its determined resistance.

The opprobrious names applied to the would-be and baffled conqueror at this time are curiously similar to the epithets hurled at Napoleon a few centuries later. He was compared to Anti-Christ himself, with demoniac attributes added, when Alexander was felt to be too mild a comparison. There was still a terrible fear of the duke's ambition, even though, in the face of all Europe, the Swiss had repulsed his men, and Neuss obstinately refused to open her gates, while the world wondered at the duke's obstinacy displayed in the wrong place. The belief expressed several times by Commines that God troubled Charles's understanding out of very pity for France, was a current rumour.

At the end of April an English embassy arrived at the camp, which was kept in a marvellous state of luxury, even though disease was not successfully curbed in the ranks. The urgent entreaty of the embassy was that Charles should raise this useless siege, fruitless as it promised to be, owing to the difficulty of cutting off the town's supplies. Edward IV was almost ready to despatch his invading army. He implored his dear brother to send him transports and to prepare to receive him when he landed. A letter from John Paston gives a glimpse into the situation [1]:

"For ffor tydyngs here ther be but ffewe saffe that the assege lastyth stylle by the Duke off Burgoyn affoor Nuse, and the Emperor hath besyged also not fferr from there a castill and another town in lykewyse wherin the Duke's men ben. And also, the Frenshe Kynge, men seye, is comen right to the water off Somme with 4000 spers; and sum men have that he woll, at the daye off brekyng off trewse, or else beffoor, sette uppon the Duks contreys heer. When I heer moor, I shall sende yowe moor tydyngs.

"The Kyngs imbassators, Sir Thomas Mongomere and the Master off the Rolls be comyng homwards ffrom Nuse; and as ffor me, I thynke I sholde be sek but iff I see it. . . .

"For it is so that to morrow I purpose to ryde in to Flaundyrs to purveye me off horse and herneys and percase I shall see the essege at Nwse er I come ageyn."

There was more reason for Charles to be heartsick at the sight than for John Paston, and he did grow weary of the further waiting and anxious, for his truce with Louis was drawing to a close. On May 22d, there was a skirmish between his troops and the imperial forces, wherein Charles claimed the victory. In reality, there was none on either side, but the semblance was sufficient to soothe

[1] *Paston Letters*, iii., 122.

his *amour propre*, and to convince him that an
accommodation with Frederic would not detract
from his dignity.

A large fleet of Dutch flatboats had been despatched to help convey the English army, thirsting for conquest, across the sea. Six thousand men in the duke's pay, too, were to be ready to meet Edward IV., and swell his escort as he marched to Rheims for his coronation. Other matters also demanded Charles's personal attention. Months had elapsed and Héricourt was unpunished—Berne had not been reproved.

René of Lorraine was formally admitted to the League of Constance on April 18, 1475, and was now ready openly to abjure the "protection" he had once accepted from Burgundy. There was a touch of old King René's theatrical taste in his grandson's method of despatching the herald who rode up to the duke's gorgeous tent of red velvet on May 10th. The man was, however, so overcome at the first view of *le Téméraire* that he hastily delivered up his letter, and threw down the bloodstained gauntlet, which he carried as a gage of war, without uttering a word. Then he fell on his knees, imploring the duke's pardon.[1] Charles was so little displeased at the signs of the impression his presence made that, instead of being angry with the man, he gave him twelve florins for his good news. The terms of the declaration of war carried by the herald were as follows:

[1] Toutey, p. 244.

"To thee, Charles of Burgundy, in behalf of the very high, etc., Duke of Lorraine, my seigneur, I announce defiance with fire and blood against thee, thy countries, thy subjects, thy allies, and other charge further have I not."[1]

The reply was straightforward:

"Herald, I have heard the exposition of thy charge, whereby thou hast given me subject for joy, and, to show you how matters are, thou shalt wear my robe with this gift, and shalt tell thy master that I will find myself briefly in his land, and my greatest fear is that I may not find him. In order that thou mayst not be afraid to return, I desire my marshal and the king-at-arms of the Toison d'Or to convoy thee in perfect safety, for I should be sorry if thou didst not make thy report to thy master as befits a good and loyal officer."

Thus was Charles pressed from the south and lured to the north. Excellent reason for obeying the order of the pope's legate that duke and emperor must lay down arms under pain of excommunication did either belligerent refuse! The armistice accepted on May 28th was followed by a nine months' truce signed on June 12th. It was a truce strictly to the advantage of Frederic and Charles. The Rhine cities, Louis XI., René of Lorraine, were alike ignored and disappointed in the expectations they had based on Frederic.

[1] *Bulletin de l'acad. royale de Belgique*, 1887.

CHAPTER XX

THE CAMPAIGNS OF 1475

"Monseigneur the chancellor, I do not know what to write to you of the English, for thus far they have done nothing but dance at St. Omer and we are not sure whether the King of England has landed. If he has, it must be with so small a force that it makes no noise, nor do the prisoners captured at Abbeville know anything, nor do they believe that there will be any English here in XL days. Tell the news to Monsg. de Comminge, and recommend my interests to him as I have confidence in him, and in Mons. de Thierry and Mons. the vice-admiral."[1]

Thus wrote Louis XI in June. Two days later and he has heard of the truce. He seizes the occasion to express to the Privy Council of Berne his real opinion of the emperor: "So Frederic has deserted us all!"[2] Well, it was not the first time! Thirty years previous, when Louis was dauphin, the emperor had tried to turn the Swiss against him. Had not God, knowing the hearts of men, inspired the brave mountaineers, Louis would have been a victim of execrable treachery. The outcome had been won-

[1] *Lettres de Louis XI.*, v., 368.
[2] *Nos omnes relinquens, Ibid.*, 371.

derful, for an eternal friendship had sprung up between him and the Swiss which must be preserved.

Meantime, Charles has made his own definite plan of the campaign which was to introduce Edward into Rheims for the coronation. The following letter from him to Edward IV. bears no date, but it was evidently written at about the time of the truce [1]:

"Honoured seigneur and brother, I recommend myself to you. I have listened carefully to your declaration through the pronotary, and understand that you do not wish to land without my advice, for which I thank you. I understand that some of your counsellors think you had better land in Guienne, others in Normandy, others again at Calais. If you choose Guienne you will be far from my assistance but my brother of Brittany could help you. Still it would be a long time before we could meet before Paris. As to Calais, you could not get enough provisions for your people nor I for mine. Nor could the two forces make juncture without attack, and my brother of Brittany would be very far from both. To my mind, your best landing is Normandy, either at the mouth of the Seine or at La Hogue. I do not doubt that you will soon gain possession of cities and places, and you will be at the right hand of my brother of Brittany and of me. Tell me how many ships you want and where you wish me to send them and I will do it."

On hearing further rumours of the actual arrival

[1] Commynes-Dupont, i., 336.

of the English, Louis hastened to Normandy to inspect the situation for himself. There he learned that his own naval forces stationed in the Channel to ward off the invaders had landed on the very day before his arrival, abandoning the task.

"When I heard that we took no action, I decided that my best plan would be to turn my people loose in Picardy and let them lay waste the country whence they [the English] expected to get their supplies."[1]

At the same time, the rumour that was permitted to be current in France was, that Charles of Burgundy had been utterly defeated at Neuss, and that there was nothing whatsoever to apprehend from him. He, meanwhile, was continuing his own preparations by strenuous endeavours to levy more troops and to obtain fresh supplies. After the signing of the convention with the emperor, the duke proceeded to Bruges to meet the Estates of Flanders. The answer to his demand for subsidies was a respectful refusal to furnish funds, on the plea that his expansion policy was ruining his lands. Counter reproaches burst from Charles. He accused the deputies of leaving him in the lurch and thus causing his failure at Neuss. Neither money, nor provisions, nor soldiers had they sent him as loyal subjects should.

"For whom does your prince labour? Is it for himself or for you, for your defence? You slumber,

[1] *Lettres*, v., 363. Louis to Dammartin.

he watches. You nestle in warmth, he is cold. You are snug in your houses while he is beaten by the wind and rain. He fasts, you gorge at your ease. . . . Henceforth you shall be nothing more than subjects under a sovereign. I am and I will be master, bearding those who oppose me."[1]

Then turning to the prelates he continued: "Do you obey diligently and without poor excuses or your temporal goods shall be confiscated." To the nobles: "Obey or you shall lose your heads and your fiefs." Finally, he addressed the deputies of the third estate in a tone full of bitterness: "And you, you eaters of good cities, if you do not obey my orders literally as my chancellor will explain them to you, you shall forfeit privileges, property, and life."

All the fervency of this adjuration failed to convince the deputies of their duty, as conceived by the orator. They declared that they had levied troops and would levy more, for defence, but that the four members of Flanders were agreed that they would contribute nothing to offensive measures. Charles must accept their decision as his sainted father had done. The details of all the aid they had given him, 2500 men for Neuss and many other contributions, were recapitulated. Flanders had been generous indeed. The concluding phrases of their answer were as follows:

"As to your last letters, requiring that within fifteen

[1] Gachard, *Doc. inéd.*, i., 249.

days every man capable of bearing arms report at Ath, these were orders impossible of execution, and unprofitable for you yourself. Your subjects are merchants, artisans, labourers, unfitted for arms. Strangers would quit the land. Commerce, in which your noble ancestors have for four hundred years maintained the land, commerce, most redoubtable seigneur, is irreconcilable with war."

This answer gave the true key to the situation. The Estates of Flanders were determined to be bled no further for schemes in which they did not sympathise. When this memorial was presented to Charles he broke out into fresh invective about the base ingratitude of the Flemish: "Take back your paper," were his last words. "Make your own answer. *Talk* as you wish, but *do* your duty." This was on July 12th. Charles had no further time to waste in argument. He was still convinced that the burghers would, in the end, yield to his demands.

With a small escort Charles left Bruges, and reached Calais on July 14th, where he had been preceded by the duchess, eager to greet her brother, who had actually landed on July 4th, with the best equipped army—about twenty-four thousand men—that had ever left the shores of England, and the latest inventions in besieging engines.

The expedition proved a wretched failure—a miserable disappointment to the English at home, who had been lavish in their contributions. Charles seems to have been put out by the place

KING RUHMREICH AND HIS DAUGHTER EHRENREICH
CHARACTERS REPRESENTING CHARLES AND MARY OF BURGUNDY
IN WOODCUT IN EARLY EDITION OF TEMDANK. POEM BY MAXIMILIAN I.

of landing. His own plan is clear from the letter quoted. He wished the two armies of Edward and himself to sweep a large stretch of territory as they marched toward each other. The one thing that he objected to was a consolidation of the two forces. Incapacity to turn an unexpected or an unwelcome situation to account was one of the duke's most deeply ingrained characteristics. He showed no inventiveness or resourcefulness. He held his own army at a distance from the English, much to the invader's chagrin, who was forced to march unaided over regions rendered inhospitable by Louis's stern orders, and outside of cities ready to hold him at bay. "If you do not put yourself in a state of security, it will be necessary to destroy the city, to our regret," was the king's message to Rheims, and the most skilful of French engineers was fully prepared to make good the words.

Open hostilities were avoided. Edward camped on the field of Agincourt, where perhaps he dreamed of his ancestor's success, but no fresh blaze of old English glory illumined his path. He did not proceed to Paris, there was no coronation at Rheims, no comfortable reception within any gates at all, for Charles was as chary as Louis himself of giving the English a foothold, though he advised Edward to accept an invitation from St. Pol to visit St. Quentin. This, however, proved another disappointment. Just as Edward was ready to enter, the gates opened to let out a troop which effectually repulsed the advancing foreigners. The Count of St. Pol had changed his mind.

"It is a miserable existence this of ours when we take toil and trouble enough to shorten our life, writing and saying things exactly opposite to our thoughts," writes the keenest observer of this elaborate network of pompous falsehoods[1] wherein every action was entangled. Louis XI trusted no one but himself, while he played with the trust of all, and his game was the safest. His fear of the invaders was soon allayed. "These English are of different metal from those whom you used to know. They keep close, they attempt nothing," he wrote to the veteran Dammartin.

It was, indeed, a patent fact that Edward was not a foe to be feared. Baffled and discouraged, he readily opened his ears to his French brother, and Louis heaped grateful recognition on every Englishman who helped incline his sovereign to peaceful negotiations. Velvet and coin did their work. Edward was easily led into the path of least resistance, and an interview between the rival kings was appointed for August 29th. Great preparations were made for their meeting on a bridge at Picquigny, across which a grating was erected. Like Pyramus and Thisbe, the two princes kissed each other through the barriers, and exchanged assurances of friendship. Edward was, indeed, so easy to convince that Louis was in absolute terror lest his English brother

[1] Commines, iv., ch. vi.

would accept his invitation to show him Paris before his return. No wonder Edward was deceived, for Louis was definite in his hospitable offers, suggesting that he would provide a confessor willing to give absolution for pleasant sins.

The duke was duly forewarned of this colloquy. On August 18th, he was staying at Peronne, whence he paid a visit to the English camp. It was ended without any intimation of Edward's change of heart towards the French king whom he had come to depose, though his plan was then ripe. On the 20th, Charles received a written communication with the news which Edward had disliked broaching orally, and was officially informed that the king had yielded to the wishes of his army, and was considering a treaty with Louis XI., wherein Edward's dear brother of Burgundy should receive honourable mention did he desire it.

On hearing these most unwelcome tidings, Charles set off for the English camp in hot haste, attended by a small escort, and nursing his wrath as he rode.[1] King Edward was rather alarmed at the duke's aspect when the latter appeared, and asked whether he would not like a private interview. Charles disregarded his question. "Is it true? Have you made peace?" he demanded. Edward's attempt at smooth explanations was blocked by a flood of invectives poured out by Charles, who remembered himself sufficiently

[1] Commines, iv., ch. viii.: Comines-Lenglet, ii., 217.

to speak in English so that the bystanders might have the full benefit of his passionate reproaches. He spared nothing, comparing the lazy, sensual, pleasure-loving monarch, whose easeful ways were rapidly increasing his weight of flesh, with the heroism of other English Edwards with whom he was proud to claim kin. As to the offers to remember his interests in the perfidious peace that perfidious Albion was about to swear with equally perfidious France, his rejection was scornful indeed. "Negotiate for *me!* Arbitrate for *me!* Is it I who wanted the French crown? Leave *me* to make my own truce. I will wait until you have been three months over sea." Among those who witnessed the scene were several Englishmen who sympathised with Charles—if we may believe Commines. "The Duke of Burgundy has said the truth," declared the Duke of Gloucester, and many agreed with him." Having given vent to his sentiments, Charles hurried away from his disappointing ally and reached Namur on the 22d, where he spent the night.

Edward troubled himself little about his brother-in-law's summary of his character. He was tired of camp hardships, and both he and his men found it very refreshing to have Amiens open her gates to them at the order of Louis XI. Food and wine were lavished upon all alike. It was a delightful experience for the English soldiers to see tables groaning with good things spread in the very streets, and to be bidden to order what they would at the taverns with no consideration for the reckoning. They enjoyed good French fare, free of charge, until their host intimated to King Edward that his men were very intoxicated and that there were limits in all things. But Louis did not spare his money or his pains until he was sure that a bloodless victory had been won. He fully realised the importance of extravagant expenditure in order to reach the goal he had set himself.

"We must have the whole sum at Amiens before Friday evening, besides what will be wanted for private gratifications to my Lord Howard, and others who have had part in the arrangement. . . . Do not fail in this that there may be no pretext for a rupture of what has been already settled."

Though they had now no rood of land, the English returned richer than they came, and they eased their *amour propre* by calling the sums that had changed hands, "tribute money." [1]

"Ryght reverend and my most tender and kynd Moodre, I recommende me to youw. Pleas it yow to weete that blessyd be God, this vyage of the kynges is fynnysshyd for thys tyme and alle the kynges ost is comen to Caleys as on Mondaye last past, that is to seye the iiij daye of Septembre, and at thys daye many

[1] The terms of the treaty provided for a seven years' truce, with international free trade and mutual assistance in civil or foreign wars of either monarch. Louis's complaisance went so far that he did not insist on Edward's renouncing the title of King of England and France.

of hys host be passyd the see in to Ingland ageyn, and in especiall my Lorde off Norfolk, and my bretheryn. . . . I also mysselyke somewhat the heyr heer; for by my trowte I was in goode heele whan I come hyddre and all hooll and to my wetyng I hadde never a better stomake in my lyffe and now in viij dayes I am crasyd ageyn." [1]

Thus wrote one Englishman from Calais and doubtless many others found the air more wholesome at home.

Charles of Burgundy was now ready to consider the affairs of Lorraine. He advised René of his intentions, in a manifesto which reached him on September 5th. The preamble contained a long list of the manifold benefits conferred upon Lorraine by the House of Burgundy. Then René was admonished to observe in every particular the terms of his own treaty with Charles, which he, René, had signed voluntarily, or the former would "make him know the difference between his friendship and his enmity."

This menace was ominous to the poor Duke of Lorraine. For on September 13th, his friend Louis XI. had signed a fresh treaty with Charles of Burgundy at Soleure, and Campobasso was marching mercenaries in Burgundian pay towards the unfortunate duchy. In other words, the French king abandoned the young protégé whom he had spared no pains to alienate from Burgun-

[1] *The Paston Letters.* Sir John Paston to his mother, Sept. 11, 1475.

The Campaigns of 1475

dian protection. It was a moment when his one interest apparently was to settle accounts with the Count of St. Pol, who had been equally treacherous in his dealings with England, Burgundy, and France.[1]

Having rested during the summer, the Burgundian troops were in fine trim when Charles marched to Nancy, taking towns on the way, and sat down before the capital in the last week of October. From his camp he wrote to the Duke of Milan:

"Very dear brother, I recommend myself to you. I have just accepted a truce with the king for nine years to come, in the form and manner contained at length in the copy of the articles which I have given to your ambassador, resident with me. . . . And be sure, *fratello mio*, that nothing would have induced me to accept the truce, had you not been comprised therein. And, similarly, you must be satisfied in all the pacts between the king and myself, just as you were comprised in the convention lately made at Neuss.

"For the rest, I have heard from your ambassador about the troops that can be furnished me, for which I am well content, praying you to continue to serve me in accordance with the promises of your ambassador. As to the coming of your brother to me [Sforza, Duc de Bari], I should be very glad. He has no reason now for delay as he can travel in Lorraine as safely as in Lombardy, as I have said to your ambassador. Pray the Lord to give you the desires of your heart.

[1] The story must be omitted here. The constable was finally apprehended, tried, and executed at Paris.

"Written in my camp at Nancy the penultimate day of October, 1475.

"CHARLES."[1]

Some trifling assistance was offered to René by Strasburg and other foes to Burgundy, but it was wholly insufficient to rescue him from his difficulties, and he was finally obliged to order the capitulation of Nancy on November 19th. The magistrates desired to hold out, but were forced by the populace to submit, and on November 30, 1475, Charles of Burgundy marched triumphantly through the gate of Craffe into the capital of Lorraine where he was received as the sovereign duke.[2]

This time Charles acted the rôle of a merciful and diplomatic conqueror. There was no cruelty permitted, and every evidence of conciliation was shown. The majority of the Lorrainers accepted the new order of things without further protest. At the end of December, Charles convened the Estates of Lorraine in the ducal palace, addressed them as his subjects of Burgundy, promised to be a good prince, demanded their attachment, confided his plans of expansion, and announced his intention of making Nancy the capital of his states. Again the duke's star rose. This acquisition seemed a sign of the reality of his dreams. Even before the fall of Nancy, his approaching

[1] *Dépêches Milanaises*, i., 253. The copy only is at Milan and there is no seal.

[2] Toutey, p. 380.

success bore fruit, inasmuch as the emperor changed the late convention into a firmer treaty signed on November 17th. Indeed had Charles died at that moment, there would have been little doubt that his dreamed-of kingdom had been simply prevented by a mere accident.

The detailed story of all that had happened in the Swiss Confederation and the Lower Union, since their formal declaration of war against Charles, is too complicated to relate. At the beginning of 1476, the situation was, briefly, that Sigismund held the debated mortgaged lands, while the Swiss allies, with Berne as the most militant member of the league, had continued to carry on offensive operations against the duke and his allies, notably the Duchess of Savoy. The conquest of Lorraine caused a panic, especially in the face of the fresh agreements between the duke and the emperor and the king.

There was a short period of hesitation, marked by a truce till January 1, 1476, between Charles and the confederates, a period when the timid among the allies urged their counsel of reconciliation at all hazards. Charles, too, seems to have desired an accord rather than hostilities, even though he still bore the Swiss a bitter grudge for Héricourt. It was probably appeals from Yolande of Savoy that decided him to open a campaign in midwinter.

"The prince has been so busy for a week past [wrote

the Milanese ambassador] in the reorganisation of his army according to new ordinances, and in the regulation of his receipts and outlays that he has scarcely given himself time to eat once in twenty-four hours. He is importuned by the Duchess of Savoy and the Count of Romont for aid against the Swiss who respect no treaty, and do not cease increasing their forces. In consequence, Duke Charles intends leaving Nancy in six days to go towards the Jura. He expects to take with him 2300 lances and 10,000 ordnance, which, joined to the feudal militia of Burgundy and Savoy, will swell his army to the number of 25,000 combatants. His operations are so planned that he will have more to gain than to lose."[1]

When Charles left Nancy on January 11th, he issued one of his grandiloquent manifestoes declaring that he was acting in behalf of all princes and seigneurs who had suffered wrong at the hands of the Swiss, and that he was ready to punish all who had provoked his just wrath by ravaging his province of Burgundy. It was rather a curious act on his part, to let his chief mercenary captain go off to make a pilgrimage just as he was on the eve of a campaign, but so he did, granting Campobasso leave of absence to visit the shrine of St. James at Compostella, a leave possibly utilised by the Italian to further the understanding with Louis XI., at which he arrived later.

On across the Jura marched the Burgundian army, while the Swiss diet came to a slow and

[1] *Dép. Milan.*, i., 266.

The Campaigns of 1476

confused decision to prepare to meet him. He did not take the route generally expected, directly towards Berne, his chief antagonist, but turned aside and attacked the little fortress of Granson. The castle was not over strong. Efforts to provision it by water failed, and, finally, on February 28th, after a brief siege, the captain of the garrison, Hans Wyler, capitulated to the duke's German forces, who represented to them that Charles was as generous as he was magnificent.

If the Milan ambassador can be trusted, the surrender was unconditional. Charles was soon on the spot. The four hundred and twelve soldiers, who had succeeded in holding the Burgundian army at bay for ten whole days, were made to march past his tent with bowed heads. Then he ordered one and all to be hanged, reserving two to help in the executions. Four hours were occupied in fulfilling these pitiless orders. Panigarola arrived at the camp on the 29th,—it was leap year, 1476,—and found this accomplished and saw the bodies hanging on the trees, but he asserts that no word was broken.[1] Charles was now absolutely confident of complete success. "*Bellorum eventus dubii sunt*," remarked the prudent Milanese, however, and he was proved right.

When the allied forces of the mountaineers finally arrived in the duke's neighbourhood a hot pitched battle ensued. The Burgundians, led by the duke in person, were thrown into utter con-

[1] *Dép. Milan.*, i., 300.

fusion. The mercenaries, terrified by the uncouth yells and battle-cries of Uri and Unterwalden, simply lost their heads and did nothing. Charles was pushed on as far as Jougne. It was not only a defeat, but a complete rout. When the Swiss came in sight of the late garrison hanged to the trees, their rage knew no bounds. In their turn they massacred, hanged, and drowned every one in Burgundian pay whom they could lay hands upon. The Burgundians saved their lives when they could, but their valuable artillery and their baggage, the mass of riches that Charles carried with him were ruthlessly sacrificed, and gathered up contemptuously as booty by the Swiss, who cared little for the tapestries and jewels though they prized the gold. Such was the battle of Granson, on the 2nd of March.

The fatal mistake committed by Charles was that he despised his enemy and underestimated his quality as well as his strength. Just before engaging in battle, the whole Swiss army fell upon their knees in prayer that the issue might be successful. This action deceived Charles into thinking that they were cowardly and his opinion was shared by his men. A contemptuous laugh broke out from the Burgundian ranks.[1]

---

[1] Jomini lays the defeat to a tactical error. "Charles had committed the fault of encamping with one wing of his army resting on the lake, the other ill-secured at the foot of a wooded mountain. Nothing is more dangerous for an army than to have one of its wings resting on an unbridged stream, on a

The Campaigns of 1476

Olivier de la Marche ends a meagre account of Granson with the following rather barren words[1]:

"In short the Duke of Burgundy lost the day and was pushed back as far as Jougne, where he stopped, and it is meet that I tell how the duke's bodyguard saved themselves . . . and reached Salins where I saw them arrive for I was not present at the battle on account of a malady I suffered. From Jougne the duke went to Noseret, and you can understand that he was very sad and melancholy at having lost the battle, where his rich baggage was stolen and his army shattered."

On March 21, 1476, Sir John Paston writes to Margaret Paston from Calais:

" As ffor tydyngs heer we her ffrom alle the worlde. . . . Item, the Duke of Burgoyne hath conqueryd Lorreyn and Queen Margreet shall nott nowe be lykelyhod have it; wherffer the Frenshe kynge cheryssheth hyr butt easelye; but afftr thys conquest off Loreyn the Duke toke grete corage to goo upon the londe off the Swechys [Swiss] to conquer them butt the berded hym att an onsett place and hathe dystrussyd hym and hathe slayne the most part of his vanwarde and wonne all hys ordynnaunce and artylrye and mor ovyr all stuffe thatt he hade in hys ost with hym; exceppte men and horse ffledde nott but they roode that nyght xx myle; and so the ryche saletts, heulmetts garters, nowchys[2] gelt and all is goone with tente pavylons and all and soo men deme hys pryde is

---

lake, or on the sea." Charles explained to Europe that he had been surprised, and his defeat was a mere bagatelle.

[1] III., 216.   [2] Embossed ornaments.

abatyd. Men tolde hym that they were ffrowarde karlys butte he wolde nott beleve it and yitt men seye that he woll to them ageyn. Gode spede them bothe."

Many of the rumours that were current represented Charles as completely prostrated by his disaster. This was only half true. His efforts to retrieve himself were immediate but, physically, he certainly showed the effects of this campaign. He was attacked by a low fever, his stomach rejected food, insomnia afflicted his nights, and dropsical swellings appeared on his legs. This condition was attributed to his fatigues and exposure in a hard climate, and to his habit of drinking warm barley-water in the morning. He was urged to use a soft feather-bed instead of his hard couch, while Yolande's own physician and one Angelo Catto watched anxiously over him. The latter claimed the credit of saving his life. Charles was not, however, fully recovered when he resumed his activities and held a review on May 9th. With all his efforts exerted in every quarter likely to yield results, the whole number of troops was but twenty thousand men. Every onlooker felt that the duke was now trying to accomplish something quite beyond his resources.

"Illustrious prince [wrote the King of Hungary[1]], we cannot sufficiently wonder that you should have been so gravely deceived and that, after having once

[1] *Dép. Milan.*, ii., 126.

found that you were lured into loss and disgrace, again you let yourself be snared in a labyrinth from which you will either never escape, or escape only with damage and shame. . . . Without risk to himself [your foe] has precipitated you into an abyss and tied you where you are exposed to the loss of your possessions and your life. . . . We exhort you to pause before incurring heavier losses and greater dangers. If fortune smiles upon you in your attack on that people, you will have the whole empire against you. In the opposite event—which God avert—it will be turned into a common tale how a mighty prince was overcome by rustics whom there would have been no honour in conquering, while to be conquered by them would be an eternal disgrace."

This plain-spoken epistle failed to reach its destination until after the prophecy had been fulfilled. Its warning would probably have been futile had Charles read it before he marched on towards Berne, on June 8th. On the road that he chose lay the town of Morat, which had made ready for his approach. A few days to reduce it, and then on to Berne was his plan. His force succeeded in holding the ground and cutting off communication with Berne for three days. On the 14th, a messenger made his way through from the beleaguered city to Berne, and all the allies were then urged to do their best. The result was encouraging. "There are three times as many as at Granson, but let no one be dismayed, with God's help we will kill them all," wrote a leader of Berne.

The encounter came on June 23d. The force

was really a formidable one. René of Lorraine was among the commanders on the side of the Swiss. It was a tremendous fight, brief as it was savage; at two o'clock the assault was made and within an hour Charles was repulsed. Almost all the infantry perished. The slain is estimated variously from ten to twenty-two thousand. Charles did not keep his vow to perish if defeated. To his assured allies he clung closely, and none had more reason to be faithful to him than Yolande of Savoy. After Granson he hastened to give the duchess his own view of the disaster:

"It has given me a singular pleasure to hear of your calmness and constancy of soul; for the thought of your affliction weighed more heavily upon me than what has befallen me . . . every day diminishes the inconvenience and proves that the loss in men is less than we thought. *Such as it is it came from a mere skirmish.* The bulk of the armies did not engage, to my great displeasure. Had they fought the victory would have been mine. There has been none on either side. God, I trust, reserves it for you and for me . . . the hope you have placed in me shall not be vain."

Thus he wrote on March 7th to encourage his anxious protégée.

After the second defeat it was to her that the duke turned again. In the very early morning after the battle of Morat, Charles paused at Morges on the Lake of Geneva, having ridden hard

[1]*Dép. Milan.*, ii., 335.

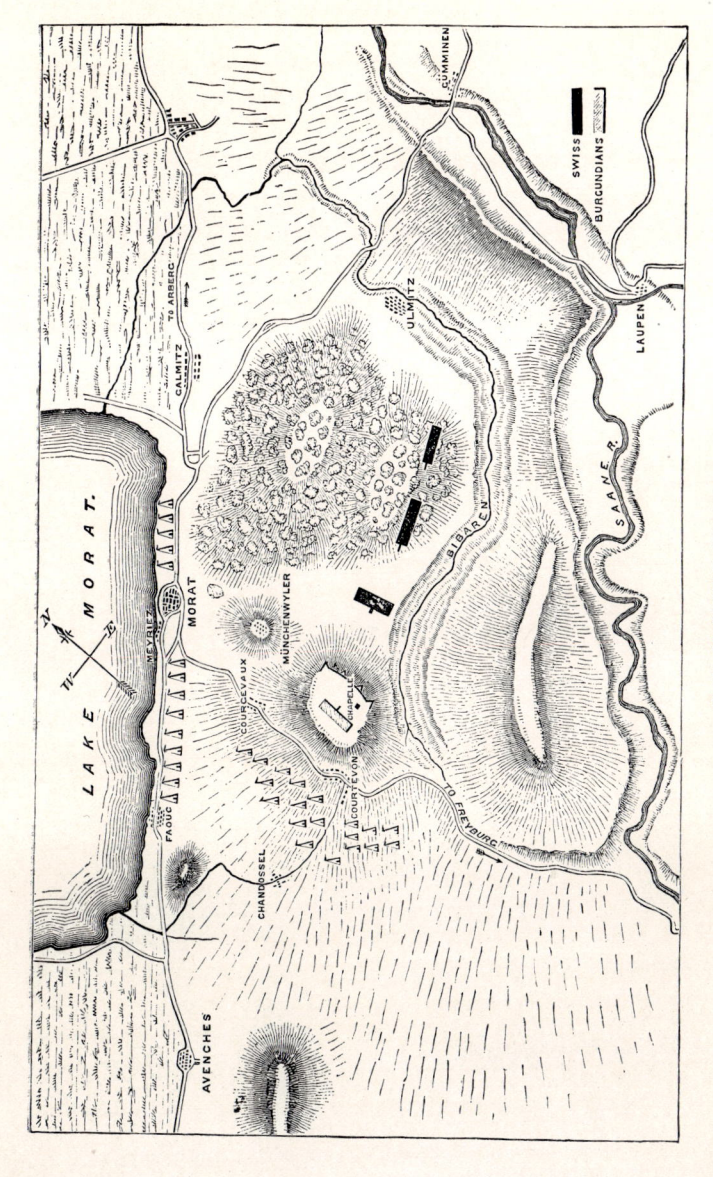

PLAN OF BATTLE OF MORAT

REPRODUCED FROM KIRK'S "CHARLES THE BOLD," BY PERMISSION OF J. B. LIPPINCOTT CO.

through the night. There he heard mass, breakfasted, rested awhile, and then rode on, reaching the castle of Gex at six o'clock in the evening, where Yolande of Savoy was awaiting his coming in full knowledge of the second disaster he had suffered.

At the foot of the staircase, attended by her ladies, Yolande was waiting to greet her disappointed friend. Charles dismounted and kissed each member of the family in order of precedence, the little duke, his brother, then the duchess, her daughter, and the ladies in waiting. Yolande had had time to move out of her own suite of apartments and have them prepared for her guest's use, and there the two talked together confidentially, while their attendants waited patiently just out of earshot.

Then Charles formally escorted his hostess to her son's room, returning to his own, showing signs of extreme fatigue. Panigarola was absent, but another Milanese was among her suite, and he pressed forward as the duke re-entered the apartment, offering to carry any message to the Duke of Milan, to be cut short with, "It is well. That is enough." Shortly afterwards, Olivier de la Marche and the Sire de Givry, commander of the Burgundians dedicated to Yolande's service, were summoned and had a long conference with Charles.

Yolande was, apparently, more communicative to the Milanese Appiano than to Charles, but he saw that she was not frank with him. "She must throw herself on the protection of France or of Milan," he wrote to his master.[1] She was, however, clear in her own mind that she would not accept Sforza's protection any more than that of Charles. She absolutely refused to identify her fortunes with the latter. She was determined to go to Geneva, but no farther. The duke remained at Gex until the 27th, and renewed his arguments to persuade her to cross the Jura with him. She was firm in adhering to her own plan. The two parties set out from the castle together, their roads lying in opposite directions, but Charles escorted his hostess about half-way to Geneva, riding beside her carriage, and continuing his persuasions in a low voice. At last he drew up his rein, gave her a farewell kiss, and rode off. He was much displeased at her determination, and he speedily resolved upon other methods of making sure of her fidelity to him. La Marche thus relates the story:[2]

"After the duke had been discomfited the second time by the Swiss before Morat, believing that he could do the thing secretly, he made a plan to kidnap Mme. of Savoy and her children and take them to Burgundy, and he ordered me, I being at Geneva, on my head to capture Mme. of Savoy and her children and bring them to him. In order to obey my prince and master I did his behest quite against my heart, and I took madame and her children near the gate of Geneva. But the Duke of Savoy was stolen away

[1] *Dép. Milan.*, ii., 295.
[2] III., 234.

The Campaigns of 1476

from me (for it was two o'clock in the night) by the means of some of our own company who were subjects of the Duke of Savoy, and, assuredly, they did no more than their duty. What I did was simply to save my life, for the duke, my master, was the kind that insisted on having his will done under penalty of losing one's head. So I took my way, and carried Mme. of Savoy behind me, and her two daughters followed and two or three of her maids, and we took the road over the mountain to reach St. Claude. I was well assured of the second son, and had him carried by a gentleman. I thought I was assured of the Duke of Savoy, but he was stolen from me as I said. As soon as we were at a distance, the people of the duchess, and especially the seigneur de Manton, had torches brought and took the duke back to Geneva, in which they had great joy. And I with Mme. of Savoy and the little boy (who was not the duke), crossed the mountain in the black night and came to a place called Mijoux, and thence to St. Claude.

"You must know that the duke gave very bad cheer to the company, and chiefly to me. I was in danger of my life because I had not brought the Duke of Savoy. Then the duke went on to Salins without speaking to me or giving me any orders. However, I escorted Mme. of Savoy after him, and he ordered me to take her to the castle of Rochefort. Thence she was taken to Rouvre in Burgundy. After that I had nothing more to do with her or her affairs."

This queer story is undoubtedly true, and the tone in which La Marche relates it indicates that he, too, was alienated by the duke's manner, and might have been more willing to lend an ear to

Louis's suggestions than he had been five years previously.

It is not evident that he played his master false or that he was cognisant of the recapture of the little duke, but he says himself that he thought the attendants were absolutely justified in it.

It is after this incident that the astute Panigarola returns and joins the duke's suite at Salins. He finds Charles a changed man, indulging in strange fits of hilarity, expressing the wish that a couple of thousand more of his troops had been killed, "French at heart" as they were. He refused to see Yolande, after thus forcibly obtaining the means of so doing, and sent her to the castle of the Sire of Rochefort for safe-keeping. Abstemious as he had been all his life, never taking wine without water, the strong Burgundy in which he now suddenly indulged went to his head.

Rumours went abroad that his mental balance was shaken. That does not seem to have been true to the extent of insanity. He was only infinitely chagrined but he certainly put on a brave front and retained his self-confidence and declared

"They are wrong if they believe me defeated. Providence has provided me with so many people and estates with such abundant resources, that many such defeats would be needed to ruin them. At the moment when the world imagines that I am annihilated, I will reopen the campaign with an army of 150,000 men." [1]

[1] *Dép. Milan*, ii., 339.

CHAPTER XXI

THE BATTLE OF NANCY

1477

IT was manifestly impossible for Charles to attempt to retrieve his fortunes without having large sums of ready money at his command. He therefore proceeded to appeal to the guardians of each and every treasury in his various states. Flanders and Burgundy were, however, the only quarters whence succour was in the least probable. The Estates of the latter duchy met, deliberated, and resolved to make no pretence nor to "yield anything contrary to the duty which every one owes to his country."[1] A certain Sieur de Jarville, accompanied by other true Burgundians, undertook to report the proceedings to Charles,—a duty usually falling to the share of the presiding officer of the ecclesiastical chamber. The message which he carried was laconic but sturdy:

"Tell Monsieur that we are humble and brave subjects and servitors, but as to what is asked in his behalf, it never has been done, it cannot be done, it never will be done."

"Small people would never dare use such lan-

[1] *Mém. de la soc. bourg. de géog. et d' hist.* Article by A. Cornereau, vi., 229.

guage," is the comment of the Burgundian chronicler, proud of the temerity of his fellow countrymen.

In the Netherlands, the individual Estates were equally emphatic in their refusal to meet the duke's wishes. Charles, therefore, resolved to call together a general assembly of deputies in the hope of finding them, collectively, more amenable. Writs of summons were issued very widely and a "States-general" was formally convened at Ghent on Friday, April 26, 1476.[1] At the last assembly of this nature, in 1473, the duke had expressly promised, in consideration of an annual grant of 500,000 crowns for six years then accorded to him, to refrain from further demands, and there was a spirit of sullen resentment in the air when this session, whose purpose was plain, was opened by Chancellor Hugonet. He set forth three points for consideration. Monseigneur wished his daughter Mary, "that most precious jewel," to join him in Burgundy. A suitable escort was necessary to ensure her safe journey and that the duke requested the States to provide. Secondly he de-

---

[1] Les états de Gand en 1476. (Gachard, *Études et notices hist. des Pays-Bas*, i., 1.)

This is a study of the report made by Gort Roelants, pensionary of Brussels, one of the deputies to the assembly of 1476. This so-called "States-general" was by no means a legislative assembly. When Philip the Good convened deputies from the various states at Bruges in 1463, it was to save himself the trouble of going to the separate capitals to ask for *aides*. Assemblies of similar nature occurred several times before 1477, when Mary of Burgundy granted the privilege of self-convention and when a constitutional rôle was assured

sired the States to endorse a levy of fresh troops to meet his immediate requirements. Further, he requested each town to equip a specified number of horse at its own expense; he demanded the service of his tenants, fief and arrière-fief; and, in addition, he required that all other men, no matter what their condition, able to bear arms, should enlist or provide a substitute. A portion of the troops should be set to guard the frontier, and the rest should be sent to the duke in Burgundy.

It was a demand pure and simple for a universal call to arms, a national levy. The duke's paternal desire to see his daughter was the flimsiest of excuses that deceived no one for a moment.

After the chancellor's exposition there was probably adjournment for discussion. The pensionary of Brussels, Gort Roelants, then acted as spokesman to present the following report, as the result of their deliberations, to the duchess-regent.

As for Mlle. of Burgundy, the deputies would ascertain the wishes of their principals, but the second request did not call for a referendum. The representatives were fully capable of settling the matter at once. Considering the heavy burdens laid on the people, and taking into account the promises made to them in 1473, that no further demands should be made on the public purse, the three Estates concurred in humbly petitioning

to the body; though not used for many years (*See* Pirenne, ii., 379.)

Monseigneur to excuse them from granting his request.

It was on a Sunday after dinner (April 28th) when this decision was communicated to the duchess in her own hotel. After a private colloquy between her and Hugonet, the chancellor told the messenger that it was quite right for the deputies to consult their principals before the heiress was permitted to leave the guardianship of her faithful subjects. That was a grave matter, but surely there was no reason why her "escort" could not be determined upon at once. In regard to the levies, Madame was not empowered to take any excuse. It was beyond her province. Since the opening of the assembly, fresh letters had arrived from the duke urging the speedy execution of his previous instructions. The chancellor then appointed a committee to meet a committee from the States at 8 A.M. on the morrow at the convent of the Augustines.

This was not satisfactory. Hugonet was speedily notified that the States did not feel empowered to appoint a committee. The most they could do was to resolve themselves into a committee of the whole. The objection to this was that a small conference was far better suited to free discussion. It was easy for unqualified persons to enter the session of a large body. The States, however, were tenacious in their opinion that their writs did not qualify them to appoint committees. Every point must be threshed out

PHILIBERT, DUKE OF SAVOY
(AFTER THE DESIGN BY MATHEY)

The Battle of Nancy

in the presence of every deputy. *Potestas delegata non deleganda est.*

There was further negotiation, and it was not until Monday afternoon that Hugonet's commissioner brought a conciliatory message that if the gentlemen were so bent on it, he would, in spite of the difficulty of discussion in an open meeting, talk over both points with them in full assembly. Again the States objected. They had no instructions whatsoever in regard to Mademoiselle, and could not discuss her movements either in public or in private session. As to levies, they repeated in detail all previous arguments, and expressed a fervent hope that Monseigneur would withdraw the request. It would, in the end, be more to Monseigneur's advantage, etc. Back and forth travelled the commissioner between States and duchess. The latter simply reiterated her dictum that Mary must certainly set forth to visit her father in May, with an adequate escort, in whose ranks must appear three prelates, three or four barons, fifty knights, and notable men from the "good towns," well armed.

The States were then resolved into a committee of the whole, for a private deliberation, an action that probably enabled them to exclude the embarrassing spectators. In preparation for this, the diligent commissioner called apart one deputy from each contingent, and expatiated on the duke's need of proof of sturdy loyalty. Seven to eight thousand combatants, besides Mademoiselle's escort and the fiefs and arrière-fiefs, Monseigneur could manage to make suffice for the present, and these must be provided. These confidences were at once reported to the assembly, which then adjourned to think over the matter during the night.[1]

When they met again on April 30th, the chancellor was ready with a new message from Madame: "Go home now, consult your principals, and return on May 15th." On the motion of some deputy, this date was changed to May 24th. Precautions were taken to prevent any binding action in the interim. Moreover, the exact phrasing of the reports to the separate groups of constituents was also agreed upon by the majority of the deputies. In this, Hainaut refused to participate, as in that province there was a reluctance to deny the obligations of the fiefs.

When the deputies reassembled a month later, Hugonet tried to weaken the effect of their answer by a suggestion that it had better not be considered the final decision, but a mere informal expression of opinion. "There were so many strangers present," etc. The States determinedly refused to be trifled with. "Madame must not be displeased if they gave the result of their deliberations in the presence of the whole assembly, not by way of opinion, but as a formal and conclusive report." Their charge was restricted to this manner of procedure. The chancellor, interrupting

[1] *Pour y penser la nuit jusques au lendemain.*

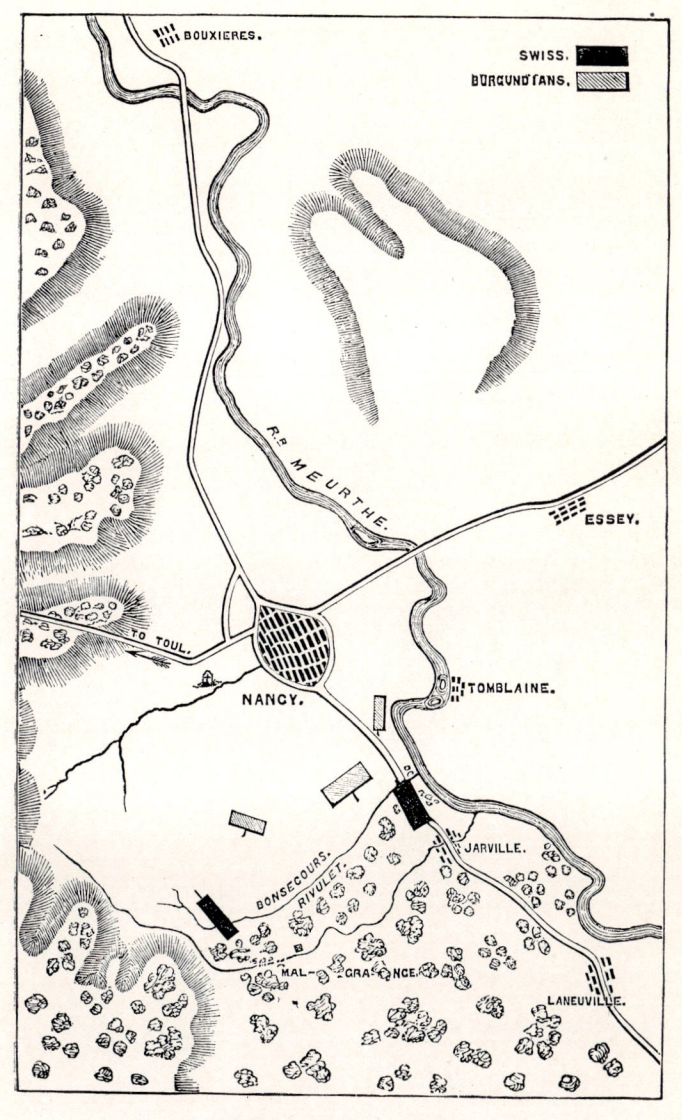

PLAN OF BATTLE OF NANCY

REPRODUCED FROM KIRK'S "CHARLES THE BOLD," BY PERMISSION OF J. B. LIPPINCOTT CO.

The Battle of Nancy 433

them, asked, since their charge was thus restricted, whether they had also been limited in the number of times they might drink on their way.[1] The answer was: "Chancellor, come now, say what you wish. The answer shall be given as it was meant to be given."

The communication was so long that its delivery took from 3 to 8 P.M. It was nothing more than a detailed apology for refusing the sovereign's demands. Several days more were consumed in unsuccessful efforts to cajole or browbeat the deputies into a more genial mood. The only concessions offered were insignificant, and to their resolution the deputies held firmly. "According to current rumour [concludes Gort Roelants's story] the ducal council would gladly have accepted a notable sum in lieu of the service of towns and of the fiefholders, but the States made no such offer."

There was evidently a hope that better results might be obtained from a new assembly,[2] but none was held and the most earnest endeavours of the duke's wife and daughter failed to arouse enthusiasm for his plans. Moreover, when there seemed a prospect that the Netherlands might be attacked from France, the sympathy of even the duchess and council for offensive operations was

[1] *S' ils n'avaient point charge limitée quantefois ils devaient boire en chemin.*

[2] Compte-rendu par Antoine Rolin, Sr. d' Aymeries, Oct. 1, 1475–Sept. 30, 1476. In the archives of Hainaut there are proofs that another assembly was confidently expected.

chilled. Not only did Margaret fail to send her husband the extra supplies demanded, but she decided to appropriate the three months' subsidy, the chief item of regular ducal revenue, for protection of the Flemish frontier—an action that made Charles very angry. Defences at home! Yes, indeed, they were necessary, but the people must provide them. The subsidy was lawfully his and he needed every penny of it. His army had not been destroyed. He was simply obliged to strengthen it. Burgundy was helping him. Flanders must do her part. They were deaf to this appeal, although a generous message was sent saying that if he were hard pressed they would go in person to rescue him from danger.

The story of the assembly of the Estates of the two Burgundies is equally interesting as a picture of the clash between sovereign will and popular unreadiness to open the carefully guarded money-boxes.[1] The deputies convened at Salins on July 8th, in the presence of the duke himself. The session was opened by Jean de Grey, the president of the *parlement* of the duchy, with a brief statement of the sovereign's needs. Then Charles took the floor, and delivered a tremendous harangue with a marvellous command of language. Panigarola declared that his allusions to parallel crises in ancient times were so apt and so fluent that it seemed as though the book of history lay opened before him and that he read from its

[1] Gingins la Sarra, ii., 354.

BATTLE OF NANCY
CONTEMPORANEOUS MINIATURE IN ABBEY OF ST. GERMAIN DES PRÉS
(COMINES-LENGLET, III.)

The Battle of Nancy

pages.[1] The impression he made was plain to see.

His demands for aid to retrieve the Swiss disasters were open and aboveboard this time. There was no such pretence put forward as the escort of Mary. The argument was that any ruler, backed by his people unanimous in their willingness to give their last jewel for public purposes, must inevitably succeed in his righteous wars, etc.

His learned and able discourse was well received, according to other reporters besides the Milanese, but there was no hearty yielding to sentiment in the reply. Four days were consumed in deliberations before that was ready on July 12th. They had certainly considered that the grant of 100,000 florins annually for six years, accorded two years previously, was their share. But in view of the duke's appeal, they would endeavour to aid him. Let him stipulate which cities he wished fortified and they would assume charge of the work. Two favours they begged—that Charles should not rashly expose his person "for he was the sole prince of his glorious House," and that he should be ready to receive overtures of peace. "We will give life and property for defence, but we implore you to take no offensive step." Charles did not, perhaps, feel the distrust of his military skill and of his judgment that these words implied.

Financial stress was not the duke's only diffi-

---

[1] *Ibid.*, 359. Scorende queste cose come avesse il libro avanti, parse ad ogniuno imprimesse bene questo suo intento.

culty in 1476. The defection of his allies continued. Yolande—that former good friend of his—was now a fervent suppliant to Louis XI., begging him to restore her to freedom and to her son's estates. Not that her restraint was in itself hard to bear. At Rouvre, whither she had been removed from Rochefort, she was free to do what she wished, except to depart. Couriers, too, were at her service apparently, who carried uninspected letters to Milan, Geneva, Nice, Turin, and to Louis XI. Commines says that she hesitated to take refuge with the last lest he should promptly return her to Burgundian "protection." Yet her brother's hatred to Charles seemed a fairly strong assurance against such action. Louis XI. was never so genial as when hearing some ill of Charles. "From what I have learned, I believe his Turk, his devil in this world, the person he loathes most intensely, is the Duke of Burgundy, with whom he can never live in amity." These words were sent by Petrasanta to the Duke of Milan,[1] who was also turning slowly, with some periods of hesitation, to an alliance with Louis, now engaged in "following the hare with a cart."[2]

On his side the king declared that he had no intention of troubling further about his obligations to the Duke of Burgundy. "He has himself broken the truce repeatedly. I can begin a

[1] Petrasanta to the Duke of Milan Aug. 12th. Quoted in Kirk, iii., 487.
[2] An Italian phrase signifying to run down his game slowly.

COLUMN COMMEMORATING CHARLES AT NANCY
AFTER THE DRAWING BY PERNOT

war when I please. But I have thought it best to temporise."

In the succeeding weeks Louis plunged deeper and deeper into negotiations with any and every one whom he could turn against Charles. In October, Sire de Chamont, governor of Champagne, —the territory that Edward IV. had failed to consign to the duke's sovereignty,—made a descent on Rouvre and rescued Yolande of Savoy. There was no attempt to stay her departure, and she was scrupulous, so it is said, in leaving money behind to pay for the Burgundian property carried off in her train—though it were nothing but an old crossbow. "Welcome, Madame the Burgundian," was the fraternal salutation which she received on her arrival at her brother's court. She replied that she was a good French woman and quite ready to obey his majesty's commands.[2]

During the summer, Charles remained at La Rivière exerting every effort to levy an army. It was no easy task, and the review held on July 27th showed a meagre return for his exertions. But he did not slacken his efforts. Lists were immediately drawn up showing the vacancies in each company, and his money stress did not prevent his offering increased pay as an extra inducement to recruits. "An excellent means of encouragement," comments Panigarola.

The necessity for his preparations was evident. An opportune legacy inherited by René of Lor-

[1] Commines, v., ch. iv.

raine enabled that dispossessed prince to work to better advantage than he had been able to do since Charles had convened the Estates of Lorraine at Nancy. Moreover, on the very day of the review of the deficient Burgundian troops, a Swiss diet at Fribourg adopted resolutions regarding a closer alliance with René.[1] Louis XI. ostensibly maintained his truce with Charles but he had intimated that a French army would wait in Dauphiné ready "to help adjust the affairs of Savoy," and, at about the same time when Yolande was at court, he gave a gracious reception to a Swiss embassy, so that René did not feel himself without support as he advanced to recover his city.

The mercenaries left by Charles at Nancy were weak and indifferent—a brief siege, and the capital of Lorraine capitulated to Duke René. Charles was too late to prevent this mortifying loss. His forces, too, were a mere shadow. Three to four thousand men rallied round him in the Franche-Comté, a few hundred joined him in Burgundy, and as he skirted the frontier of Champagne he received slight reinforcements from Luxemburg. Then came Campobasso and his mercenary troops, and the Count of Chimay with such Flemish fiefs as had, individually, respected the duke's appeal. In all, the forces at Charles's disposition amounted to about ten thousand, far fewer than those at Neuss or at Granson.

[1] Toutey calls the diet at Fribourg a veritable congress of central Europe, the first of international congresses.

The Battle of Nancy

At a diet of October 17th, the compact between René and the Swiss was confirmed, and the former was assured of efficient aid to help him repulse Charles in his advance into Lorraine. There was need. The city of Toul refused admission to both dukes, but furnished provision for Charles's troops, so that for the moment he was the better off of the two. René then proceeded to provision Nancy and to prepare it for a siege, while he himself proceeded to Pont-à-Mousson, and for several days the two adversaries were only separated by the Moselle. Charles's army was augmented daily by slight accessions from Flanders, and England, and by fragments of the garrisons of the various towns in Lorraine that had yielded to René, and the latter fell back, little by little. Charles in his turn held Pont-à-Mousson, and proceeded along the road to Nancy, not deterred by the Lorrainers.

It was on October 22nd, that Charles of Burgundy laid siege for the second time to Nancy. In thus entering into active hostilities, he was ignoring the advice of his councillors who were unanimous in begging him to devote the winter months to refitting his army in Luxemburg or Flanders. His position was really very dangerous. He had no base on which to rest as he had recovered no towns except Pont-à-Mousson. But he ignored the patent obstacles and tried assault after assault upon Nancy—all most valiantly repulsed. Within the walls, there was an amazing display of courage, energy, and good humour. As a matter of fact, the duke's reputation had waned, while the fear of his cruelty emboldened the burghers to hold out to the last ditch. Any fate would be better than falling into his hands, was the general opinion.

Throughout Lorraine, the captains of the garrisons seized every occasion to harry the Burgundians. Familiar with the lay of the land, with every cross-road and by-path, they were able to lie in wait for the foragers and to do much damage. Four hundred cavaliers, coming up from Burgundy, were attacked by one Malhortie de Rozière, and literally cut to pieces, while their horses changed sides with ease. Only a few escaped to report the fate of the others to Charles. Not long after, Malhortie, encouraged by this success, crept up to the Burgundian camp, fell upon the sleepers, and captured a goodly number of horses.

The troops on which Charles counted most confidently were Campobasso's. Several attempts were made to warn him that treachery was possible in that quarter if the commander were too much exasperated by delays in payment, too much tried by the ill-temper of his employer. But the duke persisted in being oblivious to what was passing under his eyes. Thus, while awaiting the moment for his final defection, the Italian found it possible to enter into communication with René and to retard the operations of the siege so

The Battle of Nancy 441

as to give time for the advance of the army of relief.

The weather of this year was a marked contrast to the mild season of 1473. The winter set in early and the cold became very severe, almost at once. Their sufferings made the burghers very impatient for the relief of whose coming they could get no certain assurance. The Burgundian lines were held so rigidly that the interchange of messages between the city and her friends was rendered very difficult.[1] One Suffren de Baschi tried to slip through to Nancy, to tell the besieged that René was levying troops in Switzerland and would soon be with them. Baschi fell into the duke's hands and was immediately hanged. One story says that Campobasso was among the interceders for his life and received a box on the ear for his pains, an insult that proved the last straw in his allegiance to Charles. Commines, however, declares that the Italian urged the death of the captive, fearful of the premature betrayal of his own intended treachery.

This execution was one of those arbitrary acts condemned by public opinion as contrary to the code of warfare. Intense indignation among the Lorrainers and the Swiss forced René to retaliatory measures, and he ordered the execution of all the Burgundian prisoners. One hundred and twenty bodies hung on the gibbets, each bearing an inscription to the effect that their death was

[1] Huguénin Jeune, *Hist. de la guerre de Lorraine*, p. 217.

the work of *le téméraire*. The rancour of the proceedings became terrible. No quarter was given in any engagements. Slaughter was the only thought on either side.

Towards the end of December, one Thierry, a draper of Mirecourt, proved more successful than Baschi in reaching Nancy. His information, that René's army would leave Basel on December 26th, put heart into the beseiged and the bells rang out joyfully.

Just at this epoch, there was an attempt at mediation between the combatants. The King of Portugal,[1] nephew of Isabella, appeared at his cousin's camp and implored him to put an end to the carnage, and in the name of humanity to stop a war that was horrible to all the world. In spite of his own stress, Charles managed to give his kinsman a splendid reception, but he waved aside his petition, and simply invited him to join him in his campaign.

A week sufficed for the Swiss contingent to march from Basel to Nancy, across the plains of Alsace. Meantime René had rallied about four thousand men under Lorraine captains, and to this was added an Alsatian force which had joined him by way of St.-Nicolas-du-Port. They were

[1] This monarch, Alphonse V., called the African, asking Louis XI. for assistance against Ferdinand of Castile, was refused on the score that Charles the Bold was menacing the safety of the French frontier. Alphonse's prayer for peace might have been instigated by thoughts of his own needs as well as those of humanity. (Toutey, p. 386.)

The Battle of Nancy

a rude, pitiless crowd, as they soon evinced by routing a few Burgundians out of the houses where they had hidden, and massacring them publicly. A reconnaissance, sent out by Charles, was easily put to flight.

On January 4th, Charles learned that fresh troops had reached St.-Nicolas. He showed assurance, arrogance, and negligence. His belief in his star was fully restored. He actually did not take the trouble to try once more to ascertain the exact strength of the enemy. He had commissioned the Bishop of Forli to negotiate for him at Basel, and refused to credit the statement that the Swiss were throwing in their fortunes with René. He thought that "the Child," as he contemptuously termed his adversary, had simply gone right and left to hire mercenaries, and he rather ridiculed the idea of taking such *canaille* seriously, saying that it was a host unworthy of a gentleman. Still he resolved to meet and finish them once for all.[1]

It is a fact that the Swiss reinforcements were a different and far less efficient body than the volunteers of Granson and Morat had been. French gold, scattered freely, had done its work in exciting the cupidity of every man who could bear arms. There were some staunch leaders, like Waldemar of Zürich and Rudolph de Stein, but their kind was in the minority. Berne aided with money rather than with men, but she was not

[1] Toutey, p. 387.

a generous ally as she insisted on having hostages to ensure her repayment. A venal spirit was evident in every quarter. As the troops made their way over the Jura their behaviour showed that the late splendid booty had affected them. Plunder was their aim. When René reviewed these fresh arrivals from Basel, one of his attending officers was Oswald von Thierstein, late governor of Alsace.[1] Disgraced by Sigismund he had passed over to the Duke of Lorraine, who appointed him marshal.

On that January 4th, a Saturday, Charles held a council meeting. The opinion of the wisest, already given on previous occasions, was urged again:

"Do not risk battle. René is poor. If there are no immediate engagements, his mercenaries will abandon him for lack of pay. Raise the siege and depart for Flanders and Luxemburg. The army can rest and be increased. Then at the approach of spring it will be easy to fall upon René deprived of his troops."

Charles was absolutely deaf to these arguments. He was determined on facing the issue at once. Leaving a small force to sustain the siege, he ordered the camp to be broken on the evening of the 4th and a movement made towards St.-Nicolas. He selected a ground favourable for the manipulation of a large body, and placed his

[1] See Scott's *Anne of Geierstein*. This is the man whom the author makes the appointed instrument of the *Vehmgericht* to slay Charles.

The Battle of Nancy

artillery on a plateau situated between Jarville and Neuville. It was not a good position, being hedged in on the right and in front by woods which could conceal the movements of a foe without impeding them. Only one way of retreat was open—towards Metz, whose bishop was Charles's last ally. But to reach Metz, it was necessary to cross several small streams and deceptive marshes, half frozen as they were, besides the river Meurthe, a serious obstacle with the garrison of Nancy on the flank. In short, there was ample reason to dread surprise, while in case of defeat a terrible catastrophe was more than possible. Curiously, the precise kind of difficulties which beset the field of Morat were repeated here—proof that Charles had not the qualities of a general who could learn by experience.[1]

The exact force at his disposal on this occasion has been variously estimated. Considering the ravages of the sanguinary skirmishes during the siege, and of the cold, it is probable that the actual combatants did not number more than ten thousand, all told. And only half of these were of any value—two thousand men under Galeotto, and three thousand Burgundians commanded by Charles and his immediate lieutenants. The remainder were unreliable mercenaries and the still more unreliable troops of Campobasso already pledged to the foe. La Marche estimates René's force at twelve thousand and adds: "The Duke of

[1] Toutey, p. 388.

Burgundy was far behind, for, on my conscience, he had not two thousand fighting men."[1]

The allies adopted a plan of battle proposed by a Lorrainer, Vautrin Wuisse. The first manœuvre was to divert the foe and turn him towards the woods, and then to attack his centre, which would at the same time be pressed at the front by the Lorraine forces, headed by René himself. The plan succeeded in every point. Surprised that they dared take the offensive, Charles was alert to the harsh cries of the "bull" of Uri and the "cow" of Unterwalden, which were heard across the woods. A sudden presentiment saddened him. Putting on his helmet, he accidentally knocked off the lion bearing the legend *Hoc est signum Dei*. He replaced it and plunged into the mêlée.

The onslaught was terrific. Galeotto's troops and the duke's were the only ones to make sturdy resistance. The right wing of the army gave way under the fierce assault of the Swiss. The cry, "*Sauve qui peut!*" raised possibly by Campobasso's traitors, produced a terrible rout. Three quarters of the troops were in flight, while the duke still fought on with superhuman ferocity.

Galeotto, seeing that the day was lost, protected his own mercenaries as best he could, while Campobasso completed the treason that he had plotted with René, which had been partially accomplished four days previously, and calmly took up his posi-

[1] *Mémoires*, iii., 239.

The Battle of Nancy

tion on the bridge of Bouxières on the Meurthe, to make prisoners for the sake of ransom. Then the besieged made a sudden sortie which increased the disorder. The battle proper was of short duration, with little bloodshed, but the pursuit was sanguinary in the extreme, because the Burgundian army had left no loophole open for retreat.

The Swiss pursued the fugitives hotly as far as Bouxières and inflicted carnage right and left on the route. It was easy work. The morasses were traps and the Burgundians, encumbered with their arms, found it impossible to free themselves, when they once were entangled. They fell like flies before the fury of the mountaineers. The Lorrainers and Alsatians were more humane or more mercenary, for they took prisoners instead of killing indiscriminately. Charles fought desperately to the very end. There is no doubt that he plunged into the thick of the fight and risked his life in a reckless manner, but there is absolute uncertainty as to how he met his death. It is generally accepted that the last person to see him alive was one Baptista Colonna, a page in the service of a Neapolitan captain. This lad, with an extra helmet swung over his shoulder, found himself close to the duke. He saw him surrounded by troops, noticed his horse stumble, was sure that the rider fell. The next moment, Colonna's attention was diverted to himself. He was taken prisoner and knew no more of the day's events. The figure of Charles of Burgundy disappears from the view of man. A curtain woven of vague rumour hides the closing scenes of his life.

At seven o'clock the victorious Duke of Lorraine rode into the rescued city and re-entered his palace. At the gates was heaped up a ghastly memorial of the steadfastness of the burghers in their devotion to his cause. This was a pile of the bones of the foul animals they had consumed when other food was exhausted, rather than capitulate to their liege's foe. To ascertain the fate of that foe now became René's chief anxiety, and he despatched messengers to Metz and elsewhere to find out where Charles had taken refuge. The reports were all negative. The first positive assurance that the duke was dead came from young Baptista Colonna, whom Campobasso himself introduced into René's presence on Monday evening. The page told his tale and declared that he could point out the precise place where he had seen the Duke of Burgundy fall. Accordingly, on Tuesday morning, January 7th, a party went forth from Nancy to the desolate battlefield and were guided by Colonna to the edge of a pool which he asserted confidently was the very spot where he had seen Charles. Circumstantial evidence went to give corroboration to his word, for the dozen or more bodies that lay strewn along the ground in the immediate vicinity of the pool were close friends and followers of the duke, men who would, in all probability, have stayed faithfully by their master's person, a volunteer bodyguard as long as they drew breath. These bodies were all stripped naked. Harpies had already gathered what plunder they could find, and no apparel or accoutrements were left to show the difference in rank between noble and page. But the faces were recognisable and they were identified as well-known nobles of the Burgundian court. Separated from this group by a little space at the very edge of the pool, was another naked body in still more doleful plight. The face was disfigured beyond all semblance of what it might have been in life. One cheek was bitten by wolves, one was imbedded in the frozen slime. Yet there was evidence on the poor forsaken remains that convinced the searchers that this was indeed the mortal part of the great duke. Two wounds from a pick and a blow above the ear—inflicted by "one named Humbert"—showed how death had been caused. The missing teeth corresponded to those lost by Charles, there was a scar just where he had received his wound at Montl'héry, the finger nails were long like his, a wound on the shoulder, a fistula on the groin, and an ingrowing nail were additional marks of identification,—six definite proofs in all. Among those who gazed at this wretched sight, on that January morning, were men intimately acquainted with the duke's person.

"There were his physician, a Portuguese named Mathieu, and his valets, besides Olivier de la Marche [1] and Denys his chaplain who were taken

[1] It is strange that La Marche does not make more of this

thither and there was no doubt that he was dead. It has not yet been decided where he will be buried, and to know it better it [the body] has been bathed in warm water and good wine and cleansed. In that state it was recognisable by all who had previously seen and known him. The page who had given the information was taken to the king. Had it not been for him it would never have been known what had become of him considering the state and the place where he was found."[1]

Before the body could be freed from the ice in which it was imbedded, implements had to be brought from Nancy. Four Lorraine nobles hastened to the spot, when they heard the tidings, to show honour to the man who had been their accepted lord for a brief period, and they acted as escort as the burden was carried into the town and placed in a suitable chamber in the home of one George Marquiez. There seems to have been no insult offered to the fallen man, no lack of deference in the proceedings. The very spot where the bier rested for a moment was marked with a little black cross.

scene if he were really there. His sole statement is: "The duke remained dead on the field of battle, stretched out like the poorest man in the world and I was taken and others." iii., 240.

[1] *La déconfiture de Monseigneur de Bourgogne faite par Monseigneur de Lorraine.* Comines-Lenglet, iii., 493.

This brief account was drawn up evidently before the duke's burial was known by the writer. It may have been written solely to please Louis XI. Still there is a simplicity about it that holds the attention, in spite of the fact that the story is not accepted by critical historians.

The Battle of Nancy

As the corpse was bathed, three wounds became evident—a deep cut from a halberd in the head, spear thrusts through the thighs and abdomen—proofs of the closeness of the last struggle. When all the dignity possible had been given to the miserable human fragment and the chamber hung with conventional mourning, René came thither clad in black garments. Kneeling by the bier, he said: "Would to God, fair cousin, that your misfortunes and mine had not reduced you to the condition in which I see you."

For five days the body lay in state before the high altar of the church of St. George, and the obsequies that followed were attended by René and his nobles, and the coffin was honourably placed among the ducal dead.

Yet doubt of the man's existence was not buried with the bones to which his name was given. When the Swiss turned their way homeward, their farewell words to René were: "If the Duke of Burgundy has escaped and should reopen war, tell us." "If he has assured his safety," René answered, "we will fight again when summer comes." There was no delay, however, in the division of the spoils. The Burgundian treasure was distributed among René's allies, and the ignorant soldiers received articles worth many times their pay, which they, in many cases, disposed of for an infinitesimal part of their value.

As late as January 28th, Margaret of York and Mary of Burgundy wrote to Louis XI. from Ghent:

"We are still hoping that Monseigneur is alive in the hands of his enemies." Other rumours continued to be current, not only for weeks but for years. In 1482, it was gravely recounted that the vanished duke had retired to Brucsal in Swabia, where he led an austere life, *genus vitae horridum atque asperum.* Bets were made, too, on the chances of his return.[1]

Louis XI. was a very pleasant person when news was brought him that he liked to hear. Commines and Bouchage together had told him about the defeat of Morat and had each received two hundred silver marks. It was a Seigneur de Lude who had the good luck to bring him letters from Craon recounting the battle of Nancy. It was "really difficult for the king to keep his countenance so surprised was he with joy."[2] His letter to Craon was written on January 9th and ran as follows.[3]

"M. the Count, my friend, I have received your letter and heard the good news that you impart to me, for which I thank you as much as I can. Now is the time to use all your five natural senses to deliver the duchy and county of Burgundy into my hands. If the duke be dead, do you and the governor of Champagne take your troops and put yourselves within the land, and, if you love me, keep as good order among your men as if you were in Paris, and prove that I mean to

[1] La Marche, iii., 240.
[2] Comines v., ch. x.
[3] *Lettres* vi., p. 111.

After the Battle

treat them [the Burgundians] better than any one in my realm."

The "five natural senses" of the king's lieutenant were employed most loyally to his master's service. The duchy of Burgundy returned to the French crown. Before Easter, the Estates were convened by Louis XI., and there was no longer any duke in Burgundy to be an over powerful peer in France.

With the exception of Guelders the lands acquired by Charles fell away, but the remainder as inherited by him passed under the rule of his daughter Mary, who carried her heritage into the House of Austria, through which it passed finally to the King of Spain.

On that fatal fifth of January, Charles of Burgundy had only just passed middle life. He was forty-four years, one month, and twenty-six days old, an age when a man has the right to look forward to new achievements. Every circumstance of the dreary and premature death was in glaring contrast to his prospects at his birth in 1433, in insolent contradiction to his own estimation of the obligations assumed by Fate in his behalf. In certain details of the catastrophe there are, of course, accidents. No one could have predicted that the duke whose chief title was a synonym for magnificence, that this cherished heir to his House, who had been bathed in all the luxury known to his epoch, should have thus lain in death, many hours long, unattended and uncared-for, naked and frozen on a bed of congealed mud, with a winter sky as canopy. The actual adversity as it overwhelmed him was too appalling for any foresight. But the great dream of the man's life that vanished with his vitality owed its annihilation to no mere chance of warfare. Had it not been rudely ended by the battle of Nancy, other means of destruction, inevitable and sure, would have appeared. The projected erection of a solidified kingdom stretching from the North Sea to Switzerland and possibly to the Mediterranean, one that could hold the balance of power between France and Germany, contained elements of disintegration, latent at its foundation. It is clear, from a consideration of the Duke of Burgundy and his position in the Europe of his time, that the materials which he expected to mould into a realm were a collection of sentient units. Each separate one was instinct with individual life, individual desires, conscious of its own minute past, capable of directing its own contracted future. That the hereditary title of overlord to each political unity had lodged upon a head already dignified by a plurality of similar titles, was a mere chance and viewed by the burghers in a wholly different light from that in which this same overlord regarded it. The fishers in Holland, the manufacturers in Brabant, the merchants in Flanders, the vintners in Burgundy, cared nothing for being the wings of an imperial idea. They wanted safe fishing grounds, unmolested highways of commerce, vineyards free from the tramp of armies. And with their desires fixed on these as needful, their attitude towards the political centralisation planned by their common ruler, often betrayed both ignorance and inconsistency. At various epochs some degree of imperialism for the Netherland group had been quite to popular taste. In Holland, Zealand and Hainaut, it had been conceded that Jacqueline of Bavaria was less efficient to maintain desirable conditions than her cousin of Burgundy, and the exchange of sovereigns had been effected in spite of the manifest injustice involved in the transaction. But while there was willingness to accept any advantages that might accrue to a people from the reputation of a local overlord, it was never forgotten for an instant that his relation to his subjects was as their own count and strictly limited by conditions that had long existed within each petty territory. While Charles seemed to be on the straight road towards his goal, the people within each body politic of his inherited states were profoundly preoccupied with their own local concerns, and only alive to his schemes when they feared demands upon their internal revenues for external purposes.

It does not seem probable, however, that the abstract question of the projected kingdom was ever taken very seriously among those to be directly affected by the proposed change. The bars interposed by his own subjects in the duke's progress towards royalty were obstructions to his successive steps rather than to his theory. Indeed, strenuous opposition to details was allied to a vague and passive acceptance of the whole. Moreover when the idea was phrased it was distinctly as a revival, not as a novelty. The previous existence of a kingdom of Burgundy was undoubtedly a potent factor in the degree of progress made by Charles towards conjuring into new life a reincarnation of that ancient realm. Yet it was a factor clothed with a shadow rather than with the substance of truth. Geographically there was very little in common between the dominion projected more or less definitely in 1473 and any one of the kingdoms of Burgundy as they had successively existed. That of Charles corresponded very nearly to the ancient kingdom of Lorraine. Franche-Comté was the only ground common to the territories actually held by the duke and to the latest kingdom of Burgundy. His possessions in Picardy and Alsace lay wholly beyond the limits of either Burgundy or Lorraine. But the old name survived in his ducal title, and it was that name that lent a semblance of reality to this fifteenth-century dream of a middle kingdom as outlined in the duke's mind more or less definitely or as bounded by his ambition.

In retrospect it is clear that more was requisite for the realisation of the vision of the wished-for nation, than imperial investiture of a crowned monarch with sovereignty over a group

After the Battle

of lands. A modern writer has pointed out how infinitely subtle is the vital principle of a nation, one not even to be created by common interests. A *Zollverein* is no *patria*. An element of sentiment is needful, and an element of growth.[1] The nation like the individual is the result of what has gone before. An heroic past, great men, glory that can command respect at home and abroad — that is the capital on which is based a national idea. To have wrought in common, to wish to accomplish more in the future, are essential conditions to be a people. "The existence of a nation is a plebiscite of every day, just as the existence of the individual is a perpetual affirmation of life."

Now it is evident, in summing up the salient features of this failure, that a vital principle was not germinating in the inchoate mass. Charles himself never attained the rank of a national hero. More than that, with all his individual states, he never had any nation, great or small, at his back. Personally he was a man without a country. His father, Philip, was French, pure and simple, quite as French as his grandfather, Philip the Hardy, the first Duke of Burgundy out of the House of Valois, even though Philip the Good had extended his sway to many non-French-speaking peoples and was able to use the Flemish speech if it suited his whim. But that was as a condescension and as something extraneous. The chief of French peers

[1] Renan, *Qu'est ce qu'une nation.*

remained his proudest title; his ability to influence French affairs, the task he liked best.

His son was quite different in his attitude towards France. He minimised his degree of French blood royal. More than once he boasted of his kinship with Portuguese, with English stock. He had certain characteristics of an immigrant, who has abandoned family traditions and is proudly confident that his bequest to posterity is to outshine what he has inherited. Charles was not exactly a stupid man, but he certainly was dazzled by his early surroundings into an overestimate of himself, into a conceit that was a tremendous stumbling-block in his path. He had not the kind of intelligence that would have enabled him to take at their worth the rhetorical phrases of adulation heaped upon him on festal occasions. Yet this same conceit, this very self-confidence, gave him a high conception of his duties. At his accession, he showed a sense of his responsibilities, a definite theory of conduct which he fully intended to act upon. His very belief in his own powers gave him an intrinsic honesty of purpose. He was convinced that he could maintain law, order, justice in his domain, and he fully intended to do so in a paternal way, but he left out of consideration the rights of the people, rights older than his dynasty. In his military career, too, at the outset, he evinced the strongest bent towards preserving the best conditions possible amid the brutalities of warfare. He curbed the

After the Battle

soldiers' passions, he protected women, and was as relentless towards miscreants in his ranks as towards his foe. In civil matters he exerted himself to secure impartial equity for all alike. When he gave a promise, he fully intended to make his words good. It was only in the face of repeated deceptions of the cleverer and more unscrupulous Louis XI. that Charles changed for the worse. Exasperated by the knowledge that the king's solemn pledges were given repeatedly with no intention of fulfilment, he attempted to adopt a similar policy and was singularly infelicitous in his imitation. His political methods degenerated into mere barefaced lying, softened by no graces, illumined by no clever intuition of where to draw the line. From 1472 on, the duke's word was worth no more than the king's, and words were assuredly at a discount just then. A perusal of the international correspondence of the period leaves the reader marvelling why time was wasted in covering paper, with flimsy, insincere phrases, mendacious sign-posts which gave no true indication of the road to be travelled. There are, however, differences in the art of dissimulation and Charles never attained a mastery of the science.

The adjective which has attached itself to his name in English in an inaccurate rendering of *le téméraire* which belongs to him in French. There were other terms too applied to Charles at different periods of his career. He was Charles the Hardy in his early youth, Charles the Terrible in those last months when he tried to fortify himself with wine unsuited to his constitution, but at all times he might have been called Charles the self-absorbed, Charles the solitary. There have been many men more passionate, more uncontrolled, than Charles of Burgundy, whose personal magnetism yet enabled them to win friends and to keep them, as the duke was powerless to do. The failure to command personal devotion, unquestioning loyalty, was one of his chief personal misfortunes. Philip, magnificent, lavish, debonair, found many lenient apologists for his crimes, while his son received criticism for his faults even from the faithful among his servitors. How a reflection of his bearing glows out from the mirror turned casually upon him by Commines' skilful hand! Take the glimpse of Louis XI. as he lures on St. Pol's messenger to imitate Charles. The Sire de Créville inspired by the royal interest in his narration about an incident at the court of Burgundy, puffs out his cheeks, stamps his feet in a dictatorial manner, and swears by St. George as he quotes the duke's words. Behind a screen are hidden Commines, and a Burgundian envoy aghast at hearing his liege lord so mocked. It is a time when St. Pol is trying to ride three horses at once and the French king takes this method to have Charles informed of his duplicity. "Speak louder" he says, "I grow a little deaf" and the flattered envoy repeats his dramatic performance in a way to engrave it on the memory of the duke's retainer.

TOMB OF CHARLES OF BURGUNDY, BRUGES
CHURCH OF NÔTRE DAME
(FROM A PHOTOGRAPH BY DAN FELLOWS PLATT)

After the Battle

In thus touching on the traits of his former master, Commines does not show malice or even a dislike for the duke. He is much more severe about Louis—only he found the latter easier to serve.

In his family life, too, Charles does not seem to have found any companionship that affected his life. He is lauded as a faithful husband to Isabella of Bourbon but her death seemed to make little difference. Neither she nor Margaret of York had the actual significance enjoyed by Isabella of Portugal as consort to Philip the Good with his notoriously roving fancy.

Thus at home as well as abroad the last Duke of Burgundy tried to stand alone. Perhaps his chief happiness in life was that he never knew how insufficient for his desired task he was and how the new art of printing, the birth of Erasmus of Rotterdam, were the really great events of his brief decade of sovereignty. It was his good fortune that he never knew that no splendid achievement gave significance to his device: "I have undertaken it"—*Je lay emprins*.

BIBLIOGRAPHY

THERE is an enormous mass of literature bearing upon the later years of Philip of Burgundy and the brief career of Charles the Bold. Fairly adequate bibliographies can be found in Pirenne and Molinier (see list). The following list contains the full titles of the chief works to which direct reference is made in the text but falls far short of a complete description of the matter, contemporaneous or critical, which has coloured the treatment of the subject.

When extracts have been taken from matter quoted by other writers the reference is to the later books only.

Archives curieuses de l'histoire de France. Vol. i. (Paris, 1834.) Contains *Le cabinet du roy Louis XI.; Discours du siège de Beauvais, en* 1472, etc.

BARANTE, M. DE. *Histoire des ducs de Bourgogne de la maison de Valois. Avec des remarques par le baron de Reiffenberg.* 6th ed. 10 vols. (Brussels, 1835.)

BASIN, THOMAS, 1412–1491. *Histoire des règnes de Charles VII. et de Louis XI.* (Latin text). Ed. J. E. J. Quicherat. 2 vols. (Paris, 1855.)

BEAUCOURT, G. DU FRESNE, MARQUIS DE. *Histoire de Charles VII.* 6 vols. (Paris, 1890.)

BLOK, P. J. *Eene Hollandsche stad onder de Bourgondisch-Oostenrijksche Heerschappij.* (The Hague, 1884.)

BRANTÔME, PIERRE DE BOURDEILLE, SEIGNEUR DE. *Œuvres complètes de.* Ed. Ludovic Lalanne. (Paris, 1876.)

BUDT, ADRIAN DE. *Chronicon Flandriæ.* De Smet *Corpus chron. Flandr. I.* (Brussels, 1837–65.)

BUSSIÈRE, BARON MARIE-THÉODORE DE. *Histoire de la ligue formée contre Charles le téméraire.* (Paris, 1846.)

Cent nouvelles nouvelles, Les. Édition revue sur les textes originaux, etc., par A. J. V. Le Roux de Lincy. (Paris, 1841.)

CHABEUF, H. *Deux portraits bourguignons du XV*^e *siècle.* (Dijon, 1893.) (Mémoires de la société bourguignonne de géographie et d'histoire. Vol. ix.)

CHASTELLAIN, GEORGES, 1404–1475. *Œuvres.* (Ed. Kervyn de Lettenhove.) 8 vols. (Brussels, 1863–66.)

CHMEL, JOSEPH. *Geschichte Kaiser Friedrichs IV.* 2 vols. (Hamburg, 1843.)

CHMEL, JOSEPH. *Urkunden zur Geschichte von Österreich, Steiermark,* etc. [Monumenta Habsburgica.] 2 vols. (Vienna, 1849.)

CLÉMART, PIERRE. *Jacques Cœur et Charles VII.* (Paris, 1873.)

Collection de documents inédits sur l'histoire de France. "Mélanges." (Ed. M. Champollion-Figeac.) (Paris, 1843.)

COMMINES, PHILIP DE. *The Historie of,* Englished by Thomas Dannett. Anno 1596. With an introduction by Charles Whibley. (London, 1897.)

Mémoires de Philippe de Comines, 1447–1511. Nouvelle édition par Messieurs Godefroy, augmentée par M. l'Abbé Lenglet du Fresnoy. 4 vols. Ref. (Comines-Lenglet.) (Paris, 1747.)

This edition contains many letters, documents, etc., collected by M. Lenglet du Fresnoy. Their accuracy has been impugned in many instances. Those cited have been taken with a view to the later criticism upon them.

Mémoires de Philippe de Commynes. Nouvelle édition publiée avec une introduction et des notes par Bernard de Mandrot. 2 vols. Ref. (Commynes-Mandrot.) (Paris, 1901.)

Mémoires de Philippe de Commynes. Nouvelle édition, revue sur les manuscrits de la bibliothèque royale, etc., par Mlle. Dupont. 3 vols. Ref. (Commynes-Dupont.) (Paris, 1840.)

CORNEREAU, A. *Le palais des états de Bourgogne à Dijon.* (Dijon, 1890.) (Mémoires de la soc. bourguignonne de géog. et d'hist., v.)

COURTÉPÉE, M. *Description, générale et particulière du duché de Bourgogne.* 4 vols. (Dijon, 1847.)

DESCHAMPS, EUSTACHE. *Œuvres complètes.* (Paris, 1878–1904.) (Soc. des anciens textes français.) 11 vols.

DES MAREZ, G. *L' organisation du travail à Bruxelles au XVe siècle.* (Bruxelles, 1903–04.) (Mémoires couronnés de l'acad. royale de Belgique. Vol. lxv.–lxvi.)

DEWEZ, M. *Histoire particulière des provinces belgiques sous le gouvernement des ducs et des comtes, pour servir de complément à l'histoire générale.* 3 vols. (Brussels, 1834.)

DU CLERCQ, JACQUES, 1420–1501. *Mémoires.* (Ed. Baron F. de Reiffenberg.) 4 vols. (Brussels, 1823.)

DUCLOS, CHARLES P. *Œuvres complètes de.* Nouvelle édition. 9 vols. (Paris, 1820.)

ESCOUCHY, MATHIEU D'(DE COUCY). *Chronique.* (1420?–1482+.) (Ed. G. du Fresne de Beaucourt.) 3 vols. (Paris, 1863.) (Soc. de l'hist. de France.)

FREDERICQ, PAUL. *Le rôle politique et social des ducs de Bourgogne.* (Brussels, 1875.)

FREEMAN, EDWARD A. *The Historical Geography of Europe.* 2 vols. 3d edition, edited by G. B. Berry. (London, 1903.)

GACHARD, L. P. *Analectes belgiques ou recueil de pièces inédites,* etc. Vol. i. (Brussels, 1830.)

GACHARD, L. P., Ed. *Collection des voyages des souverains des Pays-Bas.* 4 vols. (Brussels, 1830.)

GACHARD, L. P., Ed. *Documents inédits concernant l'histoire de la Belgique.* 3 vols. (Brussels, 1833.)

GACHARD, L. P. *Études et notices historiques concernant l'histoire des Pays-Bas.* 3 vols. (Brussels, 1890.)

Gesta Episcoporum Leodiensium. (Marténe Coll. Vol. iv.) (Paris, 1729.).

GINGINS LA SARRA, LE BARON DE FRÉDERIC DE, Ed. *Dépêches des ambassadeurs milanais sur les campagnes de Charles le Hardi, 1474–1477.* 2 vols. (Paris, 1858.)

GOLLUT, M. LOYS. *Les mémoires historiques de la république séquanoise et des princes de la Franche-Comté de Bourgogne.* (Arbois, 1846.)

JEUNE, HUGUÉNIN. *Histoire de la guerre de Lorraine et du siège de Nancy, par Charles le Téméraire, duc de Bourgogne, 1473–1477.* (Metz, 1837.)

KERVYN DE LETTENHOVE, LE BARON. [Ed. of works of Chastellain, Budt, etc.]; see article in *Bullétin de l'académie royale de Belgique,* 1887, etc.

KERVYN DE LETTENHOVE. *Histoire de Flandre.* 5 vols. (Brussels, 1853–54.)

KIRK, JOHN FOSTER. *History of Charles the Bold, Duke of Burgundy.* 3 vols. (Philadelphia, 1864–1868.)

LABORDE (L. E. S. J.), COMTE DE. *Les ducs de Bourgogne: Études sur les lettres, les arts et l'industrie pendant le XVe siècle*, etc. "Preuves." 3 vols. (Paris, 1849–52.)

LACOMBLET, TH. J. *Urkundenbuch für die Geschichte des Niederrheins*. 4 vols. (Düsseldorf, 1848.)

LA MARCHE, OLIVIER DE, 1422–1502. *Mémoires.* (1435–1488.) Paris, 1883–84. (Ed. Beaune et d'Arbaumont.) 3 vols.

LAVISSE, ERNEST. *Histoire de France depuis les origines jusqu'à la révolution*. Publiée avec la collaboration de MM. Bayet, Block, Carré, Kleinclausz, Langlois, Lemonnier, Luchaire, Mariéjol, Petit-Dutaillis, etc. (Paris, 1893–.)

The volume covering periods of Charles VII. and Louis XI. is written by Ch. Petit-Dutaillis, Professor at the University of Lille. (Reference used, Lavisse, IV^II.) (Paris, 1902.)

LE FÉVRE, JEAN, SEIGNEUR DE ST. RÉMY. (*Toison d'or*.) (1395–1463.) *Chronique*. 2 vols. (Paris, 1876.)

LE ROUX DE LINCY, A. J. V. *Chants historiques sur les règnes de Charles VII. et de Louis XI.*

Lettres de Louis XI. (Paris, 1883–.) (Eds., Joseph Vaesen, et Étienne Charavay,

LOOMIS, LOUISE ROPES. *Medieval Hellenism*. (Columbia University, 1906.)

MARTÉNE, EDMUND. *Veterum Scriptorum et Monumentorum, Historicorum, Dogmaticorum, Moralium, Amplissium Collectio*. Vol. iv. (Paris, 1729.)

Mémoires et documents publiés par la société d'histoire de la suisse romande. Vol. viii. "Mélanges." (Lausanne, 1849.)

MEYER, J. *Commentarii sive annales rerum Flandricarum*. (Antwerp, 1561.)

MOLINET, JEAN. *Chronique* (1474–1506.) (Paris, 1824–29.)

This is a continuation of Chastellain and is interesting especially for the siege of Neuss.

MONSTRELET, ENGUERRAND DE (d. 1453). *La Chronique*. (Paris, 1861.)

MOLINIER, AUGUSTE. *Les sources de l'histoire de France des origines aux guerres d'Italie*. Vols. iv., v., 1461–1494. (Paris, 1904.)

Neues Archiv der Gesellschaft für ältere deutsche Geschichtskunde. Vol. xxv. (Leipzig, 1900.)

INDEX

A

Abbeville, 106, 111, 143
Agincourt, battle of, 19, 407
Aire, 224, 271
Aix, 357
Alkmaar, 71, 285
Alsace, 239, 254, 256, 260, 370, 374, 386-391, 393, 395, 397, 400, 401, 442, 444, 456
Alsace, Upper, 248, 251, 254
Amboise, 106, 272, 282, 293, 298, 306
Amiens, 111, 121, 289, 290, 294, 298, 300, 311, 321, 410, 411
Amont, 43, 258, 259
Andernach, 396
Angers, 280, 305, 307
Anjou, duchy of, 118
Anjou, Margaret of, Queen of England, 101, 155, 156, 188, 264, 265, 274, 279, 280, 284, 285, 290
Anjou, René, King of, 156, 332, 367, 400
Anjou, Yolande of, *see* Vaudemont
Antwerp, 14, 180, 275, 337
Appiano, Antoine d' (Antonius de Aplano), Milanese ambassador, 423
Aragon, 38, 245, 295
Argau, 248
Armagnac, 223
Arras, Bishop of, 70
Arras, treaty of, 11-13, 15, 36, 72, 110, 221
Arson, Jehan d', 282, 284
Arthur, King, 225
Artois, 12, 14, 156, 358
Artois, Bonne of, Duchess of Burgundy, *see* Burgundy

Atclyff, William, 325
Ath, 406
Augsburg, Diet of, 349
Austria, 245, 246, 254-257, 259, 386, 388
Austria, House of, 394, 453
Austria, Maximilian, Archduke of, *see* Maximilian
Austria, Sigismund of (Count of Tyrol), 248; mortgages lands to Charles of Burgundy, 250-256, 329-331, 371, 374; resumes sovereignty of mortgaged lands, 387-394, 415, 444
Auvergne, Marshal d', 108
Auxonne, 379
Auxy, Jehan, Seigneur d', 9, 17, 18, 26, 29
Avesnes, 102, 103
Avranches, Bishop of, 206
Aydie, Odet d', 98, 305, 308, 309, 314

B

"Bad Penny," the, tax, 372, 373, 377, 380, 381
Balue, Cardinal, 206, 207, 211, 217, 224, 283
Bar, duchy of, 396
Barante, cited, 20
Bari, Duc de (Sforza), 413
Barnet, battle of, 289
Barre, Corneille de la, 103
Barrois, 156
Baschi, Suffren de, 441, 442
Basel, 60, 248, 254, 353, 375, 376, 387, 388, 392, 394, 442-444
Basel, Bishop of, 381
Basin, Thomas, cited, 355
Basse-Union, the, 375, 378, 381, 386, 393, 395, 415
Baume-les-Dames, 43

Index

Bavaria, elector of, 247
Bavaria, Stephen of, 69
Beaujeu, Lord of, 16
Beaumont, château of, 291, 317
Beauvais, siege of, 311–313
Bedford, John, Duke of, death of, 11, 72
Begars, Abbé de, 299
Belfort, 379
Bellière, Vicomte de la, 304
Berne, 59, 248, 249, 352, 376, 377, 392, 397, 400, 402, 415, 417, 421, 443
Berry, Bailiff of, 61–64
Berry, Charles of France, Duke of (Normandy and Guienne), heads League of Public Weal, 121, 124; character of, 125, 126; Normandy given to, 128, 142, 197–200, 203, 217; won over by Louis, 205, 219, 220, 282; Guienne given to, 281, 282, 294; proposed marriage of, 294–298, 333; suspicious death of, 302–304, 307–310, 314–316, 334, 344
Besançon, 60, 252, 353, 379, 380, 387, 388
Biche, Guillaume de, 89, 105, 206, 211
Biscay, Bay of, 282
Black Forest, the, 248, 254
Bladet, 291
Blamont, Count of, 393, 397
Blaumont, Seigneur de, Marshal of Burgundy, 79, 81
Boccaccio, 93
Bohemia, 245–247, 348
Bonn, 396
Borselen, Adrian van, Seigneur of Breda, 192
Borselen, Frank van (Count of Ostrevant), 9, 14, 26; death of, 323
Borselen, Henry van, 323
Boscise, 314
Bouchage, Monseigneur du, 223, 295–297, 319, 452
Boudault, Jehan, 47, 60

Boulogne, 12, 128, 286
Bourbon, Catharine of, *see* Guelders
Bourbon, Duchess of, 60, 61
Bourbon, duchy of, 118
Bourbon, Duke of, 16, 60, 61, 124, 206, 217
Bourbon, Isabella of (Countess of Charolais), *see* Charolais
Bourbon, Louis of, Bishop of Liege, 137–140, 145, 146, 212–214, 218–221
Bourges, 11, 98
Bouvignes, 139, 145, 148, 154
Bouxières, 447
Brabant, Anthony, Duke of, 14
Brabant, duchy of, 13, 14, 32, 156, 253, 358, 454
Brabant, Duke of, 181
Brandenburg, Albert, elector of, 349, 351, 352
Brandenburg, Margrave of, 247
Brantôme, Pierre de Bourdeille, Seigneur de, cited, 308, 309
Breda, 192
Brederode, Gijsbrecht of, 69–71
Breisgau, 248, 374
Bresse, Philip de, 208, 209
Brie, 219, 281
Brisac (Breisach), 251, 372, 373, 377, 379–381, 389, 391
Brittany, Duchess of, 295, 296
Brittany, duchy of, 160, 161, 363
Brittany, Francis, Duke of, joins League of Public Weal, 114, 115, 118–120, 124; ally of Charles of Burgundy, 197, 295, 296, 298, 312–314; is reconciled to Louis XI., 203, 210, 314, 315, 334
Broeck, M. van der, 198

… Index 471

Bruchsal, 452
Bruges, 2, 18–23, 38, 113, 154, 161, 179, 187, 188, 190–196, 251, 261, 268, 293, 385, 404, 406, 428
Brunette, the, 271, 272
Brussels, 18, 29, 39, 142, 153, 180, 184, 186, 243–245, 325, 379, 429
Bureau, Jehan, 98
Buren, castle of, 320
Burgundy, duchy of, 14, 156, 254, 257, 352, 358, 384, 453, 454, 456; Estates of, 427, 434, 435, 453
Burgundy, Franche-Comté of, 14
Burgundy, Anthony, Grand Bastard of, 5, 18, 123, 150, 159–161, 183, 195, 323
Burgundy, Baldwin, Bastard of, 282–284
Burgundy, Charles the Bold, (Count of Charolais), Duke of, birth of, 5, 7; elected knight of the Golden Fleece, 5–7; description of, 8, 30, 165, 166, 339–341; ancestry of, 8, 183, 269, 270, 277, 278, 291, 292, 410, 457, 458; imperial ambitions of, 10, 11, 158, 187, 247, 251, 279, 328–337, 347–361, 384, 385, 398, 414, 415, 454–457; education of, 9–11, 18, 28–30; weds Catherine of France, 16, 17; takes official part in public affairs, 18, 23, 24, 26; character of, 30, 67, 158, 166–168, 181, 187, 277, 301–303, 310, 334, 340, 359, 398, 407, 426, 440, 443, 445, 458–460; first campaign of, 37–42; entrusted with regency of Holland, 57, 58, 67, 68, 87; English sympathies of, 57, 167, 183, 188, 264–267, 271–274, 277, 278, 286, 288, 290; weds Isabella of Bourbon, 57, 58, 60–65; judicial methods of, 68, 261–263; rejoices over birth of daughter 83, 86; strained relations with his father, 86–89, 96–99, 111, 112, 119; enmity between Louis and, 86–93, 96, 113,–117, 119, 205, 271–274, 282–284, 303, 308, 309, 314, 320, 347, *et passim;* at coronation of Louis XI., 104, 105, 109; fears plots against his life, 112–117, 282–284; joins League of Public Weal, 114–119, 121; allies of, 114, 119, 124–126, 188, 197, 201, 203, 281, 282, 285, 289, 292, 293, 396, 399, 400, 403, 410, 412–415, 422, 423; letters of, to cities, 121, 220, 242, 243, 272–274, 278, 282, 363, 364; to Louis, 143, 144, 201, 205; to Duchess Isabella, 271, 272; to French council, 274, 275; to Duke of Brittany, 313, 314; to Sigismund, 388, 389; to Edward IV., 403, 407; to Duke of Milan, 413, 414; at battle of Montl'héry, 122–124, 449; armies of, 122, 140, 268, 404, 405, 420, 437–439, 445; dictates terms of treaty of Conflans, 127–129; marches against Liege, 129, 130, 140–142, 182; destroys Dinant, 139, 142, 144–153; underestimates character and strength of enemies, 158, 226, 334, 336, 370, 398, 418, 443; accedes to the dukedom, 161, 170; invested with titles, 170–172, 181, 201, 202, 244, 263, 382–387; unpopularity of, 169, 181, 184, 185, 187, 243, 254, 269–271, 278, 279, 316–

Burgundy, Charles the Bold,
—*Continued*
318, 369, 370; punishes Ghent, 170-180, 182, 185-187, 244-246; reforms of, 183-185, 258; weds Margaret of York, 183, 188-194, 201, 265, 286, 290; ducal state of, 184, 185, 276, 278, 279, 282, 342-344, 346, 398; demands *aides*, 201, 202, 268-271, 404-406, 427-434; receives Louis at Peronne, 203, 205-221; crushes revolt of Liege, 213-219, 227-234, 238, 241-244; makes treaty of Peronne, 219-221, 224, 235, 236, 281; proposed sons-in-law for, 250, 251, 329-333, 335, 347; 349, 359, 360; signs treaty of St. Omer, 251, 253, 377; takes lands from Sigismund, 251-261, 387, 388, 393; relations of, with Swiss, 253; invested with Order of the Garter, 267, 286; *Remonstrance* presented to, 269; embassies to, 276-279, 347, 360, 362, 363, 377, 398; truces of, with Louis XI., 294, 298, 300, 301, 306, 307, 315, 325, 395, 399, 412, 415, 438; besieges Beauvais, 311, 312; reverses of, 312-315, 427; acquires duchy of Guelders, 320-328, 335, 336, 350, 351, 364; negotiations between Emperor Frederic and, 328-334; interview of, with emperor at Trèves, 337-353, 364, 399; becomes "protector" of Lorraine, 347, 360, 367-370, 400, 412, 414; interferes in Cologne affairs, 365, 366, 394, 395; visits Alsace, 375-380; troubles with Alsace, 389-394; besieges Neuss, 396-399; war declared against, 397, 398, 400, 401, 415, 416; makes truce with Frederic, 400, 401, 415; defeated at Héricourt, 400, 415; besieges Nancy, 413, 414, 439-444; allies desert, 416, 424, 445; defeated at Granson, 417-420; at Morat, 421-423, 435; convenes states-general, 429-435; last battle of, 444-448; death and burial of, 448-454.

Burgundy, Cornelius, Bastard of, 5, 38

Burgundy, David of, Bishop of Utrecht, 69-71

Burgundy, Isabella of Portugal, Duchess of, 2, 4, 9, 17, 19, 21, 24, 26, 58, 81-83, 88-90, 189, 190, 193, 271, 322, 442, 461; ancestry of, 8, 183; English sympathies of, 57, 62; retires to convent, 90, 111, 139, 145, 147: burial of, 385

Burgundy, John the Fearless, Duke of, 11, 14, 201; death of, 12, 155, 156

Burgundy, Margaret, Bastard of, 56

Burgundy, Margaret of York, Duchess of, 183, 188-195, 224, 265, 286, 290, 293, 325, 328, 396, 406, 430-434, 451, 461

Burgundy, Mary of (Duchess of Austria), birth of, 81, 83; godfather of, 83, 84, 86, 90, 298; 180, 189, 428, 429, 431, 435, 451; proposed marriages for, 250, 251, 296, 297, 299, 329-333, 335, 347, 349, 359, 366, 453

Burgundy, Philip the Good, Duke of, marriages of, 2, 8; institutes Order of Golden Fleece, 2-4; children of, 5, 8, 18, 38, 51, 56, 57,

Index

Burgundy, Philip the Good, —*Continued*
69, 282; alliance of, with England, 11, 57, 201, 264, 265; signs treaty of Arras, 11–13, 15, 32; territories acquired by, 13–15, 156, 157; suppresses revolt in Bruges, 18–23; wealth and magnificence of, 30, 31, 58, 104–106, 108, 158, 160, 161, 166, 179, 183, 184, 188; crushes rebellion of Ghent, 33–44, 67, 94–96; gives Feast of the Pheasant, 46–56; plans crusade, 47, 48, 51–60, 65, 66, 68–70; chooses second wife for Charles, 57, 58, 60–65; character of, 68, 88, 115, 163–165, 171, 405, 428, 457; interferes in affairs of Utrecht, of Liege, and of Cologne, 69–71, 81, 136–138, 363; hospitality of, to dauphin, 79, 80, 82–85, 87–94, 99, 100, 102, 104, 105, 157, 161, 339, 344; influenced by the Croys, 87, 97, 98, 111, 112, 119; attends coronation of Louis XI., 103–106; illnesses of, 109–111, 148, 152, 154; witnesses punishment of Dinant, 148–152, 154; death and burial of, 154, 155, 157–161, 183, 381, 385; epitaph of, 156, 157; description of, 162, 163; popularity of, 163, 181, 243, 460, 461

Burgundy, Philip the Hardy, Duke of, 457
Burgundy, Yolande, Bastard of, 51

C

Cagnola, 107
Calabria, Duke of, *see* Lorraine
Calais, 19, 65, 100, 266, 275, 278, 286, 287, 325, 403, 406, 411, 412
Calixtus III., Pope, 70
Cambray, 16, 358
Campobasso, Antonello de, mercenary captain, 412, 416, 438; treachery of, 440–447
Canterbury, 293, 325
Casanova, Abbé de, 335
Castile, Ferdinand, King of, 75, 442
Castile, Henry IV., King of, 295
Castile, Jeanne of, 295
Cat, Gilles le, 49
Catto, Angelo, 420
Caux, 143, 314; Bailiff of, 160
Cent Nouvelles Nouvelles, les, 93
Cento Novelle, by Boccaccio, 93
Cesner, Balthasar, 356
Chambéry, 74
Chambes, Helen de, 317
Chamont, Sire de, 437
Champagne, 219, 281, 313, 396, 437, 438, 452
Channel, the, 264, 266, 275, 285, 404
Charenton, 125, 127
Charlemagne, 219, 225
Charles IV., Emperor, 248
Charles (V.) the Wise, King of France, 199
Charles VII., King of France, reconciliation of, with Philip of Burgundy, 11, 12, 15–17, 36, 110, 156; character of, 20, 72, 77, 78; letters of, 61, 62, 96; refuses to join crusade, 65, 66; breach between dauphin and, 73–79, 81, 84–86, 89, 91, 99, 101, 102; illness and death of, 101, 102; institutes standing army, 117
Charles VIII., King of France, 279, 297, 298

Charles the Simple, King of France, 210
Charmes, 369
Charny, Count de, 190
Charny, Countess de, 190
Charolais, Catherine of France, Countess of, 2, 16–18, 23, 42; death and burial of, 17, 26
Charolais, Count of, *see* Charles of Burgundy
Charolais, Isabella of Bourbon, Countess of, 58, 60–65, 81, 83, 86, 88, 89, 103; death of, 129, 461
Chassa, Jehan de, 282, 284
Chastellain, cited, 39, 40, 102, 103, 120, 162–169, 174–178, 184–186, 188, 189, 224, 277; death of, 169
Château-Chinon, 61
Châtenois, 377
Chauny, 205
Chesny, Guiot du, 295
Chevelast, Louis de, 53
Chimay, Count of, 438
Citeaux, Abbé of, 384
Clarence, Duke of, 265, 267, 272, 273, 275, 285
Cléry, 319
Cleves, Adolph, Duke of, 45, 48, 151, 191, 326
Cleves, duchy of, 348
Cleves, Marie of, Duchess of Orleans, 19, 21, 23
Cods, the (party name), 9
Colmar, 375–378
Cologne, 138, 353, 356, 357, 394, 396
Cologne, Robert, Archbishop of, 362–366, 394, 395, 398
Colonna, Baptista, 447, 448
Commines (Commynes, Comines), Philip de, enters service of Duke of Burgundy, 112, 113, 229, 230, 275, 286; defection of, 302, 316–319, 333, 334, 461; cited, 115, 117, 120, 126, 127, 211, 214–219, 231, 232, 281, 282, 284, 286– 288, 290, 291, 300–303, 307, 308, 333, 398, 408, 410, 436, 441, 452, 460
Compiègne, 80, 96, 218, 311
Compostella, 416
Conflans, treaty of, 128, 129, 138, 139, 197, 201, 203, 204, 219
Constance, 59, 387; League of, 400
Constantinople, 46, 47, 52, 55
Cordes, Monsieur de, 235
Corguilleray, 296
Cornwallis, Lord, 20
Corvinus, Matthias, King of Hungary, 246, 247
Cosmo, 131
Court, Jehan de la, 27
Coutault, Monsieur de, 258, 259
Craon, Seigneur de, 298, 301, 452
Cret, Dion du, 48
Crèvecœur, Philip of, 206
Crèvecœur, Seigneur of, 16, 271
Créville, Sire de, 460
Croy, A. de, 159
Croy, J. de, 159
Croy, Philip de, 17, 87, 94, 99, 100
Croy family, the, 7, 111, 112, 119, 291, 317, 345
Cueillotte, the (tax), 172, 177, 178
Cyprus, 245

D

Damian, 131
Dammartin, Count of, 76, 77, 98, 227, 311; letters of Louis to, 221–224, 304–307, 408
Damme, 191, 194
Dauphiné, 75, 76, 91, 438
Dauxonne, Jacquemin, 6
De Bussière, cited, 340
Décapole, Alsatian, the, 248
De la Loere, secretary, 234
Dendermonde, 89

Index

Denmark, 245, 363
Denys, Chaplain, 449
Deschamps, Eustache, *Lay de Vaillance* by, 7
Deventer, 71, 72, 79
Dieppe, 143, 314
Diesbach, Ludwig von, 209, 236
Dijon, 1-7, 161, 215, 258, 260, 323, 379, 382-387
Dinant, 139, 142, 144-147; destruction of, 142, 144-153, 241, 312
Dôle, 352, 379, 385
Dombourc, Jehan de, 25
Dompaire, 369
Dordrecht, 202
Du Clercq, cited, 40, 68, 70, 76, 77, 149, 152, 153
Duclos, cited, 296
Dunois, Count, 16
Dunois, François, 223
Du Plessis, Seigneur, 275, 280

E

Easterlings, the, 289
l'Écluse, 95, 189-191
Edward IV., King of England, 101, 156, 157, 159, 188, 264-267, 273-275, 279, 293, 294, 396; aided by Charles of Burgundy, 285-291, 293, 437; plans conquest of France, 385, 396, 398-400, 402-404, 406-408; character of, 408, 410; makes peace with Louis XI., 408-411
Edward of Lancaster, Prince of Wales, 279, 280, 285; death of, 290
Émeries, Antoine Raulin, Sire d' (Aymeries), 87, 235, 433
Engelburg, the, 372
England alliance of, with Burgundy, 11, 288, 325, 363, 385; with France, 143, 245, 408-411; French possessions of, 11, 12, 65, 72, 198, 287; commercial relations of, 145, 288, 294, 396; wars of the Roses in, 263-267, 272-274, 279, 280, 284-292
Ensisheim, 372, 373, 378, 379, 389
Épinal, 369
Erasmus, 461
Escalles, Seigneur d', 190
Escouchy, Mathieu d,' cited, 48, 54, 56, 70, 84
Estampes, Count d,' 29, 80, 81
Étampes, 124
Eu, 316, 396
Eu, Count d', 115
Ewige Richtung, the, 387
Exeter, Duke of, 286, 288
Eyb, Ludwig von, 349

F

Faret (or Farrel), Guillaume 340
Favre, Jourdain, 308
Ferrara, 363
Ferrette, county of, 251, 254, 394 *et passim*
Flanders, 14, 32, 33, 156, 161, 358, 395, 427, 434, 439, 444; Estates of, 268-271, 404-406, 428, 429; commerce of, 288, 396, 454
Flanders, Count of, 170, 171, 176
Florence 23, 192, 224
Foix, Count de, 234 295, 296
Foix, Eleanor de, 296
Foix, Gaston de, 121
Forli, Bishop of, 443
Fossombrone, Bishop of, 364, 365
Fou, Ivon du, 280
France, alliance of, with Burgundy, 11, 12, 15, 245, 325; waning power of England in, 11, 12, 65, 72, 198; changed conditions

France—*Continued*
in, 13, 72, 73, 264, 269; assembly of states-general of, 198-200, 203, 212; invasion of, 294, etc.
France, Admiral of, the, 271, 273
France, Catherine, Daughter of, *see* Charolais
France, Charles of, Duke of Berry, *see* Berry
France, Jeanne of, 61
France, Michelle of, *see* Burgundy
Franche-Comté, the, 43, 76, 379, 385, 395, 438, 456
Franchimont, 229, 242
Frankfort, 60, 65, 356, 357
Frederic, elector palatine, 247
Frederic III., Emperor, 15, 246-248, 253, 393; character of, 59, 336, 351, 353, 359, 365, 401, 402; negotiations of, with Charles of Burgundy, 328-336, 345-349, 394, 395, 399; meets Charles at Trèves, 336-357, 360, 364; description of, 341, 342, 345; signs treaty with Charles, 400, 401, 415
Fribourg, 392, 438
Friesland, 32, 69, 358; title of Lord of, 263
Friesland, West, 202

G

Gabelle, the, 33, 34, 44, 243, 395
Gachard, cited, 36 *et passim*
Galeotto, 445, 446
Garter, Order of the, 2, 159, 267, 286, 379
Gauthier, Dan, 239
Gautier, cited, 7
Gaveren, 37, 41; battle of, 39, 42, 43; treaty of, 179
Gelthauss, Johannes, 356

Genappe, 88, 91-94, 99
Geneva, 424, 425, 436
Geneva, Lake of, 422
Genoa, 23, 192
Gex, 423, 424
Ghent, 26, 31, 145, 261, 267, 268, 325, 428, 451; rebellion of, 33-39, 55, 156; submission of, 40-44, 46, 94-96; insurrection in, 170, 172-182; humiliation of, 182, 185, 186, 244-246
Gilles, Frère, 383
Givry, Sire de, 423
Gloucester, Duke of, 410
Gloucester, Humphrey, Duke of, 19
Golden Fleece, Order of the, instituted, 2-4, 157; assemblies of, 2-7, 26, 31, 55, 101, 187, 188, 190, 193, 322-324; knights of, 5-7, 20, 26, 245, 286, 322, 323, 342, 401
Gorcum, 113
Görlitz, Elizabeth of, 14
Granson, battle of, 417-419, 421, 438, 443
Grave, 320
Grenoble, 101
Grey, Jean de, 434
Groothuse, Louis de la, 271, 272, 285, 286
Groothuse, Mathys de la, 171, 174-179
Guelders, Adolf, Duke of, 320, 323; imprisonment of, 322-325
Guelders, Arnold, Duke of 69, 320-324; death of, 324, 327
Guelders, Catharine of Bourbon, Duchess of, 322
Guelders, Charles of, 324, 326, 328, 367
Guelders, duchy of, 320-326, 335, 336, 350, 351, 358, 453
Guelders, Philippa of, 326, 328
Guérin, Jean de, 150

Index

Guienne, Charles of France, Duke of, *see* Berry
Guienne, duchy of, 72, 128, 281, 282, 294, 403
Guise, 396
Guisnes, 65, 287

H

Haarlem, 202
Hagenbach, Peter von, 110, 335, 336, 354; Governor of Alsace, 239, 254, 257, 260, 370–381, 389, 390, 394; trial and execution of, 390–392
Hagenbach, Stephen von, 393, 397
Hague, The, 9, 113, 202, 263
Hainaut, 13, 14, 32, 156, 235, 239, 358, 433, 455
Ham, 206
Hanseatic League, the, 145, 285
Heers, Raes de la Rivière, Lord of, 138
Heinsberg, John of, Bishop of Liege, 137, 139
Hemricourt, Jacques de, 133
Henry IV., of Castile, 295
Henry V., King of England, 12, 19, 155
Henry VI., King of England, 11, 12, 72, 99, 101, 285, 288, 293; character of, 155, 264, 286; death of, 290, 291
Henry VII., King of England, 264
Héricourt, 397, 400, 415
Hermite, Tristan l', 79
Hesdin, 115, 224, 282–284, 330
Hesse, Hermann of, 364, 366, 398
Holland, 13, 14, 24, 69, 156, 261, 263, 285, 358, 454, 455; title of Count of, 201–203, 263
Holland, Jacqueline of Bavaria, Countess of, 9, 14, 26, 323, 455

Holland, South, 202, 203
Holland, William VI., Count of, 8
Honfleur, 273
Hooks, the (party name), 9
Houthem, 170
Howard, Lord, 411
Hugonet, Chancellor, **276**, 291, 350, 428–433
Humbercourt, Seigneur de, 211, 213, 214, 291
Hungary, 245, 246, 347, 348, 363; King of, 351, 420, 421
Huy, 137, **243**

I

Innsbruck, 248
Irma, Jean, 392
Isabella of Portugal, Duchess of Burgundy, *see* Burgundy

J

Jarville, 445
Jarville, Sieur de, 427
Jerusalem, 161
Joan of Arc, 11
Joinville, castle of, 368; treaty of, 369
Jomini, 418
Jougne, 418, 419
Jouvençal, Chancellor, 198
Juliers, Duke of, 326
Jura, the, 416, 424, 444

K

Kaisersberg, 376
Kennemerland, 71
Kervyn de Lettenhove, Baron, cited, 218, 224
Knebel, Johannes R., 376, 379

L

La Hogue, 403

Laisné, Jeanne (Fouquet), *La Hachette*, 313
Lalaing, Jacques de, prowess of, 27-29; death of, 39
La Marche, Olivier de, cited, 14, 17, 25, 26, 29, 30, 40, 42, 47-50, 54-56, 68, 70, 84, 113-116, 120, 159-162, 189-194, 232, 419, 424, 425, 445, 450; knighted, 120, 123; loyalty and zeal of, 159-161, 183, 245, 318, 319, 327, 328, 423, 425, 426
Lambert, Bishop of Tongres, 131, 132, 134
Lancaster, House of, 264, 278, 279, 286, 289, 291
Lannoy, Jehan, Seigneur de, 47
Lanternier, Jehan, 4
Laon, 223
La Rivière, 437
La Rochelle, 281
Lauffen, 378
Lauffenberg, 251
Laurentian Library, the, 224
Lausanne, 375
Lavin, Étienne de, 365
League of Constance, 400
League of Public Weal, 118-129, 142, 188, 198, 204
Le Grand, Abbé, 237
Le Gros, Jehan, 283, 284
Le Quesnoy, 96-98
Lescun, Seigneur de, 295, 296, 305
Liege, description of, 130-132, 136, 145, 227; government of, 131-135; bishop-princes of, 131-133, 135, 137, 212-214, 218-221; rebellion of, 138-140, 156, 182, 213, 214, 219-221, 363; aided by Louis XI., 138, 140, 211-213; punishment of, 141, 142, 148, 153, 182, 211, 212, 223, 228-234, 237-241, 253, 282, 312
Liege, bishopric of, 348, 352, 358

Lille, 45, 47-56, 63, 65, 112, 264, 268, 270
Limbourg, 14, 358
Livornia, 245
Loches, 208
Loisey, Anthony de, 238
Lombardy, 245, 413
London, 290, 396
Longjumeau, 122
Longueval, Hugues de, 53
Loreille, Thomas de, 160
Lorraine, duchy of, 156, 237-239, 337, 338, 347, 348, 352, 357, 366, 367, 379, 387, 414, 415, 419, 456
Lorraine, Estates of, the, 414, 438
Lorraine, Duke of, 124
Lorraine, Nicholas of Anjou, Duke of (Calabria), 126, 203, 332, 333, 366; death of, 337, 357, 366, 367
Lorraine, René, Duke of, accepts Burgundian protection, 367-370, 412, 437, 444, 446; joins league against Charles, 400, 401, 412-414, 422, 438-443, 451
Louis XI., King of France, 17; rebels against Charles VII., 73-76; marries Charlotte of Savoy, 74, 75; letters of, to Charles VII., 78, 79; to Dammartin, 221-224, 304-307, 408; to envoys, 295-301, 452; to Count de Foix, 234; to Lorenzo de' Medici, 297; to Duke of Milan, 237, 306; to Amiens, 300; to chancellor, 402; flees to Duke of Burgundy, 76-79; generosity of Duke Philip to, 81, 82, 86, 91-94, 96, 100, 157, 161, 339; is godfather of Mary of Burgundy, 83, 84, 86, 90, 298; tastes of, 91, 92, 107, 108; duplicity of, 92, 100, 101, 105, 138-140, 142, 208, 211, 228,

Index

Louis XI.—*Continued*
 231, 233–236, 271–279, 281–283, 298–300, 346, 412, 459, 460; accession of, 102–104, 170; ingratitude of, 102–105, 109, 116; character of, 106–109, 115, 408; enmity between Charles and, 114–117, 333–335, 344, 346, 348, 436; nobles in league against, 114–125, 294, 312–315; policy of, 118–121, 125, 198–201, 203; signs treaty of Conflans, 127–129; incites opposition to Charles of Burgundy, 146–148, 181, 189, 204, 205, 211, 213, 215, 281, 386, 387, 397, 416, 426, 437, 443; breaks treaties, 197–201, 203, 281, 282–284; makes visit to Peronne, 204–210, 213–219, 244; signs treaty at Peronne, 219–221, 223, 235, 236, 283; ally of the Swiss, 249, 250, 397, 399, 402, 403, 438; makes nucleus of standing army, 268; aids Earl of Warwick and Margaret of Anjou, 274–276, 290, 293; birth of son of, 279, 298; makes truce with Charles, 294, 298, 300, 305, 306, 315, 395, 399, 412, 415, 438; suspected of death of brother, 307–310, 314, 344; rewards Beauvais, 313; wins over Edward IV., 408–411; rejoices in death of Charles, 452, 453

Louvain, 79, 91, 92, 145, 181, 243; University of, 137

Lower Union, the, *see* Basse-Union

Lucerne, 376, 387

Lude, Seigneur de, 452

Luxemburg, duchy of, 14, 32, 47, 156, 337, 358, 362, 379, 387, 395, 438, 439, 444

Luxemburg, John of, 191

Luxeuil, 379

Luzine River, the, 397

Lyme, 285

Lyons, 76, 80

M

Maestricht, 212, 395

Maine, 12

Malhortie, 369

Mandrot, Bernard Édouard, editor of Commynes' *Mémoires, Jean de Roye*, etc., cited, 309

Manton, Seigneur de, 425

Marchant, Ythier, 299

Marck, Adolph de la, 86

Marne River, the, 122

Marquiez, George, 450

Mas, Gilles du, 189

Mathieu, 449

Maximilian, Archduke of Austria, 247; proposed marriage of, 250, 251, 329–331, 335, 341, 342, 347, 349, 369

Mayence, 246, 349

Mayence, Archbishop of, 247, 343, 344

Mayence, Duke of, 225

Mazilles, Jehan de, 239–242

Mechlin, 14, 180, 181, 363

Medici, Lorenzo de', 297

Metz, 336–338, 378, 445, 448

Metz, Bishop of, 445

Meurin, secretary to Louis XI., 222

Meurthe River, the, 445, 447

Meuse River, the, 148, 151, 152, 227, 228, 238

Meyer, J., cited, 34, 218, 261

Michel, the Rhetorician, cited, 58

Middelburg, 25, 202, 261, 272, 274

Milan, 245, 414, 424, 436

Milan, Duke of, 99, 237, 305, 306, 413, 436
Mirecourt, 442
Mongleive, 225
Mons, 55, 318, 333
Montbazon, 298, 300
Montereau, bridge of, 11, 12, 155
Montfort, Ulrich von, 360
Montgomery, Sir Thomas (Mongomere), 399
Montl'héry, battle of, 120, 122–124, 139, 149, 449
Monulphe, Bishop of Tongres, 130, 131
Morat, battle of, 421, 422, 424, 443, 445, 452
Morges, 422
Morvilliers, Chancellor, 112–117
Moselle River, the, 339, 354, 355, 362, 369, 439
Moutils-lès-Tours, 304
Mulhouse, 248, 254, 373–380

N

Namur, 143, 144, 152, 153, 224, 227, 322, 323, 410
Namur, county of, 14, 32, 139, 145, 156, 358
Nancy, 367, 369, 448, 450, 452; sieges of, 413, 414, 416, 438–444; battle of, 448–452, 454
Naples, 245
Naples, King of, 323
Napoleon, 398
Narbonne, Archbishop of, 16, 117–128
Nassau, Engelbert of, 323, 342
Nassau, John of, 191
Nations, the, 38, 113, 192
Nesle, 306, 308–311
Netherlands, the, 38, 132, 192, 269, 314; states-general of, 428–434
Neufchâtel, 313
Neufchâtel, Isabelle of, 51

Neuss, 364, 396–399, 404, 405, 413, 438
Neuville, 445
Nevers, 396
Nevers, Charles, Count of, 7, 112, 181
Neville, Anne, 280
Nice, 436
Nimwegen, 326–328
Norfolk, Duchess of, 192, 194, 412
Normandy, Charles of France, Duke of, *see* Berry
Normandy, duchy of, 12, 72, 109, 125, 198, 200, 271, 273, 275, 281, 311, 312, 403, 404
Norway, 245
Noseret, 419
Noyon, 205
Nuremberg, 86

O

Obernai, 376
Oise River, the, 122
Onofrio de Santa Croce, 212, 213
Orange, Prince of, 76, 79, 228
Oriole, Pierre d,' 298
Orleans, 298, 316
Orleans, duchy of, 118
Orleans, Duke of, 19–23
Osterlings, the, 192
Ostrevant, Count of, *see* Borselen
Oudenarde, 38
Ourré, Gerard, 97
Oxford, 266

P

Palatinate, the, 363
Palatine, Count, the, 254; the elector, 363, 364; Frederic, elector, 247
Panigarola, Johannes Petrus, Milanese ambassador, cited, 416, 417, 423, 426, 434, 435, 437

Paris, 11, 105, 110, 124–128, 197, 219, 237, 273, 293, 403, 407, 409
Paris, University of, 103, 125, 368
Paston, Sir John, letters of, 290, 325, 399, 411, 412, 419, 420
Paston, John, the younger (brother of above), letter of, 194–196
Paston, Margaret, 194, 290, 411, 412, 419
Pavia, 237
Pellet, Jean, 254, 258
Pepin, 131
Perdriel, Henry, 237
Périgny, 382
Périgord, 281
Peronne, interview of Louis XI. and Charles at, 203–226, 283, 409; treaty of, 219–221, 223, 237, 281–283
"Peronne, the Peace of," 224–226
Perrenet, 80
Petit–Dutaillis, Ch., author of Vol. IV[II], Lavisse, *Hist. de France, see* Lavisse.
Petitpas, Jean, 178
Petrasanta, Franciscus, Milanese ambassador, 436
Pheasant, Feast of the, 46–56
Picardy, 12, 284, 314, 404, 456
Picquigny, 408
Plessis-les-Tours, 106
Pleume, 160
Podiebrad, George, ex-king of Bohemia, 246, 247, 251
Poictiers, Alienor de, cited, 65, 81, 84
Poinsot, Jean, 254, 258
Poitiers, 293
Poland, 245, 246, 348, 363
Pont-à-Mousson, 439
Pont de Cé, 316
Porcupine, Order of the, 20, 22
Portinari, Thomas, 192

Portugal, 38, 270, 277
Portugal, Alphonse V., King of, 442
Portugal, Isabella of, Duchess of Burgundy, *see* Burgundy
Pot, Philip de, 53, 63, 64
Poucque, castle of, 37
Prussia, 245
Public Weal, War of, *see* League

Q

Quaux River, the, 42
Quercy, 281
Quiévrain, Seigneur de, 317
Quingey, Simon de, 301, 302, 307

R

Rampart, Jean, 9
Ratellois, 239
Ratisbon, 59, 60
Ravestein, Madame de, 81
Ravestein, Monseigneur de, 89
Renty, Monseigneur de, 240
Rethel, 396
Rheims, 16, 104, 170, 400, 403, 407
Rheims, Archbishop of, 16
Rheinfelden, 251
Rhine, the, 248, 355; Valley, 257
Rhinelands, the, 388, 389
Rhodes, 161
Rivers, Earl, 266
Roche, Henri de la, 308
Rochefort, 425, 426, 436
Rochefort, Sire of, 426
Rochefoucauld, 224
Roelants, Gort, 428, 429, 433
Romans, King of the, 329–332
Rome, 47, 70, 364
Romont, Count of, 416
Romorantin, 62
Roses, Wars of the, 263–267, 279, 280, 285–292

Index

Rossillon, 225
Rottelin, Marquise Hugues de, 18
Rotterdam, 461
Rouen, 143, 273, 275, 313, 314
Rousillon, 304
Rouvre, 425, 436, 437
Roye, 311
Rozière, Malhortie de, 440
Rubempré, the bastard of, 113-116
Rubempré, Jehan de, 190
Ruple, G., 220
Russia, 245

S

Saeckingen, 251, 378
St. Bavon, Abbot of, 41
Ste.-Beuve, cited, 218
St. Blaise, Abbé of, 254
St. Claude, 76, 78, 425
St. Cloud, 122
St. Denis, 122
St. Lievin, feast of, 170-179
St. Michel-sur-Loire, 297
St. Nicolas-du-Port, 442-444
St. Omer, 16, 19, 21, 100, 261, 270, 276, 279, 282, 402; treaty of, 251, 253, 329, 373, 377, 379, 387
St. Pol, Count of, 54, 97-99, 122, 127, made constable of France, 128, 151, 153, 203, 204, 206, 218, 281; treachery of, 396, 407, 408, 413, 460; execution of, 413
St. Quentin, 289, 298, 407
St. Remy, Jean le Févre, Seigneur de, 6
St. Thierry, 104
St. Trond, 140, 142, 153
Sale, Anthony de la, 93
Salesart, 239
Salins, 419, 425, 426, 434
Salisbury, Bishop of, 190,191
Savoy, Charlotte of, marries the dauphin, 74, 75, 91
Savoy, duchy of, 348, 357, 358

Savoy, dukes of, 74, 75, 100, 424, 425
Savoy, Yolande, Duchess of, 208, 295; ally of Charles the Bold, 415, 416, 420, 423; kidnapped, 424-426, 436; rescued, 437, 438
Saxony, Duke of, 351
Saxony, elector of, 246, 247
Schellhass, Karl, 356
Schiedam, 202
Schlestadt, 375, 376
Scotland, Eleanor of, wife of Sigismund of Austria, 248
Scotland, Margaret of, wife of Louis, the dauphin, 74
Seine River, the, 122, 127, 403
Sforza, Galeazzo-Maria, Duke of Milan, 423, 424
Sicily, 156, 245
Sigismund, Archduke of Austria, *see* Austria
Sigismund, Emperor, 13, 15
Sluis, 202
Snoy, Renier, cited, 357, 358
Soleure, 376, 412
Somerset, Duke of, 196, 286, 288
Somme, towns on the river, ceded to Duke of Burgundy, 12, 128, 143, 201, 281, 396, 399; redemption of towns on the, 110, 111, 117, 119, 294, 300, 303, 309, 334
Sorel, Agnes, 76-78, 81
Soulz, Rudolf de, 335
Spain, 38, 192
Spain, King of, 453
Stein, Hertnid von, 247, 349
Stein, Rudolph de, 443
Stephen, Martin, 239
Strasburg, 248, 376, 377, 392, 393, 414
Strasburg, Bishop of, 254
Stuttgart, 60
Sundgau, the, 374, 394
Swabia, 452
Swiss, the, valour of, 249-251, 256, 381, 398, 418, 421, 422; victories of, 397, 417-

Index

Swiss—*Continued*
  422, 435; allies of Louis XI., 397, 402, 403
Swiss Cantons, the, 248, 352, 371, 372, 375, 386, 387, 389; declare war against Charles the Bold, 397, 400, 415, 416, 438–448, 451
Swynaerde, 170
Sylvius, Æneas, 59

T

Talmont, Prince of, 317
Tewkesbury, battle of, 290, 293
Texel, island of, 202
Thann, 252, 372, 379, 389
Thérain, the, 311
Thérouanne, Bishop of, 69
Thierry, 442
Thierry, Monsieur de, 402
Thierstein, Oswald von, 393, 444
Thionville, 362, 365, 369
Thouan, Mme. de, 308
Thouars, Guillaume de, 319
Thurgau, 248
Tilhart, secretary to Louis XI., 297
Tongres, 140, 213; bishops of, 130, 131, 213
Tonnerre, Count of, 16
Toul, 348, 439
Touraine, 106
Tournay, 198
Tournay, Bishop of, 104
Tournehem, 287
Tours, 114, 198, 212, 283, 284, 316
Toustain, Aloysius (Toussaint), 224, 237
Toustain, Guillaume, 237
Toutey, E., cited, 438, *et passim*
Trausch, cited, 340
Tree of Gold, jousts of the, 193
Trémoille, Jehan de la, 17

Trèves, 336–354, 364, 369, 373, 385
Trèves, Archbishop of, 246, 349, 351
Tuin, 153
Turin, 436
Turks, the, capture Constantinople, 46, 47, 55; proposed crusade against, 47, 48, 51–53, 56, 65, 66, 70, 78, 79, 345, 346, 348, 350

U

Unterwalden, 418, 446
Uri, 418, 446
Ursé, Seigneur d', 295, 300, 301
Utenhove, Richard, 178
Utrecht, 69–71, 81, 137, 263, 348, 352, 358, 363

V

Vaesen, Joseph Frederic Louis (editor of *Lettres de Louis XI.*), 295, 296
Valenciennes, 323
Valois, House of, 9, 12, 457
Vaudemont, Yolande of Anjou, Duchess of, 367, 368
Vendôme, Count of, 16
Venice, 23, 192, 353, 363
Verard, Antoine, 93
Verdun, 348
Vere, 289
Vermandois, 308
Vermandois, Count de, 214
Vesoul, 258, 259, 379
Villeclerc, Demoiselle de, 77
Virnenbourg, Count of, 6
Visen, Charles de, 215
Vosges, the, 252

W

Wailly, 322
Waldemar of Zürich, 443
Waldshut, 249, 251, 252, 378
Walloon language, the, 136

Warwick, Earl of, 265–267, 271–276, 279, 280, 284–290, 323; death of, 289, 290
Wavrin, Philip de, 17
Wellington, Duke of, 210
Wenlock, governor of Calais, 275
Weymouth, 290
Wieringen, island of, 202
Woodville, Elizabeth, 266
Wuisse, Vautrin, 446
Wyler, Hans, 417

X

Xaintes, 305

Y

York, House of, 264, 289
York, Margaret of, Duchess of Burgundy, *see* Burgundy
Ypres, 207, 220, 269, 271, 272

Z

Zealand, 13, 14, 24, 32, 69, 156, 201, 202, 261, 262, 274, 289, 358, 455
Zürich, 59, 376
Zutphen, 323, **324**

*A Selection from the
Catalogue of*

G. P. PUTNAM'S SONS

**Complete Catalogues sent
on application**

Heroes of the Nations.

A SERIES of biographical studies of the lives and work of a number of representative historical characters about whom have gathered the great traditions of the Nations to which they belonged, and who have been accepted, in many instances, as types of the several National ideals. With the life of each typical character will be presented a picture of the National conditions surrounding him during his career.

The narratives are the work of writers who are recognized authorities on their several subjects, and, while thoroughly trustworthy as history, will present picturesque and dramatic "stories" of the Men and of the events connected with them.

To the Life of each "Hero" will be given one duodecimo volume, handsomely printed in large type, provided with maps and adequately illustrated according to the special requirements of the several subjects.

Nos. 1-32, each..........................$1.50
Half leather................................1.75
No. 33 and following Nos., each
                      (by mail $1.50, net 1.35)
Half leather (by mail, $1.75)..........net 1.60

For full list of volumes see next page.

HEROES OF THE NATIONS

NELSON. By W. Clark Russell.

GUSTAVUS ADOLPHUS. By C. R. L. Fletcher.

PERICLES. By Evelyn Abbott.

THEODORIC THE GOTH. By Thomas Hodgkin.

SIR PHILIP SIDNEY. By H. R. Fox-Bourne.

JULIUS CÆSAR. By W. Warde Fowler.

WYCLIF. By Lewis Sergeant.

NAPOLEON. By W. O'Connor Morris.

HENRY OF NAVARRE. By P. F. Willert.

CICERO. By J. L. Strachan-Davidson.

ABRAHAM LINCOLN. By Noah Brooks.

PRINCE HENRY (OF PORTUGAL) THE NAVIGATOR. By C. R. Beazley.

JULIAN THE PHILOSOPHER. By Alice Gardner.

LOUIS XIV. By Arthur Hassall.

CHARLES XII. By R. Nisbet Bain.

LORENZO DE' MEDICI. By Edward Armstrong.

JEANNE D'ARC. By Mrs. Oliphant.

CHRISTOPHER COLUMBUS. By Washington Irving.

ROBERT THE BRUCE. By Sir Herbert Maxwell.

HANNIBAL. By W. O'Connor Morris.

ULYSSES S. GRANT. By William Conant Church.

ROBERT E. LEE. By Henry Alexander White.

THE CID CAMPEADOR. By H. Butler Clarke.

SALADIN. By Stanley Lane-Poole.

BISMARCK. By J. W. Headlam.

ALEXANDER THE GREAT. By Benjamin I. Wheeler.

CHARLEMAGNE. By H. W. C. Davis.

OLIVER CROMWELL. By Charles Firth.

RICHELIEU. By James B. Perkins.

DANIEL O'CONNELL. By Robert Dunlop.

SAINT LOUIS (Louis IX. of France). By Frederick Perry.

LORD CHATHAM. By Walford Davis Green.

OWEN GLYNDWR. By Arthur G. Bradley.

HENRY V. By Charles L. Kingsford.

EDWARD I. By Edward Jenks.

AUGUSTUS CÆSAR. By J. B. Firth.

FREDERICK THE GREAT. By W. F. Reddaway.

WELLINGTON. By W. O'Connor Morris

CONSTANTINE THE GREAT. By J. B. Firth.

HEROES OF THE NATIONS

MOHAMMED. By D. S. Margoliouth.

CHARLES THE BOLD. By Ruth Putnam.

WASHINGTON. By J. A. Harrison.

WILLIAM THE CONQUEROR. By F. M. Stenton.

Other volumes in preparation are:

MOLTKE. By Spencer Wilkinson.

JUDAS MACCABÆUS. By Israel Abrahams.

SOBIESKI. By F. A. Pollard.

ALFRED THE TRUTHTELLER. By Frederick Perry.

FREDERICK II. By A. L. Smith.

MARLBOROUGH. By C. W. C. Oman.

RICHARD THE LION-HEARTED. By T. A. Archer.

WILLIAM THE SILENT. By Ruth Putnam.

GREGORY VII. By F. Urquhart.

New York—G. P. PUTNAM'S SONS, PUBLISHERS—London

The Story of the Nations.

IN the story form the current of each National life is distinctly indicated, and its picturesque and noteworthy periods and episodes are presented for the reader in their philosophical relation to each other as well as to universal history.

It is the plan of the writers of the different volumes to enter into the real life of the peoples, and to bring them before the reader as they actually lived, labored, and struggled—as they studied and wrote, and as they amused themselves. In carrying out this plan, the myths, with which the history of all lands begins, will not be overlooked, though these will be carefully distinguished from the actual history, so far as the labors of the accepted historical authorities have resulted in definite conclusions.

The subjects of the different volumes have been planned to cover connecting and, as far as possible, consecutive epochs or periods, so that the set when completed will present in a comprehensive narrative the chief events in the great STORY OF THE NATIONS; but it is, of course, not always practicable to issue the several volumes in their chronological order.

Nos. 1–61, each.......................... $1.50
Half leather............................... 1.75
Nos. 62 and following Nos., each (by mail, 1.50
                                     net 1.35
Half leather (by mail, $1.75)............net 1.60

For list of volumes see next page.

THE STORY OF THE NATIONS

GREECE. Prof. Jas. A. Harrison.
ROME. Arthur Gilman.
THE JEWS. Prof. James K. Hosmer.
CHALDEA. Z. A. Ragozin.
GERMANY. S. Baring-Gould.
NORWAY. Hjalmar H. Boyesen.
SPAIN. Rev. E. E. and Susan Hale.
HUNGARY. Prof. A. Vámbéry.
CARTHAGE. Prof. Alfred J. Church.
THE SARACENS. Arthur Gilman.
THE MOORS IN SPAIN. Stanley Lane-Poole.
THE NORMANS. Sarah Orne Jewett.
PERSIA. S. G. W. Benjamin.
ANCIENT EGYPT. Prof. Geo. Rawlinson.
ALEXANDER'S EMPIRE. Prof. J. P. Mahaffy.
ASSYRIA. Z. A. Ragozin.
THE GOTHS. Henry Bradley.
IRELAND. Hon. Emily Lawless.
TURKEY. Stanley Lane-Poole.
MEDIA, BABYLON, AND PERSIA. Z. A. Ragozin.
MEDIÆVAL FRANCE. Prof. Gustave Masson.
HOLLAND. Prof. J. Thorold Rogers.
MEXICO. Susan Hale.
PHŒNICIA. George Rawlinson.
THE HANSA TOWNS. Helen Zimmern.
EARLY BRITAIN. Prof. Alfred J. Church.
THE BARBARY CORSAIRS. Stanley Lane-Poole.
RUSSIA. W. R. Morfill.
THE JEWS UNDER ROME. W. D. Morrison.
SCOTLAND. John Mackintosh.
SWITZERLAND. R. Stead and Mrs. A. Hug.
PORTUGAL. H. Morse-Stephens.
THE BYZANTINE EMPIRE. C W. C. Oman.
SICILY. E. A. Freeman.
THE TUSCAN REPUBLICS Bella Duffy.
POLAND. W. R. Morfill.
PARTHIA. Geo. Rawlinson.
JAPAN. David Murray.
THE CHRISTIAN RECOVERY OF SPAIN. H. E. Watts.
AUSTRALASIA. Greville Tregarthen.
SOUTHERN AFRICA. Geo. M Theal.
VENICE. Alethea Wiel.
THE CRUSADES. T. S. Archer and C. L. Kingsford.
VEDIC INDIA. Z. A. Ragozin
BOHEMIA. C. E. Maurice.
CANADA. J. G. Bourinot.
THE BALKAN STATES. William Miller.

THE STORY OF THE NATIONS

BRITISH RULE IN INDIA. R. W. Frazer.

MODERN FRANCE. André Le Bon.

THE BRITISH EMPIRE. Alfred T. Story. Two vols.

THE FRANKS. Lewis Sergeant.

THE WEST INDIES. Amos K. Fiske.

THE PEOPLE OF ENGLAND, Justin McCarthy, M.P. Two vols.

AUSTRIA. Sidney Whitman.

CHINA. Robt. K. Douglass.

MODERN SPAIN. Major Martin A. S. Hume.

MODERN ITALY. Pietro Orsi.

THE THIRTEEN COLONIES. Helen A. Smith. Two vols.

WALES AND CORNWALL. Owen M. Edwards.

MEDIÆVAL ROME. Wm. Miller.

THE PAPAL MONARCHY. Wm. Barry.

MEDIÆVAL INDIA. Stanley Lane-Poole.

BUDDHIST INDIA. T. W. Rhys-Davids.

THE SOUTH AMERICAN REPUBLICS. Thomas C. Dawson. Two vols.

PARLIAMENTARY ENGLAND. Edward Jenks.

MEDIÆVAL ENGLAND. Mary Bateson.

THE UNITED STATES. Edward Earle Sparks. Two vols.

ENGLAND. THE COMING OF PARLIAMENT. L. Cecil Jane.

GREECE: EARLIEST TIMES TO A.D. 14. E. S. Shuckburgh.